BLUFFWORLD

Patrick Evans

BLUFFWORLD

Victoria University
of Wellington
Press

Victoria University of Wellington Press
PO Box 600, Wellington
New Zealand
vup.wgtn.ac.nz

A catalogue record is available from the
National Library of New Zealand.

ISBN 978-1-77656-311-1

Printed by Markono Print Media Pte Ltd, Singapore

Zum Bullshitter geht der Preis—

Johann Wolfgang von Goethe,
Die Leiden des jungen Werthers

I have the impression that there is an alarming amount
of bluffing in the humanities—

George Steiner,
A Long Saturday: Conversations

Time for another all-staff barbecue!

Trad

For Paul Millar

PART ONE

The Sorrows of Young Werther

Chapter 1

Have you ever noticed there's a certain kind of fly that doesn't make a sound? I'm watching one now as it moves around the light fitting above my head. They're tiny, these buzzless flies,[1] and if you watch for a while you'll see they move not in a circle but in squares or rectangles and turn right at each corner, abruptly, for no particular reason. I could watch them for hours.

I come in here each day with my laptop: sabbatical leave, Bevan calls it—he's my boss, in the bookshop across the foyer from here. Just the two cubicles, and I sit in one or the other of them like this and think about the things that've brought me here. I try to make sense of them, I try to work out whether they were always going to happen or I've just stuffed up, made bad decisions the way counsellors try to get you to see when it's far too late. But then I find I'm watching these flies instead—here's another, come out of nothing and following the first around the light—watching them mindlessly, as if there's not a brain cell left in my head. *Three* of them now, sawing their way silently around the fitting—always anticlockwise, as if they're onto something about the universe that human beings don't know.

It was always like this, to tell the truth, back in my early days as an academic, that high old time it's high time I told you about. Was that the reason my life became unstuck? Was

1   One page in and he's plagiarising already—surely he's stolen this from John Hopkins's novel *Tangier Buzzless Flies* (1972)?

it something to do with those long hours spent here staring up at these tiny noiseless flies drawing invisible squares around the light fitting on the ceiling of the English-department men's room, while almost none of my academic work got done? The word *gormless* comes to mind.

⤙⤚

My name is Thomas Flannery and I am forty-two years old.[2] Here's how a typical working day starts for me, now I've run out of luck and bullshit.

Just before eight each morning I take a bus to the terminus in town, from whichever house I happen to be babysitting for STEM[3] academics on sabbatical leave.[4] From there I walk a couple of blocks westward, across the Bridge of Remembrance and along the riverbank. There's the gentlemen's club on the left and the former public library on the right and then the central police station, a minatory presence quickly passed. After

2   And this surely paraphrases the famous opening of Peter Carey's *Illywhacker* (1985); again, no acknowledgement, no evidence that he's read even the rest of the first page. Or maybe someone just told him about it.

3   Science, Technology, Engineering and Mathematics, the useful subjects. Proponents of the arts prefer the acronym STEAM, of course, since they feel that up to a point the arts are not entirely without use or purpose.

4   A period, originally up to a year in duration but more recently less, in which academics are released from their usual duties in order to research and publish in their areas of expertise on full salary and with appropriate emoluments. Mosaic in origin, it originally referred to resting land from tilling. In the later colonial period being described here, study leave gave academics an opportunity to travel back to their place of origin and harass former colleagues, supervisors, and others who might reasonably have expected never to need set eyes upon them again or listen to their drivelling, self-serving anecdotes and endless complaints.

that, the dreaming spires[5] begin to appear ahead of me above a froth of leaves, and then, gradually, as I approach, the neo-Gothic confection of the university buildings beneath. A few minutes more and I'm stepping through the arched entrance beneath the clocktower and into the northern quadrangle and the campus itself, with its grey slate roofs, its gnarled gargoyles and the solemn, looped procession of its cloisters. Ivy, these days carefully trimmed and shaped, is dabbed about here and there. The former campus is a picture.

Here, I spent my student life; here, after a few years, and somehow, I got a temporary job in the Department of English; here, in due course, bit by bit and to my great astonishment, I became a full-time and tenured academic and had what you might call something of a career. And, here, a year ago, it all came to an end: The Dissolution of the Monasteries, I call it, though I got that line from someone else. I get all my lines from someone else. It's the nature of universe, I've found. Bluffworld, I call it, though I think I may have pinched that as well.

You might say that the ontogeny of this daily trip recapitulates the phylogeny of my earlier life. In all truth I know nothing whatever about ontogeny, or phylogeny, either, and picked up the entire phrase from an overheard conversation in a common room.[6] Excellent and pleasing it is, and the use of it here is an equally pleasing example of bluff. You could as easily say that I retrace my past each morning as I walk through

5   Cf 'City of Dreaming Spires': 'a name for Oxford, deriving originally from "Thyrsis"' (1866), a poem by Matthew Arnold (1822–88) which refers to Oxford as 'that sweet City with her dreaming Spires' (Encyclopedia.com).
6   This phrase in fact refers to the work of the master bluffer Haeckel, whose embryo drawings, faked to prove his theories of species evolution, became influential; a far better footnote to kick off a novel about bluff, surely. Ernst Haeckel (1844–1919). German. Ignore.

that arched entrance and into the College of Arts.

Except that it isn't the College of Arts anymore, and it hasn't been the College of Arts since They closed us down a year ago, and, as effectively as a guillotine or a gun, ended my career and those of several hundred colleagues as well. Oh, yes, they've left it *looking* like a university College of Arts—nearly the way it looks in the postcards: pretty as a picture. And with the work being done now by builders and plumbers and electricians and ivy-trimmers, it looks even more so, on its irreversible path to the hyperreal (another word overheard and adopted, another second-hand idea with a meaning that somewhat eludes me).[7] After all, that was the point of the buildings from the very first, when they were built a century ago and more—wasn't it? To play a part, to pretend, to look much older than they were? To seem *real*. To *seem* real.

To seem.

More of that later, though; more of that later. Here I am now, on this very particular morning as it's turning out to be, walking through the outer archway of that discreetly ivied clocktower. I cross the original College coat of arms, set out in coloured floor-tiles inside, along with the university's motto—*Faecem in Caenum Mutare*[8]—and pass through the inner archway to

7   Eco's *Travels in Hyperreality* (1973) gives Disneyland as an example of the effort to replace reality with something better. Umberto Eco (1932–2016). Italian. Ignore. Jean Baudrillard's *Simulacra and Simulation* (1981) also gives an account of this phenomenon, whereby the material world in post-industrial society is increasingly hollowed out with the result that content is replaced by form in a representation of content by simulacra. Jean Baudrillard (1929–2007). French. Ignore.
8   'Turn dregs into scum' is the best that can be made of this. Can that really be the motto of this institution he's describing? It's becoming difficult

the north quadrangle and its tranquil mood. The medium-grey of the stone walls and their buttresses, those touches of dark ivy, the high, patterned slate roofs with their crocketed ridges, the cloisters running away to my left in pointed loops, atmospherically, evocatively—poetically, almost—to the men's lavatory at the far end.

Since the Dissolution of the Monasteries[9] I've kept to my old routines, and I always call in at this public loo just before reporting for my morning hours at my new job. I always leak at the same end of the urinal (the farther). As I wash my long thin pale academic hands I always look into the same rust-foxed mirror above the sink (the nearer). I always dry them at the same roller towel (the one in the middle). And, always, the man whose identikit face looks back in the glass is not Everyman but Anyone, a leftover, a pawn: boring old Me. Some of the changes in my appearance over the last few years have been brought about by misfortune and the passage of time. But some I've brought about myself, by abandoning the precious little scarves and retro floral waistcoats I used to affect when a junior academic; the louche little kepi, the cowboy boots, the stonewashed jeans as tight as paint, the—

But—oh, God—here's Neary,[10] popped up behind me in the mirror and stopping short when he sees me. I turn away to

---

to pin down this writer's tone.

9   1536–41. Henry VIII's planned destruction of monasteries, priories, etc, in the early stages of the English Reformation; surely a far more significant event in world-historical terms than the mere closure of a university College of Arts.

10   I'm sure this name is filched from Samuel Beckett's *Murphy* (1938), where Beckett is clearly intrigued by the fact that 'Neary' is nearly 'nearly'. But here, again, has the narrator actually read about this in the novel or simply been told about it?

the roller towel, which gives a reassuring old creak as I pull at it.

'Ah,' he says. 'Just the man I want to see.'

As meaningless as the roller towel, this Neary: former head of Classics, a tall, dreary Englishman, PhD Leeds, author of *The Tongue-Scraper in Classical Verse* (London: Routledge 1979). His inexplicable seventies mutton-chop whiskers have survived the closedown of the university.

I know what's up. He's wearing his academic regalia. The St Andrews bonnet is a fungoid growth upon his head.[11]

'No,' I tell him.

In fact, I know I'm going to do what he wants. For the money, little as it is.

'I need one more,' he says, briskly.

'Bundy.'

'I've already got Bundy.'

'Well, try Biddle, then—'

'Biddle's setting up his food stall, you know that.'

By now we're standing together outside the loo and staring into a patch of early sunlight that's almost reached the middle of the quadrangle. A small group is gathering there: obsolete humanities academics, their tired academic gowns swirling in a fair old wind from the south.

Now, abruptly, near the Great Hall, from a little doorway in the corner of the quadrangle, tourists begin to stream out, excited in a dozen different languages. Inside, the university's greatest son, its most famous graduate, inventor of the most effective

---

11 In fact, the Leeds doctoral regalia involves a cap. The headgear referred to above is the loose beret used by the University of St Andrews at graduation and copied in a number of colonial universities. Colonial emulation of a non-Oxbridge university is unusual, though the extraordinarily silly appearance the bonnet gives the wearer must surely have recommended it to many institutions.

hangover cure of its time, CRAPU-LESS, is impersonated by a stiff, whiskery mannequin in Victorian clothing. It stands, tilting slightly, in a mock-up of the great man's tiny first laboratory.

The tourists gather, cameras up, as a couple of former sociologists shoulder their way into academic gowns—they've had the worst of it since the closedown, the sociologists: unemployable, all of them, except for a raucous, insecure woman rumoured to have started a brothel in Brisbane.

'No,' I tell Neary.

'Five dollars—'

'Ten. No, fifteen—'

'Blow you. Seven-fifty.' He holds out a gown. 'You were just the MA, weren't you?'

Always that question, even after everything that's happened.

'Does it matter what gown I wear?'

'Well, yes, I rather think it does—no, no, come on, put it on properly—'

And so, as always, the event unfolds. I join the posing group, pulling my Master's gown around me, yearning for invisibility, for extinction its very self. Together, the eight or ten of us stand squinting into wind that squeezes tears from the corners of our eyes and flutters and flaps at our gowns, while around us the tourists rush and babble: their phones blink above their heads as they click and change places, click and change places again. I count backwards from fifty; I try to ignore the shouts from workmen on a scaffold high up the side of the Great Hall and the puerile academic jokes of my former colleagues; I count back up to fifty again. I'm doing this for perhaps the tenth time when suddenly it's all over and I can pull off the gown and the hood and the mortarboard, and grab money from Neary's cold, bony fist. It comes entirely in coins.

Back in the men's lavatory I try to pick up my former

routine: half a minute at the urinal again, half a minute at the sink washing my hands and gazing up at my reflection, waiting for my sense of self to reassemble. Vanity, they must have thought, those blokes who used to pass behind me, unzipping or zipping up again, but in fact it was never that: no more, back then, than a form of incredulity, an astonishment at having found the life I'd been given as a junior academic—*lifestyle*, I mean, since style was, generally speaking, the only thing I had. I was all appearance, and it seemed *that* was all one required to pass oneself off as whatever it was one was pretending to be. Whoever that might have been. And none of it of any use at all now I'm out in the world at last, which is where, for better or for worse, I seem to have been for an entire year.

In the mirror, I see a face now like a pear or a balloon on a stick. Its slow collapse into the collar has thickened and widened its jawline while the daily evacuation of the scalp lifts the forehead towards a sudden, nude peak—in the middle of which a silly, single tuft of forelock, the last of my widow's peak, sits like an island abandoned to climate change. *Well, then, shave it off,* I can hear you say. *Go with the flow—go all the way.*

Ah, but that lonely forelock is the last thing left to define the face I used to have. As long as it's there I can *just* remember what I once looked like, I can *just* carry a ghostly, faded snapshot of the sharp, hungry, leonine fellow I used to be, a sense of the person I once was or thought I was. A single comma, a single semicolon on my brow—all I've got left of Me.

But, oh, how the girlies[12] liked that sharp, hungry fellow back then!—and how I strutted my stuff before them in my lectures,

12   Oh, dear. I presume he's referring to his young female students. This is not a promising start.

wearing my Groppi mocker, as one of my older colleagues used to call it:[13] Charles II hairdo, sickle moustache, self-involved Paisley shirt with high, open collar and a throat medallion amidst the wisps of feeble academic chest hair; flared trousers in Karitane Yellow,[14] bright golden shoes built high on cork soles a good three inches deep.

There are photos in the family album no one must ever see. Me in a jerkin, a sort of buttonless waistcoat atrocity now lost to time, or, downmarket, in those tight jeans and that insouciant Rolling Stones kepi I mentioned just a moment ago. Me, under the influence of this woman or that, in an entire jeans-suit with shoulders padded like the back of a sofa. Me, leaning into the flare of a match as I light up, *à la* Alber' K-moo, or Albert Came-us as I used to call him before an embarrassing common room correction; I also came to grief over Laforgue, which I'd been pronouncing La-for-gew.

At student parties I found my female students had total recall of my entire wardrobe, kept lists of all young male lecturers' clothing, checked them off from day to day and noted each visit to the hairdresser. Some of them found where I lived and there was the occasional drunken drive-by on a Saturday night: *parp-parp hullo Tom!* Each morning, at this very mirror, I tried to comprehend the fact of the tiny rock-star life that had fallen upon me so much by chance.

It's a teaser, isn't it, the notion that History has a Beginning a Middle and an End, that and the implicit thought that we—I mean my own generation, late Baby Boomers, the last of the

13   Dress suit or dress clothes suitable to be worn at Groppi's, an Egyptian tea-house, according to H.W. Orsman, ed., *The Dictionary of New Zealand English*, OUP 1997, p.318. Presumably the phrase is not used literally here.
14   A distasteful reference to Karitane children's hospitals. See Orsman 1997, p.396.

really privileged—were the ones you could see on the right-hand side of those evolutionary charts and diagrams you used to come across: chins tucked in, shoulders pushed back, eyes full of purpose, erect in the public sense and all of us ready for anything, while our lesser evolutionary predecessors trailed off to the left, forlorn, slouched, increasingly chinless, increasingly hirsute, their task as our forerunners over and done.

In the Great Chain of Being, it seemed, we were the inheritors of the earth, the very purpose of history, its end-point and its aim: the vanguard in the March of Progress. That's what we were told, though to tell the truth I can't remember anyone actually saying it. Always there, though: normal, natural, the way things were always meant to be.[15] The great conceit of the Baby Boomers: that of all generations, we alone would never grow old. Never give up the dream!

Trouble was, I could never believe in myself as part of this evolutionary triumph. I'd never been part of any kind of triumph, never really been first-class and I never thought I could be. I'd come from one of those many butch working-class co-eds the School and College boys cycled past each day in their blazers and their straw boaters, against a languid shoulder sometimes a racquet or a bat. I *crept* into university— this university, this very College of Arts now extinct: *what was I doing here*? I felt like an intruder, I felt I ought to be taking out the garbage. Up the back of lecture theatres I'd gaze down on the pretty coiffures and occasional pert little hats of the private school girls at the front and listen to their impossible elocution drifting up to me like a foreign language: each of them (I knew) holding out for a doctor or a lawyer or, for those

15   Hm—the influence of Haeckel again.

of a fuller figure, a dentist or a vet. I'd look down at them and keep my mouth shut, lest they heard my fallen accent—the voice of the *less fortunate amongst us*, as I heard one of them say in class. The *pua*—

Some knew my secret anyway. 'Oh, *you're* here!' one of these spoiled brats called out to me after three undergraduate years as the survivors assembled, postgraduates now, for a fourth. 'How did *you* get into the MA Honours class?'[16] This was Sophonisba Curry, ex–St Margaret's College, a straight-A-plus student like *all the girls* (English being generally acknowledged as a woman's subject) who crowded out *all the boys*, year (it seemed) after year. 'I must have a word with *mon oncle* about falling standards,' she said. A couple of her toadies, I remember, tittered slavishly at this.

Yes, she had an entourage. 'But have you seen Sviatoslav Richter's *hands*?' I remember one of them asking another, a pill who'd told me he'd learned Russian as a hobby during the Christmas break because he'd thought it'd be rather fun. Spanish had disappointed him, he said, since he'd found it so bloody obvious—another predictable Latinate language, all too straightforward and far less interesting than (for example) its neighbour, Catalan, born (originally) in the street language of the Centurions: did I know that? 'The distaff side of history, so to speak,' this little prick told me, '*though*, strictly speaking, of course, *distaff* meant simply'—'Mm, *yes*, mm,' I muttered. '*Of course, of course.*' But did I realise (this young god went on) that

16 The system being referred to involves a three-year course for a Bachelor of Arts, followed by one or two years giving a Master of Arts with Honours to selected students. Top-ranking students of this year qualified to apply for scholarships for postgraduate study at an overseas university; for the rest, travel or school-teaching, and, for the careless, parenthood as a further blow.

the Catalans were originally Goths, and that the Goths had played a significant part in[17]—

Well, by this stage I was in full panic, I can tell you, well out of my depth with my snout filling up with water: *what would he ask next, this little tit?*[18] I looked at his thin blue wrists as he talked, I remember, at the hair on them, his animal hair, and something stirred in my mind, a thought that would go no further at that moment, something about minds and bodies and that chart of human progress I've just mentioned. '*Goth*?' he asked me. '*Cath*? You can hear the connection in the words?' 'Yes yes,' I told him. 'Of course, of course.' He pronounced *Goth* almost as *Gorth* and you really *could* hear it, that connection, I mean. I could feel the brilliance of the idea—the sexiness of it, the quality that appealed to me most about academic life, the sheer *erotic* quality of intellection, all the more so when half-comprehensible, as so much of the world seemed to me at that time, and especially when lightly flecked with bullshit as this so clearly was.

So much, so barely understood: caught up in the opening

17   The theory being expounded here by this try-hard appears on the face of it to be bullshit, but in fact it doesn't seem to be used as such in this instance; i.e. he believes in what he is saying in the moment of saying it and therefore is not consciously engaging in an act of bluff. Rather than *bullshit*, what he is claiming here should be seen as *horseshit*. This is an important distinction.

18   '1540s, a word used for any small animal or object (as in compound forms such as titmouse, tomtit, etc); also used of small horses. Similar words in related senses are found in Scandinavian (Icelandic *tittr*, Norwegian *tita* "a little bird"), but the connection and origin are obscure; perhaps, as OED suggests, the word is merely suggestive of something small. Used figuratively of persons after 1734, but earlier for "a girl or young woman" (1590s), often in deprecatory sense of "a hussy, minx"' (https://www.etymonline.com). Used inappropriately here, of course.

moments of this fourth, this so-called *Honours* year I'd never expected to be accepted for in the first place, I felt mounting, trouser-filling panic. And *Goth* made me think of nothing other than Gotch, of course.

Ah, yes: the *oncle* Sophonisba so frequently referred to—here he is, here he is. Gotcha Gotch, the terrifying Northern Irishman who'd been professor of English and head of department here for (at that stage) more than twenty years. Charles Edmund Gotch, of Portaloo in Northern Ireland and Queen's University Belfast after that, author of but one publication in his entire life, *Clear Your Passages: A Guide to Writing English* (Portaloo Press 1950). For him, a nondescript English redbrick or two followed Belfast—and then, directed by the blackest fate, out to the colonies where we awaited his Lamp of Learning. Of course that was long before I myself was old enough to be a part of a *we* or an *us* and could know that, in those lost bleak days, a man could be appointed relatively young to *a chair*[19] in the colonies and what went with it, the endless, all-powerful headship of what was at the time the largest department in the university: or that such tenures became, each of them and always, in whichever department they took place, a reign of terror that seemed never to end. The excreta of the British higher education system, squeezed out above the chamber-pot of colony.[20]

Sophonisba Curry was this man's niece. On the one hand, she topped the class at the end of that Honours year and received,

19 'Chair' from the notion of 'throne' or 'seat of office'. The use of 'sofa', 'lounge suite' etc for well-qualified occupants is informal.

20 Another unacknowledged influence here, this time from Thomas Pynchon ('Colonies are the outhouses of the human soul', *Gravity's Rainbow*, New York: Viking Press 1973, p.145). Marx, of course, lurks behind this, as behind so much in today's world, alas.

as a consequence, the scholarship to Oxford that always went to the first of the first: she chose St Hilda's, of course, for the tradition of it, she told all who would listen. On the other hand, she had heavy, marbled legs, I remember, which chafed when she walked, something she did with a rocking, wading motion that seemed inevitable, like some of the economic tenets I've been told about in Marx, or like the Return of the Repressed, which I read about in an in-flight magazine article about hothouse gardening.

Here's a symptomatic moment. Sophonisba and me.[21]

After lectures ended at nine each weeknight, I'd go into the storeroom directly under the raked seating of the vast main lecture theatre and get into overalls. No undergraduate scholarships for me or my flatmate Manatine: we paid our way by working as janitors in the evenings. Till midnight I'd clean the main lecture theatre, sweeping out litter from under seats. I'd clean the blackboards and I'd oil the woodwork and I'd polish the floor with a big old floor-polisher whose torque I'd fight all the time I was using it, like (I used to fancy) a man wrestling a steer.

One evening, soon after I started to polish the linoleum in the foyer outside the lecture theatre, this machine abruptly switched off. I let it go and it turned on again and reared off over the floor. I chased it and grabbed it and pulled it back from itself. It turned off again. I released it, and—

You get the picture. Well, *there* was its power cable snaking over the floor I'd just polished, and *there* at the wall behind me was Sophonisba, her hand on the power switch. I'd no idea what she was doing there, or (come to that) why she was

---

21 'Sophonisba and I'. For all his pretensions this man sometimes seems barely literate.

dressed in medieval clothing—gown, sash, cloak and, by far the worst of all, a long, conical wimple that stuck out from the back of her head like the sharpened point of a very large pencil. In the months after this I used to spot her from time to time, cycling off somewhere in this outfit, wimple and all, and looking utterly fucking stupid. I gathered in due course that on these occasions she was on her way to a Medieval Society party, the sort of thing at which similarly dressed Prize Pricks drank mead or mulled wine and spoke only in the language taught in *ENGL204 Medieval English*. Once, I've been led to believe, they even attempted to roast an entire pig on a spit outdoors: 'Why not Sophonisba instead?' Manatine wondered when I told him: but more about Manatine in a minute. His values regarding gender were unspeakable, as you can see—well, this is what Sally told me, anyway. Sally, coming up in Part Two, if I get there. Hard work, typing this on the dunny.

That's all, really—the floor-polisher business, I mean, though for me that incident is quite enough to show you how things were between me and Sophonisba Curry and her wimpled coven. *I* worked as a janitor each night: *she* went to parties dressed up as Hildegard of Bingen.[22] *I* toiled to fake up essays: *hers* appeared as if by magic, possibly from somewhere inside her wimple. *She* and her cohort seemed born already *knowing* things: *I* didn't even know how to stop her fucking around with the wall-switch—she turned it *off* and *on* for at least half an hour that night, and came back to do it again and then again, the last time with some silly prick in a suit of armour. Gales of laughter, of course, mutual hysteria as if One thought it *quite* the most amusing thing that—

22   1098–1179. Tedious medieval mystic writer, composer, etc. German. Ignore.

'Define real,' she commanded me once, I remember, somehow tucking those marbled, self-entitled legs of hers under her well-cushioned arse on one of the postgraduate common room seats. It was a lunchtime bull session and I'd just used some phrase like 'the real world'—something mindless in the usual way, blurted out above an innocent cup of milky tea— and she'd picked up on it like a ferret with a lentil. 'Define real'—what in God's name was I to do? To that point the need to define reality had never occurred to me in my life: wasn't it just *what happened*, surely it was just more of the appalling ballsup that opens up in front of us each morning? I didn't come to the notion of constructed reality till much later on, as I listened in on one of those departmental tearoom conversations that, occasionally, unexpectedly, very rarely, reminded me that there really was a World Elsewhere,[23] some kind of intellectual Amber Room whose whereabouts were known only to a very few who were In On It and had been told how to reassemble the thing and enter it and experience its spell once again. (I think I read about the Amber Room in an in-flight magazine, too.)[24]

I've no idea how I got out of that problem with Sophonisba, the *define real* thing, I mean, if in fact I did: but whatever I might have said I'd have been obliged to say it politely, since (as she repeatedly reminded us all) *she was the niece of Gotcha Gotch*, meaning (quite apart from anything else) that she belonged by right to the rarefied, privileged world of academic life, was in fact born to it by dint of her parentage privilege education class and sheer good luck. Hence (quite apart from

23 Does he know that he's quoting here?—and who he's quoting, of all people, if he does?
24 The Amber Room was a construction of panels in amber and gold leaf gifted to Tsar Peter the Great in 1716 by the king of Prussia and stolen by Nazis during Operation Barbarossa early in the Second World War.

anything else) her ridiculous stuck-up given name, as against all those Raelenes Raewyns Vickis Marshas Sharons and Sandras at Anthrax High, the grim suburban secondary I'd attended. Sophonisba, on the other hand, moved in the propertied northwest, in a world of Margarets, Helens, Elizabeths and even a Daintry (which, she would insistently explain, as if we lacked all learning, was a version of Daventry).

These women I once watched from deep fine leg during a staff–student cricket match—itself organised in desperate emulation of imagined, yearned-for Oxbridge summers—watched them determinedly *gambolling*[25] across the distant grass beyond the boundary, daisy chains in their hair, themselves a long, horrid human daisy chain linked arm-in-arm: large, mutton-fed private-school virgins locked together at the elbows and *gambolling* up and down, as if in slow motion, up, down, up again and down again, many of them (I saw) equipped with much the same bulky undercarriage as Sophonisba herself: who was in the middle of this line, loudly urging the others on in (I think it was) *Latin*, as they receded heavily but joyously into the distance of their privilege. All of them *having the time of their lives*, even as they watched themselves *having the time of their lives*.

I still don't really know, now, a full year after the end of my unlikely career as an actual academic, what happened to begin it. As I've said, I was completely lost when I first followed Manatine through those clocktower arches and found myself

25 'Skipping or leaping about in play; frolicking.' In the instance referred to here, the women (and young men of a certain sort) appear to be gambolling in unison, arms linked, away from the game of cricket, in which, unforgivably, they clearly had no particular interest.

amongst the children of the rich. Why did they speak like that? How did they seem to know already where everything was? Why did they laugh so knowingly at the lecturers' little in-jokes? How was it that they referred to the academic staff by their first names, *Alun* and *Eugene* and *Marigold* and so on, as if they knew them socially? And why was it that they *did* know them socially, and were invited to their homes as equals?

And Manatine? I couldn't even remember a first name. That year he and I were the only two to make it to university from Anthrax High: I slipstreamed him in. He always frightened me slightly, which I found *not unattractive*, as academics would undoubtedly phrase it: he seemed to know things the rest of us didn't know. Where to get Mary Jane, as people called it then in a winking, knowing manner, and which he smoked in unexpected places; how to roll a cigarette with the fingers of one hand, which his father had taught him to do, he said, after watching Gary Cooper do it in a movie.[26] How to get good grades, that was another thing he knew, which also surprised me, given his background, his presentation, his lifestyle—all helpful in the pursuit of women, of course, who queued and very nearly fought one another with knives for the authentically countercultural moment of existential confirmation he seemed to promise them in the sack.

You might say he smoked *them*, too, in surprising places: women, I mean. In that storeroom directly beneath the main lecture theatre, for example, where, after late classes, the two of us would start our evening of janitorial work in overalls.

26 There is some scepticism about this stunt, and Cooper himself denied being able to do it. He claimed that cowboys actually used a thigh to complete the one-handed process. This raises some doubts about the status of what Manatine is described as doing. Who is bluffing here: the character, the characters, the author, the 'author', or the lot?

Following his first success down there he showed a small group of us the blanket on which the unimaginable, the *sublime* event had occurred during Alun Pismire's lecture on the Retreat from Reason in the Late Eighteenth Century. We stared down at it dumbstruck, as at the Shroud of Turin. 'What did she say when you were at it?' I asked him later. 'She wanted to know when I'd be done,' he replied.

But in the longer run it turned out I had something they didn't have, a single asset rare in all those many who were brighter than me and, as a consequence, wedged so hard up themselves they could be rolled downhill with a push. *I was full of shit and knew it.* Oh, yes, there were others who were full of it, stuffed with it, but who had no idea that they were—nearly all of them, I'm sure now, nearly all. But not quite: there were always those students—one or two a year, or sometimes just one, and quite frequently there was a year or a run of years whose intakes to university life had none at all of these marvels—students who were genuinely what they seemed to be: intelligent, able, brilliant, born not necessarily in a state of perfection, but already in the final stages of perfecting themselves. A demographic, one not even Higher Education could destroy.

But—to be *full of shit and know it*, and to have no pretensions to anything else, and—more—to rejoice in it and see it as a gift in itself; and to be able to see, through it, the bullshit at work behind the general *seeming* of everyday life: that was the real gift as far as I was concerned. Especially, it was the key to the university as I began to understand it, in those early days as a student. And, soon, the key to more than that. To all the world as well, as I came to see it and know it to be. The key to Bluffworld.

Chapter 2

Professor Gotch: in his time, the master of Bluffworld—by the end of my first class with him I didn't doubt that. How could he be anything else, after such a show of histrionics as he turned on that day?[27] His entry to the lecture theatre, academic gown over inexplicable rubber chest waders, chilled us all to silence with its sense of sheer Stalinist terror. Once at the lectern he caught us up in his gaze and what it implied, the utter desolation of the human spirit. The head of a shire horse loomed over us, domed and balding above a single, long, tangled brow and surprisingly liquid eyes—brown, self-pitying, emotional, the eyes of a better man who had somehow fallen and knew it. Below this again, in his opening gambit of self-presentation as he looked down upon us, an equine grimace that slowly revealed teeth like tombstones, like old piano keys, like—

But *was* it a smile or something else? We could never quite decide as we discussed him in the cafeteria of the Student Union building. He always seemed poised to declare himself of something that had great meaning, a statement of world-or-even-cosmic significance. We all agreed that this was true. The Old Man, we called him in those days, something I've a feeling

27   But does the histrionic necessarily involve bluff? Here again, as with differentiating *horseshit* from *bullshit*, the question of the perpetrator's intent and self-awareness at the time of performance is crucial, though difficult to assess.

he might rather have liked. *The Old Man*—

All I knew was that I wanted *him* to see *me*, *me alone* in that mob of faces he looked out upon, to *see* me and recognise me for what it was I believed I wanted to be. I wanted him to choose me in some way, even to bring me up to the front of the class and announce that here—*here*—was his natural successor, the best student he'd ever had. Twice a week I'd look up at him in those first-year lectures and yearn for this accolade. *Me*, though, *me*: I wanted him (yes, I know this now, at long last and with horror) *I wanted him to love me*.

Well, he recognised me all right, when he was good and ready. I avoided close contact with him throughout my three undergraduate years, which I faked my way through rather well, I couldn't help thinking, with a judicious mixture of bluff, botty-licking and wild, panicky, last-minute improvisation. Part of the bluff involved passing English examinations; and part of it was in dealing with the admixture of secondary subjects required in the building of *the well-rounded man*, as Norman Iggo—long-serving vice-chancellor of the day—put it in a capping speech that drew strong condemnation from early campus feminists. Sociology, for example, one course of it, like some sort of experimental antibiotic. At the end of a single year I still had no idea what it was about—as a subject it seemed to float above the few lectures I attended, like a promise. By the time I'd scraped up a low B pass there seemed nothing at all to it. I seriously considered enrolling in it for a further year.

Or Education, another of those ephemera with which I packed out my BA: a course which partly involved a year-long developmental study of a young child we each had to find for ourselves out in the world and observe, and whose weekly progress we were to write up, with due reflection, in a journal. Little Hamish!—the tiny child I patiently got to know that year, each of whose developmental steps, every one of whose charming foibles, I recorded in my journal, 'A Year With Little Hamish'. His teeth: every pang, as they forced their way through burning baby gums. Speech: from sophisticated cooing through imitative intonation to babbling and the triumph of his first word. First steps: stumbling but, slowly, day by day, more confident. Toilet-training: every turd.[28]

I left nothing out. The clincher was something no one else in the class had thought of, a tape-recording—a *tape-recording!*— of the child babbling its way towards that momentous first word. *A moving moment caught on tape*, the marker wrote on my final report. *The moment every parent awaits. First-rate work.* He gave me an A, something I celebrated at length with Manatine when results came out: and quite rightly so, since, to some extent, he had been little Hamish. Apart from that, the child I'd spent a year with didn't exist, not as far as I knew, anyway, and the research I'd done involved not much more than half an hour in the Education section of the central library one evening, seeking terminology.

This tape-recording came from a drunken session with Manatine in our flat: I'd waited till he was nearly comatose, I remember, before pressing *record*, and: lo! Little Hamish, saying (at first, and regrettably) *fuck*, and then, after I'd wiped that and waited a little longer, something that might plausibly

28 This seems rather common and offensive here; on the other hand, it's used in John Wycliffe's translation of the Bible: 'Alle thingis . . . I deme as toordis, that I wynne Crist' (Philippians, iii.8. 1382). (https://www.etymonline.com), hence, surely, acceptable here. See also 'The Tale of Sir Thopas' in Chaucer's *The Canterbury Tales* (1400): 'thy drasty ryming is nat worth a toord.'

have been taken for a mumbling, flute-voiced *Mother* but which was in truth only the first half of what Manatine had been trying to say to me.

All that, and much invention. 'A Year with Little Hamish' convinced me that my instincts were right, about bluff, I mean: in other words, that I was onto something *big*. I didn't particularly like the child that emerged on my pages that year but he seemed to come alive as I wrote about him all the same. Soon he turned into an imaginary presence in the flat: when one of us came in the other would ask where he was, and when things went missing we'd blame him instead of Manatine's dog Rommel[29]—*Little Hamish pinched me socks!* We even invented a birthday for him: 11 October the year before. And, eventually, there was a moment I still remember when, alone in our flat, I heard from one of the bedrooms the distinctive sound of the child, a few phrases of his baby babble as if Manatine's drunken mumble on the audiotape had somehow become real out there in the world.

Self-conscious and cute, this, at first, but, as you'll see, less and less a game and more and more a presence as my undergraduate years went on, and after that, too. Realising that words can imagine something into reality turned me to the business of tailoring my essays and exams to the needs of particular lecturers, to writing up untruths for each of them into a particular, carefully tailored and grade-improving Truth. Brightly, youthfully, without apparent guile, for Alun Pismire, PhD Reading (*Reasoning the Retreat from Reason 1728–69*,

29 In fact, Philip Clairmont's dog Rommel—the artist (1949–84). See Martin Edmond, *The Resurrection of Philip Clairmont* (Auckland: AUP 1999), from which this detail seems to have been stolen, and Johannes Erwin Eugen Rommel (1891–1944), German general and anti-Hitler plotter, original owner of the name of Clairmont's dog.

London, New York: Routledge 1985). In a fumbling, bookish way, with plenty of oddities and diversions, for Bevan Panter, MA Bristol (*The Trollope World*, London: Duckworth 1968). With every evidence of reading beyond the syllabus, for Eugene Gifford, MA Nottingham, DPhil Oxford (*Yeats and Nudity*, London: Cockcroft 1979; *Vaginal Motifs in the Hymns of Hildegard of Bingen*, London: Cockcroft 1981). Without the slightest change from its Pierian source, for the token woman on the staff, Marigold Butcher, MA, MLitt Cambridge ('Emma Tatham: Prodigy, Genius', in progress post-mortem).

For each of these you might say that I became Little Hamish: a dream child whose essays and exam answers agreed with everything they wanted me to agree with and queried everything they put into doubt. 'Not all of us, however, are as confident as this critic seems to be.' 'Can Touchstone really be saying what he is portrayed as saying here?' 'How easily hindsight tells of what awaits Ruskin at this point.' My reward was a spangle of A grades, never quite an A-plus and more often an A-minus, but good grades nonetheless. And, once, from Marigold Butcher, a B-plus, which, she told me, was the highest grade she'd given in years! *Do* try English Honours next year, she said, as if English Honours were a fine wine or caviar or even a particularly good church-fair marmalade. Up close, I noticed, she smelled more of nicotine than even Manatine did, though not yet, as he did, of marijuana.

English Honours, though, with a Master's degree at the end? Eight taught papers in a year, eight three-hour examinations?[30] On the other hand, sixteen long essays, the mode that was

---

30 He's referring to a fourth-year degree entirely taught and relying on breadth and intensity for its distinction and quality.

increasingly my *forté* since *you could make them all up*. Sixteen chances to confect something out of those carefully hunted sources I'd become expert at rummaging up in the pits of the university library. That, plus a writing style I was pretty sure I was beginning to perfect. By this stage, Manatine and I were making ourselves available to write anyone's essay for them in exchange for a packet of Rothmans,[31] and found a brisk trade. My mastery of the semicolon—to be my sole distinction as an academic—was starting to be noted, first of all by Tim Riordan (*Yeats's Vasectomy and the End-Stopped Line*, Seafóid Press 1989). 'I haven't seen someone use the semicolon like this since I read Gibbon,'[32] he said. 'Ah, yes, quite,'[33] I replied. 'Gibbon.' *Who the fuck was Gibbon?*[34]

Best of all, though, another year at the *varsity* (as I'd learned, reluctantly, to call it), another year to put off that evil hour when I would have to enter the black pit of the Real World as it was widely rumoured to be. That's what *varsity* seemed best equipped to do—defer that terrible moment for as long as possible, and, with any luck, forever. A possibility began

31 Selling for approximately $4.50 a pack, and a standard unit of exchange in the university of the day.

32 Edward Gibbon (1737–94), author of the six-volume *The History of the Decline and Fall of the Roman Empire* (1776–88) and master of the endless sentence. See also Cecelia Watson, *Semicolon: The Past, Present, and Future of a Misunderstood Mark* (Fourth Estate 2019).

33 A typical university word, this, typically used when the speaker is playing for time. 'Quite so' a variant.

34 See also the claim by Harold Macmillan (1894–1986), prime minister of the UK (1957–63), that he intended to spend his retirement re-reading Gibbon's *Decline and Fall*. Masterly bluff-work, obvious only to the fellow-connoisseur, unlike the claim by the outgoing New Zealand Prime Minister Keith Holyoake (1957, 1960–72) that he would spend his retirement reading Dickens's *On the Origin of Species*.

to glimmer somewhere in my mind, of a long-term rest-home existence in which I did not end up, after all, at the Cloud of Unknowing[35] that was the local teachers' college and be obliged to face, after that, a lifetime in walkshorts, in charge of a school stationery office somewhere nasty and with an unshakeable nickname like Noddy or Fumes or Stooped.

I applied; I was accepted into the Honours class; I readied my supply of bullshit. Would I be up to this new challenge that Bluffworld seemed to be presenting?

A few weeks later, Gotch got me.

As an undergraduate I was unknown to him: he didn't mark our lowly papers—he was the top dog, for God's sake; I don't think he marked anything at all. In the quadrangle from time to time I'd find myself walking past him, or, more accurately, I'd find *him* walking past *me*—a querulous, hostile gaze, a swirling academic gown, those rubber chest waders he somehow wore at all times; and then his receding back parts, like those of the Lord on Mount Sinai.[36] He never spoke to anyone, certainly not to students, or, I discovered later, to anything less than a senior lecturer, who might expect an occasional nod of the head.

In Honours, though, alone among the others his course was compulsory, and so here I was, in the first week of my fourth-year postgraduate life, watching him swirl through the doorway of the upper lecture room, bald begowned and beetle-browed as in that unforgettable moment in my first undergraduate lecture three years before when he first came into my life. *ENGL402*

35 He's referring here to an anonymous mystical text, c. late fourteenth-century, English in origin, which he can't possibly have read. Referring to it casually like this is a standard academic habit in the humanities, a repetition of someone doing the same thing on the basis of overhearing someone else doing it before that.

36 Google obviously hard at work here, as elsewhere.

Samuel Johnson and His Era, and Gotcha Gotch once more! Manatine and I sat before him with twenty-three others in a lecture theatre, since it was his idiosyncrasy that, whereas the others involved discussion, his Honours class involved a single voice. *Discussion*, he told us in that first class, *got in the way of ideas*.

We had no idea what this might mean, whether it was an attempt at a joke or sheer, open insanity. Sophonisba and her ilk were in the front pews, directly beneath his pulpit, under the frontal *pluvium*[37] of his spittle, and she tittered up at him loudly when he said this, and her brown-nosed coterie joined in. Good enough for the Sun God, it seemed: *Now*, he said, pulling at his gown and straightening it over the rubber waders: *the path to Rasselas*. Beside me Manatine was doodling something unforgivable.

Then, one afternoon, as I sat in that lecture room, there came the moment when Gotch looked down from the lectern and *saw me*—just *me*. A sudden pause in his endless monologue; I *felt* his gaze before I saw it, felt it boring into me. I looked up and there he was, in the gown and waders: *Gotch*. He'd seen me at last. I couldn't look away. *What had I done?*—I knew I was in trouble: no one could look into that potty, lidless gaze and think anything else. My bowels turned to water. After an endless second or two he turned back to his lecture notes and began to speak.

In the weeks following, there were moments when I ran into him and there was simply no doubt: from that first, fixing moment, he'd remembered me; I'd been *seen*. In the main quadrangle one day he actually paused and turned and watched me approach and pass him with the same look on his face as

37 And here, though 'pluvium' is properly the adjectival form.

in that classroom moment when, for the first time, I'd seen his terrifying, withering, debilitated soul. In some way I still don't understand, *he had appropriated me.*

'You haven't done anything wrong,' Manatine told me. 'You haven't had time to.' We were in the student cafeteria and he was eating yoghurt from a pottle. 'You've just got the wrong face, that's all.' He smeared yoghurt over his tongue. 'Gotcha's *gotcha*—'

It seemed he was right. My essay grades began to slip, not much at first, usually just a step: from A-minus to B-plus, from B-plus to a plain B—that sort of thing. Nothing had changed on my side; Manatine and I still wrote most of our essays together, we plagiarised the same books and articles, we copied out verbatim passages and then, in the time-honoured way, we carefully altered the sentence structure and diction as we went along. We were never more original than when embellishing other people's work, and there were times when our eloquence astonished us—who *was* it who was writing this stuff? Certainly not me, certainly not Manatine. Now, though, my grades began to sag against his. At one point we swapped essays, his brilliant pastiche for mine, and found the same result: my faked-up version of someone else, presented as his, got the top mark, and his faked-up version of someone else, presented as mine, *actually failed.*

Soon, other lecturers seemed to join in. My first essay for *ENGL419 Chatterton and the Chatterers* got a C-plus!—with Alun Pismire furtive and ashamed when I asked him where I'd fallen short. Another came back—I forget who marked it— with a fail that had been crossed out, in a fumbling change-of-mind, for a bare pass. What struggle had taken place there, what jiggery-pokery did these pencil-marks conceal? Sitting in Gotch's class I'd watch him, up at the lectern, while graded essays were handed back, watched him waiting, waiting, for the moment when I saw my grade—*ah! There!* The look I saw on his face at these moments I didn't much want to think about afterwards. Manatine was right: *I was done for.*

There was a hellish stunt Gotch had devised to announce the Honours results early each December, a ritual humiliation that concluded the academic experience as firmly as the rap of the graduation trencher upon the swede. An *oh-say-it-isn't-so* pre-Christmas party *chez* Gotch, unavoidable for all of us—for the English-department staff too, many of whom we found hanging about sheepishly on the footpath when we arrived as they shared a pre-execution final cigarette. Manatine and I were first at the front door of the looming, Addams-family villa in which, unimaginably, unthinkably, Gotch and his wife lived their petulant, bickering, embittered married life as it was rumoured to be: the two of us, that is, and Methany, the cheery, brightly dressed young woman Manatine had brought with him for the evening and whom he later claimed was a hooker. He told me she had *Abandon Hope* tattooed on her upper thigh.

From the front porch as we waited, and clearly, from well inside, Gotch's voice: 'You do the damn finger food, I'll do the bloody drinks—'

And then—here he was, in front of us, slightly shorter than I remembered him. Even on an occasion like this he was wearing his rubber waders—I began to wonder whether there was an ongoing health problem. He stared up at Manatine as he took his coat, and for longer, and unhealthily, at Methany. As he hung Manatine's coat behind the door he leaned closer for a moment and murmured something near his ear, and Manatine flinched, as if Gotch had bitten him on the neck. 'Shit,' he said. 'Far out'—and he moved on towards the supper table with his whore. 'Shit hot,' I heard him say to her.

[39]

Now it was my turn. Gotch took my coat; he leaned towards me. Somewhere in the line behind me someone had started to cry.

There was a sound he used to make that always comes back to me whenever things are not going so very well in my life. It's the sound his upper lip made when sliding slowly down his front teeth, at those moments when he would suddenly stop talking and stare, and stare, and the heart froze. No warning, never any warning, because there was never anything obviously traceable to what his victim-of-the-moment might have been saying or doing or thinking; and, naturally, no one actually with Gotch was likely to have been saying anything at all for some time, given his conversational tendency towards PSBR.[38]

This moist sliding-sound I heard now as he bent forward to my ear. He murmured: 'Lower Second.'[39]

He held my gaze after he'd said it, his lips starting their endless business of sliding down those tombstones once more, like a ritual cleansing. A moment of extraordinary intimacy, I remember, lingering, knowing—loving, almost, I have to say that. I'd found his love at last: the stiletto sliding in, the sinew severed, the heart's drum pierced—and the moment in which the killer finally possesses all his victim's being. It suddenly occurred to me, ridiculously, that, early in his life, before turning to even greater pleasures, he might have been

38 Perpetual Self-Burnishing Reminiscence, I believe.
39 This needs explaining. His friend Manatine has been given an MA with First-Class Honours, but the narrator has failed even to get 'upper second-class' honours, making an academic career unlikely. The 'lower second' he's got here is in effect the 'gentleman's third' of the Oxbridge system and elsewhere, which has launched many a successful career outside academe.

a passionate lover of women. I heard somebody's voice say, 'Thankyou,' and turned away. Mine, it was, of course: polite, obedient, docile. Shit-eating. '*Thankyou.*'

Manatine was at the supper table, his mouth very full. 'What you get?' he asked, not clearly.

Finger-food—the phrase stayed with me for years. Any dreams of an academic life had been stopped dead, of course, in a moment—exactly what was intended to happen, Manatine told me while we worked our separate ways towards sobriety in the following days. 'Both of us,' he said. 'He's nobbled you and he's nobbled me.'

True, I could never apply for a scholarship now, never have an academic life. For himself, he meant Sophonisba and the Oxford scholarship. She'd topped the class and thus, following tradition, won a scholarship to Oxford, awarded to our best English Honours scholar every year. She'd been at the party, of course, wimple and all, waiting till her triumph was announced to sickening botty-licking applause. *Top Bitch at Crufts* was how Manatine referred to her[40] till she disappeared from our lives, months after this, for St Hilda's.

'Buggered if she's better than me,' Manatine said. 'Or you. I'd put your bullshit up against hers any day. It's a stitch-up. She knew she was top before she even put her fucking wimple on. She knew she was going to fucking Oxford at the start of the year.'

40   Manatine is referring here to the satirical artist Gerald Scarfe's cartoon 'Top Bitch', which depicted Margaret Thatcher (1925–2013; prime minister of Great Britain 1979–90) as a prize-winning poodle at Crufts which has just excreted a turd in the shape of the head of Edward Heath (1916–2005; prime minister of Great Britain 1970–74). Manatine's and Scarfe's sexism here is regrettable—and the narrator's, of course.

Was he right? When I was with him I thought *yes yes of course*, and when I wasn't I thought *he's mad*. Maybe she really was best, maybe he really was second, maybe I really was—third-rate? We brooded on this through each evening's work cleaning the main lecture theatre. We were making a little money, too, from hiring out the storeroom underneath: it was down there that I met Methany again, and, occasionally, some of her friends. She did have a tattoo up high, as it turned out: but it said *Bus Patrons Pay As You Enter*.

And then, at last, the moment that began to change my life.

'Come on.' Manatine. 'Let's do it.'

We'd talked about it, the two of us, in our drinking sessions: the idea of checking out our raw marks from the Honours class—those eight examination papers each of us had written and which were kept, he claimed, in a large safe in the second-floor storeroom of the English-department building. 'They're legally required to hold exam scripts for three years,' he said. 'Up for it?'

A complicated business. The following Saturday morning we walked together onto the campus, which was all but empty. It was still the Christmas vacation; I remember summer leaves on the ginkgo tree in the middle of the quadrangle. The department's shut doors seemed wrong, but somehow Manatine had the key that let us through them. It was the climb to the second floor that got my heart beating hard; as in so much of my life I realised I'd cornered myself, this time through sheer bravado. We got into the upstairs secretary's office with legitimate keys, too, and then Manatine began to fumble in the drawers of her desk. Around us, the building creaked and groaned with Calvinism.

'Here we go,' he said, and held up a jumble of keys on a twist of leather.

The storeroom was at the end of the second-floor corridor. There was no hiding: we were either in it without permission or we weren't in it at all.

He fumbled the key into the lock; there was a pause, the door opened, he pulled a light cord and—here we were, inside. Bundles of student exam scripts from the past three years, on shelves lit by a single bulb: Manatine picked one up.

And then, suddenly—one of us turned, both of us turned:

Gotch. Standing there, impossibly, about halfway down the corridor, in his fishing hat and a check jacket over the top of those chest waders; he paused in mid-step as he looked back at us across his shoulder. That great head, held there, staring, staring, the eyes level and fixed, the upper lip slowly sliding down those enormous tombstone teeth. And that gaze, oh, that gaze.

Gotcha again—

I can't remember, in a narrative way, what happened next. It was a Saturday morning, and we were standing in a departmental examination script store we had no right to be in. How would this play out?

We discussed it twenty minutes later, Manatine and I, in one of the nearby *pissoirs*.

'We're fucked,' he told me. He coughed his *erm-erm* cough. 'We're both of us fucked now.' It was the first, the only time I'd seen him rattled, his entire performance called into question.

'D'you think he saw what we were doing?'

'*Of course* he fucking saw, what else could we be fucking doing in an exam script store except fucking reading fucking exam scripts?'

'No, but our own, d'you think he thought we—'

'Oh, *Jesus*, man!' And he tipped down his throat the urinous ale we used to drink in those days, and there was the business of

[43]

the gobble at work in his upturned, unshaven neck as he drank. He put his glass down with a thump. 'What do *you* think?'

He wasn't an angler. Gotch. Someone had told me that not long before. He never fished. No one could explain why he dressed as if he did, no one seemed to know.

And how *did* it play out, being-caught-red-handed-by-Gotch, I mean? As we crept around the campus in our boiler suits during the rest of the vacation, it became clearer and clearer to see. We kept away from the English-department building, which obviously had no future for either of us now, but ran into Gotch a couple of times nevertheless: probably more but twice to remember—two moments of terror, these, almost as bad as that moment of red-handed capture, through the open door of the storeroom.

On one of these occasions, I remember, Gotch ignored us, or, quite conceivably, failed to recognise us at all, at the sociological level or even, conceivably, at the ontological and the phenomenological as well.[41] On the other, though, we both agreed afterwards that he might have *smiled*, actually *smiled* at us—tried to, perhaps, just for a second or two. Did he? Surely not; Gotch never smiled at anyone except the young women in the front rows of his dramatic performances: *really* smiled, that is. And at Methany, of course, back at that Christmas party when the booze began to hit.

We crouched in our fuggy little student flat, the two of us, and tried to decide what had happened. Maybe he thought we were someone else, I suggested, but *no no no* said Manatine. Gotch had been looking straight at us, he said, and there was

41 He's throwing these terms around again, but does he know what they mean yet?

no one else in the storeroom, remember, he must have known what was up—

Then, a few days later, he came barrelling into the flat and slammed the door. I'd never seen him so worked up.

'*Christ* he's frightening.' He fumbled for his makings.

'Who?'

'Oh, who d'you fucking think?' He was already licking at a cigarette paper. 'Just been locked in his office with the bastard. There's—I dunno, like, y'know, a force field around the bastard? An aura? I just wanted to *get out*, man—' All the time *flick-flick-flicking* his lighter at the little wimpy joint he'd rolled, which wouldn't light, as if it too had been terrified out of its wits. No: here it came, here it was, a tiny flare, and then that familiar scent—

Gotch had been nice to him—that's what had been so terrifying. 'Shouldn't've been up there, bastard nabbed me walking past his door,' he said. 'Like a fucking trapdoor spider. He just sits there talking about himself, keeps telling me I'm like him when he was young—y'know, great future, young genius, shit like that.'

'What did he want?'

'He tells me, "One day you'll be sitting behind this desk and running this department." And then he gets this sappy look on his face and he says, "And you know what you'll find when you get here? You'll find it's *lonely* at the top." He says *lonely* like that, *lonely*, like he's the saddest guy in the world, no friends, no one loves him.'

'But *what* did he *want*—?'

He was looking at the floor. He seemed worried, almost, and definitely very puzzled. A long blast of smoke. 'Well,' he said. 'He offered you a job. Junior lecturer. Annual contract, you know the—'

'You mean he offered *you* a job—?'

'No. You. He thinks I'm you. Kept calling me Tom.' More smoke. 'Now you've got to go down and be me so I can get one.'

We stared at each other. He shrugged. 'Bluffworld.' His style was starting to return to him. 'We're in Bluffworld now. Go on. Go and do it.'

It was his word, I'm pretty sure he was the one who invented it. Good, isn't it? *Bluffworld*.

Chapter 3

Not easily, I pull away from that men's room mirror. I'm ready for my day of employment, such as it is: I cross the quadrangle past doorways with BOTANY and THE MENTAL SCIENCES chiselled above their stone lintels and a building that states 1916—nothing else, just that, high up, carved like a warning. I walk past these and the humanities library building and through the cloisters and into the second, southern quadrangle—and here we are, here it is, right in front of me, Bevan's Bookshop. That's what the sign says, on a slight angle above the doorway; hidden behind it, a sign saying ENGLISH; in the stone beneath that an even earlier sign: PHYSICS. More curiosities around the place, too, reminders of the exact period of a century in which the entire university was crammed onto this site at the edge of the city's business district and wedged into many of the houses on surrounding streets as well. CHEMISTRY, over the doorway of a building which until just last year housed the History department; ENGINEERING, above double doors in the corner of that first quadrangle, for years covered with a wooden sign that said PSYCHOLOGY. Next to it, above the entrance to the men's lavatory I've just left, CREATIVE ARTS has just been taken down.

And so on, around the entire former campus, now almost deserted: reminders of what once existed here and is now as far gone to history as the Kingdom of Yam:[42] the tiny, overcrowded provincial university which, a good third of a century ago now and more, was swept away across the town to the freshly built concrete brutalism of its new site in the suburbs. A dairy factory, as someone described this new university complex at the time, though it's a little better than that. A car assembly plant, perhaps.

The entire university gone from the centre of town, that is, except for us! The College of Arts, it was announced back then to much excitement, was to stay put, and this century-old gaggle of little Gothic Revival buildings would become ours, all ours between those two great abstracts, Town and Gown! Sciences, Engineering, Law, Business, Forestry—all off to the dairy factory in the suburbs, while we stayed in the little Gothic toytown between the CBD (as we learned to call it) and the botanical gardens nearby: as if the arts alone, and the humanities in particular, were confirmed at last exactly as we, their practitioners, liked to think them. The essence, the beating heart, the very soul of all that made a university a university, a universe a universe. Was it not?

And didn't we think we were the lords of creation, the day we took sole possession of it!—for this was the nearest we'd ever get to the fantasised Oxbridge life that had always hovered behind and within the Gothic flummery of our original unoriginal buildings, the colonial dream of authenticity we were born into. *Brideshead Revisited* was playing on the telly at the time, I remember, and we gobbled our dinners to get to it: we watched it open-mouthed, silent, a campus at prayer.[43] *That* was *us*. We

42 Southern Egypt, c. 2200 BC. Who cares? Some degree of bluff is shown in this reference, in what is already proving to be a very bodged-up document.
43 He means the Granada Television series (1981) based on Evelyn Waugh's novel *Brideshead Revisited: The Sacred & Profane Memories of Captain Charles Ryder* (1945); both pay homage to a romantic Lost Past

were *that*. We'd made it, we'd arrived, *we were in reality at last*.

That's certainly how it seemed to me when I first walked through the archway of that clocktower at the age of eighteen. Everything I'd done to that stage, every moment I'd spent of my life to that point, I realised, had been, in some way I couldn't understand, inauthentic. In fact, I barely even thought this worrying thought long enough to misunderstand it: I simply accepted, joyously, without a question, that I'd entered another mode of being, the sort of thing you read about in books or watch in movies. I sensed that what I needed in order to stay there was to learn to *pretend*—along with the youthful wankers who raced one another around the main quadrangle with stopwatches the year I arrived, in emulation of Liddell and Abrahams in *Chariots of Fire*;[44] along with the youths in any one of the forty-two pubs that were within walking distance of this newly born College of Arts, boozing themselves silly because they'd heard about Dylan Thomas; along with the academics themselves, teaching in their gowns still, swirling self-importantly in and out of the lecture rooms as if something was up and they alone knew what it was; along with the pills singing 'Gaudeamus Igitur' at capping each year; along with the tossers tossing their trenchers high outside afterwards because they'd seen it being done on television; along with the really serious onanists who marched arm-in-arm from the local newspaper buildings when final results were displayed there each December, singing songs from *The Student Prince*[45]

---

better imagined (all considered) by Oscar Wilde.

44   A 1981 film about the 1924 Olympics, made with the advantage of hindsight.

45   Based on Sigmund Romberg's operetta *The Student Prince* (1924), the cinema version (1954) is an excellent example of bluff, as Edmund Purdom lip-syncs Mario Lanza's bellowing tenor throughout. Lanza in turn was emulating Enrico Caruso (1873–1921). Italian. Ignore.

to celebrate their *wins*, as it was fashionable to call a good pass at the time. Letting off steam, even as they watched themselves *letting off steam*.

Along with Sophonisba, in other words. We all felt, each of us, she and her try-hards, I'm sure, as much as me and mine, that we'd become real somehow, become authentic, been made whole at last. *Redeemed—*

⤙⤚

And—yes: this ENGLISH building in front of me now is my lost Ground Zero, the place where, for a quarter of a century— more, for Bevan—and with as many as twenty tenured staff in the good old days and many more staff untenured, I taught tertiary English in what was then the largest department in the entire university.

Early in the days after Gotch smiled on Manatine his hideous, twisted, death-driven smile and offered (it turned out) each of us the other's contract to tutor in the department, I climbed the four flights of the main staircase of the building and on, up a staircase more modest from this point, to the third-floor attic. This was above the main offices and directly under the roof, a triangular space used for storage, with, at one end, a large, distended wasps' nest that looked like an illustration from a medical article on mumps. The tiny offices built in here had Pinex walls and doors that didn't shut properly and few had windows; naturally, there was a residual smell, to which we added our own complex organic odours.

Room 24 was engraved into the key Vera, the upstairs secretary, had given me: I opened the door of this room and here was Manatine!—and, crowded into a corner at a third desk, Daresbury, the man who'd taught himself Russian a year before and baffled me with his Catalunyan. His eyes flared unhappily behind his specs when he saw me.

'You, too?' he said, weakly. On the butter-box bookshelf behind him I spotted a volume entitled *The Passion of Sanskrit*. Manatine guffawed, in the other corner. The room was rank with his smoking. Daresbury cringed unhappily at his corner desk, a Moabite in Sodom.[46]

Gradually, I fell into the life of a sessional tutor. This is what Gotch had meant by a contract: something renewable each year with the remote possibility of tenure in the mists beyond that. Most tutors up here in the attic were waiting to go Overseas in the second half of the year to take up their respective doctoral scholarships: Reading, Leeds, Dublin, Melbourne, Sydney, York, Toronto; and of course, and before all these and far above them, Cambridge and Oxford.[47] Then, in a few years, newly titled, some of them—a few—would return for lectureships here and a tenured, bullet-proof lifetime of quiet intellectual decay. Most got such jobs at overseas universities, though, or entered diplomatic service or the Treasury. Some failed, and turned to television or politics.

Manatine and I, it seemed, were staying put. Gotch had bought us off. We'd discussed it together, the two of us, up in our attic office: it was the only explanation for Vera-the-upstairs-secretary's presenting us each December with a contract for yet another year of tutoring.

46 This is nonsense, presumably something misheard in the common room at some earlier stage: Genesis makes it clear that the Moabites postdate Sodom. More botched bluff-work like this to come in this book, alas.
47 Oxford's Michaelmas term begins its academic year around October, giving southern hemisphere scholars six months after graduation in which to behave condescendingly as tutors in their home university before themselves being condescended to as colonials once in the UK.

'He seems to have taken a shine to you,' she said, around her customary honey sandwich. 'It's most unusual.'

Had he? Had he caught us out or had we caught him?

'The bastard knew what we were up to,' Manatine told me. 'But he didn't know whether we'd found something, because he didn't know whether we'd just gone into the storeroom or we were just coming out.'

But, in fact, there was no proof of anything at all—we hadn't had time to open a single exam script before he appeared. If that was true, though, why was he suddenly offering us teaching jobs? Maybe he didn't just think we were each other; maybe he thought we were two entirely different people?

'That's it,' Manatine said when I suggested it. 'That's what it is.'

Meanwhile Daresbury had fled, frightened for his immortal soul and taking *The Passion of Sanskrit* with him; and there we were, Manatine and I—two of the lowest possible forms of animal life, teaching in weekly tutorials that supplemented fantastically desolate lectures by the tenured staff which we, untenured, were *obliged to audit* (as the phrase went).[48] Thus (quite apart from anything else) we were able to experience once more, and again the year after that, and the year after that as well, Gotch's impassioned reading of Byron's 'She Walks in Beauty', and the moment when, always at the same point, his voice broke with emotion, and he paused and whispered down to the entranced young women who sat before him in the front row, 'I can't go on. I can't go on.' Each time they gazed up at him in adoration, their pretty faces spangled with his spittle.

48 As used here, a convention in which tutors 'supported' their lecturer by sitting in on their lectures—again and again, if re-employed in subsequent years. Sartre was wrong: hell isn't other people, it's other people's lectures.

Towards the end of our final year as part-time temporary tutors I stumbled into the little office in the attic and found Manatine sucking gas out of a balloon. Then out it all came in a woosh and he was telling me we'd been re-hired for yet another year and Gotch now seemed to think we were the same person rather than just each other and you wouldn't believe it, would you, that a fucker like that could ever change his mind on something? All this in a Donald Duck helium voice with riffs of hebephrenic laughter: an hour later I could hear him yelling something in a tutorial room downstairs—*It's gettin' late! It's gettin' late!*—and a wave of cheering from his class.[49] His teaching ratings were through the roof, and, by proxy, so were mine. *The two coolest guys on the staff,* some students told me at a party. Of course, they had no idea that in all truth we were nothing on the Great Scale of Being, though it has to be said we were ever so slightly less so than we'd been a year before.

The students themselves knew nothing, too—nothing at all about anything very much, as far as I could see—and to them we posed as young gods, Manatine and I and the other tutors as well. Soon, in that extraordinary alchemy which bullshit never fails to bring about, we *were* gods. By *seeming* to be what the youngsters wanted—oh, so urgently, and with a yearning that was even more than sexual—we *became* the ideal lovers of their dreams. The stage beyond that began when I came upon Manatine in Room 24 interviewing a first-year student in such a way that I had to leave him to his relentless questioning. We became what the young wanted us to be, and watched ourselves

49 He's got something wrong here: helium has no hallucinogenic properties. A chink in the author's bluff-work, it seems. Or is Manatine bluffing, is he pretending to be hallucinating? Hard to tell.

watching them watching us as we did. *I don't know what you see in me*, I remember a naked young scholar whispering up at me on someone's upstairs bed during someone's downstairs party. I looked down, I remember, on the ripeness of her flesh, upon *the anonymous abundance of her youth.*[50]

And, yes, indeed we *were* all *chaps*, those of us in the little row of hutches up there in the attic at the top of the English-department building, and across the corridor all the doctoral students were *chaps* as well. These doctoral *chaps* were a year or two older than us and a class apart; and, hence, were given the three attic rooms farthest from the wasps' nest and with small half-dormer windows that took in afternoon sunlight. Unlike us, these earnest young men never horsed around or (it seemed) took any time off at all. For them, the charms of Jolene, our plump, pretty downstairs secretary, remained undiscussed as far as we could tell, even unnoticed: the rattle of their cash-register typewriters never ceased except when one or other of them slipped out for a pee or a pie before darting earnestly back to work. Occasionally one or another of these scholar–monks might nod at us in passing, but more often than not they swept on, their minds on higher things: levitating, almost, as they thought upon those doctoral theses they were so busy *writing up*.

But what was it they were *writing up*; what did a doctoral student in English *write about*, in that unimaginable status so far above our own?[51] I knew I couldn't be a tutor forever, going

50 On the other hand, this bluff-work is exemplary: the italicised words sound like a literary quotation but nothing can actually be pinned down from them: the mark, it has to be admitted, of the master bluffer-bullshitter. On the other hand, he seems not to understand the implications of what he's describing—no moral sense evident here, or elsewhere, either.
51 This status, it should be noted, was lower than that of the tutors who

from contract to contract: to qualify for a lifetime in this strange combination of gentleman's club and sheltered workshop I'd have to acquire a doctoral degree from somewhere or other—in other words I'd have to become one of those monks upstairs, with a topic and a typewriter and, most of all, someone to supervise me, one of the continuing staff willing to put in the effort involved in doing—well, not so very much, as far as I could gather.

What was it, I used to wonder, that I'd find myself *writing up* in the event that I found this combination? *At the writing-up stage yet?* some kindly old buffer would ask me in the tearoom, for something to say, and across the room Manatine would guffaw, and I'd say *oh, still annotating* and try not to catch his eye. *Ah*, the old buffer would say, as if I'd cleared up a great mystery that had consumed him for some time. *You're at the note-taking stage.*

This threatening little tearoom was a floor below our noisy, noisome little attic and was made worse by a portrait of Gotch's distant and long-dead predecessor, Sir Donald Borin, which hung like an X-ray on one of the longer walls. Gotch's lair was across the corridor, next to Vera-the-upstairs-secretary's office. It had taken a while for any of us on the *distaff side* of the attic (as I overheard one of the senior lecturers describe us) to creep down and into the dusty, fubsy little room with its cluttered sink, its sad, looming water heater, the unchanging, out-of-date notices on its unchanging, out-of-date noticeboard, and its aged, buckled linoleum the colour of trodden gum. What if one of the lecturers

---

were preparing to go off to *doctoral study Overseas*; whose status in turn was lower than that of former tutors who had completed *doctoral studies Overseas and returned*; whose status was less again than that of those who had completed *doctoral studies Overseas and remained there*. Whose status was less, it goes without saying, than that of anyone who was *Overseas and had never been here in the first place.*

asked a difficult question in there, something that required an answer featuring knowledge, content—thought, even?

No fear of that, as it turned out: when I finally made the plunge—well, here they were, these lecturers and senior lecturers: men who had taught me, all of them, discussing *how to concrete a garage floor*. I relaxed.[52] Even Borin's portrait seemed a little less threatening, his tiny rat's-eyes a little less mad. As things transpired, the problem wasn't ours: after we'd begun to tiptoe into the common room, as some called it, for morning and afternoon tea, it was the lecturers who seemed afraid—slightly of both of us but really of Manatine with his loud, confident voice. Conversation fell away whenever we came into the room—as it did whenever Gotch turned up—until we began to melt the ice with charming conversation and an ability to feign interest in the SSRM.[53]

By the middle term of that first year the temperature had thawed sufficiently that we were able to go through the ritual known as FNT;[54] these followed by maidenly blushes as on old-fashioned wedding-nights, when couples used to meet *virgo intacta*. No one called Gotch by his first name, though, and in truth no one called him anything behind his back but his surname, *Gotch*, like that, abruptly, like a belch. Otherwise nothing at all, just pronouns, as in *he's downstairs with Jolene*, or code, as in *look out, the fucker's coming up the stairs*.

Yes, there *were* other things we called him, obvious childish insults like *arsehole* and *prick*, and *Brontosaurus Rex*, which didn't stick; and then there was Houston, the tall American

52 The trick is to hose the ground before you pour the concrete: give it a good soak before you start, take care to keep the water up to it during the pour, as it is called, and let the float be your friend.
53 Sustained Self-Referential Monologue.
54 First Name Titters ('Call me Alun'; 'Call me Gene', etc).

cowboy who turned up after a while and who, exotically, used to call Gotch, retrospectively, a *bass-turd*, and once, memorably, a *fucken asshole.*

More of Houston soon. Houston and his gun. It's time for me to tell you about the next significant step my career took for me. I don't want to, since I still can't write about it without blushing. But since it reinforces the main thesis of this book, namely that real things can be made out of bullshit—that bluff is, in effect, the origin of all things, the universal solvent, the *aqua vita*, the *lingua franca*, the only genuine global currency, the Bitcoin of Bullshit—I'm willing to push on with it.

Here we go.

In due course, somewhere in that first year, at morning or afternoon tea, I found myself sitting next to one of those young gods from the doctoral side of the attic, a man whose room (as I glimpsed a couple of times) contained far too many books as well as mountain-climbing gear and an enormous poster of Edmund Hillary. Cocks was his name, one which you have to admit had a certain ring to it, as if just waiting for that higher title to fulfil its promise. He was well thought of, I knew that, this future *Dr Cocks*, this *Professor Cocks* as he was destined surely to be: *a coming man*, I overheard a reader telling a senior lecturer as they spluttered side-by-side at the stainless-steel urinal in the downstairs lavatory. Cocks was one of those demographic geniuses I mentioned earlier, one of those accidents who simply can't help themselves—naturally brilliant, naturally gifted. He was more than a little odd in his ways, too: an academic career seemed inevitable.

What, I murmured after a minute or two of sitting next to this haughty, mute young paragon, might be the subject of his doctoral research?

The tearoom chairs went around three of the walls, facing in as at a Shaker wedding.[55] Three or four of the senior teaching staff sat there, watching. There was a long silence, as if I hadn't spoken. Cocks stared ahead; you'd have thought I was on the opposite side of the room instead of at his shoulder.

Then: 'Hugh Selwyn Mauberley, at the moment,' he replied, suddenly and still looking ahead. He spoke as if to someone else, possibly someone not even present, and with just a hint of contempt in his voice—disdain, even, the life-blood of academic life.

There was a pause, I remember, on this dreadful occasion as it was about to become. At that stage, I had not the slightest notion who Hugh Selwyn Mauberley was. No, that's not true: I'd heard of him, vaguely, at second-hand or third, and knew to associate him with Literature. There were so many I knew like this, floating names and little more: Blake, Jonson, Meredith, Tennyson, Thackeray, Donne, Austen, Galsworthy—George Herbert,[56] too, whom I inadvertently referred to as Victor Herbert in an otherwise blameless essay *pasticcio* in my second year: the marker underlined this and scribbled *Naughty Marietta?* in the margin.[57] I'd definitely heard of Shakespeare though I hadn't read much more of him than I'd read of any of the others and in fact (perhaps) somewhat less; I could never quite work out what

55 Where does he get this from? The turn of the United Society of Believers to be misrepresented, apparently. Sloppy bluff-work, written off the top of his head.

56 George Herbert (1593–1633), Welsh poet and clergyman.

57 Victor Herbert (1859–1924): Irish-American musician, composer of the music for 'Naughty Marietta' (1910), a light operetta, and others. The narrator clearly had no idea who Victor Herbert was at the time mentioned, the name coming to him out of the cultural sludge. No intention to bluff is detectable here.

was going on. I certainly saw that Zeffirelli movie, dragged there twice by different women. I can't recall whether I read *Tess of the d'Urbervilles* or saw the movie; the same with *Tom Jones* and *Barry Lyndon*. I read quite a lot of either *Jane Eyre* or *Wuthering Heights* but not both, and even at the best of times still can't remember which one Mr Rochester is in. And one day I overheard Bevan Panter and Alun Pismire discussing a scene in one of Hardy's novels—where a mother replaces tablecloth, cups, saucers and so on even as her son and his lady friend take their afternoon tea on and with them—and began to drop it into conversations or lectures myself, with what I felt was a pleasing vagueness ('And doesn't Hardy have somewhere that marvellous scene where the mother changes the tablecloth—'). No idea which one it's from, otherwise I might have read it.[58]

So, you might say that, back in the tearoom, Hugh Selwyn Mauberley's name rang a bell for me but no more. I'd no idea what he might've written. I looked for a hint, a clue, something—anything—in order to improvise a little more, my usual technique in surviving life in Bluffworld. From his portrait across the room the late Professor Borin stared at me pitilessly out of the past. Beneath him, the older lecturers sat watching, listening. Waiting. Knitting at the foot of the guillotine. Waiting for the severed head to drop.

I decided to take a punt.

'Good old Hugh,' I ventured, cautiously.

Silence. No one was helping me out.

'I've always meant to read all of him,' I heard my voice say—helplessly, simply without hope by now.

---

58 *A Pair of Blue Eyes* (1873), in fact. The narrator's claim that he might have read this novel if he'd traced it is straightforward bullshit rather than bluff, in that it has no meaningful purpose.

I still can't write that without blushing. Such an awful moment, such an awful, awful moment. I remember a sort of splutter from one of the people opposite and I remember tea being spilled. No one *said* anything; they simply stood and drained their miserable cups and stacked them for Jolene the downstairs secretary to wash and dry, and left without saying a thing. They couldn't even be bothered to laugh at me out loud, but you might say there was an air of Suppressed Amusement. *Priceless, simply priceless!*

As to this Cocks, he stood, after perhaps fifty inscrutable seconds, and walked across to the single window of the tearoom and stood there, gazing out: presumably at the Government Life clock, which was a daringly digital feature atop the Government Life building half a mile away, across town. He *checked the time*, as they say; and then he, too, turned and made for the door.

He paused, though, halfway to it, and stopped in front of me: he bent and seized my hand. Very deliberately, he shook it up and down, twice, carefully, as with a dim child from Old Tinnie's special class back at Anthrax High. I remember the cold lizard feel of his palm, the bony grip of his fingers.

'The very best of luck with the remainder of your career,' he said.

And left.

I'd no idea what I'd done, but I knew it was something disastrous. I took it up the stairs to the attic and Manatine and his marijuana fug. As I came through the door he rolled his head towards me and reached out his hand with the tiny joint in his bronzed fingertips, and I shook my head, and he reapplied the wispy remnant to his mouth.

'Who the fuck is Hugh Selwyn Mauberley?'

He slumped forward and the front legs of the hoop-backed dining chair he was sitting on came clattering down with him onto the lino. He blew a long, liquid squirt of smoke across the room, like a flame-thrower.

'You kidding me?'

'Yeah. No.'

And I told him what had happened. As I spoke, his mouth began to tear open on one side, slowly yanking up a smile.

'Well.' He took another drag from the tiny remains of his joint. He held it in for twenty seconds and then blew smoke out carefully, slowly. He coughed, once. 'You've gone and made a proper prick of yourself, haven't you?'

I remember my throat tightening when he said this. *What the hell had I done?*

'He's a fucking *imaginary character*, you dumb fuckwit,' he said. 'In a fucking *poem*. By Ezra fucking *Pound*. You did Modern Poets with Giff, didn't you?'

Well, I did, more or less, but I'd steered clear of EP, as Eugene Gifford used to call Ezra Pound in the Modern Poetry course we'd taken with him the year before. EP had seemed rather difficult to me, vague and dispersed—you had to read him, too, which made things rather problematic. *ENGL426 Poetry and Modernism* had been one of the papers I'd skidded by on, rather, aided by the well-disposed Gifford himself, who once claimed, when I'd become a junior colleague, to have marked a particular student's essay minutes before while looking out of the window. Much laughter in the common room: *priceless, simply priceless.*

As his student I'd avoided EP, but on the other hand I'd managed to rummage up a few words to say on HD,[59] sufficient,

59   Hilda Doolittle (1886–1961), poet, editor and associate of Ezra Pound (1885–1972), poet, editor, fascist sympathiser, anti-semite, social credit enthusiast and bluffer-bullshitter *extraordinaire*.

anyway, for Gifford to give the essay that contained them rather a good mark, quite conceivably looking out of the window as he did so. I'd written hardly a word of it myself, of course, though it was all my own work in the sense that cobbling together a decently plagiarised essay is no pushover—I mean an essay that gives absolutely nothing away. Well, the one I managed to concoct for Giff—'HD and the Greeks' it was called, the same as the long journal article I'd worked it up from—seemed bullet-proof by the time I was done with it. Even Manatine, bullshit supremo, was impressed. He read it through carefully: 'Well,' he said when he was done. 'He's smart if he picks it.'

The thing is, he *did* pick it, Gifford, something I didn't realise for a good long time, well into my years as his colleague. He picked it, and he gave it an excellent mark—*because* he'd picked it, I came to realise, *because* he knew it was plagiarised: because he knew that, by plagiarising it, I'd seen something of the world he'd seen and understood and lived in. 'He was telling you, *welcome aboard*,' Sally said years later, when we'd become a couple and I was discussing the business with her. 'He was acknowledging that you're a player. You know, qualified for Bluffworld.' Because, yes, Sally understood that term I'm using so freely here, and she was the one who told me I was the biggest bullshit artist she'd ever met and by far the best, far better than Manatine, even, whom she loathed the sound of and who, she told me, was a bad lot.

Good old Sally—dear old Sally. I'm so sorry about the other women. Gifford's wife in particular. All this comes later, of course.

Chapter 4

Up the stone steps now, into the foyer and across to the door of Bevan's Bookshop, which activates a bell when it's opened—here it goes: *ping!* At the counter, Bevan himself, poring over whatever's in front of him and not looking up. For an hour it'll be the two of us till our regulars start drifting in. There he was at the start of my university career; here he is at the stop.

Old Bevan. It turned out that when the axe fell, he of all people managed to save something from the ruins. Older colleagues retired, younger colleagues retrained to peddle insurance. Marigold Butcher sold Avon Cosmetics from door to door in the north-western suburbs—she herself, presumably, representing *Before.* Boodle, the rubicund Devonshire man who collected railway stuff, got a job on the new tourist tram system in the middle of town. Perry was already back in Toronto starting his own business; Gifford had a dedicated chair at Brown–Rice; Bundy got a job in a shopping mall picking up litter while dressed as a Tower of London Beefeater; Biddle became a nude model. The truly desperate became secondary-school teachers.

And the rest of us? Well, we simply improvised from day to day, guiding foreign tourists around the ghost of the campus, posing for souvenir photographs, punting the bastards up and down the river nearby at a couple of dollars each time. Now and then, when fear began to gnaw at me, I'd look through Situations Vacant. *Not a job, dear God—please, not secondary teaching—*

And then the phone rang. Sally?

I seized it. 'Darling—?' There was a pause, and then Bevan's unmistakable Pommy accent. 'Sorry. Bevan? Thought you were—'

We met the next morning at the abandoned English department.

'Heard the latest? Chap in Philosophy's just tried to shoot himself in the head on the Beautifying Society bench in the Botanical Gardens. Apparently, he feels there's a viable argument he might have missed.'

He let us into the building with a big, unexpected key. We stood inside.

'*Les lauriers sont coupés*,'[60] he said. 'Spooky, isn't it?' His voice echoed, ever so slightly. Familiar things were gone or stacked, walls were a series of blanks where remembered things used to be; except I found I couldn't remember them. A tutorial list on a surviving noticeboard offered a plangent moment.

We climbed the stairs, looking at nameplates yet to be taken from doors and a staff photo from twenty years ago which looked like something from Max Nordau.[61]

'I'm glad it's over,' he was saying. 'It's been like Henry's time—you know, the monks, waiting for the dissolution? But I don't think we have to be like that.'

'Like what—?'

'This might be the opportunity of a lifetime—you know, *To strive, to seek, to find, and not to yield*—?[62] All this rot we've

60 A reference to *Les Lauriers sont coupés* (1887), novel by Édouard Dujardin (1861–1949). French. Ignore.

61 Surprising that he's heard of Nordau's *Entartung* [*Degeneration*] (1892), which contained, among other things, photographs of cretins, morons and imbeciles. Max Nordau (1849–1923). German. Ignore.

62 The final line of Alfred Lord Tennyson's poem 'Ulysses' (1842) about

been teaching, it must mean something, mustn't it, otherwise what've we been doing these last twenty-five years?'

It was as we were coming down the stairs again that he told me he'd leased the two teaching rooms to the right of the main entrance foyer, plus two adjacent offices abandoned by former colleagues: Tim Riordan, the Yeats specialist I mentioned a while ago, and Pat Hazard (*Introducing Maori Literature in English*, Wellington: VUP 1985), who was bit of a joke—he kept trying to bring postcolonialism into the English syllabus! 'Yes, I know these people write in English,' I remember someone saying in one of our staff meetings—Basil Shortbread, it was (*Shakespeare's Lads*, NY: Manson & Harris 1973). 'But are they really *English*?' Which rather put an end to silly old Pat's argument, I'd have thought; except that he *would* go on and on about it, till he—

What was this Bevan had just said?

'A second-hand *bookshop*?'

He stood there, smirking around his pipe. '"Bevan's Bookshop"—sounds good, doesn't it? Come on.'

I followed him out: we bustled across the second quadrangle, still a couple of academics, me behind him, always junior. He was taking me to the library, the building that divides the first quadrangle from the second and is modelled on the Bodleian at Oxford but a quarter-sized or smaller and minus the tower. Only the windows seemed to be possibly authentic to the original: tall and stately, and admitting a grave light on the interior as if illuminating history itself.

In there, I slipstreamed him up squeaking metal stairs. We stood on the second level, our modest little academic chests

---

the hero of Homer's *Iliad*, Odysseus, seeking adventure in old age. The poem's first three words ('It little profits') seem appropriate to the proposed second-hand bookshop.

heaving in and out, in and out.

It took him a minute to speak.

'There.' It came out in a gasp. He pointed to a sprawl of books on the floor. 'Our future.'

Just library books, nondescript, dull covers, higgledy-piggledy: I stared at them. And then it began to occur to me— *surely he wasn't—*?

He was—he had! I listened to him, to his almost-excited almost-babble. The really valuable books had already been sold to overseas interests, he said, for a lot of money. This was our chance with the rest! *Get ahead, make a killing, run the opposition out of town*: all the clichés he seemed to have taken to already in the transition from faded academic to faded seller of books.

A pause, when he was done.

'So,' I asked him. 'How are you going to get all these down to the bookshop?'

He tilted his head back and pretended to laugh, *chuff chuff chuff*. I waited him out, I remember, my eyes on the books. Our future, he'd said.

Back then, our future seemed to be about doctoral theses.[63]

---

63 A doctoral dissertation is a work of original scholarly research of no more than 80,000 words to be written on any topic appropriate to the candidate's area of study and supervised by a university staff member unfamiliar with that area. The supervisor's task is to ensure that the candidate does not disturb the supervisor's own scholarly work, which, apart from the pursuit of ongoing promotion and regular periods of funded leave, consists almost entirely of marking undergraduate essays. Any methods are acceptable for the supervisor to keep the doctoral student at bay, including pretending not to be in his office when the doctoral student knocks at the supervisor's

'Write one or die,' Manatine told me as the third term dawned and we began to talk about what might happen next. There was no guarantee Gotch would keep on renewing our annual contracts: but, then, given that moment at the door of the exam script storeroom, no guarantee he wouldn't, either. Feigning doctoral study might give us a little more *cred*, we decided, and in Manatine's case would help him hold on to the three-year internal scholarship his first-class degree had given him. To my astonishment, he chose Bevan Panter as his supervisor and Trollope as his topic—'A Defamiliarising Poetic: Anthony Trollope and His Kind' was the title, which seemed to me worth the degree in itself.

'No idea,' he said, when I asked him what it meant. 'The trick is to keep people away from the bastard—d'*you* want to read something with a title like that?'

But Bevan, Bevan Panter of all people as a supervisor? The most boring lecturer in the department, the university—the universe, quite possibly: him?[64]

'Think about it,' was all Manatine would say.

I did. Soon after, I found a topic. Or it found me. Things began to work together more and more smoothly, always the sign that bullshit is at work—bullshit on a large scale, bullshit for the ages. Cosmic bullshit, even.

I can remember the moment as if it happened this morning: LOCAL STUDENT DIES IN ALPINE FALL. Manatine told

---

door, cursory reading of the beginnings and endings of submitted material, and, in the case that the supervisor has not read the student's work-in-progress at all, outright bluff. Up to a certain point, discreet publication of part, but not all, of the supervisee's research under the supervisor's name is not entirely discouraged.

64 'He'.

me, up in our noxious little attic office when I got there first thing in the afternoon. He looked terrible and for a few seconds I thought he was in shock and grieving. But it turned out he'd been on the piss.

Cocks. Fallen from near the top of Mount Blimit, all twelve thousand foot of it: so Manatine told me as he yawned and stretched. Fallen, unroped, to his death.

'There's where Ezra Pound gets you,' he said. 'Ten thousand fucking feet, imagine it.[65] I dunno. Should've stuck to T.S. Eliot.' He stood up. 'Got the munchies,' he said, at the door. 'Want some chips?'

Cocks—*Cocks*. My *bête noir*.

One of them.

'No, thanks,' I said.

I sat there after he'd gone, I remember, not knowing what to think. *Cocks. What had I done?*—well, that's how it felt.

What *had* I done?

'Let's have a look in his room.' Manatine again, when he came back with his pottle of chips. 'What sort of typewriter'd he have?'

I remembered the invasion of the exam script storeroom and how that had played out. I followed him across the corridor and into Cocks's room. Apart from the wasps we were the only two creatures in the attic. The Hillary poster; another, advertising a lecture, 'Reclaiming Gondwanaland', about reversing continental drift; the mountaineering equipment; under the monkish light of a dormer window, Cocks's desk. I didn't know what to think about all this. Dead, his great academic future with him. Professor Cocks.

---

65   In fact, over 3000 metres. The language used here and elsewhere in this text is, again, regrettable.

'Take a look at this.' Manatine, crouched over Cocks's typewriter. 'Electric bastard.' One of those golf-ball typewriters, state of the art back then: Manatine was pulling its plug from the wall. 'Any prick could pinch that now, couldn't they,' he said. 'Can't have that.'

Together we stripped Cocks's desk and the bookshelf and the walls, though not the Edmund Hillary poster above his desk, which we agreed was far too hearty. In five minutes we took everything we could see of Cocks's academic life and put it in our little room across the corridor.

We sat there. Manatine rolled a *spliff*, as I'd noticed he'd started calling them lately.

He licked the paper and looked across at me. 'What about the climbing gear?'

'That's theft.'

'Research-related. We're looking after it.' He stood up. 'The boots and the parka. They're research-related too.'

He came back with these and a large cardboard box.

'Missed this.' He put it on my desk. 'On his shelf at the back. Poor fucker's notes or something. What d'you reckon?'

I opened the box. Folders, single typed pages, carefully written notes, photocopied articles, Venn diagrams showing how one part of the Cantos related to another, slips of coloured paper carefully glued to mark significant places, often with a single Delphic word written in Cocks's soft, curiously unformed handwriting—'*Rapallo.*' '*The great Muss.*' '*Establish these first.*' '*LII–LXXI Chinese and John Adams cantos—really dull.*' '*Established.*' The world of a relentless, methodical mind, far finer than mine: logical, remorseless, intimidating. Dead.

I stared into the box. An entire doctoral thesis in skeleton form. No, no, far better than that, I found as I began to read: large parts had been *written up*, and these (as I skimmed back and forth) seemed quite plausible—and, added up, more than halfway to those magical 80,000 words.

I let the wodge of paper flop back in the box.

Manatine, sitting there, staring at me.

'Go on,' he said.

'Go on, what?'

'Poor fucker's dead. He can't use it.'

I stared down at the box on my knees. 'I can't.'

'Yes, you can.'

'He's still up there in the snow.'

'He's going to defrost and walk in?'

'They'll smell a rat. Suddenly I'm interested in Ezra Pound? I don't know anything about him. I can't understand the bastard.'

Manatine leaned forward, carefully. There were times when he really did seem to come from a different order of being.

'*Hommage*,' he said.

'*Hommage*?'

'*Cheeses*, you really are *dumb. You* and *Cocks* were *really close*—'

'He was a stuck-up prick, I hardly knew the bastard—'

'I know that, but this is what you say—you go to them downstairs and you say, you tell them—what was his first name?'

'Buggered if I know.'

'Well, find out. Find out and say you want to finish his work because you were close. As an act of hommage. Tell them it's barely started. They won't know, PhD supervisors never read anything. No one's ever read anything I've ever written.'

'But you haven't written anything yet.'

'Exactly—'

And so on. Improbable. Impossible. Irresistible—Mephistopheles himself. Who was I to do anything other than what he told me to do? There are times, he said, as he began to wear me down, when life simply presents itself to you. It mightn't be what you expect it to be, but that's exactly why you need to step towards it. This is one of those moments.

It had such a ring to it, this pronouncement, it was so self-evidently a monumental piece of export-quality bullshit that I knew it had to be taken seriously. I decided there and then to hijack Cocks's thesis. It seemed magnificent, that decision, once made, even heroic—all of history pressing behind it, like an impending bowel movement. And who could say it might give me anything less than the next forty years of my life? More? Because he was right: there on my lap was the promise of an academic career spent safe from the real world.

All I had to do was bluff—

Gifford next. He'd been Cocks's supervisor, after all. I found him at his desk, reading a book called *A New Discourse upon a Stale Subject*.[66] Yes, he said, appalling, the death of our top internal doctoral student. He sat slightly side-on as I began my pitch, looking away but turning back now and then to spy on me with his cool, unblinking northern gaze. I rattled on. I think I might have said that Cocks had had a great career ahead of him. Or maybe I said that we would not see his like again.

'Mm. Mm.' He turned back towards me. 'I'd no idea you and he were such friends. You and Cocks.'

'Oh, yes. Inseparable. Sandford and Merton.'

It was a shock to me, this, coming out as it did—the title of a book I'd never even seen but which had somehow come to

66 Sir John Harington (1560–1612), *A New Discourse upon a Stale Subject: The Metamorphosis of Ajax* (1596), which discusses his invention of the flush toilet ('Ajax'/'a jakes' in his title).

my mind in the moment: evidence of the bullshit nature of the universe itself, a thing I'd long suspected. *The History of Sandford and Merton!*[67] I could see I'd impressed him, mentioning this, though it took many years more to understand that it stirred him not as a thing I knew *but as bluff-work*, and that even as early as this he was onto my larger purposes. He'd seen through me and—himself a master bluffer—wanted me, an apprentice bluffer, to follow him. Was that it?[68]

'Yes,' he said, after I'd made my pitch with due emphasis upon both the funerary aspects of the proposal and the service I'd be doing to the discipline of English. 'Yes, I think that's a goer. I think you could go ahead with this.'

And then he told me he was going on leave for a year, and that I'd have to find another supervisor for that period. Who did he recommend, I asked him: Dr Panter, he replied.

Bevan Panter again.

Old Bevan—?

I'd almost said that to Gifford, I was so taken off my guard. *But*: here was the final stamp, I realised years later, of his approval. Manatine was right: who better to supervise a project

67 Thomas Day, *The History of Sandford and Merton*, a children's book serially published in England 1783–89. Although it was widely distributed throughout the British Empire in the nineteenth century, it is difficult to see how the protagonist here would have any knowledge of it. Very complex bluff-work here, difficult to pick apart, because apparently to some degree external to the bluffer.

68 The term 'bluff-work' used here and adopted in these footnotes seems to be modelled on Sigmund Freud's 'dream-work' in *The Interpretation of Dreams* (1913), which refers to the unconscious work of patterning that gives dreams their sense of purpose and meaning. This linkage suggests that, with varying levels of awareness, 'bluff-work' operates in precisely the same way, and that bluff-work frequently completes and fulfils dream-work's implications and potentials in everyday life.

so full of bluff and bullshit than a man who knew nothing whatever about its subject matter?

Bevan Panter was the man.

And, thus, I became a doctoral student, and Bevan, also unquestioningly, became my supervisor. For twenty-five years this man had taught everything stupefying that fiction could provide, in classes famous for their tundral bleakness. Now here was I, about to start fumbling along beside him, untenured, improvising, relying on his inexplicable patronage for renewals of fellowships and one-year contracts, all the time keeping aloft the slowly deflating balloon of my doctorate, sole guarantee of the career I'd set my mind on long before, as soon as I'd seen the extraordinary lifestyle that academia involved—that feeling of the gentleman's club best embodied by Bevan himself. That sense of the sheltered workshop, too, which, again, and to no small extent, he also *bodied forth*, as I'm sure he would have put it himself. I kept this thought ahead of me as I pushed through each day, the cold winds from the local teacher-training college blowing hard behind me, urging me on, and up, and away.

Yet all the time I was treading on eggs. As I'm sure you've picked up, almost everything I know and say comes from here and there—movies, a glimpse of someone else's page, an in-flight magazine, an overheard conversation, those few moments in academic seminars when my butterfly attention manages to settle on something for more than ten seconds. I never contributed to these seminars, never spoke—was never silly enough to try—but I found that, afterwards, although I could never grasp anything of their argument, their *phrases* invariably stayed with me, whole sentences—conversations, even, like Post-It notes that had stuck to me as I passed. There was little to get in the way, after all: like a tape recorder I'd take them in, like a tape recorder I'd send them back out, quite often surprising myself at what I said—that Sandford-and-Merton moment with Gifford: a good example. Who spoke the words I was speaking? Who spoke them before that?

We enter the Lacanian Real every time we screw and we fall back into language when we finish: I can remember telling that to a young woman I was—well, entering the Lacanian Real[69] with one night on a waterbed, not long after I overheard someone talking about it. Gifford it came from, I think, in our little departmental tearoom; whoever it was, it went down a treat in the sack, I can tell you. *There'll never be a revolution in Germany because there are too many signs saying KEEP OFF THE GRASS. History repeats itself, the first time as tragedy, the second as farce. History was not made behind men's backs.* A thousand times I've used those and a dozen other one-liners from Groucho's older brother; but where did I get them from, who is it I'm mindlessly repeating here? It has to be someone, because I've never read a word of Marx except the first part of that essay about commodifying a chair, which I confess I found hard to follow although I think I got the general drift— you know, the work is caught up in the wood and so on. Yet there I'd be, quoting him in lectures! Where it always went down a treat, as with the young *femme horizontale* I did the Lacan routine with.

69   Jacques Lacan (1901–81), psychoanalyst, psychiatrist. 'The Lacanian Real' is conceived as a kind of negative sublime 'beyond' language and the rational. Although Lacan was undoubtedly a bullshitter *extraordinaire*, Jean Baudrillard (see footnote 7 above) challenged him for primacy in statements like the following: 'Here in the transversality of the desert and the irony of geology, the transpolitical finds its generic, mental space.' Brilliant bluff-work, quoted by Rob Doyle in a review of Jean Baudrillard's *America* (1986), *The Irish Times*, 2 March 2019. Was Baudrillard responsible for the waterbed joke? Or was it Lacan? Both French. Ignore.

And, in turn, where did I get *that* phrase from, *femme horizontale*, given that I neither speak nor read a word of French? Again, from repeating the men and women around me in our tinpot little academic community—Gifford, Riordan, Back Passage and their ilk. And they, by and large, were repeating other people, who mimicked yet others still. Where does it all come from, who started this business off? Has *anyone* ever said anything original? Not me, certainly. And where did I get the joke I made that night with the young *femme horizontale?*— about how you always get one stroke free on a waterbed? Not mine, not mine, although she certainly thought it was. Who owns it all, where does it start?

Oh, yes, one more thing: Cocks's first name. I went to his funeral, dragged along by others, by guilt—by shame, guilt's subtler, more private bed-mate. The funeral was all grieving climbers, I remember, and the coffin—a gesture, of course, since Cocks's body was still up there, entombed in the ice— had a mountaineering axe on it and a pair of climbing boots and a knitted hat. His family was present: I took care not to look at them.

Anyway, it turned out Cocks's first name was Hamish.

This took me aback. There was something about my reaction I didn't quite understand. The boy I invented for that pass in *EDU102 Principles of Education*—I'd ushered him into the world, and now he'd been ushered back out again. Something like that. All nonsense, of course, but I kept thinking about it. What was the connection? Was there a connection?[70]

70 No, of course not. What's he playing at, trying to be profound?

In the bookshop's rear workroom I shrug off my backpack and the fine leather jacket I stole at a literary party. Ahead of me lies a day far longer than any I worked as an academic but with a break for lunch, and, always, the chance of one of those errands that might keep me out of the disused library and the bookshop for as long as I can possibly stretch it.

Through the workroom door I observe Bevan from behind: the sparse, stringy hair, the bottle shoulders, the dreadful khaki shorts. Sometimes I see him caught by a book, lost in the middle of the shop with his mouth slightly open, his curved Petersen pipe pulling down his solemn Habsburg upper lip.[71]

Yesterday, when I found him like this, I eased the duster out of his hands and began flicking it around the shelves beside him. He looked up, and re-entered the twenty-first century.

'Theodore Watts-Dunton.' He turned the book so I could see the grubby gold leaf of the printed name. 'Know him?'

I didn't, of course. 'Oh him,' I said, and began to dust at shin level, head down—minimising eye-contact like this is crucial to bluff-work, though it's important to use prolonged eye contact once the bluff has succeeded, to convey the depth of one's sincerity.

He put the book back. 'So many of them. The not-so-great tradition.'

I dragged the duster over its unimportant spine. *The Coming of Love: Rhona Boswell's Story and Other Poems.* These are Bevan's favourites, the also-rans of English literature, the Duntons and the Goldsworthy Lowes Dickinsons and the Catherine Gores; he ran a postgraduate course on them for years that I struggled through in my time.

---

71 Again, this phrase isn't his—another unacknowledged theft, this time from Warwick Deeping, *Two Black Sheep* (Knopf 1933), p.123. How does he know about a forgotten book like this?

'You can't understand the great without understanding the not-so-great,' he'd say. At other times he'd talk about whales and minnows. I wondered sometimes whether he identified with them, the minnows, whether he saw some link between his second-rate academic existence and the forgotten struggles of a thousand Grub Street poetasters throughout the world. 'You can't have a literary tradition without people like these,' I remember him telling a roomful of yawning students, and I can remember the sudden image I had when he said this, of a Darwinian humus of failure in the—well—the *Garden of Literature*. 'Never underestimate them,' he told us. 'Now and then you get a really great second-rater like Trollope. Dylan Thomas, he came right out with it and *said* he was a second-rater.'[72]

Now, Bevan is a second-rate seller of second-hand books— worse: hardly anyone comes here to buy. I realised this after only a week. A year on and we've settled to a more-or-less serious clientele, a handful of people who appear at the same time of day or week. They try to borrow, sometimes they steal, occasionally they even buy.

As I stood with the feather duster in my hand yesterday, one of them came in, the wild-haired, wild-eyed, rouged-up wife of a former engineering professor, who drops by early each morning to read a chapter of Iris Murdoch.

'*A Severed Head*,' Bevan murmured, the first time he saw me looking at her. 'That's what she's got up to. Appropriate, don't you think?'

'D'you think she's going to buy it—?'

'Nearly sold one this morning, just before you came in.

---

72 'A second-rate Charles Laughton' was the actual phrase. See Isabella Beeton, *Dylan Thomas: The Limericks*, John Thomas 1975, p.212.

Almost had it in the bag, almost closed the deal—then he lost interest and walked away.'

He always tries to sound like a big-league businessman but in fact he sees each customer almost as a potential thief, someone who might destroy the perfection of his reliquary of ancient tomes, his House of Literature. On Day One, I remember, he caught me making my first sale, some old volume you'd only ever use to prop up a piano, and he was almost in tears. Ah, Literature! Art!

Chapter 5

To form the bookshop Bevan's had the wall taken out between the two tutorial teaching rooms. The bookshelves around the walls come from the abandoned library, others have been sawn roughly in half to make displays. Tables, draped with black cloth and scattered with books; BIOGRAPHY, HISTORY, HOME-MAKING, COOKERY on signs cut from cardboard. In marker pen and Bevan's tall, uncertain capitals they add to the jumble-sale feel of Bevan's Bookshop.

I slip past him and into the workroom at the back, where a tiny electric heater is frying the air in front of itself, its glow as orange-dark as Betelgeuse.[73] The heater produces much the same smell I remember from his study: clothing, feet, too many books in too small a space. Now a self-employed shaman practises holistic medicine there. In Biddle's former study there's a potter; Boodle's is leased by a colour therapist; Gifford's by a lawyer who uses the adjacent former tearoom— scene of my humiliation by Cocks—as well. Roy Perry, the ironic Canadian senior lecturer who shot back to Canada the day the music died and became a multi-millionaire within (it seemed) days, has had his corner study taken over by a transactional analyst. Gotch goes unremembered in his former office, which—delightfully—has become home to a wymmin's

---

73 Google, again. An increasingly dingy star in the constellation of Orion.

group. My former office, on the ground floor, is now an ashram: from time to time we hear a droning chant.

Often, I think of these newcomers piled above us on two floors and an attic, all of them doing their unimaginable non-academic thing. From time to time they drop by, and the bookshop hosts a saffron-robed visitor or a transactional analysand, a clay-fisted potter, or even, now and then, a wymmin. And I dust and sort and answer the phone and, each day, cart wheelbarrow-loads of stock from the disused university library nearby, which diminishes, bit by bit—the three-tiered mezzanine, the long metal tables, the catalogues, the issuing desk all going one by one, and me somehow and inadvertently a tiny part of the force that is slowly, relentlessly, emptying the whole place out. An entire university college, a small, complete universe, disappearing in instalments.

><><

With the theft of Cocks's thesis Manatine and I graduated to his room, bringing the electric typewriter back to it and the climbing gear and everything else we'd liberated a couple of weeks before. Here was an office with a window plus two filing cabinets and two bookshelves; but, also, the ghost of Cocks: something to do with the light from that single window, high in the half-dormer. All bullshit, according to Manatine, who fearlessly set up his desk beneath its wan, ecclesiastical light: 'The fucker's dead and gone.' He licked and rolled and lit some stuff he said was becoming available from the American base out at the airport. 'Gimme Cocks's box.' He set about its contents. 'We might each of us get a thesis out of this shit.' He coughed and huffed on his *spliff*.

From that point we worked on Cocks's remains and lived on staffroom biscuits, ticking Gotch's initials on the honesty sheet for each one: Manatine's pages increased as the biscuits diminished, as if the two were a single thing. 'Some for you, some for me,' he told me after a few weeks, staring at one of Cocks's pages and crunching a Chocolate Thin. 'I've used a lot of the second half, I've changed *Pound* to *Trollope* and *poem* to *novel*. It just has to *resemble* a thesis, remember, it doesn't actually have to be one.'

'Right.'

'And I've flushed the stuff about the influence of Browning.'

'Why?'

'*Cheeses*, man—*Browning* and the *narrative lyric?*'

I could *take his point*, as they used to say downstairs in the tearoom. Meanwhile, what was I supposed to do with the half he'd left to me? Could I really fake it up to the required length on a topic I knew nothing whatever about, the way he seemed to be doing with his?

When I asked him this his answer had a touch of genius to it, genius and sheer insanity, the signature fuel-mix, always, of his mind.

'A *woman?*' I said. 'Mauberley is a *woman*—?'

'It's in the poem, it's in the poem.'

'I haven't read the poem.'

'Well nor have I but it's obvious, isn't it? Write about that.'

'It's unprovable. You can't prove it.'

'Of *course* you can't prove it—that's what the unprovable's *there* for.' His wild, proselytising, in-from-the-desert gaze. 'That's what the entire discipline *is*, for fuck's sake, it's just a series of assertions.' A drag on his spliff. 'It doesn't have to be *right*, it just has to be *daring*.' Coils of smoke, drifting around his head. 'And *emotional*, it has to be *emotional*.'

We both knew Henry James's view that, in art, emotions are the meaning. Manatine had overheard Gifford telling someone that in the tearoom.

Every time I revisited Cocks's box, though, I recoiled from what was actually in it. *Pound and the autobiographical self. What is Mauberley's and what is Pound's? Mauberley's visionary poetic. The meaning of Pound's 'Medallion'.* All this in the dead man's hand, mincing across the note-paper, showing paths for me to take—all of them non-starters, I knew that each night I took these pages home and sat there glumly shuffling them about. Gradually, I gave up hope. When Rommel got hold of them one evening I let him, and sat there watching him tear them to shreds and pee on them as well. Who cared? I'd met my match, I'd reached my ceiling, I'd run out of gas. I could see the gates of the local teachers' college opening in front of me, hear the sound of the school bell, feel the breeze up the walkshorts. And you couldn't even flog the bastards anymore.

Then, a summons to Gotch's room. I remember the sense of internal organic collapse, the quick dash to the downstairs men's room to throw up. In there too was David Peach (*Hemingway's Balls*, Fedora College Press 1989)—a local who'd taught American literature so long he had a strong Midwest US accent. 'Caught a bug?' he asked; 'Gotch,' I replied, and he turned and fled, as if he, too, might catch it.

Back upstairs I crept into Gotch's office. He looked up, from the far side of his desk.

'Ah,' he said. 'Cocks, isn't it?'

I could feel my head nodding, a spasmodic, involuntary death-rattle *yes yes yes*—

He pointed to a seat. I sat. The small sculpture on his desk, of two hands bound at the wrist with chains. The Kelly-Tarlton-Sea-Life-Aquarium sounds of his post-lunch interior.

He stared at me: those eyes, drilling into mine point-blank, with their complex messages about the slow destruction of the human capacity for love. He began to talk, at length—his early years, how I reminded him of himself when young, his hopes and fears for the future.

He leaned closer.

'I did it for you,' he murmured.

I had no idea what he was talking about. But, oh, the intimacy, the hideous closeness of it—like the moment he shafted me at that end-of-year party a few years before, but different this time, slightly changed. I was starting to realise there was something even worse than his unearned enmity, his cruelty, his bottomless capacity for vindictiveness. *There was the terror of the proximity of him, of his approval, his attention. The miasmal horror of his love.*

Two days later Manatine walked into our office and tossed a letter into my lap.

'In the tutors' pigeonhole downstairs.'

It was addressed to Cocks. I opened it.

A formal offer of a tenured lectureship, with salary and conditions outlined, including completion of a PhD thesis within three years.

'Congratulations. About time you got some recognition.'

'But it's addressed to Cocks, it's got his name on it—he thought I was Cocks. Downstairs. In his room.'

'Well, there you go. You're Cocks. The job's yours.'

'But Cocks is *dead*.'

'Yes, but *Gotch* isn't, so it doesn't matter to him who is, does it?'

'It's got Cocks's *name* on the letter—look. Hamish Cocks.'

Manatine stared at it. 'Just a detail,' he said. He tugged it from my fingers. 'Leave this with me.'

'What are you going to do, sign Cocks's name again?' After

all, he'd perfected Cocks's signature each time we'd signed in at Forty Wanks, the *magasin du frappe* in Bangor Street, just as I'd perfected Gotch's there and sometimes Daresbury's as well. 'I still need a postgrad thesis. How in hell am I going to do that?'

He reached around to his desk and dumped something on the floor between us. A manila folder: a mess of typed A4 pages slewed out as it hit the lino, like a fan of cards. It took me a second to realise what he was showing me.

'You've finished?'

He nodded. 'Just needs typing up.' Rolling a joint now.

'That's *quick*—'

A shrug. 'What you think?'

What did I think? I stared down at the thing. I was appalled, envious, angry, dismayed—I'd hardly been able to write a word the way he'd obviously done, buffing up Cocks's remains. He'd done it and I hadn't—couldn't. I'd been found out at last. I was *farcie*, utterly *farcie*.

He shoved the folder across to me with the side of his foot.

'It's yours.' Leaning back, taking a drag.

I sat there staring at him.

'Go on,' he said. 'I don't need it.'

'You don't need a postgrad thesis?' I picked it up, opened the folder, straightened the papers, looked at the first page. 'Reads really well.'

'That bit's Cocks. Try further on.'

I gave it a skim, a really deep skim, for nearly a minute. The thing seemed to work brilliantly. Now and then Trollope's name came up, obviously pasted over Pound's, and there were titles changed as well—but who could tell, overall, who would know it was a forgery? That's how it seemed to me.

'Why don't you want it?'

'I'm off.'

Again, a second or two of staring at him, listening to his *erm-erm*. He couldn't possibly mean this, could he?

'You're *leaving*—?'

'*I* don't want to turn into one of those fuckers downstairs.'

'What's wrong with them?'

He pushed away from me in his seat. 'For God's sake.'

'Gifford's all right.'

'Gifford's as fucked as the rest of them, he's worse. The reason he seems okay is he's just fucked in a different way.' He pointed his finger at me. 'This place is starting to *eat you out*— if it wasn't, you'd see it.'

'How's it starting to eat me out?'

'You're losing your hair.'

I couldn't believe it! Nonsense, of course. Why would he say a thing like that?

He shook his head. 'It's how they *do* it to you. They change the way you look once they realise they've got you. They make you look like all the rest of the needy fuckers.' He pulled back and squinted at me, as if I were a painting. 'Back Passage,' he said. 'You're starting to look like Back Passage.'

I was appalled—I couldn't believe he'd said it! Back Passage, of all people, Back Passage from Romance Languages?

'*I'm* not going to end up like Back Passage!'

'You *will*, you've only just started. It's what they do, they start to work on you—'

'Who's *they*—?' I'd always wanted to know this.

'See, you just don't know *anything*. Because you're being sucked *into* it. People think it just happens, but it's being done *to you*. By *them*.'

Them. Over the years I've often thought about Manatine's *Them*. Stoner logic, you'd say. But, on the other hand, he'd been right before. I looked down at the folder on my lap, I felt its weight, the substance of it, the substance *in* it. He'd never let me down before. Now he was explaining to me what to do next, how I should change *Trollope* back to *Pound* and the title back to Cocks's—mad stuff, yes, but on the other hand *he'd never been wrong before. Ever.*

I sat there, staring at the folder on my lap.

'Go on,' he said. 'If *that's* what you want to do to yourself, *there's* the way in. Accept the job, wait three years to the deadline, hand this in, and there's your tenure confirmed.'

I lifted it, I held the thing up, I clutched it to my breast. My heart thudded against the thin, used cardboard. He was busy telling me what he was going to do next, where he was going to do it and when. I hardly heard a word. A new life ahead of me. A lifetime in a sheltered workshop, a lifetime in a gentlemen's club. Guaranteed.

'You'll be back,' I told him when he'd finished. 'You'll be back.'

I could feel my heart beating *hard* inside the lurid paisley of my shirt.

Tenure. Unsackable.

At midday I slip down the saucered front steps of the building and leave Bevan to his customary lunch: two chapters of Trollope and the contents of the brown paper bag provided daily by his wife. Onion sandwiches, as a rule; and, also repeating, *The Last Chronicle of Barset*, for the fiftieth time perhaps and always featuring Bevan's favourite moment, the unexpected death of the terrible Mrs Proudie, found with her arm locked around a bedpost. I know about this simply because Bevan reads it out to me each time it comes around again. I've never read any

Trollope myself. I've certainly taught him, though.

Through the cloisters again, and here's Biddle setting up his baked potato stall for the lunchtime tourists. The dean of Arts he once was, an extraordinary political mandarin so high-powered he did no teaching and spoke to almost none. Now here he is, testy as ever, hurrying his stall together before the first of the tourists arrives, his striped apron tied fast, the wind troubling his straw boater. I feel sorry for him, and always stop at his cart. He nods curtly as he clanks the counter down and into place—still self-conscious, I think, at the turn his life has taken, still in shock at his fall, still taken aback, most of all, by having to talk to people.

'One?' he asks, looking away over my head.

'Please,' I say, still the junior lecturer.

His big fleshy hands, fumbling a knife through a steaming spud, dolloping cream cheese, handing the potato over. He takes my money looking away and wrestling his shoulders about within his jacket, a habit I remember from faculty meetings, over which he presided from a massive chair like a throne.

Now he's turning and bending to serve a couple of tourists who've come up beside me. They can hardly reach his counter. 'Baked potatoes,' I hear him bawling impatiently into the southerly wind. 'Hot baked potatoes!'

Across the quadrangle workmen are eating their lunch at the foot of scaffolding that goes up and up the side of the Great Hall; above their heads a loose tarpaulin flaps like a sail, giving me a sudden, literal sense of *something in the air*, the strangest feeling that everything is changing in directions I can't see. The world, going its way without me! I'm through the clocktower portal now and here's a tram clattering up like the ones you see on old postcards of the town, a replica made in South Korea. It's painted bright red-and-yellow and carries signs for businesses long gone—Armstrongs, Beaths, Cuddon Stewart Agencies. I step aboard, still gobbling at my spud; a clang and we start rolling towards the centre of town and the Cathedral. Ahead, another spoof tram, coming towards us with its antlers rippling and sparkling against the overhead wires, tourists aboard like those around me now, amongst whose dainty frottage I snatch at a swaying handgrip. And look who's here in front of me, clipping tickets from the little organ-grinder's gadget against his paunch, his tram conductor's kepi tipped saucily over his brow: Ron Boodle (*Literary Modernism in Late Medieval England*, New York: Dutton 1971)!

'G'day cocker,' he calls, cheerily, over tourists' heads; his knees give expertly to an unexpected lurch and he winds out another ticket for a punter, looking down through his little granny glasses.

We've got to the bridge now and I can see workmen, over to the right, ticking past us in the middle distance like figures in an old movie. Boodle's beside me now, grinding out a ticket as if from his very navel, swaying about, balancing like a surfer. 'They're taking it down,' he's telling me. 'That statue—when people start missing it they'll put it back.'

Now we're entering the canyon of hotels that leads to the Square, we're nearly in the Square, the Cathedral's up ahead, its great wooden doors are wide open, we're in the Square, we're rumbling across it—

He's moving away from me, Boodle, swaying into the awe-struck babble of the travelling circus. 'Except it won't be exactly the same statue,' he calls back. 'It'll be, you know, a new one exactly like the old one.'

Our mechanical Tower of Babel chugs across the Square on its unstoppable path towards the splayed doors: now the tram begins to slide under the shadow of the Cathedral and into the foyer, and we crawl into the cool remembered sanctity of the nave, with its solemn, religious light. I look around, up, down, as cameras fire off around me. The tram stops at last. I step down after the tourists. On either side, boutiques where the side-aisles were, above them a mezzanine with more boutiques and cafés. To the left, from one of the little chapels in the northern transept, a bridal couple is emerging, she a tiny Asian in white dress and veil, he a tiny ditto in a tux: they smile and bow and smile. Another bridal pair is moving into the doorway the first two have just come from, like a change of shift. I can smell coffee.

Behind me, a loud clang!—I watch the tram turn hard, into the northern transept, past opened doors. The Cathedral's shadow slides up and over it and Boodle's gone into the sunshine, with an informal parting gesture. In here I'm left with the churchy light and echo, the same spooky feel to things as in the abandoned humanities library. People everywhere, chattering, pushing against me, gabbling at each other—wedding parties, tour groups with guides, locals with their peasant European faces, Polynesians. Everywhere, the Sound of Muzak.

There. Built into a side chapel. The Han Kin, most popular Chinese eatery in town, as packed as ever—and here's Mrs Wang, the proprietor, amid a scribble of diners: *No! No!* she's saying as she jabs her finger at the menu. *This is not what you have!* Such behaviour is thought to guarantee the authenticity of the cuisine.

This is where we'd meet in our early days together, me and Sally, in the years before she went north. It was a few blocks away then, in a building that's since come down; here it is, remade: the noise, the smells, the proprietor. I sometimes see Sally in here with her new television friends—hoping she'll see me, hoping she won't. She's not here today: that's what I'm busy not saying.

PART TWO

Venusberg

Chapter 6

And here it is again, the squawk of the pneumatic muscle on the men's-room door—it catches me every time. I look up. Those tiny flies, half a dozen of them now, still working their way around and around the light fitting. Who is it, this time? Holding my breath, sitting here: footsteps, fumbling, and then the familiar sound I used to hear through the wall each day I was in the office on the other side of the wall.

There's a slight vertical gap worn between the cubicle door and its frame: I ease up from the lavatory seat and apply an eye to this, taking care not to fart.[74]

Garland—Garland, surely, standing there unzipping, unzipped, pelvis pushed forward in the usual gunslinger's stance of the male leaker. What's *he* doing here? *Fucking third Rockingham administration*, he hissed at me years ago from the left end of this very urinal as I stood at its right. And, when I look blank: *What I'm trying to bloody teach. The Marquess of Rockingham*[75]*—see, you don't know what I'm talking about and you're staff—how am I supposed to make anything of it for these fucking cretins?*

74 Got him again—someone must have pointed this out to him in Walker Percy's novel *The Moviegoer* (1961).
75 Presumably Garland is referring to Charles Watson-Wentworth, prime minister of Great Britain in 1765–66 and 1782. Details of his Whig administrations have proven fascinating and relevant to young students of history throughout the British Empire, though less so recently.

And he flung out without washing his hands, a detail that stayed with me: out, and in due course discovered lecture-and-tutorial timetabling, for which he showed an unexpected flair, and then, little by little, the *jouissance* of the spreadsheet. He'd found his way out of the chores of teaching and research and into the magical fourth dimension of managerial administration. That was towards the end of Norman Iggo's time as vice-chancellor, as the changes that were to sweep us all away were just beginning, unrecognisable then even though we can see now they were there in plain sight. Oh, how young we seemed back then, how naïve, how arrogant!

But Garland, it seemed, embraced the tide of history. One by one his academic chores fell away from him, one by one his management responsibilities filled their place. Out in the quadrangle he'd bustle past us importantly, absorbed in spreadsheets taut between fingertips and thumbs, the day-to-day actualities of mere academic life now behind him. Soon he abandoned us here in town and strode off to the main campus out in the suburbs, where he began to move *up* and *up* the brutalist tower of the Registry building, briskly, from smaller office to larger, acquiring personal assistants as he rose. Eventually he began to appear regularly at the side of the vice-chancellor at Senate meetings, nodding and whispering to the great man, passing him scribbled little notes, turning away confidently to patter silent, urgent, confidential messages into a laptop, all the time with those grubby, unwashed hands. On one occasion I'm sure I even saw him shake his head at the boss: *No*, he seemed to be saying. *No, you can't do that.* And the boss seemed to pause, and reflect, and then he nodded, too.

Now here he is, Garland, zipping up his fly. *Will he wash his hands this time, though?* I crouch forward at the gap in the doorway, mouth-breathing slightly: he steps down from the urinal and turns away. A quick flirt with the sink and he's out and gone—the fourth or fifth of this type I've seen around here this week: men in suits with phones at their ears and hairstyles not casually arrived at. What are they doing here, these people, what are they up to?

⌖⌖

A new year, and suddenly—out of nothing, it seemed at the time, I remember—there I was, a newly tenured lecturer in the Department of English. On *tenure-track*,[76] the phrase seemed to be: confirmation requiring completion of a doctoral thesis within three years. *Nil perspirandum*: did I not have Manatine's thesis left to me, requiring no more than a tidy-up? I put the problem out of my mind and turned to the perks of the job: a ground-floor office of my own with a junior lecturer's entitlement—lino, two-drawer pine desk, bookshelf, single filing cabinet, unparalleled vistas of the boiler-house wall immediately beyond the window. Best of all, the men's downstairs lavatory, right next to my office. Soon I began to identify various colleagues' signature performances through the lath-and-plaster—not least the extraordinary efforts of Gotch himself, in whose hard-fought daily cannonade I began to sense something of his favourite teaching topic, Arnold's Empedocles on Etna, struggling with Doubt.

Getting on tenure-track meant that I began to reflect light. Older staff who'd ignored me as a tutor suddenly began to speak

---

76   A regrettable Americanism which, like so much else from that source, seems to have penetrated our tertiary institutions. In this case it simply refers to the fact that our hero must finish a doctoral dissertation within an agreed period in order to confirm his continuing appointment.

to me as a lecturer, although without giving reliable evidence that they knew who I was. Even I was unsure who Gotch thought he might have appointed, so I put all three nameplates on my door: Cocks's, Manatine's and my own. Alun Pismire would peer at these whenever he went past to his office. Soon he began to drop by at the end of each day to talk about himself while leaning against the door-frame, all the time looking around my room for possible further occupants. *Sherry?* he suggested on one of these visits, unexpectedly, and we went next door to his room, where he revealed a decanter of inexpensive liquid. Riordan appeared after a while and then Basil Shortbread and Norman Bonesaw. After a while I realised we were *doing the Oxbridge thing*, a pale imitation of something we'd read about somewhere and copied as if it were real, like the building we were doing it in. The gossip flowed—Gotch's latest driving disaster, the prof from Astronomy who'd got locked overnight in a cupboard, the man in Physics rumoured to have a portable toilet in his office. *This is it*, I thought, *the life of the scholar. Made it at last!*

Suddenly, people began to invite me to dinner. I remember the excitement of the first of what were to be many invitations from colleagues as they *brought me into the fold*—which is how each of them put it, laboriously, in their turn. At the Pismires', Alun made a complex Incan dish which caused immediate and widespread flatulence among his guests; afterwards someone really let fly above a sofa spring—following which, urgently, loudly, we all began to discuss the lot of the liberal in Western society. A few weeks later and here was an invitation from Marigold Butcher, who made a jolly roast-beef-and-Yorkshire-pud sort of dinner with plenty of root vegetables she'd grown in her own garden plus a steamed plum duff she must have trapped and killed herself. As we were leaving she went into the garden in gumboots and returned with an armful of homegrown chard, which she wrapped in newspaper and thrust upon us, all the time observed by a fierce little one-eyed pug called Pugin.

After that, an invitation from Basil Shortbread to the heart of a gated community, where he made a tittering revelation of a male partner called Aart, a tremulous, decrepit, pinned-together Dutch youth of possibly sixty. There was a cat, too, called Penis Envy: *Male owners only*, Basil chortled, naughtily, pleased with himself. Meanwhile Aart made us a meal that seemed to have no beginning, middle or end, just a series of palatal feints on stoneware by Clarice Cliff; a slight sweetening confirmed, eventually, that dessert was upon us. *Chez* Bevan and Iris Panter, out in the countryside, the meal was from *The Jeffrey Dahmer Cookbook*;[77] at Biddle's it didn't arrive at all and survivors had to make up for it afterwards, self-consciously, at a rather *louche* pie-cart near the centre of town. All the same, munching a fried egg sandwich with my colleagues, our collars up against the midnight wind from the sea as we discussed whether the new secretary in French was up for it,[78] I couldn't help feeling once again that I really *was* in the ruck of things, really *had* arrived as an academic—

Bit by bit I fell into the routine of a tenured lecturer. Five days a week I'd walk through that clocktower archway and into the northern quadrangle with its not-so-great Great Hall, the imitation Bodleian straight ahead and those looped cloisters to the left with the men's lavatory at their end. After my ritual pause there, into the southern quadrangle I'd go and

77 Jeffrey Dahmer (1960–94), US serial killer, cannibal, food-writer.
78 Starting to feel uncomfortable with this men's-locker-room sort of thing? Very common amongst male academics of the period but not entirely consistent with endemically poor upper-body strength, poor posture, pot bellies, large posteriors and, in certain cases, rudimentary development elsewhere.

to the erstwhile Physics building and the strange little fish-tank known as *The Department of English*. There, I continued to teach amiable, awkward, harmless young folk in one or other of the two downstairs tutorial rooms that are joined now as Bevan's Bookshop, or in antique, woody lecture rooms up tight spiral staircases. I'd been employed as a generalist: I'd take classes on anything and everything, from books I hadn't read till the night before to books I hadn't even *heard* of till the night before. I was getting better and better at doing this. *Lets us have our say*—a comment on an early teaching survey. *Doesn't tell us what to think.*

Soon I passed the greatest test of all for a young lecturer in English literature—teaching the two plays of George Farquhar without losing class control—and gave close scrutiny to the first chapters, and, more frequently, the first pages, or even the opening paragraphs, of many a great master. When I told Gifford I'd just spent an entire class on the opening sentence of *Moby-Dick*,[79] he told me I'd turned *ejaculatio praecox* into a mode of literary criticism. I had to look that up but then used the line frequently myself. Not bad, is it?

I became something of a connoisseur of this up-front approach, and still maintain that page one of *Pride and Prejudice* is beyond comparison in the entire English canon. Or maybe it's *Sense and Sensibility* I'm thinking of. After a little of this I began to wonder if there might be an opening here, I mean an area of specialisation for publication purposes. I imagined an article titled (say) 'Making a Start: Decision-Making Processes in the Creative Act', or even a book called something like *Opening the Batting. Committing* was another title I liked, despite someone telling me once I seemed to think commitment meant staying the night.

79 'Call me Ishmael.'

Apart from Gifford, though—who seemed to be thought a bit of a *parvenu* for publishing so much, and in such good northern hemisphere journals, too—no one in the department published anything much at all. At one point (Gifford confided this to me in my first year *on tenure-track*) one of the old chaps, a man who, unthinkably, had been there *even before Gotch*, had taken him aside to suggest on behalf of other senior staff that he might tone things down a little and stop this embarrassing business of publishing so much. *Showing us up!*—that's when I knew I'd arrived, when Gifford let that slip to me in his dry, despairing little office, the one the lawyer's in now, right above the bookshop. *Historyless*, was his word for them: it didn't mean *ahistorical*. 'Even the tearoom noticeboard doesn't change,' he said. 'Notice that? Never anything new on it. They'd take it down if there was.'

What we studied did it to people, he told me, and the way we taught the humanities was wrong. And that was the first moment I thought of what we were doing as other than simply *what had been immemorially done*—thought of it as something that might actually be bad for you. I remember watching Donald Tyrdie (*Bawdy in the Sermons of Thomas Hooker*, London: Purist Publishing Group 1964)[80] trying to mount a bicycle in a street nearby and stuffing it up every time. As I watched him floundering about—his right leg was actually *through the bike frame* at one point—I began to realise that *that* was the reason he was having trouble with his bike, with the university, with the universe—the fact that he'd written a book with a title like that.

80 Thomas Hooker (1586–1647). An English founder of Connecticut. Preacher, prolific writer on religious matters. *The Soul's Exaltation* (1638) and *A Brief Exposition of the Lord's Prayer* (1645) were bestsellers in their time.

*

With my improved status I began to spend more time in the little tearoom. Minus Gotch, minus Manatine, minus Cocks, it seemed slightly bigger, slightly less intimidating, simply the home of conversations that had neither beginning nor middle nor end. There was a milk-on-tea debate, for example, which came and went over weeks and months and, eventually, years: it moved from one group to another like the plague—or, worse, plaque. There was a second ongoing debate, more obscure and centring on a wild, semi-coherent member of the Russian department, about seaweed, and a third, more furtive but insistent all the same, about vapour trails. I'd no idea they contained barium and manganese and so on—did you? Someone really ought to look into it.

Apart from these, Bevan Panter told me at regular intervals that Bristol was once known as *Bristow*,[81] and, more interestingly but also often, that his elderly aunts in England used to refer to Anthony Trollope as *Mister Trollopey*.[82] To avoid unfortunate associations, he always added whenever he came up with this, and then he always laughed the same mirthless, chuffing laugh and rubbed his bony hands together in the same way he always did when laughing his mirthless, chuffing laugh. Pat Hazard kept pushing his African and Indian writers till he became friendless, a pariah—Postcolonial Pat, they were calling him these days, with Gifford his only friend. Basil Shortbread told me Tennyson was the last known to use the word 'rathe' rather than 'rather' or 'rathest' in a poem, and then told me again a

81 This assertion is correct, astonishingly enough.
82 This, too; i.e. that Trollope's name was thus pronounced in order to euphemise the more unfortunate implications when it was restricted to merely two syllables. Finding two correct assertions in a row is astonishing in a book like this.

little later, and again after that; and I said *Really?* each time he did.[83] Each time Marigold Butcher drained her cup and set off to lecture she'd say, 'A pint of port and a pistol,' and I never knew why.[84] Each time Farting Harry Toothill from History appeared at the tearoom door Alun Pismire would make his *fort–da* joke.[85] Roland Sentance (*Colloquialism in Paradise Lost*, Kutner & Sons 1968), that old buffer who asked if I was still *writing up* on my first day in the tearoom, asked me the same question at regular intervals after that and seemed just as satisfied each time I told him I hadn't quite reached that stage yet. He himself had never published anything in his life, he confided to me, except for a short piece in *Notes and Queries*.[86] Overseas visitors were always shown a laminated copy of this immortal half-page, which he'd pinned to his office door, and another, similarly timeworn, on the tearoom noticeboard. Several of them professed to find it *not uninteresting*. Something about bees in Thomas Hardy.

Each day passed like the next, till I thought of Nietzsche's Eternal Return[87]—just the phrase: I know nothing about

83   True again!—in 'Lancelot and Elaine' (1859), *Idylls of the King* (1859–85), l.330.
84   The hero at his most theatrically romantic in Goethe's *Die Leiden des jungen Werthers* (1774, 1787). Johann Wolfgang von Goethe (1749–1832). German. Ignore.
85   Refers to Sigmund Freud's analysis in *Beyond the Pleasure Principle* (1920) of a repetitious 'there–gone' game played by his grandson; Pismire's play on words here is a little askance from this and not a bad one.
86   *Notes and Queries* (OUP 1849–) is what its title suggests, a quarterly which records brief articles informative of 'English language and literature, lexicography, history, and scholarly antiquarianism'. Rather more interesting to read than most literary journals, as it happens, though sometimes referred to as *Quotes and Nearlies*.
87   The theory of the perpetual recurrence of events in an infinite universe

Nietzsche apart from that story I overheard in the tearoom once, about him sheltering from a storm inside a shepherd's hut and finding a man slaughtering an animal in there. I remembered Nietzsche's pale-blue-wristed academic's excitement at the blood and the violence, and how hearing that excited *me*, too. I'd begun to make something of a study of academic wrists, as you might have noticed.

One day, without thinking, perhaps to show I'd made some progress at last when he asked his question yet again, I told this Roland Sentance that, yes, yes, I was in fact *writing up* at last; and he seemed just as satisfied as at all those times I'd told him I wasn't. *This fellow's writing up*, he informed the next man through the door, or maybe it was Marigold Butcher instead, or Vera the upstairs secretary or Jolene the downstairs secretary, come in to wash our cups and saucers; but whoever it was seemed just as pleased for me. *Writing up!*

And that was the episode which reminded me it was high time I took a look at that blank cheque Manatine had left me. I found his manila folder and settled in with my office door ajar and my feet up on my desk to demonstrate the laid-back, ironic quality I wished to project to any passing student—the quintessentially Oxbridgean pose that the whole academic business was a bit of a bore but something to be endured for the sake of appearances.

I opened the folder and began a more substantial flick-through than I'd done that first time in front of Manatine; in fact, I gave it a damn good skim.

It took a few minutes to get past Cocks's dull, logical

---

developed from about 1882 by the philosopher Friedrich Nietzsche (1844–1900). German. Ignore.

opening chapter and let the text settle into me. Then, suddenly, I drove over a body on the road. *What in the name of God was this?* A world lit by the mad, flickering strobe light of Manatine's prose—the dazzling, addled world of the dope smoker and consumer of all those other things I'd been too chicken to follow him into over the years, those belts and needles and the stuff up the nose, and (once, he told me) a magical suppository of astonishing proportions and spectacular effect.

I began to shuffle through the pages, feeling my innards tightening, my heart rate lifting. Trollope's name began to appear, and Pound's, too—but a Pound changed, from time to time a woman, occasionally a man again, now and then both. An entire chapter argued that the younger writer had influenced the older after his death; in the next chapter both were trapped in a U-boat suspended beneath the sea as depth charges sank around them. All through this, the steady underdrift of Cocks's original was like the remains of a shipwreck far below, hard to make out through great drifts of discarded plastic but there, undeniably there.[88]

I read all this with my mouth sagged open as if on the verge of a great revelation just a turn of a page away—the truth, the *absolute truth* of literature; even the very truth of life itself. Each fresh page I turned blew that feeling away again—here he was now, writing about the bombing of Dresden, the guttering flames below the bombers, the mounting firestorm—but then, suddenly, we were back in the sunken submarine, at the bottom of the sea and somehow in the company of Friedrich Nietzsche himself—

88 The quality of the writing is really falling away now—this is a very poor attempt to say what he wants to say, clogged with metaphor, always a sign of a writer sinking out of his depth.

I let the thing slide out of my hands and slop onto the floor. Its pages spewed out in a fan again and Rommel, who I'd inherited, pricked up his ears and licked his lips with his lollopy pink tongue. I shoved the folder towards him with the side of my foot. *Go on*, I whispered. There was a skein of drool from one side of his mouth, not unlike his former owner's at moments of self-induced stress. *Go on.*

I sat there watching Rommel eyeing it, licking his lips. On the other side of my office wall, Atkinson, one of the tutors, started up—I could always tell it was him, with that relentless rattle-on-the-metal of a man who knew where he was going in life. I stared through the window at the side of the boiler-house till he was done. I could hear my heart beating, *thump, thump, thump.* Submission time ahead, and nothing, *nothing* to show for it. *I should have known, I should have known.* Everything changed in a matter of minutes, my borrowed postgraduate degree drifting away, my tenured career falling like a shot duck. *What was I going to do, what was going to happen to me?*

The answer came in a dream. Manatine appeared to me quite distinctly, fabulously dressed in robes and a turban: he might even have been levitating a little.

That familiar *hem-hem* cough, and then he began to whisper to me, *blotto voce.* In the dream I strained to hear him. *Everything is connected, everything is one*—

I jerked half-awake. My office door was open. I wondered whether anyone had spotted me. Then I was completely half-awake. What was it he'd just told me? *Give it to Bevan?* Did he really tell me that? Give this potty *faux*-thesis draft to someone else as if it was mine? *Tell him it's finished*, he'd said. I straightened in my chair. I could still hear the voice. *Then steal it back off him.* Something like that.

Was it me thinking this or was it really Manatine?

Didn't matter. Here I was, five minutes later, outside Bevan's office door like a sleepwalker; here I was, tapping on it, and here was Bevan's reedy Bristow voice calling out *yes* on the other side; and now here I was, stepping into that familiar used-odour-eater smell.

I held Manatine's mad thesis out to him in its manila folder. It pulsed with its own awfulness.

He took it from me, aghast. 'What's this?' He stared down at it like a man in shock.

'The final draft of my thesis.' I was feeling more confident now. 'I think I'm there, I think I'm done.' My palms wiped themselves against each other in front of me, an involuntary dusting-off gesture they'd thought of themselves.

'Final *draft?*' He opened the folder and pushed his fingers through a page or two. His eyes flickered up to me and away. 'Well done,' he muttered. 'Well done.' His expression was rat-like, furtive. He snapped the folder shut and put it on his desktop, well to one side. He put a book on top of it, then a coffee mug. *Yes—*

'Of course, I'm very busy at the moment,' he said. 'Not much time for reading things.'

'Oh, quite, quite.'

'Everything seems to have a habit of landing on my desk and avoiding certain other people's.'

'I've noticed that.'

'No names no pack-drill, naturally.'

'Naturally.'

'I mean, I wonder sometimes if they think we're coolies[89]—'

'Oh, they do, I'm sure they do.'

---

89   Straight from Anthony Powell, *What's Become of Waring* (1939).

That's all it took. I slipped away knowing I'd really rattled him. *Misprision accomplished.*

A couple of days, and then I checked the lecture timetable in Vera's office. Yet one more time I asked her if it was honey sandwiches for lunch again and yet one more time she said yes, in fact it was, and showed me; and, indeed, it really *was* honey in her sandwiches.[90]

'Who are you looking for?' she asked, not particularly distinctly, and when I told her she said, 'Two o'clock. Room 15.'

I followed Bevan there and watched him fumble at the lecture-room door. Once he was in I heard his Bristow drone start on the other side, and waited a few seconds till students began to slip out of the fire door at the rear of the lecture room, one or two at first and then pairs, then groups of them, huddled together like boat people. Another class underway.

Now, back to the department building and up the staircase with Manatine's keys in my hand. I slid into Bevan's room with my heart drumming the way it had all those years ago in front of the departmental safe. There—the manila folder, full of Manatine's mad ravings, exactly where I'd left it, on the right side of Bevan's desk under two books and an empty coffee mug whose brown, dried interior bespoke the utter pointlessness of human existence. *Just fetching Bevan his lecture notes*, I'd planned to say if someone saw me in there. No one saw me in there.

Back in my office downstairs I hid the folder and its contents

90   The phrasing here echoes a scene in Nikolai Gogol's novel *Dead Souls* (1842) in which the protagonist and his friends inspect a horse that is said to have thrown its shoe: 'And indeed the horse had thrown its shoe.' Again, no acknowledgement, of course. Who's he got it from this time, who's he overheard talking about this scene? Back Passage, at a best guess, in the tearoom.

behind my bookcase. I straightened, I folded my arms and leaned back, I looked out at the blank wall of the boiler-house again. I'd taken to doing this sort of thing recently, I noticed, striking poses out of the blue. Maybe Manatine had been right, maybe this business did take you over bit by bit—the academic life, I mean. This particular pose, for example, seemed to suggest an introspective bent, a moment of scholarly reflection. Whether or not I was actually reflecting was less clear. All I was aware of at that moment was the sound of Donald Tyrdie through the wall, his glum, intermittent, well-meaning splutter.

The next step, I knew, was for me to do—nothing. My forté, of course. So simple, now it had begun—nothing for three months! No need to look at Manatine's potty thesis again, feel its sick sense of seduction, hear its wild and whirling words.[91] I knew Bevan wouldn't mention it to me again if *I* didn't. In a month or two I'd go back to him, and if I played the game properly after that I might really be able to take the wretched thing out from behind my bookcase and give it to Rommel to rip up and pee on again. And then? Ah, that really was a gamble; but I was beginning to get an idea of it now, a glimpse of something in the future. Of Manatine's master plan, if that was what it really was—was it? Or was it mine? Who was calling the shots here?

After a month, a little more, I struck. By now I was even clearer in what I was doing—confident, a little ruthless, even. Becoming an academic, perhaps.

My knuckles fairly rattled on Bevan's office door.

'Your *thesis* draft?' he asked when I was in.

---

91 We all know where these ones come from. A slightly less furtive theft, for a change.

He looked around the room—he had no idea what I was talking about, you could tell. But when I explained a bit more I could see it coming back to him in panicky flashbacks. He stood and began to look around his desk, his palms flopping uselessly among the books, the papers, the unmarked essays, all the time his head jerking about like a chicken's. 'I'm sure I had it here somewhere.'

He sat down again.

'No hurry.'

'No, but this is very annoying—I mean, I've been intending to make a start on it—' He picked up a book from his desk, and put it down again, assertively.

'No rush.'

'Of course, I've been very busy lately. Things seem to land on my desk and not certain others'.'

'Oh, quite. I've noticed that.'

'No names no pack-drill, naturally—I mean, sometimes I wonder if they think we're coolies—'

Yes, I did feel bad about this, but not *bad-bad-bad*. I watched him pick up a tower of unmarked essays, put it down, lift a copy of *Is He Popenjoy?* and reveal an elderly packet of sandwiches flattened underneath. I thought of Manatine's thesis draft, wedged behind the bookcase in my study.

'I must've left it at home,' he said.

'Yes,' I said. 'You must have.'

After a few weeks of this struggling back and forth with the wheelbarrow I start to take library books home with me each evening—a few at a time, no room for more in my tiny backpack. It feels like shoplifting. James Stern the first time,

The Hidden Damage (London: Chelsea Press 1947)—Auden in postwar Germany; some nice pix. Max Weber, *Economy and Society: An Outline of Interpretive Psychology* (New York: Bedminster Press 1968)—terrifying, unreadable, not a single photo to help me out. The next night, Donald Davie, *Articulate Energy: An Inquiry into the Syntax of English Poetry* (London: Routledge and Kegan Paul 1976): I can't get past its bright blue dustjacket and the used, torn despair of it—all those fumbling, baffled hands, all those dents from being thrown against walls. After that, William Empson, *Seven Types of Ambiguity* (London: Chatto & Windus 1930): dustjacket long gone, brown leather cover bared. I try a few paragraphs and give up. Well, the first paragraph, anyway.

These days I'm house-sitting for Magnus Furz, ex-German-department, and his *de facto* Blodwyn. Last month I was house-sitting for the Pismires in the made-over state house they're reduced to these days, and for two months before that I was warming myself at Basil Shortbread's gas-heated hearth before Aart returned from The Hague to put their apartment on the market. And before *that* I was in Marigold Butcher's ancient ruin while she pursued Round 125 of an ongoing, perfervid encounter with (it was rumoured) the famous English landscape architect Dame Dora Packet. Marigold died soon after this, probably to save expense.

Currently Magnus and Blodwyn are in Bavaria, leaving their elegant home for me to explore, with its expensive whiteware, furnishings and artwork. *Pitching your tent in the houses of the diaspora*, Magnus calls my lifestyle: it sounds like something from the Bible, but naturally I've no idea whether it is or not.[92] I presume he means I'm refusing to commit myself to life minus

92 Not.

Sally, having failed to commit myself to life with her. I sit each evening as I do now, in Magnus's massive leather armchair, and work my way through whatever I've just brought home with me. *Season of the Jew* (New York: Norton 1987)—Maurice Shadbolt: now *there's* a chap who *really could* write. Another Giorgio Agamben, *The Open: Man and Animal* (Redwood: Stanford University Press 2004), and a third edition of John Farrant's classic, *The Care and Maintenance of Swimming Pools* (Oxford University Press 1973).

And all through this, five evenings a week, Sally is in the room with me, on the Furzes' enormous wall-mounted Sanyo. The back of her head, most of the time, and, whenever the camera focuses on her victim-of-the-night, past the back of her left ear, too; though often there's a reverse shot and then there she is, all of her, Sally, my Sally with her own current affairs programme, *Cut 'em Off!*—named for its main stunt, in which she does just that, cuts the sound on her interviewees when she thinks they're talking bullshit. After our years together, she told me, she has a fine sense of exactly when to flick the switch. Caught bluffing, victims have their mouths taped shut by female assistants dressed as Atwood's handmaidens; the fifth time and she operates a trapdoor from a button beneath her desk. This last atrocity rarely occurs—her guests are far too terrified to bluff—but is eagerly anticipated each evening by her vast viewing public. Last week she sent the Minister of Finance backwards down the hole for a shifty answer on debt indicator trends.

Sally at forty-one—confident, commanding, the woman she was always destined to become long before she took possession of me all those years ago: a public figure popping up in glossy lifestyle magazines, interviewing world leaders, reporting from hotspots overseas, rumoured for a career in politics or diplomacy. Always in the glossies she's with Yousef, my successor as her Significant Other and a diplomat of some sort, a man who's been shot at and shot, and, spectacularly, held hostage with a dozen others in an embassy somewhere for forty days and forty nights. Images of him, images of Sally in shades and a headscarf, holding her daughter, a tiny, imperturbable child, as she reports back from the World while on the spot, her voice tightened each night with grief and anxiety. A woman in the gulf-stream of History, being washed into the bewildering world that seems to be making itself up for us now day by day—the global woman: larger than life, *real* only as *real* seems now to be. The final thing she tells us as her show closes each evening is her diet for the day. Grains, pulses, soya, miso; *kale, kale, kale, kale.*

Chapter 7

Next morning, here I am, on the third floor of what's left of the humanities library, loading the barrow again. The real thing in its time, this building, designed a hundred years ago while the tiny colonial university was assembling its neo-Gothic toytown confection. It was Bevan who told me the model for this particular piece of colonial flummery: you could find small fake Bodleian libraries like ours on campuses anywhere in the West, he said. The original Bodleian didn't feature temporary metal shelving as ours did, though, against which our small imitations of large imitations of classical busts looked particularly out of place. *Cotton Vitellius Meccano*, I essayed in the tearoom once, when we were discussing this— hopefully, faking up a learned joke. But someone immediately protested, quite sharply, that Cotton Vitellius was not to be found at the Bodleian: was I not aware of this? A couple of exchanged looks across the room, a smirk or two: priceless, *simply priceless*.

All that common room nonsense, gone, done for, tearoom lecture room library and all. Each day I've been bumping ten, fifteen of these barrow-loads across to the service elevator and down to the ground floor, stopping to pick up spillage, and eventually pushing each load to the bookshop and up the wheelchair ramp. There's something about all this that disturbs me, something beyond the obvious memories of the fight, back then, to keep the place open. For all my philistinism (Sally's word) the truth is that I find myself increasingly disturbed at what's been done.

Reversing the tide of history, Bevan says; but what will *really* happen to these abandoned books? Here's one in front of me now, on the worn felt flooring of the library: Walter Benjamin, *Reflections: Essays, Aphorisms, Autobiographical Writings* (New York: Schocken Books 1986). Here's another: T.S. Eliot, *The Sacred Wood: Essays on Poetry and Criticism* (Methuen & Co 1920). Up at my nostrils this one has a hint of must and decay the Benjamin hasn't yet begun to acquire, but which all books come to in the end.

And that's what's really getting to me. It's nothing to do with the contents—you've read this far, d'you *really* think I've opened either of these before? No, it's everything to do with the feel of them, the weight of them, the smell of this tomb, the light from the tall leaded windows on the north side now the fluorescents have gone. Beneath this, books seem to give up the fight—pages curl shut like dead men's fingers, book covers open as their contents clench up. Left behind, they turn scarred and dog-eared as if something invisible goes on twisting their covers. It's taken all that's happened this year for me to begin to understand that they're things, they're alive—with their *joints* and their *tails* and their *spines*. That they're—well, people, even.[93]

I said this to Bevan one evening as we crouched here in the half-stripped library, working late in the early days and always overwhelmed by what it was we'd set ourselves to do. It was the first time I'd become aware of the plaintiveness of everything

93 All very fine and plausible, this, but clearly filched from Catherine Chidgey's novel *Golden Deeds* (VUP 2000), in theme and in detail. Shameless, shameless.

that was happening, and what I said seemed strange, silly, once it blurted itself out. But he understood it straight away. 'As good almost kill a man as kill a good book,' he said straight back. 'For books are not absolutely dead things, but do contain a potency of life in them to be as active as that soul was whose progeny they are.' And then he nodded, knowingly, one scholar reminding another of something they'd both known long and held dear: and—also scholarly—reminding me too of his feat of memory. For good and bad, an academic to his bones.

Oh, how I wish I could have shot straight back to him: 'Milton! *Areopagitica*!' Once more I had that sense I always had in the tearoom when someone pulled the stunt he'd just pulled, that I really was in some kind of community of scholars—that, and the sheer *sexiness* of it: fleetingly in that Amber room once more. But there was the slight problem that, of course, I'd read neither *Areopagitica* nor anything else by its author and knew little of him except that he'd been blind—deaf, I'd thought at first, but later I checked on Wikipedia and he was definitely blind, Milton. It's only because Bevan showed me the quotation back in the bookshop that I knew where it came from at all!—I forgot it straight away, of course.[94]

'That's what we have to remember when we're doing this,' he told me another time, as our frail, puny, contemptible little academic arms were trying to lift a massive elephant's turd of humanities books stacked in the wheelbarrow. 'All these writers.' His little pigeon chest, puffing in and out. 'We're trying to prevent their deaths.' He gestured at the barrow and the books sliding off it. I remember we both stopped when he

94 If he forgot it straight away, how does it come to be here on the page? What is he up to here, what has he just let slip? Here we see bluff-work falling away into mere bullshit.

said that. We waited for his breathing to settle a little. 'Saving lives,' he said. 'We're saving lives.'

><><

And, back in the fake common room, the milk-in-tea debate went on and on. Milk First seemed to be the default mode, the refuge of the Roundheads, men of action who tended towards the-teabag-on-the-milk and the-boiling-water-on-the-teabag and then a quick hot slurp before dashing away to change the world. Milk Second was for the Cavaliers, the traditionalists who could spare a leisurely six minutes for the pot to draw and its temperature to fall just enough for the tea, once poured, to receive the kiss of the milk unscalded.

Basil Shortbread seemed to be the great defender of this group, with a shifting arrangement of supporters around the room.

'Pouring it onto the tea doesn't cook it,' I heard him say one afternoon. 'It has a different taste from when you pour the milk in first.' He'd said this several times before, too, but to a different audience, a small group apparently more sceptical than these Milk Second followers, as they seemed to be.

Through the smoke of her eternal cigarillo I saw Marigold Butcher nodding to herself. 'Then surely the issue is the *taste*,' I heard her say. 'Surely the issue is whether the *taste* of the cooked milk is the standard we're using here.'

Now another voice, breaking in—I couldn't believe the life-and-death urgency of it: 'But—*both* methods—can't you see this?—cook the milk?' The man sat back, looking eager, pleased with himself. Warren Puttance, PhD Melbourne (*Rural Australian Attitudes to Settler Latticework 1882–1915*, Sydney: UAP 1989). 'Surely,' he said.

'Quite.' Marigold again. 'But in different ways, do you agree?'

'I find it very difficult to accept'—someone else now, just a voice behind me—'that the *volume* of scalding *tea* on the *milk* has no *effect*.'

Ah. Professor Leon Becker-Paysage L-ès-l, University of Paris, M-ès-l, Université Louis-Ferdinand Céline (*Écrire sur le massage: Proust et le pénis*, Paris: Gallimard 1965)—a small, tired Belgian who always wore binder twine around his lower trousers for the bicycle ride to work late each morning and kept it there, plodding around the campus like Worzel Gummidge.[95] He occasionally visited our tearoom and got himself tangled up with Gifford, who liked to toy with him. Here they were, weeks after Gifford got back from his year of leave on the nudist beaches of Lower Normandy.

'So, you're arguing that Luther wrote ninety-five theses because he was constipated?'

'Of course he did. Of course he did. It was a release for him.' Gifford, sitting opposite Back Passage, his expression unreadable. 'You can hear it in the language.'

'But it's not the same in German.' Alun Pismire. His face was creased with concern. He sat forward in his chair, urgently, each arm out a little from his body and his thumbs and fingertips touching like those of the Buddha.[96] 'In German it'd have been— I don't know—*kot*, Luther would've most probably used *kot*.'

'He was a priest. The language would have been Latin. He'd have called it *faeces*.'

95 Dishevelled, imaginary scarecrow figure from British children's fiction, identified with numerous politicians and academics over the years, not always to their disadvantage.
96 A good example of standard bluff-work—'the Buddha' (rather than just plain 'Buddha') suggesting superior knowledge without actually having any.

A brilliant parry this, pure Gifford. He was very, very good.

Back Passage nodded, and shifted in his seat as he did, as if he'd just got rid of something whose time had come. 'From the Latin for dregs,' he said. 'Wine dregs.'

In the far corner, the eternal debate went on. Milk First had been rallying lately but Basil seemed to be making a fighting comeback. 'It's an *aesthetic* issue,' he was saying. 'Quite apart from anything else. It belongs to the history of *gustation*.'

'Do you *really* think it was an issue before tea got here—? To Europe, I mean—?' Christopher Shrike from French; PhD University of London (*La Soixante-neuf parmi les Pieds-Noir*, Savina: Formentera University Press 1969). There was a portable record player on his lap.

'Naturally! They moved from the tea ceremony to Dr Johnson's dish of tea in a decade—'

'But there's no milk in the Japanese tea ceremony—'

'Of course! My point exactly!'

Over to the left, Gifford again, as he began to toy with Back Passage. 'But we live in an economy of language,' I heard him say. 'We can't get away from it.'

'Languages.' Back Passage, perspiring a little. 'Languages.'

'No. Language. Singular. It's an important distinction.'

Brilliant. Brilliant. What could this possibly mean? And how could anyone ever know? Export-quality bullshit.

'Of course.' Mordecai Himmelfart from German, Leopold-Franzens University of Innsbruck, Austria (*The Romantic Prolapse*, Bayck College Press 1979). 'Of course, of course.'

'Language,' said Back Passage. 'Yes, language, not languages. Of course. I take your point. Quite.'

Advantage Gifford. His face was inscrutable, as unreadable as ever. The Zip boiler in the corner gave a watery, surging little belch, as if it, too, was part of the debate.

*

Yes, he was back, Gifford, after a year away on leave, and immediately the department became a different place, more exciting, more electric, just that little bit more *dangerous*— almost as I'd imagined a real department of English to be, out there in the world. He'd come back through the US, where his publisher had given him a fresh book contract, he told me in his office. Behind him there were new photos on his noticeboard, of naked youths with gloomy, pendulous genitalia.

His latest book would have a rather contentious topic, he said; he'd let us know what that was, he said, in due course.

I pressed him for a hint, a clue, and he said *shit*.

I'd no idea what to make of that.

A pause. He was taking books and folders out of his briefcase.

He looked up.

'How's the PhD thesis going?'

I breathed in. 'Well, actually, it got lost. The final draft.'

His eyebrows went up. 'Really?' He stared at me. '*Got* lost?'

'My PC ate it. I—I hadn't made a copy.' I breathed out again and waited.

Still staring at me, that bloodless gaze. I tried to hold on to it.[97]

He dropped it. He returned to his books and folders. 'Back to square one, then?'

Whew. I looked away, out of the window. 9:51, on the

97 An interesting strategy here—by saying so little, our man has rather skillfully implied to Gifford that he's trying to protect Bevan for losing the thesis and is thus showing character, when he himself has arranged its 'loss'. The important thing is that Gifford, no fool, seems to swallow this. Successful bluff-work of some quality! Perhaps our hero is maturing a little, as he practises to deceive.

Government Life clock.

I breathed in. 'I've got a new topic,' I told him. 'Something different. It's going really rather well.'

A few weeks before when I'd come to the end of the road with Manatine's botched thesis draft and realised I had no more chance of a doctoral degree and consequent career-for-life, nowhere to go and no idea what to do next—I found myself watching Marigold Butcher in the tearoom. There she was across from me, lighting up the trillionth cigarillo of her life and chatting up a recent new appointment, an awkward young dark-haired little thing called Amanda Cupmark—skinny, anxious, bitten fingernails and all the rest of it. Flat chest. She had a blue plastic tube in one hand and it took me several minutes to realise what it was. *Really? Was that* what she was holding? PhD Leeds, apparently, on some woman writer or other. She was nodding *mm, mm*, as Marigold told her about her own work on Emma Tatham—God, was it possible *two* people in the world knew about this meaningless, forgotten writer?[98] 'Oh, *years*,' Marigold was telling her now, laughing out great gasps of tobacco smoke all over this new woman, whose fingers, I saw, clenched her plastic holder with each puff, as if the holder, too, was a cigarillo.[99] 'I've been researching it for twenty years!' Marigold was telling her. Another great toot of smoke, like a tugboat. 'One has to make sure these things are properly *founded*,' she said, and laughed again, *ho ho ho.*

98   Emma Tatham (1829–55), *The Dream of Pythagoras and Other Poems* (1858). Well-regarded in her time, for example by Matthew Arnold; less so here, it seems, though almost certainly on the basis of no knowledge of the text whatever.

99   Subjunctive mood required here—'as if it, too, were'—but he doesn't seem to know about that sort of thing any more than the pronoun business. And he's supposed to have been a lecturer in English!

Ping!—I could almost hear it in my mind. Of course—of *course*—*that* was the answer! Wasn't it? An endless project, a life's-work—more than that: something that becomes so much a part of the department's collective being that no one ever questions it any more than they question the corridor wallpaper. Something that never has an end but which validates you as an active researcher all the same, someone who means business but never actually does any. Yes! *That* sounded like *me*—someone *talking the talk*, as Marigold was doing right now all over this poor, asphyxiated woman: *talking the talk*, but never quite *walking the walk*. 'Not a thesis but an antithesis,' Gifford said when I told him about it. 'Like Byzantium, always about to fall.' These were such good lines I used them ever after, until I overheard someone accusing him of stealing them from me.

This was the point when I began to sense that he was onto me, that he knew I was bullshitting, *and approved*—knew that this Robert Byng of mine *didn't actually exist* but at the same time came close to the core of what the entire literary project was about—rang so many bells in minds nurtured on the humanities that he *might as well have existed—should* have existed, even. That his nonexistence completed the canon—the entire project of the Western humanities, even.

I've still no idea how the name popped into my mind. Robert Byng? I remember asking around the department, that day he first came to me. Mystified looks. Familiar, someone said; rings a bell, said someone else. Then at morning tea this young Amanda person suggested *The Dictionary of National Biography*—wryly, I couldn't help noticing, as if it should've been my first thought. *Yes, yes, of course*: almost straight away I remembered forgetting it. In the mournful light of the fake Bodleian I worked the first two volumes' sere pages, assisted in due course by a research librarian, who told me the third volume had been mislaid. A relief, when I heard this: endlessly turning the pages of volumes one and two had not been my idea of time well spent. Real scholarship at last!—thanks for the warning.

Eventually, though, this sad, undervalued librarian rang me in my room: volume three had been found! I crossed the uneven asphalt of the second quadrangle again—the very path along which, years later, I've been carting all those wretched, doomed books in the opposite direction. 'There,' the librarian told me, with an off-hand gesture that conveyed a certain bitterness about the way his life was playing out. 'The 1895–1900 volume.' And he left me to it, not entirely without a trace of contempt.

And I found my man almost straight away—no, not Robert Byng—no sign of him anywhere in these volumes—but someone real: Robert *Baron* (1593–1639). One particular word caught my eye as I skimmed and skidded my way through the entry: *Baron, Robert, poet and dramatist, claims distinction as the most successful of plagiarists*—what was this? *With so much judgment did he steal that his thefts passed unrecognised for more than a century after his death.* I can still remember the moment I read this, the *belt* in the chest. *Whole passages of 'The Cyprian Academy' and Baron's other works are taken, with scarcely a pretence of alteration, from the first edition of Milton's minor poems, first published in 1645 and as yet almost unknown.*[100]

Finally, further down the page, the clincher: *there is no evidence that he took his degree.*

I stood there, caught in the fakery of that strange, nostalgic light. Boswell had found his Johnson: by some alchemy he had

---

100 If Baron died in 1639, how could he have plagiarised poems published in 1645? Inferior bluff-work evident here, descending into common-or-garden bullshit once more.

come out of the air and landed at my feet. *I* was *his*, *he* belonged to *me*. Robert Baron. I could see what to do straight away. If I decided to fake up a doctoral thesis on *him*, I'd have to find what he'd written and then I'd have to read it. Worse, I'd have to find all the silly crap written *about* him in the four hundred years since he was alive and read *that*, too. It'd be like all those days I'd just spent with the *DNB*, but multiplied by a thousand. *Out of the question—*

But what if, under my hands, in my treatment of him, Robert Baron became Robert Byng?—what if I pinched Robert Baron's story, stole from the same sources he stole from, and made others up?[101] What if I plagiarised the plagiariser?

I stood there, so excited I wasn't quite able to breathe properly. I kept swallowing and swallowing as if I'd caught myself out. But the thing was, I knew I'd never be caught—because (a) I'd just had substantial evidence that Bevan, as my supervisor, would never read anything I wrote, and (b) the purpose of this project was, of course, that it would never be completed any more than Marigold's, never put to examination, never exposed at the end because there would be no end. It would always hang there, a staff PhD thesis-in-progress, interminable by definition, something to be mentioned from time to time, presented as work-in-progress at the occasional research seminars Gifford had drummed up in the department—why, I could see the titles now: 'Robert Byng: The Sincerest Form of Flattery'; 'Milton's Borrowings from Byng'; 'The Laying on of Hands: Byng's "Mirza", out of Denham's

101 Has he pinched this idea from Thomas Pynchon's novel *The Crying of Lot 49* (1965), which contains a ten-page synopsis of an invented Jacobean play, *The Courier's Tragedy*, by an equally fictitious playwright, Richard Wharfinger? Surely an unconscious memory at work here, possibly of an overheard common-room discussion involving his Americanist colleague David Peach, whom he mentions in Chapter 5 and elsewhere.

"Sophy", out of Jonson's "Cataline"'. God, even an article on the man, there was even the possibility of an article! Cutting out historical fact frees one so completely—a conference, even, what about a conference, an international conference on Robert Byng?

I closed the *DNB*. I stood there, straight-backed, square-shouldered, firm-jawed. I felt omnipotent, godlike—*no, no, I felt like Manatine. Like Gifford, even.* Wasn't all this worthy of them at their best? Hadn't I, simply in conceiving this, inherited their mantle? And who else to supervise it than Bevan Panter? How lucky I was, I came to see over the following years, to have him there: always accepting my excuses, never wishing to read what I never wished to write. The words *I'm working up a long introductory chapter at the moment*, with its crucial first adjective, were always quite enough to keep him at bay. And, in the common room, the occasional remark dropped into a group of senior colleagues about the difficulties of balancing teaching and research, how responsibility to *the kids* was the reality of teaching, whatever the pull of scholarship: these were enough to keep them at bay as well. I got a long way on a concerned frown and a piece of paper in my hand. Not, to tell the truth, that anyone really cared what I was doing or, indeed, what anyone else was doing, either. Oh, it was a different age, all right. And I was in this world, it increasingly seemed, for the long haul. Bluffworld!

And, here, on cue, came Houston at last, our first Charles Edmund Gotch Memorial Writing Fellow—yes, yes, Gotch himself had gone at last, abruptly, after a shocking accident involving a shooting stick.[102] Tim Riordan was running the

---

102 Another theft—this time from *Private Eye* and its account of the death of its columnist, the bibulous journalist Lunchtime O'Booze.

department now, on a three-year rotating basis; he'd brought in the writing fellowship *in memoriam* to a great man, he'd told us at a staff meeting. Stifled laughter: we all knew Gotch had been setting it up himself! Creative writing was upon us, too, as we sensed the need to catch up with *the ineluctable development of the discipline.* Tim's phrase.

Creative writing—a whiff of dung: I sensed an opening. More bluff-work! This Houston claimed to have an MFA in creative writing himself, from a college in Moscow, Idaho, plus a long residency here with *citizenship application in process.* Something like that; no one knew quite how he came to be our first writing fellow. Gotch had interviewed him in a tearoom somewhere in the far north, apparently, where Houston told us he'd fled after being driven out of the States *tarred 'n' feathered 'n' on a pole*—an anti-Polaris protestor, he told us, though on another occasion he said it'd been to do with drugs and sometime after that he told us it was espionage. The CIA, he said, or perhaps it was the FBI.

His first name was Estes but he told us to call him Zac. Or maybe that was the other way about, too: no one was quite sure, about the man, about his name or, as things unfolded, about anything else to do with him, either. We simply called him Houston, as if referring to the entire city in Texas and the Johnson Space Center as well, and through this began to think of him—well, I did, anyway—as one of those classic Apollo astronauts, Buzz Aldrin or Gene Cernan perhaps: a flinty, hardened space cowboy, athlete, scientist and intellectual all in one, a right-stuff Aquarian who'd somehow achieved splash-down in the Registry building's busy little water feature.

However it might have been that Houston had come among us with his Stetson, his lanky jeans and his Redneck Rivieras, he did it with a wife called, curiously, LaPeste, as in

K-moo;[103] but, no, said Houston, there was some Chicano in her background and that explained it. Fuck's sake nobody's perfect, he told us. LaPeste was not with us long: some kind of crisis required her to recast her relationship with her older children, who were not (we gathered) Houston's goddamn problem, and maybe not even his goddamn children, either. Dumb mafaka gone stuck up a Taco Bell, he muttered to me in the tearoom one day: for a moment I thought a son had got someone pregnant, but it turned out he'd been here all the time. We hadn't met him, LaPeste told me, because he'd been at home spending quality time with his penis.

The lack of central heating here had encouraged LaPeste's departure—that and the way the sun crossed the wrong part of the sky. 'Is that east or fucken what?' she was heard to say, exasperatedly pointing elsewhere. 'Estes, where you goddamn taken me this time?' He for his part asked why we didn't heat our goddamn homes, as he sat rubbing his long, bony cowboy hands between his long, bony cowboy thighs in the tearoom-that-still-thought-itself-a-common-room. This was after he'd said he'd walked a goddamn hour that morning lookin' for fucken flapjacks. Englishmen on either side of him, shifting uncomfortably in their seats, gazes averted, dipping their little beaks at their cups like caged birds.

He intrigued me. For a start, he made me think of Manatine, who by this time had been gone at least three years and maybe four. There was a rumour he'd been travelling the country selling illegal stimulants whilst working for an international publishing firm that specialised in books about dogs, another

103 Albert Camus's *La Peste* (1947) tells of a plague in the French Algerian city of Oran.

that he was in Spain hanging around the bull-rings, a third that he was directing *As You Like It* in Tbilisi. Twice I was sure I'd spotted him back here in town, once driving a plumber's van and then in a gang of maintenance staff going *down down down* into the basement of the English department. I called out and ran after him, and he turned and—

Well, that's when I thought there was something of Houston to him—just in that single hurried look back across a shoulder-strap of his overalls before he disappeared into the abyss. After all, wasn't this exactly the sort of thing Manatine might do?—pose as a lanky American who (it was beginning to seem) was posing as somebody else?

The first time we got drunk—Houston and I and a couple of others who'd set up a self-conscious bad-boy poker evening at someone's suburban home—I remember *layin'* on the floor near his corpse and gazing at his long, oblique, shut-down face. *Is it you?* I hissed at him, and shook his shoulder just as I used to shake Manatine's, back in the bowels of our student flat whenever the wheels fell off. *Sure fucken thing*, he muttered back—I'm certain of that, I swear he said that, his lips barely moved but I was sure. Of course, in the dull grey light of day the thought seemed ridiculous, one man turning into an entirely different human being just like that, cell for cell: it was the sort of thing that happened in movies. But then Houston, whoever he was, seemed always to be *not quite himself*, even more so than the rest of us.

Take his writerly *oeuvre*, for a start. Nowhere in our library catalogue could I find a single work by anyone called Houston, E. or even Houston, Z. I asked at the enquiry desk, a librarian made a search: nothing. A pseudonym, then? I stood on the third floor of the humanities library and gazed at the stacked shelves of the North American literature section: how could

I check every one of these books, every author photograph on every dustjacket? 'Why don't you just ask him,' someone suggested—Amanda Cupmark again. 'Ask him what he's written.'

'All kinda shit,' he told me. 'In m'fucken trunks.'

Waiting for his boat to dock I prowled the library shelves. J.D. Salinger, was he J.D. Salinger? I looked at the long, wounded face on the back flap of *The Catcher in the Rye* (Boston: Little, Brown 1951). Possibly, possibly: not unlike. Or might he be John Updike, who stared back at me from the rear cover of *Rabbit Redux* (London: Deutsch 1971)? *Or might he be*—I lit up when I thought of this—*Thomas Pynchon himself, a man even more famously reclusive than Salinger?* I stared at the back cover of *Gravity's Rainbow* (New York: Viking Press 1973), where there was *no picture at all*—conclusive, surely; surely that was the clincher?

But—were Houston's teeth as bad as Pynchon's were rumoured to be? Was his skin bad enough to be Updike's? Was he shell-shocked enough to be Salinger? *Or was he Manatine after at all?*

LaPeste's return to Moscow was followed by the Houstons' version of a custody dispute: neither party wanted the children. 'Says they're not *of her body*,' he told me after a particularly heated phone exchange with her. 'Says the *bass*-turds are mine, says they came with the goddamn marriage. I tell her, *what goddamn marriage?*' Soon he was back in Moscow, Idaho, on compassionate grounds, to *recast his relationship with LaPeste*. Just before he left he tossed his house keys at me: 'Feed the fucken cat for me would ya?' He was gone, and I moved into the beachside residence they'd rented in the hope that things might be slightly warmer there. I began house-sitting a house

Houston had been house-sitting for someone who might very well have been house-sitting it for somebody else: for all I knew the entire building had broken free of the anchor of ownership. And desk-sitting a desk, too, a large *escritoire* beneath a window with a fine view of the beach and the surf, and a golf-ball typewriter on it as well as the usual writerly junk; a photo of some beautiful lost woman, a half-eaten donut—that sort of thing. Either Houston was pretending to be a writer, or he really was one. Or (the thought occurred after I'd been there a couple of days) the person he was renting it from was a writer.

Or Manatine. The golf-ball typewriter, after all, was surely the one he'd pinched from Cocks's remaining effects. I sat there staring at it as the surf glittered beyond the tinted windows of the little study. The thought stayed with me all the time I was *chez* Houston. So, too, my thoughts regarding the cat, which turned out to be a dog when I arrived on the first evening— surely Rommel, Manatine's pooch, who'd gone missing. Wasn't it? Was it?

Best of all, though, was a system of pigeonholes at the back of the desk, each of which had a label. ARGUMENTS was one, and next to it, predictably, RECONCILIATIONS. JOKES was another, but these turned out to be little better than what you get in Christmas crackers—'*Why does one never go hungry at the seaside?*'—that sort of thing.[104]

The slips of paper in the other pigeonholes were more interesting. *Fuck up pie-face* was a note from inside the ARGUMENTS pigeonhole, together with *Uninterested? I'm not even disinterested*: bits and pieces from long-past domestic bust-ups scribbled verbatim, I suppose, hot from the writer's vivid daily life. Ditto the stuff in the other dozen or so pigeonholes:

104 'Because of the sand which is there.' Do try to keep up.

COOKING TOGETHER (*shirr the eggs like Henry James*), IN THE BATH WITH HER (*rubber duck—disappears—surfaces again—no, plastic*) and so on. My favourite was from the pigeonhole labelled SCREWING: *I'm speaking for a higher kind of love*—scribbled down seconds after utterance, I imagine, but definitely the best: a sort of magnificence in it, I felt, something heroic, a glint of the Twilight of the Gods.

There was a page of typescript wound into the golf-ball typewriter, too, and, naturally, I rolled it up and began to read it. A description of a young woman, *roan-haired, wide-shouldered, grey eyes, slim-hipped like a boy*—there was more, not much but enough to ignite something for me straight away rather as *a higher kind of love* had done: almost as if I'd written the words myself, as if they'd come out of me in some way and the woman being described was something to do with *me*. Next to the typewriter there was a pile of typescript and I began to read that, too, sitting at the desk as the beach vista faded in the evening light. You know very well I'm not much of a reader, but I did manage a good twenty pages—well, fifteen—ten—and by the time I was done she was *there*, this imaginary woman who'd been written onto the page. I could see her as if she was right in front of me like a physical, material being. *Where did you come from?*—I can remember saying that, out loud. Laura, her name. *Laura*—

The entire experience worked on me—the desk, the typewriter, the paper, the act of writing, the woman written. I'd always been aware of this process, of course, the Miracle of Creation and so on, but here it was, in front of me, the nuts and bolts of it. I carefully rolled the page of typescript out and a blank page in, and typed a few exploratory words of my own—just nonsense of course, the usual stream of semi-consciousness. As the sun set I began to see myself reflected in the darkening pane of glass in front of me: *the writer at work*. I typed, and watched myself type, and typed another paragraph of nonsense and watched myself watching myself doing it. Yes, not bad—promising, even: youthful still, yet a little haggard, a little abstracted. I knew the image needed more work.

Around this unfamiliar house I found and filched a few items for myself—a gossamer silk scarf (a touch that had never occurred to me before), and a second, which I tied, loosely, around a pale straw hat I found in a cupboard. Wearing this I felt particularly solid back at the desk as I sat there tapping away at nothing very much and watching the beach fading beyond my reflection.

I looked exactly like the young man in the typescript, I had no doubt about that. Like a narrator, like a writer. *So* Jeremy Irons.

Wednesday morning now: I've almost filled my third barrow-load of the day and here comes Bevan, clanking up the service lift. 'You can forget that,' he calls as he steps out. 'Give me a hand with this.' *This* is a trolley he's brought up with him, a large black metal box, open-sided, looking primitive but sturdy on four double castors. There are push–pull handles at each end and a trademark on the side.

'A Samson trolley—got it off the chaps stripping Classics out.'

Together, not easily, we rumble the thing from the elevator and around the stacks while he tells me how it'll halve the time and make our job so much easier. Will it? Side by side, we begin to stack books onto its tray—too many at first, as if some overnight magic has put muscle on our weedy bodies. He's still telling me how simple the job'll be from now on when some of the books start spilling through the open sides of the trolley; we wedge them back in, carefully, one by one. Then we push and pull at the thing and nothing much happens except more books fall off, so we swap ends and pull and push, by which time there're enough books on the floor for us to move the trolley just a little, and then, bit by bit, a little more.

Slowly we get it across to the service lift, more spillage along the way—by the time we stop at the ground floor there's fewer books on than off. We push out into the quadrangle and stop, and stand there gasping at each other. A workman high up a building calls something out, a couple of words. It takes a good five minutes to get the trolley across and halfway up the wheelchair ramp in front of the bookshop, and when we do it starts rolling back down again. I ferry the books in by hand, a dozen at a time, and then I go back for the ones that have fallen behind us in the quadrangle. In the bookshop Bevan stacks them, books on books on top of books, using one of the two little storerooms, Tim Riordan's former office—there's no more space out in the shop.

'How many of these d'you think we've sold?'

'Oh, don't worry, we sold *The Sermons of John Donne* this morning. Volume three.'

'A lot more to go. Up there in the library.'

'I know, I know.' He's looking around for somewhere to put half a dozen Dickenses held compressed between his palms. 'There's still a market. Remember, we sold a Beryl Bainbridge just last week. *Young Adolf*—you know, the one about Hitler young in Liverpool?'[105]

---

105 This is no joke—*Young Adolf* (1978) covers the Fuehrer's early years with his older half-brother, a waiter living in Liverpool, including the accidental scarring which, according to Bainbridge, caused Hitler to grow his hair over his brow and that small moustache.

Now *Master Humphrey's Clock* slides between Bevan's fingers and to the floor. A pause and then, slowly, thoughtfully, *Martin Chuzzlewit*. Then *Bleak House*. Books, splattered on the ancient linoleum. *Little Dorrit* down there now—*Little Torrid*, I used to call it years ago, trying to persuade a class it was a sex romp.

Tim's back room looks so much smaller than when he was there. We're filling it with traditional stuff—Bevan's idea—right back to those three-volume bastards nobody could read. Our great tradition, he calls it. Cultural capital.[106]

'We'll have to find somewhere else to put the lesser stuff, we can't just throw it away.' He points out to the foyer beyond the shop doors. 'We're going to have to stack some out there.'

'In the foyer? But we don't rent that space?'

'I'll have a word with the folk upstairs. I'm not thinking long term.' I follow him out with the empty, rattling trolley. 'Just a few. Two-or-three-deep, perhaps, up against the wall. Nothing more than that.'

Back in the shop a despairing man with no upper teeth has a book in his hand. Might he, will he?

---

106 I presume he's referring to works such as Samuel Richardson's *Pamela* (1740), Henry Fielding's *The History of Tom Jones, a Foundling* (1749), and, of course, Laurence Sterne, *The Life and Opinions of Tristram Shandy, Gentleman* (1759). There are many others in the category mentioned here: lengthy, multi-volume, yes, but wonderfully sustained works of the imagination. Sterne's great classic in particular should be of more interest to the protagonist here than it seems to be—but, then, all those pages, all those words. Even one of his 'deep skims' wouldn't be quite enough.

Chapter 8

All the time we're ferrying the books across the quadrangle the builders are about; we can hear them, their rough calls to one another and their distant hammering, the squawk of wrenching panels, the persistent, dental whine of their tile saws, the long, slapping fall of a severed plank. Occasionally, as we creep the laden Samson trolley across the quadrangle, shedding our usual trail of books, one of these men calls out to us from the roof of Old Chemistry or up above the cloisters, where they're doing something that involves a wet saw. We try to ignore them but they keep at it. At one point one of them calls out *want a hand?* and drops a rubber glove down: his mates laugh themselves silly at this. I give them a placatory wave, but it's hardly an evening with Oscar Wilde.

A few days later, we're stuck about halfway between the bookshop and the former library when two of these men stop us. I can see the terror start up on Bevan's face, just a flicker.

'How y'doin' there, cobber?' Amiable enough. Inside the man's overalls his belly is like a drum but carried high, suggesting strength, not the terminal sedentary decline of the academic.

The other man is younger, skinny inside his overalls. 'What's this?' he says. He opens one of the books. 'Fuck me dead.'

Bernard Williams, *Ethics and the Limits of Philosophy* (Cambridge: Harvard University Press 1985). I know these details because I was trying to get a piece of dried jam off its cover just minutes ago. I wish I could tell you the Dewey[107] number but I think it's under the jam.

Bevan's still caught motionless at one end of the Samson trolley. His eyes flare behind the milky lenses of his specs. 'Bernard Williams,' he says—blurts; I see he can't stop himself. 'Moral philosophy. The limits of the humanities.' He licks his lips. 'D'you know his work?'

The younger man looks up from the book. 'Yous read this shit?'

'As a rule.' I can hear the tightness in Bevan's voice.

'Come on, Dylan.' This from the man with the belly. They *heave* themselves at the trolley—Bevan and I step back and off they go, more books hitting the ground behind them, the whole thing rattling across the uneven asphalt as they bend hard behind it, heads down, big football legs pumping. We follow them, gathering up the spillage, and for a moment I smell the work on them. Together they force the Samson up the wooden wheelchair-ramp by the stairs at the foyer entrance: *up* the trolley goes and *in* just like that! A loud cheer from their mates on top of Old Chemistry; one of them starts a slow handclap, another calls something down, *doin' a bit of work for a change*, that sort of thing.

Now the three men come out again, the one with the belly dusting his big hands together: 'There you go, mate,' he says, and he gives us a wink as he walks past us and off. I can't tell you how good that makes me feel. Mate![108]

107 Wrong—the Dewey numbering system is used in public libraries only. The books he refers to here and following would have Library of Congress numbers. Ignorance or bluff?—probably a mixture of both.
108 All very well, this, but it's pretty much straight out of George Orwell's *Down and Out in Paris and London* (1933). A plain steal. Also whiffs of Katherine Mansfield's short story 'The Garden Party' (1922), Hemingway,

We stand in the foyer, puffing like goldfish. Books, stacked out here now next to the bookshop door and hard up against the wall, two-deep right now but anyone can see we'll have to go wider to go higher. Less than a third of the library cleared by now; what's left would fill this floor and the next.

I push the empty trolley back across the asphalt. Through the cloisters I can see Leary organising another photoshoot in the north quadrangle. This time Alun Pismire is there, looking older and scruffier than I remember him, and Colin Tudge from Fine Arts; others as well, in their tatty flapping gowns.

The evening after I became a writer at Houston's twice-borrowed house, I walked the man I'd created to a barbecue nearby wearing borrowed scarves borrowed hat and all. I could almost feel the twinge of a novel coming—was this what it was to be an artist, was I entering an authentic experience at last, after all these years? Did inspiration simply arrive, when one found one's muse? Or was it the other way around?

The party house was being renovated and the layout was a little unpredictable. I knew hardly anyone there except the host, and I barely knew him. Dave Brubeck on the stereo as I went in; then, the further problem of placing the Cold Duck amongst the drinks on the kitchen table in a way that hid its label, and, after that, the usual game of spot-the-scotch. Instead, magically, there was the woman I'd just been reading about the night before! Laura! Can you believe that? I saw her straight away, standing across the room from me against the darkening

---

Steinbeck, Dreiser and others. Shameless.

windows and almost exactly as I'd imagined her from the page: slighter, perhaps, as if still in the business of being created out of thin air—was that it?—and, naturally, with the face of an angel. Someone else's heroine, and now, it seemed, becoming mine—*and*, when I asked her, with the *very same name* she'd had in the novel! Extraordinary! She really *was* Laura!

And didn't she *like* it, this heroine, this Laura, when I let slip, as if casually, that I was an artist. *Writer, writer*, I murmured, and lit a cigarette, shading the flare of the match with my hand in the manner of K-moo. *Seeking experience*, I told her, *or letting it seek me*. Well, she really liked *that*, too, although I'm no clearer on what it means now I've written it down than I was when I said it all those years ago.

Fine by her, though, she couldn't believe her luck: a *writer*—! I stood there giving her the goods, in fact the whole routine, the heavy swigging of the fag between walnut-coloured knuckles, the distracted looks stage left as if I were still back there with the Muse. All Standard Manatine, of course; I was simply doing a version of one of his routines, which were themselves versions of other versions that went back to Adam's first hump with Eve, his mouth still stuffed with half-chewed Cox's Orange.

All the same, I knew a few things myself. *Faux* diffidence, for example, the tiniest stammer, the slightest hesitation as if One is not quite sure of the spoken word itself, not used to Mere Mortal Language and thus operating on a different plane of Pure Thought. Utter bullshit, of course, but it turned the trick with this Laura all right. I managed the stammer down into little more than a hesitation and I was playing her like a harp, a trout, a fiddle—she simply couldn't wait, this splendid young woman, for the next pearl to slither from between my lips! And—oh, God—I felt so *real*, so *authentic*. When she agreed to come home with me an hour later it was as if she expected to meet Mnemosyne[109] herself when she got there.

'The place'll be a bit untidy,' I warned her. 'Rilke?—*The Notebooks?*—you remember what he says about the artist's need for chaos?' And as she looked at me, amazed that one small head could carry all it knew,[110] I remembered Magnus Furz, who'd first told me about this: 'The growth of art out of chaos: *you must read Malte*'.[111] He was right, Magnus, I must, and I still should because I haven't yet and my chances are beginning to narrow somewhat. On the other hand, I've recommended the book to dozens of people in the years since: *You must read Malte*, I've told them, though naturally I try to keep Magnus's thick Bavarian accent out of it.

All the time I was telling her this she stood there with the long dark rippled glass of the window throwing back for me the eagerness of her face and the eagerness of mine at the pleasing girl I saw, the set of her shoulders, the fall of *her roan-coloured hair* (the very words I'd read the night before). Lovely eyes, slightly hurt and a darker grey than I'd expected— exactly as she'd been written. Were they really grey at all, though? Blue, almost, and staring back at me as if she'd never known anything quite like this moment, never met anyone quite like the man they saw. Quite right, of course: I caught a tiny glimpse of myself in the darkened, glittering windows and I have to say I looked at my dishevelled, *roué* best: every inch a hero.

109 Google again.
110 He's used this before, smuggling it in, typically, as his own; but we all know where he's stolen it from.
111 *The Notebooks of Malte Laurids Brigge* (1910), Rainer Maria Rilke (1875–1926). A fictional account of the artist's life. Bohemian–Austrian. Ignore.

I gazed down at her. 'All that.' I gestured towards the black mirror of the windows. 'The Lacanian Real.'

Her eyes widened. I could see she knew what I was referring to but not that it was utter bullshit. The Lacanian Real, she murmured. She gazed up at me. We held our gaze, under the fatherly protection of the great Jacques himself. We stood there.

I turned away.

I knew what I was doing. I wasn't pulling back. I was 'pulling back'. I was beginning The Move.

'I'm sorry—'

She followed me. 'What's wrong?'

'You remind me so much of someone else—'

'Who—?'

I shrugged, I turned away.

'Where is she?'

I hesitated for a second. A pause, an awful pause. I could see the moment in her eyes.

'I'm sorry.'

Another pause. Looking up at me.

'Who was she—?'

Bingo—

'Don't ask.' This delivered with a wry, sad smile. I watched her work it out, I watched her mouth fall open, slowly.

'That's the trouble.' I took her shoulders, very gently. 'I'd really like to sleep with you.'

I could hear a faint huskiness in my voice. I could hear the catch of her breath. She looked up at me.

'Just sleep. Just the two of us.'

This wasn't just any old proposition, I could see her beginning to understand this: it was going to be a rite of passage for us both, an act of *shared making*. The thing that had just begun to grow between us had already transcended the physical and I could see she knew that to sleep together like this, innocently, in each other's arms like children—just sleep—would be a true, an *authentic* celebration of—

'Just *sleep* with me—?'

'Just sleep.'

I looked down at her. She looked up at me.

Never known it not to work.

She slipped away after that—just for a few minutes, she said, to freshen up in the bathroom. As I waited I looked out at the crash of the surf in the fading light with a thrill coming and going in my chest. I thought of the people back at the party desperately trying to score when here I was, on a promise.

I turned back, looked around—where the hell had she got to, this Laura of mine?

I slipped into the hallway and crouched outside the bathroom door, listening. Nothing.

I rattled the doorknob: *hullo?—hullo?*

Silence.

I eased the door open, looked in, stepped back, looked around. What? Where? I tried the other rooms, I looked for her outside.

I stopped on the lawn. She'd gone back to the party, that was it—freshening up in the bathroom over there.

Really?

Back at the party house I walked up the drive and peered into a darkened window as I passed. How was I supposed to know I was looking into a bedroom that was halfway through being turned into a bathroom? It took a few seconds for my eyes to adjust to the darkness, and then to the fact that there was someone in there and that it was a panicky young woman perched on the throne with her knickers stretched across her quads like a rubber band.

'Piss off,' she yelled at me. 'I'm on the fucking toilet—'

I withdrew, I worked my way back to the living room, the party, the *faux* bacon, the toy sausages. Maybe Laura was in here—but instead, after a few minutes, the toilet woman emerged. She looked angry when she saw me, not badly so but definitely pissed off. Straight away I felt the pull of this. I have no explanation. I turned after her when she went past and onto the patio.

'Get a good look?' she called, from over by the barbecue.

'Not really. Thought it was a chap at first.'

'Oh yes fuck you.'

This, it turned out, was Sally. Not my type, but on the other hand I had to admit I found her *not unattractive*, and that *that* had something to do with the way I'd caught her in the most fundamental of activities. Didn't it? Just the animal body? Oh, yes, and the anger, of course. There was that, always with Sally there was that. *Grrr—*

I strolled over.

'Front potties or back potties?'

She *stared* at me.

'*What*—?'

A look that froze the soul.

That was it: our first meeting, and my first experience of the rinse of terror that did so much to bond us over the next many years. She came from the same world I'd flirted with all those years before when I invented Little Hamish in *EDU102*, a stunt which enraged and appalled her when I told her about it—she even threatened to report me to the authorities, and she always held it over me in the ongoing knife-fight our relationship was to become. God, I came to love her. Did I? What does love mean? Does it mean death? Sally was death, of a certain sort. Wait and see.

'A writer?' she said, when we got to that stage of the game.

'Writing, writing.' I turned away, as if distracted. 'It's a vocation, not a job. My daily work is at the varsity.'

But hers was in Sociology as I've said, and it turned out that she'd nearly finished writing her thesis whereas I hadn't even begun mine. Naturally I told her I had: What's it about? she wanted to know. Robert Byng, I told her. We were post-party and back *chez* Houston by the time we got to this stage, me and this mysterious Laura who had somehow turned into Sally, made of the earth. Clothes everywhere, the clothes basket on the clothes, the cat on the clothes basket, the second cat on the first; and that's just the sofa accounted for. Rommel was locked in the laundry in a sea of piddle. He was silent, so far.

I showed her the typewriter, told her about the novel-in-progress, showed her the title on the top page of the stack. I watched her lean down to the little wooden pigeonholes at the rear—exactly what I wanted her to do next.

'"Arguments",' she said. '"Reconciliations"—?' She looked back at me, her hair falling away in a curtain[112]—the very words on the page in the typewriter. She pointed at the MAKING LOVE pigeonhole. 'Not much happening there—?'

'Hardest thing of all to write about,' I told her, which though not entirely original is a reasonably good recovery, you have to admit. She was leaning forward: her bottom pressed against the canvas of her jeans in the shape of an inverted heart.[113] 'You're confronting the Lacanian Real when you try to write about that.' For a second or two she didn't say anything and

112 Oh, dear.
113 For goodness' sake. This is sub–Mills & Boon.

for a second or less I wondered if I'd got it wrong. It *was* the *Lacanian* Real, wasn't it? And not someone else's? The price of bluff is eternal vigilance.

She was still looking at the labelled pigeonholes. 'I see how this works,' she said. 'When you have an argument with someone—you—?'

'Write it down and file it away. That's right.'

'And then it goes—?'

'Into what I write.'

On the sofa the second cat was standing, stretching up into one of Dali's long-legged elephants and quivering at us, his tail a question mark. He decided on Sally. She took his big soft dumb eager head in her hands.

'That one's called Penis Envy—'

'You have a cat called Penis Envy—?'

'Only for male owners—'

It's not bad, old Basil's line, and certainly good enough for a guffaw from her: quite a mannish, horsey laugh, I must say, in three descending notes, *HA Ha ha*, like that. I was doing well: you know what it means when you can get a woman to laugh. They say they say.

But when she did laugh, and in the manner described, Rommel started barking out in the laundry, and, off guard, I found myself having to explain who he was and why he was there. And when I'd done *that*, she asked his name. And when I told her *she hit the roof*, she absolutely *hit the roof. Are you aware who Rommel was? Have you actually heard of the Nazis?*—that sort of thing. It's not my dog, I kept telling her, I didn't name the fucking thing: but when I said who had she said *Who's Manatine*, like that, and when I told her a bit about him she said straight off he was no good for me and all the rest of it. *Sick*, she said over her shoulder as she stalked out to the taxi.

Only a very sick mind, an *infantile* mind, could call a dog *that*. And she was right, of *course* he had a sick mind. I'd hardly been hanging around Manatine to better myself, had I?

In the next few weeks, and inevitably, the climactic disaster crept towards me. A book launch; a *faux*–Left Bank bookshop in the middle of town; thought of Laura; an idle few minutes spent flicking pages among the displays and—every twenty seconds or so—looking up to see if she might possibly be there. *Sharing Her*, the title of the book-to-be-launched, on a startlingly explicit cover which people kept coming back to peep at, furtively, throughout the evening. No Laura, though, and few else I knew. The crowd tumesced, engorged, the cheap plonk sprayed, I mopped up at the buffet, carb-loading crackers and cream cheese.[114]

And then, the official desolations began: here was the bookshop proprietor, there was his voice. I munched and munched and looked about myself as I did, and after a while this proprietor introduced someone else, who spoke at length and then introduced someone else again. Were we getting anywhere? A couple of minutes and I suddenly realised that this was it, this was the main act—the author himself, this small, tired, slightly despairing man with an obvious toupée. It seemed to have torque, just a little: I watched it take a nanosecond to catch up each time he moved his head while he read, as if it was on ball bearings. So, this was the writer whose house I was babysitting, was it?

As he spoke, though, his Laura came to life for me once more—she'd never gone far off in the first place—but somehow Sally did too, as if she was part of the deal. I hadn't seen her since that evening at Houston's when Rommel had rather got

---

114 The imagery he's using here is pointless. What is the effect he's trying to achieve?

in the way of things. That, I remember thinking at the time, was that—but now, suddenly—dear God—here she was again, as this ur-Houston was reading, and with the effect of having sprung out of his words. She *materialised*. I gazed at her across the room, at her strong basketballer's body, her strawberry-blond hair, her sceptical gaze. *There* on the page was the woman being read about, who'd set this business off, and *here* was the woman who seemed to stand in for her in this muddy, unsatisfactory, sit-on-the-toilet world. Laura, the mystery-that-is-woman born of literature, a woman made of words. Sally, significantly less mysterious and made out of everything that was left. And *here*, present, in the real world. Oh, God.

She spotted me across the room, straight after the reading. '*You*,' she called out, and pointed a sharp, witchy finger at me. She pushed through bodies, right up to me, she *shirtfronted me*, as they say in politics and school-teaching. 'I *wondered* where you'd got to. You are a fucking *impostor*, you know that?' She had a copy of *Sharing Her* in her hand and she shoved it at me, right in front of everyone, right in my face till it squished my nose. 'D'you want to sign the fucking thing for me? Don't be put off by the fact someone else wrote it.'

Sally terrified me. Fear was to be at the heart of my relationship with her. We were living together within a week. Looks quick on the page?—pretty quick for me when it happened, I can tell you. No idea how it came about, either, nothing to help me reconstruct the moves. She shifted into Houston's house on the beach, the unanchored writer's-home-minus-a-writer-and-minus-an-owner: she just walked in the back door of this lost unloved house with a couple of bags. Trauma occludes much of my memory of this period in my life; all I can recall is a Then and after that a Now with nothing much between, and that as far as the Now went,

Sally seemed to be cleaning it. The kitchen cupboards first, then the rest of the kitchen including the interior of the dishwasher, which I hadn't actually noticed up to that stage of Being There—the entire dishwasher, that is, not just the interior. No matter: on she went, through the kitchen and then the rest of the house like Sherman through the Shenandoah.[115]

It all came to a head when she got rid of Rommel.

I came home one evening and the laundry was scrubbed out, scrubbed clean: windows open, a breeze rinsing through, washed cleaning-rags on the line—yet another room of the house smelling of Janola and not a dog turd in sight. You could've done open-heart surgery on the floor.

It took twenty seconds more to realise what was missing, and to ask where he was, and for her to tell me.

'Down to the vet?' I couldn't believe it. 'You just—'

'Had him euthanased. He was disgusting.'

Euthanased—was it even a proper word?[116] 'You didn't even—'

'Tom, he was all wrong. He was filthy, he wasn't housetrained. I just couldn't live with him. And the name—'

'I didn't call him that. It wasn't me who—'

115 Here, he's confusing the Shenandoah Valley, devasted by troops of Union General Philip Sheridan (1831–88) in September 1864, and Savannah, Georgia, terminus of the 'March to the Sea' a couple of months later by troops of Union General William Tecumseh Sherman (1820–91). Ignorance, confident reliance on hearsay and faulty memory are at work here, inevitable components of bluff-work.

116 No: more commonly 'euthanised'. A termination usually practised on non-human animals, but more recently voluntary euthanasia has been advocated by some to relieve human suffering. Involuntary euthanasia also has its advocates; see for example, George Bernard Shaw, *Prefaces* (London: Constable and Co 1934), p.296: 'If they are not fit to live, kill them in a decent human [sic] way.'

'Yes, I know who it was. That awful man Ross.' Somehow she'd decided that was his first name, Ross of all things—Ross Manatine! 'Your sicko friend.'

Why the terror? Why the cleaning? What could she possibly see in a man like me? It'd occurred to me already that, somehow, inexplicably, she liked me, but *why*? Was I her *little bit of rough*, was that it, did I seem like a loose shaggy dog of a poet to her social scientist mind? Was that it? When I'd never written a thing of my own in my life? And, anyway, look at what she did with loose shaggy dogs!

I'd wonder this into the darkness as I lay beside her each night, gripping her to myself as if I'd never let her go. I couldn't get enough of her, once I was in and caught. I'd used the same technique I used with Laura, suggesting at the conclusion of a crepuscular stroll (I dropped that word in, *crepuscular*, but she didn't react) that we sleep together, just sleep—and she swept it aside with her basketballer's arm. 'What's the point of that?' she said, far too loudly for the suburbs. 'People go to bed to fuck, don't they?'

I remembered the young student in that upstairs party bedroom years before: *I don't see what you see in me.* I was solving the puzzle of her bra strap at the time, I remember; was Sally solving the puzzle of mine?

'There's no puzzle,' I mumbled amidst the confessional chaos of the bedsheets one night, as I lay beside her in the recovery position.

'What?' she said, into the dark. 'What do you mean?'

'I have no mystery. There's nothing to find out about me.'

Silence. Then:

'I never said there was. There's nothing much to find out about anyone, is there? Certainly not you.'

In the darkness I thought that one through. How could

that possibly be true, how could she think that, what was the puzzle she thought I wasn't presenting to her? What was the puzzle I thought she wasn't presenting to me?

>╍╍╍<

Here I am, pushing into the bookshop past a man who's coming out to the tinkle of the doorbell; his belly brushes against me as he squeezes by and into the foyer and down the steps.

'Rainin' thunderpumps, mate,' he says to me over his shoulder. The big chap who pushed the Samson trolley for us the other day—Harrison, I heard someone calling him. He splashes big boots in puddles as he walks off. There's a book in his hand.

Bevan's behind the counter inside. 'You're not going to believe this—he asked me if we had any books by Robert Tressell!'

'Oh? Really?' *Who the hell is Robert Tressell?*

'And we did, in the back room. *The Ragged-Trousered Philanthropists!*'

'You're kidding me—'

'And guess where he comes from? Hastings! He's a house-painter from Hastings, and it turns out his favourite book is *about* house-painters from Hastings, written *by* a house-painter from Hastings!'[117]

I'm in the back workroom by now, Riordan's old office, hanging up my wet coat and hat. They piddle rainwater onto *Enemies of the Enlightenment* and *Proust and Signs* and down onto *Le Grand Meaulnes* and *Thomas E. Dewey and His Times* and then *The Moviegoer* and the floor. Bevan's reading

117 Robert Noonan/Tressell (1870–1911) sign-writer, house-painter, paper-hanger, socialist and author of *The Ragged-Trousered Philanthropists* (1914).

something out loud, declaiming it to an empty shop. Poetry: he's reading out a poem from an open book in front of him.

'Mm,' I say when he's finished. 'Quite.'

He holds the book up to me through the doorway. 'Arnold? "The Scholar Gipsy"?'

Arnold who? Oh. Ah. Yes. Always meant to read it.

'*Who, tired of knocking at preferment's door, One summer-morn forsook His friends, and went to learn the gipsy-lore? And roam'd the world with that wild brotherhood*'—he's reciting it now, book shut head back eyes closed. I pretend to listen. It's still raining.

He stops, and opens his eyes, and stares at me meaningfully. '*But came to Oxford and his friends no more*—?'

'Yes, yes—'

'D'you see what I mean?'

'Oh, quite.' I don't, of course, in fact I've no idea what he's going on about, I really don't.

'*Wild brotherhood?*—don't you think that applies?' He waves towards the windows, the quadrangle outside, the abandoned library, the rain, the world. 'To them?'

'Oh—Harrison and his mates? Jason? Dylan?'

'Well, don't you?' He's over at the window now, peering out into the rain, speaking back to me across his shoulder.

'Scholar gipsies? Well, I—'

'I had no idea, you know, the thought of them reading a book, but then I thought, that's silly, that's condescending—I said to him, take as many books as you like—your workmates, too, as long as they bring them back. It'll open up a new world for them.'

Past Bevan's head I can see Jason out there, loading something into the back of a white van. His hood is up against the rain. He's looking furtive.

Chapter 9

Out in the foyer, the pile is becoming bigger. I'm stacking the books just next to the bookshop door, where Bevan says they'll be a good advert for our treasure-chest of cracked, bumped, edge-worn stock. I'm not so sure he's right, but I try to keep a tidy pile of them all the same, biggest on top and none of them more than three-deep from the wall. So far so good.

'Keep them in order,' Bevan told me when I started stacking out here. 'Y'know, alphabetical, genre and so on.' I've decided the best way to do this is to start back on the library mezzanine shelf by shelf and follow the order that's already there. But I can't help wondering how they're all going to fit in, how I'll keep any order.

One day as we're dusting in the shop he stops and pulls a book out of the shelves.

'*Redgauntlet*.' He takes out a large, loose handkerchief and parps at his nose. 'Now *there's* a read for you.'

I know it's Walter Scott but only because I had it in my hands a moment ago—I, who've delivered entire lectures on books I'd never read, I, who always told students the first chapter of any novel is the one that repays the closest scrutiny, the first page of any chapter where the author really lets it all hang out, the first paragraph—

'Quite. Oh, quite.'

'That scene at the coronation with the Young Pretender[118] in the gallery, watching George II being crowned in his place?'

'Yes—yes! George II! That's right!'

I haven't the faintest idea who Charles Stuart was or what he's written, though when I look it up a little later (as I always do when caught like this), I realise that I've known it all along. I take in a few facts off Wikipedia, then renew the conversation as soon as I can.

'Died in his daughter's arms, didn't he—'

'Charles?' You can see he's been living *Redgauntlet* since we spoke. 'Yes! Yes!—that's right, a hopeless drunk. Terrible complexion—smallpox, poor fellow—and a permanently disappointed look, apparently, but then who'd blame him for that, you know, *the man who would be king?*' He pauses and stands there with paperbacks held compressed between his palms. 'Thackeray, too, of course. *Henry Esmond*—'

'Oh, quite!'

'Trying to smuggle the Old Pretender onto the throne. Of course, the thing is, they don't tell it like that—Scott and Thackeray—'[119]

---

118 Charles Edward Stuart (1720–88), 'the Young Pretender', second-to-last direct Stuart claimant to the throne of Great Britain and Ireland and an interesting variant of the bluffer. Bonnie Prince Charlie, as he became known, was effectively disinherited as a consequence of the Glorious Revolution of 1688, but, as oldest grandson of a reigning monarch, was a genuine claimant to the throne of England. A bullshitter, possibly not: but capable of bluff-work at particular moments, almost certainly.

119 Bevan is referring to Thackeray's novel *The History of Henry Esmond* (1852), which contains a fictional version of an unsuccessful attempt to put James Francis Edward Stuart (1688–1766), the 'Old Pretender', onto the throne of England following the death of Queen Anne in 1714. Thackeray's novel *Vanity Fair* (1847) is a masterclass in the study of bluff-work in the England of the Napoleonic era.

'No, of course—'

'—and that really is the point, isn't it, the point of that entire way of writing. An alternative universe that's totally convincing but didn't really happen. I mean, there's no evidence Charles was even *in* the country in 1728 let alone at the coronation of the Elector—'

No?—good to hear; about to make a major blooper there. 'Quite.'

'The world as we would wish it to be.' He says it dreamily. I remember him using the phrase in class several times, the moments when he would drift off with the same look. 'Isn't it remarkable, the way a line of words—you must have thought this yourself as a writer—d'you know what I mean—?'

'Oh, quite.'

'How it can set off all that stuff that bloke Iser[120] talks about—you know, that marvellous chemistry between eye and page—you know what I mean—?'

'Quite. Quite so—'

'It's genuine magic, it's the only real magic left in the world—and look what we've got instead, look what we've come down to.' And he stands there, surrounded by piles of books that represent about a quarter of the old library's holdings by now, a quarter of them shelved and only a quarter of those likely to be sold over the next quarter of a century. 'I mean, all that *life*, apart from anything else, all that imaginative life—a writer like *you'd* know what I mean by *that*, I'm sure . . .'

Later, back in the bookshop, I watch him trying to talk a

---

120 Wolfgang Iser (1926–2007). Literary scholar: *The Act of Reading: A Theory of Aesthetic Response* (Johns Hopkins 1978), thought by some to announce the beginning of the decline of aestheticism in literary criticism. German. Ignore.

customer out of buying a book. He's shaking his head, pointing to flaws. Sometimes he bids his clients down—'No, no, you don't want to pay that much for it, that'd be silly.' Bevan's Bookshop is making a *transaction*! Someone is *buying a book*! I observe the elderly buyer through the door. Oh, the shabby side of the humanities, the down-at-heels quality of second-hand books and the third-hand people who buy them, the lonely bedsits across the city in which they sit, reading, waiting, hoping their phone will ring.

⌒⌒

Early in our time together Sally and I ran into Gifford at the local supermarket on a Saturday. He was the last person I thought to see there, pushing a trolley with kids in it. Naturally, the kids were behaving badly. Ferko and Gergely, he told me. *Ferko?* I said. *Really?* and Sally gave me a kick on the leg, low down, hard.

Now a woman came up, cradling four packets of long-roll toilet paper. I looked straight into her eyes; she looked straight back into mine; she looked away; etcetera. She dumped the toilet rolls into the trolley and began to separate the children, pulling them apart like someone tearing a stale bun in two.[121]

Over the top of this Gifford said, 'Meet Laura.'

Laura? I stared. Sally gave me another poke in the shins.

Laura said, '*Eugene*—'

'Well, that's your name, isn't it?' He was looking away somewhere. To us, over his shoulder, 'Lára in English. Acute accent above the *a*.'

Sally said, 'Lovely to meet you, Lára.'

---

121 That's not bad, that bun image—wonder which writer he got it from?

I said, 'Sally, this is Eugene Gifford.'

Gifford said, 'Hullo, Sally.' He looked at her, hard.

Lára was Hungarian. I got this out of her while Gifford was asking Sally about the social sciences, which he told her went as far back as Epicurus. Lára was telling me yes, yes, the children's names were Hungarian, too. When she said their names, they sounded completely different from the way Gifford had said them.

'Now, Ferko,' she said to one of the little fuckers. 'There's going to be a big consequence.' An accent, a slight slub to her voice when she talked, something going on at one side of her mouth; light olive skin, a profile to slay for. So, this was Gifford's woman, was it? Mitteleuropean exotic.

'Come on, Ferks,' Gifford was saying. 'Give it a bone, old chap.'

'What a striking woman,' Sally said later, amongst the Fine & Specialty Cheeses.

'Didn't really notice. What'd you kick my leg for—?'

'Back there? Because I'm a striking woman.'

'Ha ha.'

'And you're as bad as her kids.'

'Fucker and Gurgly—?'

Later, at the checkout, she said, 'Remember what Lára told her kids, Tom. There's going to be consequences.' I'd no idea what she meant, no idea at all.

And then, a couple of days later, they invited us to dinner! By this stage I'd been at various colleagues' dining tables but the Giffords had never been at any of them and seemed not to hold similar desolations of their own. Now, here was this scribbled note in my pigeonhole—I tapped on several office doors to boast, but was progressively disconcerted to find that several of the people I waved my invitation at had invitations of their own to wave back at me.

Sally wasn't able to come. 'That's my seminar night,' she said. 'We're strong enough to go to different things.' 'Quite so,' I told her. 'Quite so.' We'd talked all this stuff through, of course. Time together and time apart. Trust, and so on.

The Giffords, it turned out, lived in a somewhat *déclassé* area—one more piece of information you couldn't really pin down. Getting out of our car outside his house I ran into the Pismires getting out of theirs and, a moment later, the Riordans doing the same: they'd brought Amanda Cupmark with them, who told us she was having her menstrual period. Together, we went up the perfectly unexceptional path to the perfectly unexceptional bungalow in which (it seemed) the Giffords lived.

Lára Gifford answered the door. I felt a slight stirring in my loins when I saw her.[122] Was it because she was Lára or because she was Laura? Clearly, given this and Amanda's announcement, it was going to be a complicated evening.

'Come!' she told us, brightly, over-brightly: again, that neurotic teasing at the sides of her mouth. We followed her into a tight hallway which had a too-large grandfather clock and the muffled, outraged sounds of Fucker and Gurgly, strapped down early.

Through a doorway to a living room with a dining table at the near end, and Gifford, carefully putting out paper napkins.[123]

He looked up as we came in.

We stopped, progressively; we slammed up against one another like rolling stock at the buffers: Alun at the front with

122 Oh, dear. And he claims to have taught creative writing.
123 Paper napkins—say no more.

[154]

his arms out on either side as if to register the collective shock of it all, his wife hard in behind him, then the Riordans, then Amanda, then, at the back, me. We clattered into each other, we collected there rammed together and astonished, bottles of plonk swinging in our hands.

'Gene!'

Smiles now, breaking out amongst us, and laughter; we all started to laugh at once, I remember; a festive jollity burst out like champagne uncorked. I'd never seen any of us as happy before and I've never seen any of us happier since!—any one of this group of colleagues, most of whom loathed and despised one another. Alun proffered his bottle of Riesling and said how inadequate it was for the occasion, Tim Riordan rubbed his palms together and said *no no no it looked pretty damn good* to *him*, and then they both laughed at this as if it was something from *Billy Connolly Live*—laughed like madmen, the two of them, and clung an arm around each other's shoulders and *laughed* and *laughed* and *laughed* like two men on the *ganja*. Gifford, it seemed, had brought them together at last—their wives, too, after a few seconds, as the hysteria seized them— and me as well, as if we'd all caught a plague that had blown in through the window. Even Amanda Cupmark joined in, with a series of high, echolalic titters.

He was stark naked, you see. Gifford. Not a stitch on at his own dinner party, not a thing, and here we all were, pretending that there was. I looked at his lean, unexpected body, his waxwork flesh, the hard, dark little nipples, the light run of hair *down down down*, till—I looked away, I caught someone's eye and turned back—and there it was again, in front of me, perky, bouncing, unavoidable and clearly determined to host the evening. Now Alun was saying something stupid again and here was Tim doubling over and slapping his thigh and laughing again but this time in a way that was different—serious and difficult and with a touch of despair to it, something wild and verging on mania, even; I remember a flutter of panic as I listened.

And all through this here was Amanda, banging him on his back. You all right? Gifford enquired politely in his light Yorkshire tenor, looking up for a moment as he bent to work a corkscrew into the bottle of Riesling trapped between his knees. I watched the turn of the screw, tried to focus on its work, focus hard—till once again I found myself gazing at his silly meaningless bobble: and then away, away, anywhere-but-there. It was something which, now seen, could never be unseen.[124]

What was it Alun had just said, though?—by now Amanda was in the kitchen where Miranda Pismire and Yvette Riordan were talking with Lára; here we were, just the chaps, suddenly, somehow, discussing the Anxiety of Influence. *The Anxiety of Influence?*—we clutched at it gratefully, all of us, like shipwrecked men struggling in the water.[125] *Harold Bloom, the strong ancestor, misprision, the personalised counter-sublime*—it seemed there was nothing we couldn't find to say about these things, each of us hanging on to one another's words like immigrants but with bursts of wild, meaningless laughter whenever Gifford spoke.

124 An echo of Vladimir Nabokov's description of seeing a ship's funnel between buildings in *Speak, Memory* (London: Victor Gollancz 1951): 'which the finder cannot unsee once it has been seen,' etc. How has it got here?

125 In *The Anxiety of Influence: A theory of Poetry* (1973), Harold Bloom (1930–2019) argues for the influence of past poets on existing poets and the pressure simply to 'rewrite' influential poetry as their own. His interest is in how 'strong' poets have resisted this influence. This sounds like a source for our narrator's sketchy references throughout to the Ocean of Literature, etc, filtered through a thousand intermediaries till it reached him standing near the door during some common-room conversation.

'Somewhat over-elaborated,' I remember he said of Bloom's book at some point, and we guffawed like country bumpkins. 'Isn't kenosis part of the Atkins diet?' one of us was asking, wildly, blindly—it's silly enough to have been me—even as the doorbell sounded again and we parted to let Gifford through to answer it, all the time watching one another taking care not stare at his—well, at his *prancing buttocks*, which was a phrase that slopped up into my mind from somewhere in the Ocean of Literature. Jane Austen, possibly; but then did she do bare bums? Not sure.[126] Meanwhile, here was Gifford coming back from the front door, bringing with him the Puttances, both of them rigid with shock: Warren numbly gripping his bottle of Cold Duck, Ava a tremulous bowl of dip.

The evening unfolded. Oh, the relief when we were called to the table: just Gifford's bare head and torso to deal with now. *The Anxiety of Influence* had run its path and we were clutching at bits and pieces of it now, remnants—no matter, no matter: Gifford to the rescue!—had any of us caught up with the man business? We listened, pretending to know what he was talking about. After a minute I pricked up my ears: *a literary bullshit artist who'd been found out but had got away with it?* I needed to know more about this!—oh, *de Man*, so *that's* who he was talking about?[127] Yes, I'd heard of this prick, vaguely, very vaguely. I nodded knowledgeably as Gifford told us more and his wife set out prawn cocktails.

126 Unlikely. Try instead *The Complete Works of D.H. Lawrence* (Wordsworth Editions 1994, p.7). 'Virgin Youth': 'I / Would worship thee, letting my buttocks prance', etc.
127 Paul de Man (1919–83). Influential literary critic, Professor of the Humanities at Yale, posthumously revealed to have authored a number of anti-Semitic articles during the Second World War and to have been involved in financial malpractice. Belgian. Ignore.

Then, suddenly, he was up and out of his seat to refill our glasses and here it was again, inspired by the prawns. He stood between each of us in turn with his carafe, none of us daring to look left or right as the Cold Duck tinkled into the glass: here it was, next to my left ear; now it was next to my right. I held my breath as Gifford told us about the contradictions inherent in Derrida's fundamental assumption, the flaw that gave the entire game away. *Really?* I heard someone say; and someone else said *D'you think so?* as if they meant it, and there was a blast of loud, unhappy laughter. The dinner party was turning into a parlour game of hunt-the-thimble; except that in this case the thimble was the very thing we were all agreeing not to see.

I stared across at Lára: how did she put up with this? Alun had taken over now and the room rocked with laughter over nothing very much at all—a new professor of Japanese who couldn't speak it: how would this affect his teaching? And the chap in Linguistics who'd been found to have been dead in his office for some time: extended study leave, somebody said, and we even laughed at *that*—at anything, as Gifford was up, was down, was up again and down again till his wife brought in the second course. And—oh, God—*it was a roast chicken on a platter.* He stood yet again, and picked up a carving knife and began to sharpen it, swiping the blade left and right. The greatest challenge of the evening: watching a naked man carve a chicken.

Throughout, I watched his wife. Unreadable, but there'd been a moment—nothing more—when our eyes met along the table and I was sure we'd made a connection. Had we?

Later, as we all lazed uneasily back at the table with biscuits and cheese and Ava Puttance's onion dip, I stood up and followed Lára into the kitchen. She was in the far corner with her back to me. In her window reflection I could see a hankie at her nose. When she turned and saw me her face crumpled and she let me hold her against my shoulder. I looked around—Gifford's voice from the other room—I looked back. I was away here, I was *in*, I could feel that; this was a situation I could work on. Empathy, that'd do the trick, empathy always gets the job done. She was still crying, she was trembling, I could feel that. I put my face into her hair and held her, gently, trying hard to pretend to care. The scent of the conditioner she used, and something else that was subtler than that, something that was just *her*. I was dying for a fag.

Afterwards, four of us gathered at the cars outside the house, four men smoking underneath a streetlight, collars up against the wind. Oh, yes, and Amanda Cupmark, slightly to one side, waiting.

'Poe.'

'What?'

'"The Purloined Letter".'[128]

'What *are* you talking about?'

'Oh, I see what you mean—the object hidden in plain sight.'

'Yes—yes, when no one's looking for it. Right.'

'No, but he *is* looking for it, that's the point of the story, surely? Inspector Dupin? In the Poe story? He *is* looking for it?'

'What's this book he's meant to be writing, anyway? Gifford? Anyone know what it's about?'

'That he's got a contract for? Some forbidden topic but he won't say.'

'Flogging. It'll be about flogging.'

---

128 A short story by Edgar Allan Poe (1809–49) concerning a search for a missing letter hidden in plain sight and which has occasioned extraordinary hyper-analysis by over-excited Continental literary critics.

Laughter, confident male laughter beneath a streetlight.

I cleared my throat. I didn't tell them what he'd told me.

'*Why* didn't any of us blow his cover? Eugene? *Why* didn't one of us just say, *why the hell've you got your dick out?*'

I can't remember who asked this: the fundamental question of the evening, of course. It wasn't me, anyway. And no answer forthcoming: a moment of silence, of self-loathing. *To strive, to seek, to find, and not to yield*—hmph.[129] We'd all pretended, we'd all—well, covered up for him, I suppose. That seemed to point to something fundamental about us, about academic culture itself. Naturally, I've no idea what it is.

Throughout this I flicked glances back at the house. Lára, I wanted one last glimpse of Lára—and there she was, at their kitchen window: just a second of her. We'd made some connection just now, she and I. Hadn't we?

'Castration,' someone was saying behind me. 'It's about castration.'

'Well, he didn't look particularly castrated to me!'

Deep male laughter again, men's shoulders bobbing about. Amanda Cupmark to one side, looking embarrassed, looking down, looking away, looking up at the stars. Waiting patiently to be taken home by someone else, I realised later, much later, although the full meaning of that escaped me, too. Being with her always seemed to tap my shoulder with a significance I couldn't quite get—as if I ought to feel guilty or something. I found this irritating. Guilty of what, for God's sake?

I told Sally when she got back from her chemical castration study group. I described Gifford's performance and I made

---

129 Tennyson's 'Ulysses' again (though not the hmph part). See footnote 62.

the hunt-the-thimble remark, too, but she took no notice of it. There was just one thing she wanted to know.

'Like a horse,' I told her. 'Built like a horse.'

'He *can't* be, he's an academic.'

'He *is*. Most of us are the same, most men are normal.'

'They're *not*, some of them are fatter, some of them are longer. Anyway, yours is shorter because they cut the end off it—'

Etcetera. We were a couple by now, we did things together, we had conversations like that in bed. Almost daily we argued, often wildly, angrily, till I became frightened and drew back; at other times we hit it off, although there was one difficulty I had with her that I find rather awkward to mention here. An Ongoing Delicate Reservation, you might say. More later. Perhaps.

At this stage we'd left the writer's house I'd been babysitting for Houston and were at the Riordans' while Tim and Yvette were overseas on his sabbatical leave. Together Sally and I enjoyed an eco-friendly home that seemed to live and breathe for us. A roof of solar tiles; rainfall collecting in a vast tank outside; walls made of failed doctoral theses recycled and compacted; a composting toilet that terrified me and which Sally made a roster for, so we could take turns raking it out. When it was my turn I always pretended. A slight smell began. I denied it was there. Then I said it was an odour not a smell. That seemed to take care of it, for the time being at least.

An ideal background for pretending to write a novel. *A Higher Kind of Love*, I'd decided to call it: Laura its heroine, of course, though a heroine somewhat qualified by Sally's growing presence in my life—by Lára's, too. I'd talk to Sally about it often: the problems of making a start, of writing with integrity, of waiting till the writing began to speak. And to others as well, colleagues at work, and students who sat in awe in the student cafeteria as I spoke: a real live writer, there in front of them! Gradually, steadily, I was becoming established as an author. All I needed now was to write something.

It was at the Riordans', too, that Sally helped me read my first real book—right through, I mean. *Really* read it. I watched her eating up titles like *Male Sex Offenders* and *Dishonest People*—right through, *boom*, in a sitting sometimes, with a list of notes scribbled down when she was done. And not just textbooks: she read fiction, too, lying back on a couch with her lips moving and the pages turning every seven seconds—Ali Smith and Toni Morrison, other women. I watched her and I thought of the books I'd never quite got around to reading or had abandoned partway through, of the *bluffing* that my teaching involved—all those books I've faked it with in front of classes who were busy faking it back. Being with Sally was making me see things like this. She was so *real*. You couldn't bullshit her, I realised that early on. This thought made me feel very strange. 'You've got so much *potential*,' she told me. 'I don't know why you piss around so much.' That scared me, I can tell you. Potential? Me? Aren't we all just faking it?

Anyway, all this boosting made me decide to try to read a novel right through. I don't mean just any old novel—don't get me wrong, I've read novels all right, read them right through, quite a few of them. Dozens—well, a few dozen. All of Maurice Shadbolt. No, I mean one of those hard-bound hard-work generally-agreed-to-be-great novels people talk about but never actually read, that's what I had in mind. *War and Peace. The Idiot. The Red and the Black. Ulysses. Don Quixote.* I decided I'd really try to get through one of those big bastards.

Proust, I decided, it'd be Proust. I'd read Proust.[130]

Yes. Proust. Who'd always seemed so forbidding I'd never bothered even to pretend to have read him. As with all Great Literature, I'd gambled on the probability that no one else had, either, or few or none, and that as a consequence I'd be able to bluff my way through any discussion that might come up. In the humanities library I found the whole lot, the Scott Moncrieff version that everyone pretends to have read. Quite apart from anything else, how could one man simply *write so much?*—a testament to bedsores and solitary fumblings. Well, anyway, I settled on the first volume and set to. *Swann's Way.* Proust. Scott Moncrieff. The whole shooting match, as Bevan was wont to say (he was also wont to say *wont*, too).

A turning point in my life. I sense that's what you're thinking. It's time for such a moment, surely, although bringing it up two-thirds of the way through the book might've been better than here, which is less than halfway. Our Hero Comes To His Senses At Last!—like Emma in *Emma*, you might say, which I *almost* completed early in my career, in an effort to *cut the mustard* and be like my new colleagues—you know, well-read, able to cite chapter-and-verse the way Bevan and the rest of them used to do—but which I couldn't quite knock off after all when *push* came to *shove.* What *is* all this about irony in Jane Austen, anyway?

Proust, though. *Swann's Way.* I sat down and forced myself to read at least ten pages of it a day. Soon I began to fall short and make excuses but after brisk exchanges with Sally I'd be back in harness again, her boot up my bum. I kept at it and

130 Marcel Proust (1871–1922). Author of the interminable *À la recherche du temps perdu* (1913–27), which no one has actually read to its end, though many claim to have done so. French. Ignore.

kept at it, and so, it seems, did she. And to tell the truth I could make neither head nor tail of this *Swann's Way* business, I really couldn't. Six months of boredom and puzzlement, six months of absolute bafflement at what-in-God's-name-was-going-on as each fresh page opened up its mannered, irritating *minutiae* to me. *Oh, God, what was he up to this time? Which boring bastard was he writing about now? Who the hell cared what was going on in this eminently fuck-free novel?* I slowly began to understand why, of the seven volumes of *À la recherche*, only the first, the one I was trying to read, looked fattened and dog-eared and the rest as if they'd just arrived fresh from the publisher—no one who'd survived Round One in their right mind was ever going to get off his stool for rounds Two to Seven, were they? And I don't care what anyone says: I'm not ashamed to say so.

No, that's completely wrong: I *am* ashamed when I read that back. Because with Sally urging me on, and on and on, I *did* get to the end of *Swann's Way*—I pulled an all-nighter, a series of all-nighters, I read till I was punch-drunk with reading, just to get rid of the bloody thing and rebuild my life. And the moment I got there everything changed. Such an extraordinary feeling, as I closed the book for the last time and realised I'd never have to open it again—exhaustion, relief, elation. And disbelief: could I really have done this—had I really survived my greatest self-imposed ordeal? *I've done it! I've read an entire volume of Proust!* I called out to Sally, or maybe she wasn't there—I called that out and burst into tears, overwhelmed at what I'd just experienced, the greatness of Proust's art, the transformative power of Literature itself. I realised I'd just had the greatest six months of my life.

Well, that's what I told people, anyway, and I also told them it'd taken one month to read not six; and after a while it became true—true to *me*, *my* truth: I'd feel the emotion of it welling up as I spoke and I could see it registering with them the moment they saw my hankie begin to dab at my eyes. I've just re-read it for the third time, I'd tell them. *À la recherche.* Yes, all seven volumes. In French, yes. It's exactly as I remember it, it's a masterpiece, it's wonderful, I couldn't put it down.

What d'you mean, you haven't read it?

With writing I've never read, on the other hand, I find I've got a far better sense of things, a special gift of empathy—Hardy, for example, the writer-I've-never-read whom I've always thought I'd appreciate most if I had. I've just come across one of his while I'm dusting in the foyer—*The Mayor of Casterbridge*, with that great opening scene of the reddleman slowly approaching from the middle distance of a green field. I remember it from the movie. Or was that in *Jude the Obscure*? I think the one he's in might have a longer title. Or shorter. One of the two. No matter: here he is in my hands again, here once more is the familiar feel of his cover, the glossy nubble of his cloth, the mysterious low-church smell of those entombed nineteenth-century pages. Ah, the silent mystery of the uncut page, that metaphysical, hypothetical world that floats inside, *virgo intacta*—everything that could possibly be. I take care to put him in my backpack so I can place him on my bedside table tonight, reverently, next to the King James Bible I never read during my religious period one Easter years ago.

Later, as we're shutting up shop, the Canadian potter stops by. He rummages through one end of the pile.

'Hey,' he says. 'Whaddya know, *The Manticore*.'

'The who?'

'Robertson Davies. My favourite.'

'Oh—yes, he's good, isn't he?'
'What's your favourite novel of his?'
'That one there. *The Manticore.*'
'Yeah, isn't it just great?'
And off he goes with it.
Who the hell is Robertson Davies?
In the shop, Bevan, parping his nose.

Chapter 10

The Riordans have sold their environmentally sensitive house, solar panels and all; they're in a beach cottage up the coast writing dialogue for a television series about a gay detective with an artificial head. Bevan tells me this as we stand outside the workroom-that-once-was-Tim's-office, now so crammed with books we can hardly open the door. The book pile out in the foyer has grown to four or five rows deep, perhaps a dozen books high in places. Keep on bringing them over, Bevan tells me, brightly, and from time to time he gives me a hand with the trolley—Harrison and some of the other tradies do, too, with their usual brief inspections of each load and their usual sceptical remarks about what's in it.

And every day he takes away some books, Harrison—*The Defeat of the Spanish Armada*, Garrett Mattingly, that's one; I remember the cover from up in the stacks. *Bomber Command*, Max Hastings, that's another. Off they go, books like that, but I'm not sure they ever come back. He takes one or two when Bevan's around and more when it's just me—Jason and a couple of the others are in and out, too; sometimes they come in twice a day. I never say anything about it. Twenty books gone, twenty less to stack.

All the same, at ten or a dozen trolley-loads a day, the stack in the foyer keeps growing. For a while I manage to keep up some kind of order in it: very basic, fiction–nonfiction–poetry–philosophy–drama as five rows become six and six become seven. But then there's the Monday we turn up to work and there's been a book-slide over the weekend and they're sprawled halfway across the foyer. When I start to re-stack them, try to find the lost order—suddenly, abruptly, I give up. Stuff it; what are we doing with these books, anyway? Oh, that's right, saving the humanities. And I don't fuss quite so much about order after that. They're all over the place. And more books going, you can see that each morning.

Anyway, this is what I'm getting to: right at the end of the day, when I've brought the last trolley-load down from the library, the silliest thing happens: a book bites me. Seriously!— that's what it feels like, a little soft nip, nothing more but a bite all the same. The bloody thing starts to slide off the corner of the row I've just been stacking, Dewey 821 English Poetry, and out goes my hand to stop it—and the damn thing gives my fingers a quick hard little nip! Nothing much, as I say, but it does make me pull away for a second all the same. Like being nipped by a crab's claw when you reach into a tank. A good firm bite, like a warning. Isn't that silly, isn't that mad?

I stare down at it: *The Meaning of Meaning.*[131] I've eyed this book furtively over the years in the library, the faded gilt in the title, the uninviting purple-blue wall of its cocked, rolled, edgeworn cover.[132] Here it is, inviting attention at last. What's it

131 *The Meaning of Meaning: A Study of the Influence of Language upon Thought and of the Science of Symbolism* by C.K. Ogden and I.A. Richards (London: Kegan Paul 1923). Note also Paul B. Diederich, 'The Meaning of "The Meaning of Meaning"', *The English Journal*, Vol.30, No.1, pp.31–6; and Eugene Gifford, 'The meaning of "The Meaning of *The Meaning of Meaning*"' in *The English Journal*, Vol.30, No.3, pp.201–10.
132 He's showing off his (superficial) knowledge of the terms of the second-hand-book trade here: the first two simply refer to cover-edges which are pushed in, the third to covers which are—well, worn at the edges.

saying to me? I pick it up, gingerly, hold it up to my nose: nothing much, just the usual foxy-mildew phase of any old edition. I turn it over, turn it back, give it a bloody good why-not shake.

And a slip of paper falls out—a single cigarette paper, very thin, flattened out. I pick it up. Two words written on it: *Ultima Sigaretta.*[133] That's all. I sit staring at this via my thirty-dollar supermarket spectacles. Even I can translate it. *Last cigarette.* A voice speaking to me from the past, giving me a warning, a special message, just for me. What's it saying? *Give up the smokes?* Thinking this makes me nervous. I light a fag, inhale, look around. How did C.K. Ogden and I.A. Richards know I smoke?

After a long time, Houston returned from the States, abruptly, minus LaPeste and with his mood (it was generally agreed) somewhat lowered. In the tearoom he brooded in a corner rather than telling jokes about farm animals; we could hear him talking to himself, loudly, angrily, alone in his room; he said *fuck* and *ass* even more often than before and also *asshole*, to the dismay of those thus identified. He seemed to be turning more and more into his performance of himself.

By now his year as Gotch Memorial Writing Fellow was almost gone, completely wasted, and a successor had been appointed on the basis of a single application photo (wheelchair, monocle, quill).[134] Houston hung around all the same, past

133 This, somehow, is straight from Italo Svevo, *Confessione di Zeno* (1923), even the detail of the paper dropping out of a book. How could an idiot like this possibly know about a book like that?
134 This is obviously an attempt to mimic Vladimir Nabokov's famous parenthesis in *Lolita* (1955)—'(picnic, lightning)'—believed to be the shortest in literary history. Yet again, how could a man like this know two

year's end and into the new; he kept the same office and sat in the tearoom morning and afternoon drinking the frightful coffee the downstairs secretary made, to which she always added mustard after misreading a tip in the *Women's Weekly*.

Our self-conscious little poker evenings resumed. *Ah'm afraid ah'm gonna have to raise the stakes a little here, gentlemen,* he said on the first night back, slapping a card on the baize. The money on the table bounced as he did this—coins, just coins, but money all the same. He'd insisted on it as he shuffled the cards: *What the fuck we doin' here? Still playin' for matchsticks—?* We looked around ourselves: good question. So, we fumbled out our loose change and found after a few minutes that, even in small amounts, playing for money felt different: more real, more dangerous—even more so than the duty-free whiskey he'd brought back with him, which was called *Tennessee Tiger Water* and whose label showed a tiger peeing into a bottle of the product.

At the end of the evening I was *down* a little (as I learned to say), but less so than the other two of the four of us: *Whaddya know, I cleaned up!* was Houston's contribution. Twenty bucks he made from me that first night back on the baize, somehow; on the other hand, it'd seemed a better evening, all in all, once it was done. I returned to the Riordans' financially *down*, rather than *up*, but emotionally *up*, rather than *down*.

And, once again, to Sally, who had long been abed and fast asleep. *No*, she mumbled when I got in beside her, and, when I persisted, *no* again, and the third time she sat up in the darkness and said, *Tom, we've discussed this.* Then she said *You've been drinking* and, when I spilled the beans, *Gambling?—how much?* I confessed, in a brave, high-pitched squeak. She sat up. *Ten*

---

things about this writer (see footnote 124), let alone one?

dollars? She turned the bedside light on. *Have we discussed this? Tom?*

By this stage in our *shared life project* even I could see—crudely, instinctively, like a pig—something of what was happening in this new life that had suddenly begun to happen itself around me during the last year and a half. She was *making a man of me*—or, as she would say, *a person.* It'd stunned me how quickly and thoroughly she'd come into my life after that frightening encounter at the book launch; it stunned me even more how little resistance I'd put up when she did. My being had simply crumpled and folded around hers like a large, partially cooked pudding—junket, perhaps, or blancmange or tapioca.[135] What could she see (I remember wondering) in someone who so much resembled an old-fashioned kids' dessert?

Once again Manatine was there to tell me. Not as a gaudy apparition this time—in fact I couldn't help thinking he looked just a touch down-at-heel—and, as far as I could see, no longer levitating at any point. But, otherwise, here he was, in my dreams again—though this time as I lay next to Sally, something which made me feel more than a little odd when he was done and I was awake again and there she was beside me in the dark. I listened to the rhythmic lilt of her breathing,[136] now familiar, reassuring, meaning she was asleep and unable, for the time being, to continue her life's work on me. For that, in essence, was what Manatine had just been telling me about. Wasn't it? I'd struggled to follow him. *She's spotted you,*

135 Of these, tapioca pudding is probably the least revolting given the resemblance of the others mentioned here to cooked fish-eyes. But it's a close-run thing, as the Duke of Wellington is said to have said after the Battle of Waterloo.
136 These attempts at literary heightening are getting more and more irritating.

he'd said, just a minute before. His voice was muffled, as if he was eating a pie at the same time. *She's onto you, you're her project. You're fucked.* Why? Why? *Look in her notebook.* In her notebook? *In her bag. She's onto you, y'dumb fuck.*

What did he mean? She had a secret, that's what he meant. There was something she was withholding from me, in her bag, something she kept in the orange collector shoulder-bag which had come into the relationship with her along with two suitcases, a laundry basket and a Bullworker[137]—oh, and cleaning equipment, there was that, of course, and the iron and the ironing board and an indoor clothes rack. And a sofa that turned into a bed but only when Sally made it turn into a bed. This shoulder-bag of hers always seemed to be bigger on the inside than the outside; Gifford called it *the widow's cruse* when he saw it over her shoulder in the college grounds one day, a phrase which meant nothing at all to me when she told me about it. He's thinking of the *OT,* Sally said, and when I said OTT? she said *Old Testament, Tom, not Over the Top,* in her patient Old Tinny's Special Class voice. Then she explained what a cruse was, which I also didn't know, and then she smiled to herself, which is what she always did when she'd had to explain something to me. And then she got on with the business of preparing a *cauliflower roast,* as she called it—we were *on our path from vegetarianism to veganism* at the time, another step we'd agreed, apparently, to take together. There was an all-night service station around the corner, I discovered, which served up doomsday-prepper hot dogs.

Two mysteries, then. One, she had a past. Knowing about the *OT,* I mean. 'From childhood,' she said, but she wouldn't say

137 A metal compressor tube used by hearty, optimistic people, apparently, in isometric physical exercises.

more. 'Brethren?' I asked. 'Seventh Day? Is that how you know the Bible?' No good, though. She just got on with it. 'There is no past,' she said. 'It's always moving away from us. That's what we have to remember. There's just the presenting problem, we work on what's in front of us day by day. If it isn't functional we correct it.' And, on another occasion, 'Tom, there's just *now*. That's what we work with. *Now*. We just change the behaviour, it's all about behaviour. We grow into our new behaviour if we decide that's what's required.'

And the second mystery was that collector bag. Each evening I'd stare across the room as it leaned against her armchair, fatter one day, thinner the next, but always containing the big, brutal laptop computer she'd brought home from the Department of Sociology. I'd never seen one of these things before and had no idea how to use one—was barely functional on the boxy little Mackintosh my job inflicted on me. Each evening I'd sit watching her dabbling her fingers on its keyboard with the telly muted. Her sociology thesis was done and published—Gifford helped arrange this, through his North American contacts. What was she writing now? Was it about me? How could I find out? As far as my own project was concerned, I'd hit a writer's block—well, to tell the truth I hadn't quite started, really. Not quite. A starter's block, perhaps.

And all the time, Houston went on hanging about the Department of English between morning and afternoon tea, just like a real academic. Giving lectures, even: here was his voice as I passed a lecture room; there he was, as I eased its rear exit door open, wandering about in front of the lectern and jabbing his finger at twenty or thirty students, his Stetson on the back of his head. Behind him, sketched out simply on the whiteboard, a UFO: *They gonna have a good hard time explainin'*

[173]

that, I heard him say, and there was belch of happy laughter from his class.

I went to see him in his office, which was borrowed from a blurred little man who simply never came in except for our monthly staff meetings, at which he never spoke, even if asked a direct question; in fact, we had no reliable evidence he could speak at all. He was rumoured to be a world expert on the poet Sturge Moore. 'Sturge *who*?' I remember Houston saying, when I told him this. 'Never heard of him.' 'Never heard of Sturge Moore?' I asked, almost by reflex—but of course at that stage I hadn't, either. I looked him up afterwards, just in case. Brother of G.E. Moore, philosopher. Who? What? Anyone out there?

Houston's door was open. I stopped and looked in. He was crouched at the window with his eyes squinted-up like Clint Eastwood's in *Unforgiven* or possibly *City Heat*. He was aiming something—oh, God, a *rifle*, he was aiming a *rifle* into the Privileged Visitors Carpark two storeys below—

My heart started juddering. Shit, Houston—

Down there, two maths lecturers, trying to get away from Farting Harry Toothill.

He stood up: it wasn't a rifle after all!—oh thank God, thank God—but instead a long packet, a long brown paper package. He held it up: 'Curtain rails.' He crouched down and pointed it through the window again. 'Lee Harvey fucken Oswald, man,' he said, over his shoulder. 'Fucken American *hero*—'

Somewhere around this time, too, Gifford broke cover. We'd known about his mysterious project for a while now, the one with a book contract; now he gave a public seminar on it. *Gifford Talks Shite*, the posters said; the seminar room was crammed. The poster, it transpired, referred to his proposed book, which started with Aristophanes and Petronius and scooped up any writer whose potty-training was anywhere near as dodgy as I suspect his own might have been—Herrick, Harrington, Swift, even Nadine Gordimer. Scatology, the name of the mode, and *Shite* the book's title, plain and simple.[138] He was well into writing it, he told us; he was particularly pleased with the chapter on W.C. Williams.

'It's a form of the Abject,' he said afterwards, back in the *Senior Common Room*, as a sign on its door now proclaimed the tearoom to be. 'It touches on the Lacanian Real.'

Bevan was sitting across from him with his knobbly lived-in red-and-white legs disappearing into those dreadful baggy khaki shorts. They were arguing over something Gifford had just said in his lecture.

'I thought it was disgusting.' Bevan pecked at one of the onion sandwiches that always made his afternoon tutorials so taxing for students.

'It's saying the unsayable,' Gifford said. 'It's about the boundaries of language. It's about what you can and can't say.'

'It's about *shitting*—'

Bevan's knees, working against each other, his left arm knotted against his chest, his mouth taking another quick angry peck at his sandwich. On it went, Bevan and Gifford, Gifford and others. I got left behind fairly early on, just as I had during the seminar, when I'd become mesmerised by the gear-changes in Gifford's Adam's apple as he spoke—no, really, it was quite something, you should have seen it—

'It's a rupture in the fabric of reality,' Gifford was saying.

138 Gifford's study seems to have begun a trend: see Jeff Persels and Russell Ganim (eds.), *Fecal Matters in Early Modern Literature and Art: Studies in Scatology* (*Studies in European Cultural Transition*), 2004; and also Peter J. Smith's *Between Two Stools: Scatology and Its Representations* (Manchester University Press 2012).

'It's what psychotics live in all the time—it's just a blast of pure affect, how to write about that, that's the issue.'

'Yes, but in *Enid Blyton*?'

Bevan *slammed* his lunchbox shut. He stood and walked out. The door went off behind him, *bang!*

Someone said, 'A blast of pure affect.' A guffaw of self-satisfied, bookish laughter. *Priceless, simply priceless!*

Gifford stood up. 'Got a film crew coming by,' he said. 'On the news tonight.'

We watched him together that evening, Sally and I, whilst sharing a bowlful of a greenish, snot-like substance. 'He presents well,' she said. 'Glad I'm not married to him.'

On telly Gifford's voice sounded different, deeper, richer, his pauses seemed more weighted, more significant. Even the books in the bookcase behind him had more colour, more order than I remembered them in his office. On his desktop his hands seemed large, manly, his fingers loosely interlocked in a way that suggested a brooding power. *Laugh?* he was saying, and he ducked his head forward at the interviewer; his eyebrows lifted. *Are you seriously suggesting the disposal of waste is something to laugh at? Wouldn't you think that in fact I'm writing about one of the central challenges of our times—?*

'Brilliant.' She clapped her hands beside me. 'He's brilliant.'

'He trained me.' I slid out of the bed and took the empty bowl and the spoons from her. 'Might just stroll down to the corner and back.'

'Again?' She stared at me, beadily. 'You're not buying cigarettes at the service station, are you?'

'Ciggies? No, I'm not buying ciggies.'

How strange, to be telling the truth for a change. I looked at her as she lay there, hands behind her head, elbows up, and thought again, momentarily, of my Ongoing Delicate Reservation.

Eventually, Tim Riordan rang from Trieste: back in a month. The composting toilet problem had metastasised by now and Sally had a couple of professionals in to look at it. You could hear them outside as she was talking to Tim. Bring the *what?* one of them was shouting at the other. The *what?*

'We need a new start,' she said, as soon as she was done with Tim. 'Not rental, a place of our own.'

'Really?'

I was trying to sound noncommittal. It sounded like *rilly?* Commitment, she meant. *Rilly? Commitment?* I could feel my throat tightening.

Instead, I got ahead of her and found a rental in a *déclassé* area out near the airport—not a colleague's this time, just the standard thing. We lasted a month. What sent us packing was the small ceramic nameplates on the bedroom doors. One, sickeningly, read *Mom & Pop*—but on the kid's, worse: *Hamish.*

'We *have* to get out of here—'

'Oh, God, Tom, this Hamish thing is silly, it's *so* silly.'

'He's after me—'

'*Who?* Who *is* this *he* you keep talking about?'

It was odd, then, once I finally broke into her secret, to find that name again. Not in her laptop—that remained impenetrable—but in a spring-backed notebook she left behind when she went to the main campus one Saturday afternoon. By then all I'd managed was a seminar on Robert Byng, which, lightly attended as it was, had gone very well, I thought— light attendance being the point—and the man himself was thickening up in my mind as time went by, becoming a fact like all the other facts in the world: made up. Elsewhere, too, it seemed; I had a couple of queries about him from overseas.

I opened the notebook. *The Story of Little Hamish*—her title, it seemed, written in pencil at the start and underlined twice. Little Hamish? Wasn't Little Hamish mine—hadn't I invented him? What the hell was going on? *A taxonomy of the challenges facing young women in a reactionary society today*, that was the general area she was working in, she'd told me, and to tell the truth I hadn't been terribly interested in it when she did. What was *taxonomy* supposed to mean, anyway? I made a feeble joke about taxis, and she looked at me with pity in her eyes, genuine pity, and said nothing.

H. is poor at sustained and connected thought, though improving with discipline. Initially it seemed Ganser syndrome might be indicated. In a strange way that's unexpected, H. seems in fact not to be delusional—Sally's words, scrawled in the red notebook. I looked around. What was Ganser syndrome? I tried Wikipedia: *A rare dissociative disorder characterised by nonsensical or wrong answers to questions and other dissociative symptoms such as fugue, amnesia or conversion disorder, often with visual pseudo-hallucinations and a decreased state of consciousness.*

She was well ahead of me, I could see that—hard work, I'd found, keeping two imaginary projects going at once. I put her notebook back and wiped my hands together, uneasily. This must have been what Manatine meant in the dream. How could he have known about it, though? Wasn't it just a dream, anyway? And who was this poor prick she was writing about—where'd she found a weirdo like *that*?

Back from leave, Tim Riordan began another term as head of department. In his first three years he'd insisted on running things from his downstairs office—the one we were to store all those books in years later when it became part of the bookshop.

'He's shown us he's one of the boys,' Gifford said. 'But he knows we want a touch of the whip so he's turning into Gotch. Remember—a bird flew in search of a cage.'

Which was rather nicely put, I had to admit.[139]

Now, at the start of this second term, Tim moved upstairs to Gotch's old office. When I went to settle the bill for replacing the composting toilet, there he was behind Gotch's desk. I felt that familiar, low-down twinge. How did this power thing work? He'd begun to sign his inter-office emails *TR* and sometimes just *R*, like Gotch's abrupt, Napoleonic *G-for-God*. He was talking more and more about himself, his sacrifices, the price he was paying for being head of department—here he was now, starting up as soon as I sat in front of him with my chequebook and pen. It was like the good old days; I could feel myself tuning out as he began to talk, *zzzzzzz* . . .

Now, suddenly, though, he was talking about Houston. I came to and resurfaced.

'*Employing* him? As a lecturer? Houston? *Rilly?*'

Tim nodded, gravely. He'd developed an increasingly professorial manner, I'd noticed, even though he was but a *Reader*,[140] one step down from professor and marooned there despite having recently published *Why Yeats's Hair Matters* (Seafóid Press 1994).

'We're employing him on contract. There may be a place opening up.' He looked around, he lowered his voice. 'Certain

---

139 Of course it's nicely put!—it's one of Kafka's aphorisms.

140 A rank below professor, still used in some British universities and the colonies and devised to acknowledge achievement in scholarly publication but tacitly to indicate that the recipient is thought unlikely to receive a personal chair because of insufficient dishevelment, paranoia, vindictiveness, etc.

people around here whose days are numbered, between you and me.'

I couldn't help smirking. Postcolonial Pat! About time. Lately he'd been pushing Pacific writing, for God's sake!

'It's the future, I'm afraid, it's the choice-architecture we're confronted with.' Tim nodded at himself again. 'What with Norman going and so on. The gig economy.'[141]

Ah, yes: Norman Iggo, retiring at last after a phenomenal length of time as vice-chancellor, thirty years, something like that—even he couldn't remember how long, he told us, as he laughed his agreeable, honking laugh. A lifetime, and taking an entire age with him, it was generally agreed, though at that stage none of us had any idea what that might mean.

'Bums on seats,' Tim said. 'It's going to matter more and more. The dean advises that our departmental SSR is trending a little low.'

Dean? I'd no idea we had one. And what was an SSR?[142]

'The important thing is, Houston tells us he's been through this before at Moscow, Idaho. When they tried to contract the staff base there.'

Contract the staff base? What did *that* mean?[143]

'Just rumours so far. Not clear what the new man will have in mind when he turns up.' He set his jaw and turned his head to one side, his hands positioned well on the desk, firm but not clenched—rather like Gifford's on the telly. 'I'm thinking

141 Originally used by jazz musicians to denote a brief playing contract, 'gig' is now used widely to denote an economy which uses short-term contracts in order to reduce costs by removing the concept of salaries, tenure and other traditional attributes of employment. Increasingly popular in academic life, particularly in female employment.
142 Staff–Student Ratio. Alas.
143 For God's sake, what does he think it means?

ahead, taking precautions.' His head creaked back towards me, like an Easter Island statue being winched around on ropes. 'You're our creative man on the staff,' he said. 'All those short stories you've brought out? This novel of yours, how's that coming along?'

Ah, yes, *A Higher Kind of Love*. So difficult to get the opening pages right in a longer work of fiction. As for short stories—a few years ago I'd claimed I had some under a pseudonym in *The London Magazine*, and someone told me, yes, yes, they'd read them—is that *you*? Word got about: *I'd been published Overseas!* I really did mean to write a story of my own someday, I really did—I'd got a great idea for one, about a lonely old woman no one loved.

I tuned into Tim again—what was this? A creative *writing* course? A creative writing *stream*? An eventual MFA in creative writing? Me and Houston? We were going to set this up and teach it?

Rilly?

'I don't want you to give up on the Byng thing,' Tim was saying. 'You're widely acknowledged as a leader in Byng Studies now. I want you to go ahead with a conference here next year.'

'Oh, quite.' My voice had found itself again. A *conference* here? 'Quite so.'

'But if you and Chet could team up together and—'

Chet—?

'Quite.'

'He's running a course on American literature for us at the moment. While David Peach is away on leave.' His head began to turn away from me as he reached for the profile shot once more. 'I really don't think it's a matter of lowering the standards. Teaching this American stuff. Seems to bring 'em in. The punters.' *Punters* was new, too, or newish.

Straight away I checked Houston out again, from the rear exit door of the lecture room I'd found him in last time—yes, there he was again, as if he'd never left, the class in front of him much bigger now. The UFO was gone from the whiteboard, replaced by a proliferation of lines, a scrawl of a car moving away from a child's drawing of a building labelled TEXAS BOOK SUPPOSITORY. 'And now,' I heard him say. 'The moment that broke the back of the twentieth fucken century.' Again, a happy blast of laughter from his class. Bums on seats, bums on seats. It had begun.

I told Sally. 'Creative *writing* teachers?' she said. 'But you haven't published anything yet. Nor's he—has he? Houston?'

She had a point. I'd never pinned him down on this matter, either. His trunks just never arrived.

'I don't understand it, Tom. Shouldn't you be able to get a job just about anywhere in the world? With this Byng thing? Aren't you—what did Tim call you? The Robert Byng man? This big conference he wants you to organise? The book you're writing—?'

'Oh, yes—the book—'

'I mean, shouldn't you be walking into any job you want? Just like that—?'

And she tried to snap her fingers, but they were moist and slid one off the other without a sound. Given the moment, it seemed appropriate. A failed mid-air finger-snap. My life.

I breathed in deeply, let it come back out again, tried to feel the *prana*. I'd read about this a few days before, in *Harness Racing Tips*.

It was around here that I betrayed her for the first time. Like an automaton, from Sally to someone who definitely wasn't Sally.

And, Lord, d'you know, I can't even remember who it was? Just someone I'd known before, I remember that; some brief flare-up from the past, a body owned by a flight attendant as I think she was or might have been or was about to become. Something to do with airlines. Anyway, I rang her, and later, in the anonymous bedroom of her anonymous shrug of a *pied-à-terre* amidst a row of anonymous *pieds-à-terre*, she told me she'd always known it wasn't really over between us, always known I'd come back into her life again one day. And come again I did.

And then, like the young man in the limerick, I went.[144] Yes, heartless, I know, and no, I'm not happy about it, least of all writing it down like that for all to see. Generally speaking I'm not happy with myself in any of what I'm telling you, not at all. I can't even remember the woman's name, either; but the trouble is *I don't think I could remember it at the time*—gripped together and hard at it, our faces averted from each other as I tried to hump Sally off to a suitable distance. Had I *ever* known this woman's name? *Darling* goes a long way, of course, in anonymous encounters such as these, and should never be underrated.

A pilot—it's coming back to me now. *That's* what this woman told me she was. An airline pilot. That's it.

I took care to shower afterwards at the main campus gym and sprayed myself with Rut. Magnus Furz was there, bending naked to dry his feet. I looked away. I hadn't realised Germany was still divided.

144 It seems he's referencing here the story of the young man from Kent; no need for further details. The tastelessness of this and the event he is describing barely needs comment.

Back home I smelled good but felt strange. 'What's wrong?' Sally asked as soon as I came in, and that shook me up badly, I can tell you. 'Wrong?' I said, in a Vienna Boys' Choir voice. I began to feel a tickle at the back of my throat.[145] 'I might be coming down with something,' I told her. It just occurred to me, even the fingers up to the neck, the dry cough, twice. I couldn't tell whether I was sick or not. I knew that if you get shingles and piles at the same time you might be turning into a house. But I'd been bullshitting so long I could never tell whether I was really ill or just pretending.[146] I can see dying is going to present quite a problem for me.

That night I watched her undressing at the end of the bed. Freckles, on her arms and shoulders and behind her neck, a real drift of them, and then, abruptly, her extraordinarily pale skin, bluish in certain lights, almost iridescent and seeming to change as she moved. She was naked now: the wholeness of her, her *womanness*. Was that it? I could hardly look at her. I was terrified—to be thinking like this, even, to be thinking properly—*almost* properly. Like an adult, she'd say if I told her, I knew that. Why had I betrayed her? What was happening to me?

Later, in bed, I found myself blurting out my Ongoing Delicate Reservation at last—it just happened: here it came, like a pimple bursting. As I blundered through it she *displayed*

145 'The liar's quinsy'—W.H. Auden in his poem 'Petition'. It seems that obvious literary associations like this never occur to this extraordinarily unlettered man, let alone the possibility that, here, literature really does seem to be working through him, something of which he claims elsewhere he is aware.

146 This is stolen, in theme if not in words, from Nathanael West's novel *The Day of the Locust* (1939)—a thematic theft not a literal one, but a theft nonetheless.

her listening skills, and when I'd finished she rolled away from me.

'No,' she said. 'You shave yours. Go on.'

'*I'm* not shaving mine, I'm a man.'

'What's the difference?'

'Men never shave their armpits.'

'Because it's natural?'

'Well, it is.'

'Define natural.'

Define real. Sophonisba.

Why was I always being outflanked by women who were smarter than me?

Because they were smarter than me.

'Natural is—what people do.' Grasping at straws now, of course, moving backwards, attempting yet another tactical withdrawal. 'It's what they always do. People. Then it's—natural.'

'It's natural so it must be natural?' She swiped me lightly across the brow with *The Sexual Politics of Meat*. 'There's nothing *to* you,' she said. 'I've just realised. For a while I didn't see it. You're completely empty, you really are completely empty.'

It didn't hurt because she didn't say it to hurt, you could see that. She was beginning to understand the full depth of my shallowness, that was what was happening. I wondered what had taken her so long. Wasn't she the one, though, who'd told me no one had a core, that it was what we did that defined us? Besides, it wasn't true I was completely empty. Hadn't she told me a hundred times I was full of shit?

She had her arms around me high up, she was kissing me where the book had scuffed me. She was fiddling around up there, she was fondling my hair—she really liked me, you can see that. There was more, though, I began to sense more. I struggled up. I was starting to understand a tiny something of my confusion, I was beginning to know my life-sentence:

To endure the full horror of being loved by a good woman.

I could feel her nails on my scalp. She was stroking my head, she was fondling my neck.

She stopped.

'Ooh, look,' she said. 'You're going bald.'

PART THREE

Götterdämmerung

Chapter 11

Here I am, typing this in one of the cubicles when—*boom!*—the outer men's-room door flings open, *hard*, and a man thumps in below the squawk of the pneumatic muscle. I can hear the metal in his soles striking the abject, pitted lino: one of the tradies. Harrison? Whoever he is, he's into the cubicle next to me—doesn't shut the door, doesn't pull the seat up: instead, he starts giving the cubicle walls a bloody good shake!—the whole thing, my side and his. He stands there shaking them *left* and *right* and *forward* and *back*, and then he *bangs* his hands on them—

Beside me the toilet roll bounces on its fitting. The laptop slides about on my knees, I clutch at things.

'Oy!'

I look up. Big chipped nails, fingers gripping the top of the cubicle wall: hands, wrists, black tangled hair. A scramble and now here's a face—bulging eyes, horrid nostrils.

He stares down into the cubicle.

'What the fuck you up to?'

I manage a coprophagous smile.[147]

'I'm—writing a book. A novel.'

It sounds ridiculous, of course. What *am* I doing here?

'Writing a *book*—?' He stares at the laptop, he looks around and down again. 'This is a *crapper*, mate.'

---

147 'Coprophagous'—? Where does he get this from? Better than his earlier, more vulgar version.

Now he drops back on the other side and gives the wall another manly slap: the toilet roll bounces right off its holder this time and onto my lap.

His voice comes back to me. 'These're all going anyway.'

'What—?'

'The lot.' Another slap, another rattle; the sound of his boots to the door. I hear him stop. 'Gettin' a revamp,' he calls back.

'What about the bookshop out there?'

'Whole fucken thing.'

I call out to him. 'The whole men's room?'

'Whole shebang. Whole building.'

What's this? Everyone knows what a toilet revamp means— the start of yet another managerial change process, yet another blow to the soul of an institution. Everyone knows they start by removing the men's urinals.

Sally was right, I *had* started to lose my hair. By means of a complex system of interacting mirrors only the follically challenged could ever devise I checked her out, and stared, appalled, at what she'd seen: a coin-sized patch of naked skin on the crown of my head, a swirl of hair thinning around it. *How could this be happening?* Was *this* the start of my long path to life in Bevan's Bookshop?

Or might something even bigger be happening? *We're in the early stages of an epistemic change*, Gifford told us.[148] *It started,*

---

148 I presume Gifford's referring here to Michel Foucault, *The Order of Things* (1966), which argues for a series of historical periods each united by shared assumptions about thought and speech, and that he's suggesting the tumultuous year of 1989 represents the start of a transition to (in Foucault's terms) a fourth episteme. Note how this concept is trivialised into 'paradigm shift' in managerial discourse. Dear God, no wonder our hero is confused.

oh, around ten years ago. The World Wide Web, the Berlin Wall, Tiananmen Square, the collapse of the Soviet Union, the rise of vulture capitalism—and more, but as far as I was concerned all this amounted to yet another fast ride on the back of his intellectual motorbike, yet another tumble at the first bend. I turned up the volume. *This is something they'll be talking about in five hundred years,* he said, and then he laughed and said *if there is another five hundred years,* and his studio audience laughed along with him. *If there's another They!*—here they started to clap, so much did they like whatever it was they were liking or thinking they liked or being told to like. *Public intellection gets sexier and sexier the less people understand it,* he used to tell me. *The less they know the more their bodies come into play and then they get horny and want to be fucked by an idea. Works better than champagne.*[149]

Yes: now our sole international jetsetter, Gifford—the sheer audacity of *Shite,* its grossness, had kicked him out and into the coprophagous world. These days he was on our screens more often than in the department corridor, looking leaner than before, aviator glasses cast off for a pair of squinty ski frames, hair chiselled, tinted, sculpted, blown, his face tanned, his teeth bonded: Gifford, commodified and caught in the eternity of cyberspace. *You've really written a book about doodoos?* was the first thing the host asked him on one of the late-night shows:

149 'Sapiosexual' seems to be the term currently used for what Gifford is describing here. The claim itself is an excellent example of the tendency to simple assertion in the humanities, where, by and large, nothing can actually be proven. See for example K.K. Ruthven, *Faking Literature* (2001), where he asserts that the Bank of England's issuing of paper money in place of gold nearly three hundred years ago might have begun the decline of the fiduciary relationship between language and material reality. Brilliant bluff-work—itself the topic of Ruthven's book—but unprovable, of course.

Yes, but literary doodoos was Gifford's silken reply, and the Yanks went wild for that—went wild for all of him. *The States is where it's at*, he told us when he came back from his book tour, which had started with a sardonic review in *Time* magazine and an interview on one of the late shows. His American publishers had given him a contract for another book, too, he told us— you'll never *believe* what they wanted him to write about next!

All in all, what you might call a successful literary movement, a load of shit that got him a personal chair at our little university and, eventually, just before the Dissolution of the Monasteries, a better one in the States—you can look him up on their website, you can catch up with him doing the rounds on CNN and elsewhere. 'A personal chair,' I remember someone telling me. 'Should've been a commode—might have to change Lára's name to Celia Schitz.'[150] I had to look that one up, of course, or maybe someone explained it to me. Maybe it was him.[151]

Meanwhile things were getting out of hand with his strange, pretty wife. We'd begun with trysts in sordid motels, each trying to find out what the other was into. 'Oh, sleaze,' she said when I asked her. 'I tell you yes because you're sleazy.' I was quite chuffed, I must say!—you don't often get a compliment like that. Soon, though, we moved from squalor to terror—a particular kind of terror: I couldn't believe my *ears* when she first pitched her brilliant new idea to me in the last of those tired motels.

150 An uncalled-for reference to Dean Swift's equally uncalled-for poem, 'The Lady's Dressing Room'; no further details required. On the other hand, the joke mentioned here is of a higher standard than most in this book.
151 'he'. Subjective nominative case.

'*My* place?' I stared at her. 'You mean where I live? In the bed where I—'

'You and—'

'*Me* and *Sally*—?'

'*Igen*, yeah. Where you two *fasz*.'

'*Fasz*—?'

'Yeah!'—and she bounced her pelvis a couple of times beneath the tired motel sheets, bump-bump. '*You* know—?'

'You want us to—*fasz*—in the same place Sally and—?'

'Yeah!' Bright, eager. Another couple of bounces under the bedding. '*Mf–mf*—'

'No.' I couldn't believe it. 'No, it's just not going to happen.'

Instead, as it transpired, we bonked in *her* bed—*chez* Gifford, site of the nude dinner party, home to that grandfather clock and, it turned out, more. Don't ask me how we got there, how she talked me into it, but when we did I found they had a His and a Hers like the Furzes. She showed me his His: a narrow, military cot, a severe metal desk strewn with the usual academic nonsense—books, papers, jars of pens and pencils, a surprisingly elderly PC. 'He never draws the curtains,' she told me. 'And see the silly photos on his noticeboard!' I looked, and looked away. 'Isn't he strange?' she said.

Her bedroom had a queen-size bed, mysterious, exotic. Between the bedrooms there was a gestural *en suite* with two toilets.[152] 'The small one's for washing babies in?' I asked. 'For washing babies out,' she said, and went on plumping the large square flat pillows on the bed, which her mother had sent her from Hungary, apparently, along with brightly patterned bedding and a wooden bedhead that matched it, and a long wooden trunk that matched the bedhead and curtains that

152 A toilet and a bidet, obviously. Our man seems rather untravelled.

matched the long wooden trunk. 'Peasant stuff,' she told me. 'Made for tourist.'

Good enough for me, though: in a way I both liked and disliked at the same time, this stuff loomed over me whenever I lay in her bed, which smelled of something foreign, exotic, a scent that was on her body, too, every time I held her close to me, locked in middle Europe. In her *otherness*—a concept Gifford himself had introduced me to, as it happened. Was he *really* across town at the lido with Fucker and Gurgly, as she claimed each time we lay in her bed? Or might he burst in on us any minute now, and was that part of her plan—or was he right next door in the kids' room, listening with a stopwatch and his cellphone up against the wall—would they get together after I'd gone, Lára and him,[153] and compare notes?

Paprika, it might've been paprika, that smell, though that's a bit obvious. Whatever it was I can smell it now, even as I'm writing here in this lavatory cubicle: the smoky smell of a world beginning to change. I can see that now, a little, some of it.

Or am I just imagining all this Twilight of the Gods stuff, am I making it all up? Little enough at the time to tell us our boat might rock till the moment when, slowly at first then quicker then quickly, we all began to tumble out of it. Any rumours that did pop up became mixed in with the other tittle-tattle that makes a university day—the gossip, the rumour-mongering, the back-stabbing and betrayal that make the humanities human.[154]

For decades, successive governments had been threatening to do something about tertiary education, so that when a new lot

153 'he'.
154 This can't possibly be original to him—who's he quoting here?

arrived in office, indignant lefties blurred by years of opposition, no one took much notice. There was to be an audit of publicly funded institutions by some *international services provider* or other, it was said: no one was sure which one or whether all tertiary institutions were to be targeted or some, and, if some, which—*so what*, we told one another: hadn't we survived a dozen audits like that?—*come and get us!* Then, another change in the wind: only selected universities and polytechnics might close. We'd heard *that* one before, too, and laughed all the way to one or another of those forty-two pubs that lay around our comfortable, leafy little townsite college campus. *Bring it on!* we cried, half-pissed or worse. *Make our day!*

Time went by: Armageddon went in and out of focus, and in again and out again and in again once more. The century turned, the buzz of rumour became part of our lives, part of the static that went with being an academic: they say, they say, heard the latest? All polytechs and none of the universities were closing; all universities and none of the polytechs were closing; some departments were closing; some individuals were going in some of the departments; all staff above fifty were going; all staff under forty were going; staff between forty and fifty were the ones for the chop—no; it was the arts faculties that were closing down across the country after all—as if!—or, a month or two later, only the arts faculties were to survive, turned into stand-alone liberal arts colleges like our very own—no no no, that was wrong: the universities were to be brought together, that was it, they were to be merged with the polytechs; the country would have one big, titanic university, interconnected like a lunar colony and wired up as a smart city of course of course, ready for interstellar travel and more. Tomorrow, the future, tomorrow, the stars—

*

Enter, with these words, our new vice-chancellor, Norman Iggo's replacement, known from the first, and inevitably, as *Super-Iggo*. I've forgotten his actual name if I ever knew it, and no one I've asked since has been able to *assist me on this matter*—as Super-Iggo himself would undoubtedly have put it, through *one spokesperson* and preferably *more by an order of magnitude*.[155]

But his name didn't matter: he was eager, optimistic, outgoing, *clean*—clean as if he'd just been broken out of his packaging and assembled with Loctite model-airplane adhesive. A fine spray held his steel-grey hair in a standard managerial cut, as we came to understand these things: carefully dishevelled but only just, as if ruffled by a single breath of wind and no more. A curious, bronzed, humectant[156] quality to his skin, presidential teeth; a series of weightless business suits, perfectly cut and all of them dark except for a double-breasted ensemble in cream linen which he wore with a grave, calculated irony to those more casual events, barbecues and so on, that involved students and junior staff: the only things missing were boater and cane. Each day, a fresh tie in solemn blue or black, or the gaudy devil-may-care rag that went with the creamy-white outfit together with boat shoes or brogues. At those times his shirt cuffs, normally exposed a precise two centimetres beyond his jacket sleeves, were folded back exactly three times up each smoothed forearm, neat as napkins; his jacket was off and held behind him over one shoulder with a single finger through its tag to chime with the rolled cuffs in representing (we decided) informality—or, as we began, step by step, to understand it, 'informality'. I yearned to plunge my face into the vanilla ice cream of his shirtfront.

155 Meaning, in this case, multiplied by ten. Why can't he say that?
156 What's this? Meaning that it retains moisture; but what is the use of this *recherché* word meant to achieve? Are we meant to be impressed by this?

He came, this Super-Iggo, from some enormous North-American mega-college, New Orleans or New Mexico or New Brunswick and who cares? Whichever it was, we soon began to understand that in some curious way which challenged ontology and phenomenology alike[157] he was still back there, that his mind had not accompanied his body in his long, long plane trip across the Pacific, the sun never setting before him as in-flight breakfast followed in-flight breakfast till backward reeled the mind.[158] At his welcome reception someone described him as a *change agent*, and this went around the entire university in minutes. It was the first time any of us had heard the phrase: touchingly, naively, no one had the slightest idea what it meant.

That day, this Super-Iggo outlined for us his *vision going forward*—the first time I'd heard that phrase, too, the first of the drip-drip of the strange foreign language—as much an invention as Newspeak and Nadsat and Klingon, Gifford told me—that would soon drown so much of our native English and then our way of thinking, and, in the end, all that was left of our minds. We listened as he told us of the university he intended to create, a *cyber-smart campus* teeming with foreign students, the sons of sheikhs and the daughters of Asian magnates sitting in *cyber-cafés* plugged into an *increasingly wired-up world* in an *increasingly wired-up solar system*. Friends! Colleagues! Scholar-managers! he cried, with passion, in his *outro*, as he called it, presumably because it was at the other end of his speech from his *intro*.[159]

And the first time he said that, his words took me for a moment, caught me off-guard—I felt them lift me suddenly as

157 There he goes again. Just words.
158 Filched from Wolcott Gibbs this time, talking about the early *Time* magazine: 'Backward ran sentences until reeled the mind.'
159 'Outro' originates in music performance, evidently, possibly in rock music.

if I were quitting the world forever, rising into the mesosphere in which Super-Iggo seemed to live and onto the slowly turning world of that cycle-wheel space station in *2001: A Space Odyssey*, Richard Strauss Friedrich Nietzsche *Thus Spake Zarathustra* and all:[160] weightless, spinning, slowly and majestically, just for a few moments, a few seconds, even; and then my toes bumped back down to the lino once more and, softly, my heels, and I was restored to myself, gently, gram by gram, as in the newly refurbished Registry *elevator* that so recently had been no more than a *lift*. What was it, what had this Super-Iggo just said— what was the thing he'd just told us, the secret he'd just shared as if we were all of us his closest friends? I felt as if I'd woken from a dream, with nothing remaining that was solid, nothing to hold on to, but with all that *yearning* left over for whatever it was that might once have been and still could be. I'd felt so *good* up there, so *right*, so *whole*; but I had no idea where I'd just been taken. Heaven, it'd felt like a kind of heaven—like a huge, glittering mall that had no end, where you might shop till you drop and then rise to shop a little more.

I began to follow him around, to experience the passing festival of his clothing, to see the blur of personal assistants and brown-nosers hovering around him wherever he went like a haze of midges, to watch his lustre increasing as he moved further away from me—with each pace more charismatic, glistening more with presence, his talk packed more with knowledge and wisdom, his voice a buttery baritone reeling off facts, figures, *data*. He radiated power and presence, he was *in the moment*—he *made* the moment: *he was reality itself*. Fully

160 See footnote 87 above; here, a reference to Nietzsche's *Also sprach Zarathustra* (1883–91), itself much referenced in Stanley Kubrick's messianic movie *2001: A Space Odyssey* (1968).

mediated onscreen, we found when the time came, he was truly, truly the *Big Swinging Dick*.[161]

Even in small groups he was much the same, his words as ravishing as ever, his language always turning into something else even as he spoke it, a thing that had no name. I became dazed, bewitched, entranced: *more*, I wanted *more*. I listened to him speaking to a group of engineers in one of those touching 1970s buildings of the main campus, poured concrete and dark wood and copper detailing and so on, parts of an heroic idea of the future caught forever in the past.[162] And even *they* seemed entranced, these practical unimaginative folk sitting in their khaki walkshorts, their ankle-socks inside their roman sandals and their plastic lunch boxes on their knees: even *they* seemed captured by the magic of this man and his talk. He held their attention so utterly he could have been the Vampire jet engine[163] rumoured to be bolted to the floor of the Mechanical Engineering department, or a Pratt truss on a bridge[164]—or even a box of Meccano.[165]

This was just *made* for me, this was *my* kind of world; I realised I'd been waiting for this all my life. *This guy was talking my kind of shit.* 'I've never heard anyone like this,' I told Sally. 'You've got to hear him.' And along she came to an address he made in the Town Hall, part of a *conversazione*, whatever that was; and as we sat there and listened I could feel her scepticism melting away—from *Sally*, even from sceptical social scientist *Sally*—

---

161 Alas. Alas. Sometimes, in this novel, the worlds of Shakespeare, Milton, Tennyson *et al.* seem far, far away.
162 This phrase is stolen, obviously—it can't be his.
163 In fact, the de Havilland Goblin turbojet engine.
164 Much work on Google evident here.
165 A child's assembly toy invented in England. Not to be confused with Erector, also by Meccano but more suitable for teenagers.

Late that evening we discussed this Super-Iggo, excitedly, at the kitchen table in the shambolic kitchen of Parsifal Oates (*Stamped Out: The Loss of a Print Culture*, New Haven 1996) and his wife Irina (*Stalin at the Easel: Original Oil Paintings 1922–30*, New York 1992), both of them art historians, both of them on leave in Kiev for six months, and whose house was in our care. I'd taken to smoking a pipe—we'd talked it through, Sally and I, and it felt right, transgressive but not threatening.[166] I stalked about, reinforcing my points with the pipe-stem *jab-jab-jab* and feeling more real than I had in years, and excited, too, as if I were in a movie I was watching at the same time I was acting in it. That brow of mine, furrowed while Sally had her say; my riposte when she was done—crisp, articulate, informed, gender-sensitive; that posture I found my body had struck when delivering it—leaning forward but not aggressively, ready to make the pipe-jabbing gesture once again to reinforce whatever it was that might have passed as the point I was trying to make, assuming that I had a point to make at all.

By now Sally was no longer a tutor in the Department of Sociology but, somehow, working part-time in the advertising section of a local television network while she completed a new project back at home she told me she wasn't ready to tell me about. Super-Iggo lifted us up together, though. We'd no idea what we were talking about, but that didn't matter. More and more it was going to be just words from now on, we both knew that.

'It's like he can see into the future, it's like he's—'

'Yes!—*yes*! Like he's got there before the *rest* of us—'

'Before the whole *world*, the entire fucking *planet*—'

'And when he reels off those figures like that—'

---

166 Straight out of Don DeLillo, *White Noise* (Viking Press 1985).

'I *know*! I *know*! And then he flicked onto those *pie-charts*!'

'I mean, how can he—'

'I *know*! I *know*!'

'*Change*, he's talking about *change*—'

'He's talking about changes, too.'

'That's the same thing. It's the—'

'No, it's different, *changes* means something else. *Change* is something that's always going to happen in the future. *Change* is good. It doesn't mean anything. It's just general. *Changes* is bad.'

'Why?'

'Because *changes* happen *now*. In the *present*. To *people*. *Change* is always *about* to happen but it never does. That's why it's good. We need *change*.'

'You're *right*! Change is crucial—'

'But we don't need changes—'

'No. No. We don't.'

'I don't think he's mentioned changes yet.'

'No. Just change. Right.'

'Right.'[167]

We were really becoming a couple, the two of us, you can see that, we were able to spend *time together and time apart* because we were *growing more and more* of our *composite self*. That, at any rate, was what Sally explained to me in weekly sessions in which we discussed where each of us thought we'd got to as a couple at that point. 'It happens in any successful relationship,' she told me. 'Any relationship is an organism, it grows. It

---

167 Much of this scene is a poor imitation of an exchange in Richard Yates's novel *Revolutionary Road* (1961)—from quite early in the book, so quite conceivably glimpsed by our man in passing.

mustn't be over-watered, it has to be nursed along.' She even drew a Venn diagram headed *Our Ongoing Relationship*, our version of a pie-chart, with a SALLY circle and a TOM circle. The part where the circles overlapped she labelled US. 'Look!' she said, and drew some more circles that showed US getting bigger and bigger and the other two, the SALLY and the TOM, fading away to nothing. 'That's our US, moving forward!'[168]

I stared down uneasily at US travelling irreversibly across her page, left to right, hand in hand, remorselessly becoming a WE. Time together and time apart. Best friends for life. Enjoying each other's differences. You're either in or you're out. *Commitment*—yes!—crucial, of course, to any healthy relationship, that and any of these words; crucial, quite possibly, even to the very core of it. I'd heard about this.

The thing that worried me, of course, was the SHE that was missing from the Venn diagram, and the fact that (as even I was beginning to see) SHE wasn't really missing at all. SHE was at the heart of everything—Lára, I mean, Lára Gifford and whatever else I had going on behind the scenes at the time to keep my spirits up. Even those crude service-station hot dogs I stuffed down myself four or five evenings a week—the stale bun, the severed-member saveloy, the squeeze of mustard and the dash of tomato sauce, all of which I consumed, furtively, gobbling, hood up, crouched against the wind and the rain on the service-station forecourt—*bring it on!*—even they were part of what helped me return to Sally each time I did and climb into her Venn diagram once more, to continue our shared march across the pie-chart to whatever moment of cold fusion lay ahead. It was part of what made me clutch her to myself at

168 Not to be confused with going forward, which implies not necessarily a plan or a purpose but simply the passage of time.

night as if I would *never let her go*, it was part of what made me *really, really need her*. And I understood none of it. *Oh, God, please don't let her go away*—which woman was I saying that to at any given point? Which one of many, to tell the truth?

Here's Lára-and-me in the middle of a day, with Gifford off teaching an Honours class on (possibly) HD and EP, and Sally in town stabilising the advertising breaks in the evening's programme, which was where she'd got to in her television career.

'There.' Lára, pointing across her bedroom.

Up *there*? She couldn't really mean it, could she?

Here she was now, scrambling across the room to the cupboard, pulling things down from it—a great tumble of stacked pillows and cushions, now a mighty crash of the cardboard box that came down with them. Computer parts all over the floor, a packet of lightbulbs, batteries rolling around her feet: her lithe swimmer's body, the muscles at play in her back.

'There?'

'Up *there*—?'

Mad, she was mad. Sex and danger—I was beginning to work it out: the terrifying combo that explained what happened in those places she'd started taking me once we'd left motels behind. The cupboard top was beyond us that first afternoon in her bedroom but it was nothing compared to the terror of what she unfolded for me from there—the stab-in-the-guts every time a car slowed or stopped outside her house, every time someone knocked on the door of my office at work once she'd talked me into trying it there—oh, and that ten-minute break in a lecture room after one class had gone out and before the next came in, oh, God, the horror of that! *I could lose my fucking job*, I kept thinking as we clutched at each other in the corner cupboard I'd persuaded her into once I heard students coming down the corridor for the next class. And, then, the fifty-minute wait in there, crouched half-naked in the darkness, listening to the halting, shuffling lecture on the other side of the cupboard door, on *forewash and swash zone processes on local beaches*. Lára, all the time holding on invisibly to my *pénisz*, as she'd told me it was called back in *Magyarország*, which she'd told me was the Hungarian name for Hungary. *Fogaskerék*, she giggled, and waggled my Woodrow Wilson[169] about in her fist—'gear-lever', apparently. *Shhhh*, I hissed at her, and I could hear her tittering back, *t-t-t-t*. *How did we not get caught, how did I not get fired?*

Oh, and there was worse to come, far worse, once we were out of the cupboard and I could see that triangular sharp beautiful face again, those green eyes staring back at me—*just the wrong colour*: bright red, they should have been, they should have said *STOP!* But instead they were green and said to me *GO*, and I did, on and on, to the end, the terrible end.

On the other hand, Sally-and-me, any early evening during these times: in the supermarket, me behind the trolley, head back, spine straight, buttocks lightly clenched, pushing after her cautiously as she guided us down the aisles with one fingertip on the front rail of the cart, expertly steering us among other couples equally aware of the need to shop without damaging the environment. Or me, coming up the driveway of whichever away-on-leave colleague's home we were babysitting at the time, my heart beating almost through my shirtfront at the thought of being with her again. Sally, the love of my life. Was she? Was this love at last? Walking together in the park hand-in-hand, kicking

169 Woodrow Wilson (1856–1924), 28th president of the United States. Involved America in the Great War, Versailles, the League of Nations, etc. His connection with the narrator's penis is unclear.

our way through the fallen autumn leaves, oak and sycamore, beech, talking about the things that mattered—my job, her job, the state of the world. And all the time she was writing, writing, and smiling up at me whenever I passed. What was it, what was it about? Long, long afterwards I came to see the truth. This was her service-station hot dog. The secret thing that kept her going.

Somewhere, somehow, I knew what I was doing. I was bonking Lára to get a distance on screwing the air hostess, who I'd bonked to get a distance on Sally. Now I needed to get a distance on Lára. So I rang the air hostess again; and *boy*, was that a dumb move. I still don't know what part of it I got wrong! I'd taken a gamble and called her Chantelle—was that it, had I got that right? I was sure it'd come back to me at last, I was sure that was her name. Or was it calling her *darling* that—well, *screwed the pooch*, as Manatine used to say? This was a little way into the conversation, when I was trying to, you know, salvage the call. I just didn't know what'd got into her, still don't—she was like a different person! *Using* you? I asked her, when we'd got to the bitter-recrimination stage. *In exactly what way am I using you?*— but it was no good, there was no getting any sense from her. In the end I hung up in case she was about to hang up on me. You know the drill, you know how it goes—high school stuff. Feeble.

I'm not particularly proud of any of this, by the way. In case you were wondering.

⋙⋘

I'm working my duster through the shelves beneath Bevan's THOUGHT-PROVOKERS sign and here's *Seven Types of Ambiguity* again. I pick it up and flick-flick that leather cover. Calfskin?

'Buckram,' Bevan says when I show him, and rubs the cover with his sleeve. 'With something else mixed in to stiffen it up. Books haven't been bound in calf for years—if you want something animal you'd have to go back to—I don't know— one of the Waverley novels.'

He points to shelves labelled, disastrously, TALES OF DERRING-DO. *The Heart of Midlothian. Peveril of the Peak. Quentin Durward.* I bring *Rob Roy* back for him. He opens it: 'I was a kid when I read this the first time, couldn't put it down.' He wipes a palm across a page. 'There you go. Vellum. Calfskin.'

I stare at the thing. *Calfskin*—

'Of course it could be a pig or a goat, they used anything back then and called it calfskin.'

All this in my ear and I'm just staring at the page. Why didn't I think about this sort of thing before? *We're saving lives*, I can remember Bevan saying when we were pushing the books across the quadrangle.

And all the time, the question of where we're going to keep these *not-quite-dead-things* while they're still alive? All those books, piles of them in Bevan's storeroom by now, and behind the display area, too, and out in the foyer. I'm beginning to smell their special smell every time I go around the shop with the feather duster: the smell of rescued books. All the time scratching my hands, my wrists too and up my arms.

I show Bevan. He's got a cold in his head again, just slight but you can tell by his eyes, or maybe it's just the same old cold he had the week before. I raise my hands and wrists to him like a man in handcuffs: look! And he holds his up the same way: look!—red like mine, and scratched.

'*Snap!*' he says.[170]

He means the books, of course. My doctor tells me so, when I go to see him. 'What's your line of work,' he asks me, and when I tell him I'm a rare-books recycling consultative engineer he says, 'Well, there you are, case closed.' He gives me a hydrocortisone ointment with steroids and that takes the itch away, some of it, but it doesn't stop much of anything else. If anything, the rash gets worse. *Scratch scratch scratch. Scratch scratch scratch.*

I show Bevan. 'It's off the books. The doctor told me. He said wear gloves.'

'And a mask.' He's blowing his nose again. 'We'll both have to take precautions, by the look of it.' His cold's got worse, except it isn't a cold, of course, I'm starting to realise that by now.

After he's gone, a book falls off the pile. *The Road*. Cormac McCarthy. I kick it across the floor. The dustjacket comes off. I kick that across the floor, too. It tears.

170 A children's card game suitable for family entertainment and mentioned here, presumably, in reference to the delighted cry made when players discover identical cards in their respective hands.

Chapter 12

Another week and the smell gets worse. That wymmin from upstairs is the first to complain. Know anything about these? she asks one day, while I'm smoking yet another *Ultima Sigaretta* on the front steps. *They're stinking the place out.* Like the books were animals and came here to shelter and mate and bite, and poop in corners. A few days later she clumps past again. 'Oh, by the way, you'll be getting a letter from upstairs in the next couple of days,' she calls out, and lurches up the staircase. 'Cease and desist,' she calls back at me, with a look that somewhat chills the soul. She's got a backside on her like a steer.[171]

I tell Bevan. 'Cease and desist?' He's over in the corner, where I used to sit back in the day, a lordly young tutor with thick dark hair that fell forward over one eye, peek-a-boo. 'Sounds serious.' Flicking the duster and adjusting each book, lining it up with the next as if it matters, as if the whole doomed, stuffy venture matters.

Later that week, here's an envelope under the bookshop door. Bevan opens it and stands there with the feather duster over his shoulder and the letter almost at the tip of his nose.

---

171 Despicable. Here, somehow, he manages to offend two completely different interest groups: first, those of the fuller figure; and, second, vegans the world over (whose figures tend on the whole to be somewhat less full).

Then he hands it over to me. Fancy letterhead, name and so on—they're almost always called Richard or Richards, have you noticed that about lawyers? This one's called Robin Richards.

'Cease and desist,' Bevan says. 'They've got a cheek. It says, "following complaints from the building's tenants."'

Together we walk out to the foyer. It's obvious who's behind this. She's been going round knocking on doors, stirring people up.

'Well, there's no more room in the shop.'

'I *know* that.' He's peering at the pile of books. 'Some of them are gone. Don't you think?' A couple of Patrick Whites've gone? *The Tree of Man* and—'

'*Riders in the Chariot*.' He's right, I know that because I stopped and read a few pages of that very book the other day, just the start, of course, and I remember being stunned by the description of the run-down house and the lonely woman who'd been brought up in it and how it was collapsing. So *significant*, so *meaningful*.

Meanwhile Bevan's backing off to get a better view of the pile. 'Four or five dozen,' he says. 'Gone since last night.'

He's probably right. The Patrick Whites definitely, though. Apart from him, at least a couple of hundred others, and the same the next day, when we check the book-stack again: definitely smaller. We stand there by the pile.

'Couple of hundred this time. More.'

The wymmin—the former wymmin. She's got a key same as us, she must've been in after we closed the shop on Saturday afternoon—I can see it happening, a group of them, hurrying armfuls of books and dropping them into—what? Into whatever it was, and scurrying back for more. I can see them doing it.

And Super-Iggo?—well, we simply couldn't get enough of him. We drank him in, each of us, any of us, all of us, till we made no further sense. Wherever I went the talk was of this new wonder, what he'd just said or was said to have said or was about to say, what he wore while he was saying it, which of his retinue was with him when he did and which of them wasn't and why, and whether any of this might *mean* something, might add up to something really big as it was sure to, *bound* to—wasn't it? We were besotted, we were smitten, we were hypnotised; we were, every one of us, in love.

Soon, a class of soothsayers emerged from amongst us: interpreters, translators, village explainers,[172] people who claimed to have spoken to the great man or to have heard him speak or spoken to people who'd heard him and thus were *on the inside* and *in the know*—people who told us what he'd really meant whenever he paused, whenever he paused and smiled, whenever he smiled but failed to pause or paused but failed to smile. They explained for us the semiotics of his daily wardrobe. Later, one of them explained to me what *semiotics* meant.[173]

Then: *The Quinquennium, he's thinking ahead to the Quinquennium*—I can't remember which of these sages came up with this, the first insider tip that went around, but I can remember the man's firm common-room nod through the oily

172 Gertrude Stein's phrase, describing Ezra Pound. Our narrator seems to have a number of brief phrases like this which he's memorised from things overheard, not so much for the purposes of this book as to bluff his way through academic life—a common practice in universities throughout the world, I expect.

173 The science of signs—of anything that communicates meaning. In this case, the white suit and what it might signify.

vapour from his coffee cup. Of *course—of course!* The words ran around the place: the Quinquennium! The great man was preparing for the Quinquennium! Quick, we needed to get our ducks in a row for—

What in the name of God was a quinquennium?

A five-year planning period with a rolling horizon, someone said, Reg Pye it was, from Theatre and Film—another of these sages thrown up by the Moment, one of these insiders we gathered around and listened to, rapt, whenever he began, gravely, to speak. Back in my office I wrote those words down, *quinquennium* and *rolling horizon*. After a moment of reflection, I wrote *rolling five-year horizon* and felt a tingle of excitement in my chest as I did. That phrase was *mine*! *I* owned it![174]

Rolling five-year horizon—

There was something for me here, I began to sense that, something in the new world this Super-Iggo had brought with him that I could sense conspiring itself towards me, around me, something I instinctively half understood. *The power of words detached from meaning*—or in the *process* of detaching, perhaps, while they still had a fly-dirt smear of meaning left in them, still with possibility but also the beginnings of instability, too, the opening chords to a true, glorious emptiness. I began to list them as I heard them, these words and phrases that'd started up around me, those moments (especially) when Super-Iggo spoke and by speaking took us to the places he took us to. He was a *poet*, that was the thing to remember, the man was a *poet*. I understood this of him from the moment someone

174 In fact, he's as deluded as ever—it's a commonly used expression which goes back to the Early Management Period, itself part of what has been argued to be a second phase in the evolution of the theory of management. See Rita Gunther McGrath, 'Management's Three Eras: A Brief History', *Harvard Business Review*, https://hbr.org.

[211]

else pointed it out to me—Justin Beadsman, it was, one of our recent appointments, who told us he'd been through this sort of thing *back at home*. It's like listening to Shelley, this Beadsman said. That's what you've got to think of, that's how you've got to see him. As a poet, he meant, a poet speaking the language of the new world he was opening up to us—the new universe, as it seemed to be. Thrilling times, thrilling times. *Lord*, they were magnificent; *God*, they were sublime.

Quinquennium. Rolling horizon.

Rolling five-year horizon—

Houston, though, had a different take. He, too, had seen it all before; back stateside, he told us during one of our card evenings. Our host that night was Vernon Plummer from Civil Engineering, whose wife refused to acknowledge us when we came in, four men she'd never met before, and *slammed* drawers and cupboards in the kitchen all the time we sat in the living room being flensed at the baize. After each round Houston raked coins towards himself like a croupier, all the time with (of course) a poker face.

Naturally, it was Super-Iggo we talked about through all this. He'd just called a *whole-house meeting for the end of the week*—what did this mean, what did it portend? *Whole-house*: another of his phrases, seductive, professional, alluring, not quite meaningless but moving away from meaning without yet leaving it entirely behind. *Whole-house, wholemeal, in-house, out-house, full house—whorehouse*, even. They were all in there, rattling about, full of echoes. Yes, poetry, a sort of poetry!

When he'd filled his pockets Houston stood, abruptly. A couple of coins bounced down his front to the floor; he kicked one of his Redneck Rivieras at them.

'Come on out.'

We followed him into the *yard*, as he called it. The Plummer family washing hung inert, eloquent, in the darkness, on a rotary clothesline with pale wooden arms—an image from de Chirico, perhaps, or even early-mid-period Picasso.[175]

Houston pointed past this and up to the laden skies.

'What? What?'

We all stared: van Gogh stars dripped from the firmament. Houston's forefinger stayed fixed on one point in them, past the despairing dangle of a laundered athletic support.

'What?'

'Hale–Bopp. Remember him?'

'Hale–Bopp? That's a while ago, Zac.'

'What the hell is this? What are we talking about?' Ray Densem from Forestry, a man forever in walkshorts, even on a chilly night like this. 'Why're you showing us this, Chet?'

Houston kept pointing. 'See him up there?'

'Who?'

'Hale–Bopp. He's still up there.'

'Hale–Bopp was the comet, wasn't it?' Murray Chote, a crystallographer from Chemistry, his hands dug deep in his pockets and his fingers jingling his car keys. He was looking around us, uneasily, while I kept staring at *the starry heavens above me*, as Kant would have it.[176]

---

175 Journeyman bullshit here rather than bluff-work, requiring no more than one of our man's 'deep skims' through Google, etc. Note the attempts to simulate genuine bluff-work, though, with the use of 'perhaps' and 'early mid-period', symptomatic bluff-work codes to imply greater background knowledge than is actually possessed. Giorgio de Chirico (1888–1978), Italian; Pablo Picasso (1881–1973), Spanish. Ignore.

176 Good Lord!—is he pretending to have read *Critique of Pure Reason* (1781) now? '[T]he starry heavens above me and the moral law within me' is the original phrase. Wikipedia—the only explanation for this man's

'That's what this is all about.' Still portentous, Houston, still pointing upward with his spare hand.

I took a shot up his arm. The stars, doing their star thing. What was the man getting at?

A moment, just a moment of unease as we all stared up beside the washing—well, for me, certainly. What *was* the man pointing at? Then, behind us, a muffled, furtive flatulism. Chote, I think—yes, Chote. Bloody scientists.

Houston's Hale–Bopp thing stayed with me. It made me go outside a couple of evenings later in the week—alone, which didn't help. A little cloudy the first time and a little breezy the second: but, both times, there were the stars, winking down at me.[177] Nothing much to it, except that the second time I was out there and just as I was turning to go back in, I saw something—a movement, a tiny blink in the darkness, barely a smudge, and then it was gone.

Did I? Was it?

He'd certainly put something into my mind. I went back indoors and checked out this Hale–Bopp thing of his online and the whole crazy business that attached to it, the death-cult that went up to the spacecraft behind the comet and so on— remember?[178]

---

improbable erudition. Hard to tell whether the tone of this piece ('as Kant would have it' etc) is ironic or not, but, whichever it is, here's an excellent example of everyday academic bluff-work, tossed off and left behind at pace. Immanuel Kant (1724–1804). German. Ignore.

177 Oh dear, oh dear—and a sentence or two later he's talking about creative writing! As bad as the stars 'dripping from the firmament' a page earlier.

178 The Hale–Bopp comet, named for its discoverers, passed by Earth in 1997 and gained added attention when thirty-nine members of the

I became intrigued. I took to sitting in on Houston's lectures, which seemed to be helping considerably with the departmental SSR problem Riordan had told me about. This time, the quarter-filled lecture room of my first glimpse of Houston teaching was crammed to the walls, the usual oafish figures now rebranded,[179] apparently, as clients.[180]

'UFOs?' Sally demanded that evening, when I told her. 'How is that creative writing?'

'Well, it's not all UFOs. Sometimes he talks about the Kennedy assassination—'

'Oh, for God's sake!'

'Imagination, he's developing their imaginations—'

That's what Houston had told me when I asked the same question. No writing at all required in his half of the course—part of its attractiveness to our young scholars, no doubt. I tried to keep the writing demands down in my half, too, to encourage oracy,[181] which he told me about and which sounded full of pedagogical promise. More and more I found myself grading students on pure attendance—participation is so important, after all. Soon, I was requiring just a single creative work from these *clients* for a pass, and found myself pleasantly surprised by what some of them came up with. The best by far was a story about a clerk in a legal office who suddenly shuts down and tells his boss

---

Heaven's Gate cult, based in California, used phenobarbital to commit suicide *en masse* in order to pass, disembodied, to a spacecraft they believed to be following the comet, where they expected to enter a higher level of consciousness. Of course, our man gets this jumbled up here and again when he mentions it a few pages further on.

179 'Rebranded'—sad, sad.

180 Ugh.

181 A term devised in Britain during the 1960s to formalise and simulate control of ongoing and uncontrollable classroom noise.

no, he'd prefer not to—not to do the work he's just been handed, in other words, and not to do anything afterwards, either—and he ends up in jail! A brilliant, enigmatic piece far beyond the student's years.[182] 'I'd prefer not to'—the words stayed with me. I gave him a very high mark, of course, to distinguish it from the fairly high marks I'd given other students.

Staff–student Ratio. Rebranded. Clients.

Oracy.

Rolling five-year horizon—

As for me-and-Sally—well, things had moved on, as you might have detected from our brief exchange above. She was less patient with my workplace anecdotes, I'd noticed that: *Get a life* was a phrase she used more frequently, and after a while *Get into the real world, for God's sake!* There were a couple of others as well. These days she flew north each Friday morning, achingly early, and early each following Monday she'd return after a weekend at Viscera Television: suddenly, she was training as a production assistant for current affairs. She did other things, too, which she told me about each Monday evening, excitedly, but to be honest I didn't really listen. These days there was only one thing I wanted of her once she was back. I'd listen to her rattling on about her weekend, I'd watch her rippling her fingertips at the keyboard of that laptop of hers with a pencil clamped between her jaws, I'd wait while she did her kitchen stuff and her bathroom stuff and doused our lights one by one—and, then, here it was, here she was: Sally in my arms again, in the sack, and *me* anchored to *her* once more. To her Sally-smell, to the Sallyness of her body. *Mmmm . . .*

---

182 He really hasn't read a lot, our man, has he? See also Thomas Berger, *Vital Parts* (1970).

I knew in my dumb oink-oink way that *that* was what all this was about, *that* was what I needed of her: those strong, predictable limbs, that shadowless response to a world which seemed to me increasingly out to stuff one up. Familiarity, predictability—stolidity, almost; and, as much as anything else, her sensible, no-nonsense approach to the Act of Darkness itself, her methodical response to the gloomy panting waddle-and-crump of everyday common-or-garden bonking. Always different, always the same.

As I lay beside her in the recovery position one night, she started fiddling with my face. I was talking to her, at her—about Super-Iggo, of course, but also about an audit of departmental floor space recently announced. Three men like triplets with smartphones had turned up and demanded to see our departmental library. Departmental library? What was that? Did we have one? We ran from office to office, all of us, as these earnest, interchangeable young men used a sort of electronic pistol to measure our corridor for length width height. Then—

I stopped. What was Sally doing with my face?

She was staring down at me with her mouth open. I could see a little harp-string of saliva down there at the back, near her uvula, a word I always feel unsure of. 'I wondered how you'd look with your nose slightly across, that's all.'

'You weren't listening—'

'Yes I was!—*departmental-library-just-your-photocopying-room-measured-it-anyway.*' All this with a finger on my nose as if about to move Queen to d4.

'But the photocopying room's full of *junk*, we store stuff there we don't know what to *do* with—'

'Mm—'

'It's the size of a toilet cubicle—'

'Mm—'

'—and they're charging us for it, we have to actually *pay* for our own *space.*'

'Standard managerial practice, they charge for use now.' Another push at the side of my nose. 'It's just a little bit off-centre, that's the thing. Your nose. I've always thought if I could just—'

'Aah!' Me, pulling away, sitting up. 'What are you—'

Sally, kneeling next to me, peering at my face, reaching out again. 'Stay still.'

'Are you serious?'

'It's one of the tricks I learned up there. At Viscera. Key showed me when she was doing my hair.' She'd tried out in front of the camera, that was the other thing, and now she was *making her move*, as they say in careers. *Key* was what they called the makeup person. Fakeup, Sally called it. *Key* did the *fakeup*. More new words.

Key. Fakeup.

Oracy.

Rolling five-year horizon—

Meanwhile, back in my other life, Lára was becoming fascinated with my Woodrow Wilson. 'It's still up when it's down!' she said, crouching over me and fiddling it about. Another time she said, *'Are you my Jewish boy?'* and that rattled me a second or two, rattled me badly, as if she'd opened a door in front of me that had far too much on the other side. Thinking of it terrified me.

Another time after that, she rattled me from another direction. We were lying there after completing what a few moments before had seemed far more important than it had turned out to be; she was gazing at me point blank. Then—

'Poor Tamás, so afraid of yourself, so afraid of women.'

'*I* am?' Even pointing at myself, finger-in-the-chest, in case she didn't know which one I was. '*Me*—?' *Moi*, I almost said *moi* there.

'I know there've been a lot of women but if you weren't afraid of them so much there'd be just the one and she wouldn't be me.'

'Wouldn't be—'

'Just a sad unhappy one. A bastard case.'

'Basket case.'

'*Igen*, yeah, basket case.'

Ersebet Balogh, her maiden name, she told me when I asked; or, in fact, Balogh Ersebet when she was back at home. Eastern name order, surname first, the only European country to do this, she said: back to front as in Asia. Nobody knew where the Hungarians came from, apparently—they weren't like anyone around them; same with their ethnicity, she said, and the language, too. And *Balogh* meant *left-hander*, so she was born back-to-front twice over—wasn't she? I knew what she meant, sort of, but there were times when I didn't, I really didn't.

Was that her or was that me? She'd certainly taken me to some strange places. One of them was a railway walk-through in one of the suburbs—a few feet wide, pedestrians only, with the rails on massive bearers directly above our heads as we waited for the first, distant sound, the premonitory quiver of the rails. Then—there it was, the music we were waiting for, there it was and *here it came, here it came, the terror of it, a thousand tons of metal coming down the track at us, it was closing, it was close, it was closer, it was on us, it*—

All I could remember afterwards was the singing of the rails above our heads as the train went over, and then the shudder of the bolts in the sleepers as if the whole bloody thing was coming apart, engine-carriages-track-and-all. The *noise*, taking away everything, taking away my *me* till it was gone—and then her face below mine, staring up at me as we fumbled and pushed at each other: green-eyed, mad. What were we doing here underneath a train track at three in the afternoon when she was supposed to be picking up Fucker and Gurgly from school? And *I* was supposed to be giving a class in twenty minutes, on *plot, form and narrative method*? Above us, the rails, still singing and humming with the oblique message the train had left behind; beneath them, the two of us, clutching each other, terrified, our hearts bouncing together.

She went on calling me Tamás. I quite liked the acute accent, same as hers, and that rough slub to her voice when she said it, slight but enough to give a special taste to whatever we were doing. It made me feel as if there was a third person present and she was talking to him by talking to me, meaning I could take time off from the tiresome business of being whoever-I-am and feel more finished, more rounded—more whole, even. More like a character in a book or on the screen, you might say. She'd talk about people I didn't know as if I did, and put me in stories that made less and less sense as we went on, as if she was turning me into somebody else. Tamás.

She raised the stakes. The train underpass ritual became more. Now it was night-time and we were up on the track above the underpass, and I was cold and scared as hell. The late train was about to come through and she wanted us to lie there till we felt that first premonitory thrum in the rails that meant the train was on its way, and then we—

Lying there scared shitless, Lára somehow on top of me, the first thrill coming down the rails from a thousand metres off—there—the tremor in the back of my neck, in the metal beneath my calves—was it? She was holding me down, thin, wiry little fists like pipe-grips on my wrists; I couldn't shift her, she had the strength of the insane and there, there, you could hear the fucking train now, it really was—

Then:

Kimerült.

It just came out of me, like a cough or a belch, as we scrambled down the embankment, terrified at ourselves and long before the train got anywhere near. We crouched there as it went rocking and blazing past above our heads—yellow lit windows, I remember, and faces flickering by, bent over iPhones—

Kimerült—

Twice.

I stared down at her. She was staring back up at me, she was lying back in the wet grass at the bottom of the bank. God, I was frightened, I was terrified—

'*Magyarul beszélsz?*'

I nodded a dumb-fuck nod. I had no idea what she was asking me. 'A little.' It was true, though, I was shagged out. What on, wait on, how did I know I'd told her that I was? *Kimerült.* Tired, exhausted. It'd just come out. What was happening?

That night I crouched in front of the bathroom mirror, pushing and pulling at my face. I wasn't shaving so often these days and I looked swarthy, unkempt, a man on the run. She was taking me somewhere, I knew that, I was in the grip of something that was hers. *Are you my Jewish boy?* That was part of it, that was one of the things she was putting in my mind, I knew that. But there was Sally, too, and Houston as well. I moved a hand up to my face, which was starting to look like somebody else's. *Whose, whose—?*

After the Cease and Desist letter I decide to take matters into my own hands—climb the stairs, have it out with the lawyer, that sort of thing. Up there the former-tearoom door's open and in I go with scarcely a tap-tap-tap, kidding myself I'll see Marigold still in there, chewing on her cigarillo, or Basil drinking tea with his little finger out. Instead, of course, a desk and filing cabinets, the usual lawyer stuff, and here's this Robin Richards person—is it? The lawyer?

He looks up at me. Much younger than I expected. 'Can I help?'

'You sent us a letter. Downstairs. The bookshop. Cease and desist.'

'Oh, so we did, so we did. Hold on—' and he puts his head into an open doorway that's cut into the former-tearoom wall about where Borin's portrait used to hang.

I can hear him talking to someone in there, in what used to be Gifford's office.

He turns back and gestures me in. 'Two minutes?' he whispers.

And guess who's behind the desk when I go in—the wymmin! What the hell is *she* doing here—I mean, isn't she meant to be off somewhere sticking pins into wax?

You might be quicker than me on the uptake here, by the way, but I'm not.

'You're one of the wymmin,' I tell her.

'One of the *what*—?'

'Wymmin. The wymmin's group that meets around here. *You* know—you've got a room somewhere but I can't find it?' She's staring at me, just *staring*. 'Large, heavily built women?' Staring, staring. 'You meet and you'—what *do* they do?—I'm gesturing in front of her—'I don't know—stick pins into'—a shrug—'wax models of men's balls?' Another shrug, to end it.

The awful thing is that through all this there's a part of me that's slowly registering what's actually going on here even as the rest of me is travelling, as you can see, in the opposite direction. We're passing each other even though both of us are me.

'You're not a wymmin,' I hear my voice telling her into the silence. That's where all this ends up. Oh, Lord.

A pause, as they say in Literary Fiction.

She leans forward, her hands at prayer.

'A number of the tenants of this building agree that your book dump is cluttering and befouling the non-rental area downstairs.' A measured, soulless voice that can mean only one thing: death itself. 'The landlord of this building agrees it's a nuisance. On the tenants' behalf I've sent you the letter which you've just told me you've received. It's expected that you act on it.' She turns and points to a frame on the wall behind her. 'Oh, and I'm a Barrister and Solicitor of the High Court, by the way. Not a giant lesbian feminist, which is what you seem to be imagining.'

A further pause. It's rather hard to know what to say to this. She's certainly got a point.

She nods towards the door. 'My PA says he can smell you in his office. Your pile of mouldy rubbish. We can smell it up the staircase.'

I'm standing there. You can see the Government Life digital display from her east window. Two o'clock neat. Her PA, is he? Now he's behind me, whispering at her: *Next appointment's here, Robin—*

I leave the room but stop at the outer door, the old tearoom door. 'That's not mouldy rubbish,' I call back to her. 'It's the remains of Western civilisation.' It just pops into my mind as if Bevan's saying it for me. No one's taking any notice, of course; there's just the sound of her PA—Oh, you're *welcome, my pleasure,* do *come in.*

'It's our *heritage,*' I yell back at them.

Her door *snaps* shut, as if upon the knackers.

Chapter 13

At Cathedral Mall again, with Bevan's ridiculous string bag of books banging against my thigh. It's the last thing I can think of to trim our book pile—I tried Books for Africa but the online page was dead. After that Bevan suggested Books for Prisoners and held up *One Hundred Years of Solitude.* He wasn't joking but I didn't realise that till afterwards. Anyway, here I am, trying to give the bloody things away, shoppers drifting past me as if I'm invisible.

Halfway down the nave, though, here's a young woman stopping in front of me, just like that, *boom.* Her face reassembles itself for me: one of my recent students, Tegan, Tayla, something like that. Tyler, that's it.

She's staring at me—she's shocked, you can see that.

'Tom? she whispers. 'Are you all right?'

'Yes! Yes! Fine!'

'Has something happened?'

A minute later it's over and I'm adjusting the string bag. I look up: here's an odd-looking coot in a sock hat, staring back at me over a string bag. *Me*—in a dainty boutique mirror! I pull away: now I'm shoving one of my books in the face of an oncoming ripple of young kids, pre-teens—who simply brush past me. More kids behind them, Asians this time, but they melt around me too and suddenly I'm in the middle of a small family group.

'Try one of these?' I hold the book up—but they walk past me too. The man mutters something as he pushes his horrid little kids ahead of him: *Gave at the office*, no eye contact. A quick look: what've I been offering them?—oh, God: Coleridge and Wordsworth, *Lyrical Ballads*. I'm going to have to do better than that. Muzak throughout all this, Manhattan Sinus: *doo-dah-ah-doo-dah-ah-doo-dah—*

I press on up the nave. Here, in the midst of things, people watch an Asian masseur working thumbs like soup-spoons into the neck and shoulders of a man who sounds like a football being pumped up; after that another crowd gathers around a chap in a white coat who's gloving up at a stall offering free invasive examinations. Beyond them, almost at the transept, more people, in an open cafeteria space with a sign that reads *The Font*; they're milling around, shouting, calling out—and here's poor old Godwin in the middle of them—Godwin Puttock (*The Mortal Afflatus: Flatulence in Catullus' Time*, Madison: UMP 1999), now a second-language teacher and completely out of his depth, perspiring in the ruck of the everyday. He holds up a cup and saucer: 'Everyone got a cup of tea?' Then he spots me and looks away, ashamed, and I look down, ashamed too, for him, for both of us. I move on, my bag of books bumping at my knee with each step.

Dah-dah-de-dah-dah. Xtra Penis?

Suddenly I'm in front of the Han Kin. It's closed: lights off, signs down, chairs on tables. Now, and suddenly, another rowdy mess of the young—teens with their feral blood-smell, their noise, the aggression in them and the fear behind that. I can't stop myself, I've got my hand up and *oh God what am I doing* I'm offering them a rather nicely made volume I'd no idea I'd brought with me—good God, Denton Welch, *In Youth is Pleasure*—

It stops them short. 'What the fuck's this?' One of them grabs the thing and there's a belch of laughter from his mates—

he frisbees the book away, across the mall: Denton Welch, flying high, high in the air to the sounds of Xtra Penis. 'Fuckin' mental!' one of the little pricks calls out, and his mates think that's pretty good, too. And they're off, bumptious little spotty arrogant pricks pushing through shoppers, bustling away, full of themselves, desperate. One of them turns back and jerks a fist in front of his fly. 'Fuckin' pedo!'

Now a couple of cops, strolling towards me, up the mall. 'What you got there, mate?' one of them calls out.

'Books.'

'Got a permit? Need a permit to sell anything along here, mate.' The other copper, looking away, humming along with the muzak.

'I'm not selling them.' The urge to join in, the awareness of it: *Doo-doo-d'dah-daah—*

'You handing out tracts—?'

'Literary books.' It sounds like a perversion.

D'dah-dah-do-doo—

'*Library* books?' The second cop's interested now. He stops humming. 'Givin' away *library* books?'

'Well—yes, they are, they're literary library books—surplus to requirements, that's the thing.' And I try to explain it all to them, the university, the closedown, the cleanout. When I say *the humanities* it sounds like the language of the Ik.[183]

Xtra Penis is finished; Lunar Toilet now. *Bm-bm-bm-bm—*

'Givin' away books?' the first copper. He seems bemused. 'What you want to do that for?'

That question again. What *do* I want to do it for? *Bm-bm-bm-bm—*

'We're preserving our heritage,' I tell him. It sounds terrible

183 Who? Not on Google. Not anywhere. Bluff-work concealing bullshit.

out here in the world, among people, just ridiculous. What can it possibly mean?

'Tell you what you want to do,' the second copper says. 'Swap 'em. Give 'em away.'

'Give them away?'

'They're all round town, mate. Book exchanges. You just dump 'em there and people just take 'em home.'

'Not much free these days,' the first cop says. He's looking around and tapping one bunched fist on top of the other.

'Got a John Grisham there the other day.' The first cop. 'Read him?'

'Yes.' No. Now, though, the second cop's telling me about a fridge. 'Where's this?'

'Four Oaks. Out by the hills. This old bus shelter, got a fridge full of books. That's what y'want to do with 'em. Stick 'em in the fridge.'

Out of nothing, Robert Byng came back into my life. Since his immaculate conception all those years before in the reference section of the university library he'd slowly faded to a ghost. 'Keeping me busy!' I'd say back then, if Basil Shortbread or Clem Bodyrot ran out of anecdotes about C.S. Lewis snubbing them at Magdalen and asked about my research instead; and they'd nod *yes-yes* as if Byng had actually existed. Then older staff began to retire completely, one by one, and of course Postcolonial Pat got his comeuppance at last *thank God*; and as each of them went they took a piece of Byng with them, plus all those lost years when I was refining my bluff, learning to seem, becoming what might be thought, in certain lights, a mature academic. I outlasted them, and got tenure simply by being there. When new, younger colleagues like Amanda Cupmark and Justin Beadsman started to turn up I must have seemed almost as antique as the portraits of Borin and (now) Gotcha Gotch that hung on the tearoom wall. Of *course* I was just plain old *Mr* Flannery, MA, DL,[184] academic warm body—guardian of the departmental refrigerator and that tiny departmental library now we were thought to have one, organiser of the Christmas party quiz and still master of the Gibbonian semicolon! Every academic department in the world had someone like me.

At first, these youngsters asked me for advice—on publication, for example—and I'd tell them what people like Pismire and Gifford had told me years before. 'Try *Notes and Queries*,' I'd say. 'I had something in there a while back on bees in Thomas Hardy.' Just like a real academic—I certainly felt real, just in the moment of saying it, no more. Then one day I overreached myself and recommended the *Tamarack Review* for publication—the name just popped into my mind; I must have seen it somewhere—and Beadsman told me the *Tamarack Review* had closed down twenty years before. More, he said, and stared at me. He kept on staring, far longer than he needed to, I thought; a bit like Travis Bickle in *Taxi Driver*. Oops.

A week or two after this the little prick struck again, *hors du bleu*, as our French friends put it.[185] He got me one morning *sans* breakfast and crouching, mouth crammed, above the biscuit tin in the Charles Edmund Gotch Memorial Common Room as it'd now become.

'Robert Byng?' he asked. 'Remind me who he is?'

---

184 Surely he doesn't mean 'Driving Licence', does he? Used occasionally by job applicants a little light on academic achievement. Shades of the old BA (Failed).

185 As his online translation engine puts it. This man is not multilingual.

For years now, moments like this had been cockpit drill for me: I'd barely had to think. I raised an eyebrow to him. '*Really?*' A meaningful pause as I munched. '*Mirza?*' Munch-munch. 'Out of Denham's *Sophy?*' Munch-munch-munch. 'Out of Jonson's *Cataline?*'[186] Now the other eyebrow up as I swallowed. 'No? *Cataline His Conspiracy*—?'

As good a name-dropping smokescreen as you're likely to see, I'd like to think; but hearing Byng's name again was disconcerting all the same. There was a smart-arsed, undescended-penis quality to this Beadsman. 'If you part your comb-over over any further down,' he told me soon after we met, 'you'll have to start doing it below your ear.' Yes, his disdain had a touch of Daresbury and Cocks about it, but as a different sort of reminder of our colonial place. '*Love* your Great Hall,' he said when we took him through our neo-Gothic fantasy campus on his first day. '*Very* cute, *very* dainty.' And he laughed out loud when we showed him our tearoom-that-thought-itself-a-common-room. 'Beats the Old Common Room back at Balliol!' he told us—yes, Oxford, of *course*, which is why he'd been appointed in the first place. Oxford! Cambridge! I knew no good could come of it, but who'd listen to me?

Now, here we were, in that very tearoom he'd laughed at, with Gotch and Borin gazing pitilessly from their frames on the wall and the same tired Zip boiler in the corner making its ruminative noises, *thrrrp, thrrrp.*

'John Denham,' Beadsman was saying. 'Yes, that topographical stuff, "Cooper's Hill" and so on—that what you mean?'[187]

186 Ben Jonson (1572–1637), English playwright and poet, author of the Jacobean tragedy *Cataline, His Conspiracy* (1611).
187 Sir John Denham (1614/15–1669), Anglo-Irish poet and courtier. 'Cooper's Hill' was his best-known poem, describing what has subsequently become the site of occasionally violent cheese-rolling competitions.

'Quite. Quite.' I could feel myself shifting on my chair.

'Tell me again the Byng connection—? Because he was quite influential, wasn't he, Denham, I mean formally speaking, quite apart from the landscape thing which some say anticipates the Romantics but I don't, not for a minute—'

'Quite so, quite so.'

Thrrrp, from the Zip.

'So, you're saying this Byng fellow was influenced by him—?'

'Quite. Quite.'

'What's the connection?' Staring right at me. Was this another *Tamarack* moment, had he rumbled me again: or was it simply the eagerness of youth? No, he looked like a shit to me.

'Well—the thing about Byng is that he was—influential, he was certainly influential, but he—he—didn't actually write that much.'

'Ah.' Still gazing at me. 'The invisible hand.'

'Quite! His influence was—well, it was so indirect it's more obvious in, you-know'—here I made a weak gesture around a room with almost nothing in it—'what other people wrote.'

I could see Beadsman's eyes narrow when I said this. 'They were influenced by what he *wasn't* writing—?'

'Mm.' Firmly. I pulled myself up a bit in my chair. There was something here, I could sense that, something was forming itself inside the rubbish I was talking.

'Keats?' He leaned forward. 'A sort of negative capability thing?'[188] I could see he was interested. 'So, in effect you *are* arguing for a kind of early romanticism in—what're his dates?

---

188 'Negative capability' describes the argument by the poet John Keats (1795–1821) for a poetic based on instinct, subjectivity and uncertainty rather than logic and planning, a poetic that conjures the sublime.

This Byng fellow?'

What *were* his dates? I shifted about. On the plain bum-polished wood of the seat, I was dancing cheek to cheek.

'*Baromság.*'

It just came out. He *stared* at me.

Thrrrp, from the Zip.

A day later, beneath the railway underpass again, I asked Lára, urgently, what *Baromság* meant.

She stared up at me. 'Bollock,' she said. 'It means bollock.'

'Bollocks? You mean bollocks?'

'*Igen*, yeah, two of them.'

So, I'd been right. I stared back down at her. I'd just said *bollocks* to a junior colleague. In Hungarian.

But it turned out Beadsman didn't seem to mind at all! 'So—*így beszélsz magyarul?*' he said the morning after that, when he caught me breakfasting in the tearoom again. 'Me, too! Picked up a smattering when I was in Pécs, summer before last—know the little college there—?'

'Mm, mm.' My head nodding, my voice thick with chocolate thins.

'Expect you know more than I do—these days I don't read anything not in French or Italian. Now, does this Byng chap have some Hungarian connection, is that it—is that why I haven't been able to track him down?'

This was getting serious. There were others coming into the tearoom now; this could go anywhere. Amanda Cupmark, staring at me, reproachfully.

Thrrrp, from the Zip.

'Because the executive dean's asked me to be your *kifutófiúja*, you see.'

Dogsbody. It meant *dogsbody*, God knows how I knew that but I did. I knew nothing about Robert Byng and the seventeenth century, but I knew, somehow, that *kifutófiúja* meant *dogsbody*—or (it just came to me) *whipping-boy*. I listened, appalled, as this bumptious, self-satisfied young twerp told me Tim had asked him to help me get my Byng conference going at last—for the department, Tim had told him: we needed some PR to show the VC we were RA.[189]

So here he was again, Robert Byng, come back to torment me. What was I to do? I sat there, munching biscuits and watching this little Beadsman prick across my teacup as he talked at me, partly in Hungarian, partly in English. What kind of name was Justin, anyway, what sort of woman would even bother with a man called *Justin*?

Soon after this we had another poker evening—I forget whose house this time—and, in due course, another night-time trip out to somebody's back garden. Just Houston and me this time, side by side in the night and arking mightily onto the unremembered academic's strawberry patch. 'Mary Jane,' he said. 'Does that to ya.' And then, as we were zipping up, he started jabbing a finger into the night sky again and we were back where we'd been at Vernon Plummer's, staring up at the stars.

Nothing. I gazed up, around, about.

Nothing.

Then:

'There.' Pointing, pointing.

'Where?'

'There—'

189 Public Relations; Vice-Chancellor; Research Active.

And this time there was something, I swear it, I saw a *thing* moving quite slowly across the sky and down to the right, just moving but at the same time as if it wasn't moving, either. And not a sound, that was the thing that frightened me most— terrified me. I couldn't move.

Gone in a blink. Was it? What?

We stood there. My heart was going *thump thump thump* so high in my chest it was in my throat. Well, you know what I mean.

'See that? Kind of a fucken disc thing?'

'Yes, but it was more of a flying wing thing, wasn't it? With different coloured lights underneath?'

'Yeah, I seen the lights but, like, more of a disc-type thing—'

'With a winking light underneath? D'you see that—?'

'Don't see no winkin' light, man—'

Had we seen anything at all? The next morning, I drove past the house whose yard we'd stood in and looked for a mark—scorched earth, or a crop circle next to the recycling bins. Something. Anything. Nothing, though, nothing. My heart, still pumping away. Extraterrestrial visitors!

In the next few days, new beings began to appear on our campus. No announcements, no warnings, no explanations, nothing in the media; it was almost as if they'd always been amongst us but we hadn't quite noticed till we came back from our long summer break. And when we did—here they were, inexplicable men and women hurrying around with phones to their ears, each of them far too well-dressed to be an academic let alone a human being. Instead, they wore dark suits like a uniform, charcoal to grey, the women little different from the men, their jackets just as padded at the shoulders, their hair pulled up or cut or tinted a steely gunmetal grey.[190] Who *were* these people? *What were they doing here?* Dozens of them, more, in offices also new and built where a row of teaching rooms had been—hadn't they? Before the summer break? On the ground floor of Old Chemistry, as they seemed to be calling it now, where the Department of Classics had been and Music Performance, too? Or had things always been like this?

'Each college is getting a management hub,' Ray Densem told me—that Forestry chap I met at Vernon Plummer's poker table. 'Science is already started.'

'Since when were we colleges?'

'Over the summer break—where've you been? The entire university's divided up now, six colleges, six executive deans, six of everything. They want a flat structure across the university to duplicate the central administrative structure. Operation Expand, it's called.'

Flat structure.

Operation Expand.

Rolling five-year horizon.

I couldn't believe what Ray was telling me. Six more of *everything*? Six more financial managers, six more school managers, six more HR departments, IT departments, Marketing and Outreach? All with their teams? Janitors? Works and Services? Security?

'What's that going to cost? All those new salaries and offices?'

'Apparently they'll pay for themselves by the end of the Quinquennium.'

Meet you at the Hub—that's what they were being encouraged

190 Straight from Michael Ende's novel *Momo* (1973) (also known as *The Grey Gentlemen* and *The Gentlemen in Grey*).

to say out there on the main campus, he told us. They were trying to establish a new culture in the university, something more professional, more corporate. When I asked who *they* were, he said *the new corporate culture. They're trying to establish it.*

Hi! Drop by the Hub! Have a great day at the Hub!

I *dropped by* our new *College of Arts Hub*, a reception space with adjacent small offices that seemed to have sprung up where an old, tiered lecture theatre had been before the summer break. No sign of that now, and not only no sign of it but no *sign* of any sign of it, either—nothing to show it had ever been there in the first place. Each new office looked slightly, carefully worn, as if it already possessed a tiny past of its own—framed desk-photos of children and grandchildren in one, a pair of oars crossed on the wall of another, in a third a print of a Spitfire flying low above a ploughed field. I said hi to Jan at reception, who showed me how to help myself to coffee using a *state-of-the-art point-of-use direct-vent water-heater* in the *breakout lagoon* and introduced me to the College Office Manager, who was *also* called Jan! You wouldn't believe it!—Jan the First and Jan the Second! Guess which one's which!—and so on; much giddy laughter. Meanwhile, through a glass wall nearby, a team of identical men, bent together in a huddle. They straightened up as one: black T-shirts, MARKETING & OUTREACH! across the front of every one of them.

I watched them as I drank my coffee. A team-bonding session, Jan told me, the first Jan—the receptionist Jan. I asked her whether she remembered the tiered lecture room that had been right here, where this College Hub now stood. 'Tiered lecture room?' she said, and laughed. 'That's going back a bit, isn't it! Before my time!' I asked others: some remembered, some didn't. The more I asked the more it became like the Amber Room as I knew it from those images online—gorgeous, fabulous, out of this world—and the more it seemed it had never really quite existed, as if it was something that should have been, even if it never had.

Super-Iggo's whole-house meetings were held in a vast main-campus lecture theatre called CG17b, like an exoplanet. Here was more of that sense of a break in time, a cosmic hiccup.

'Brown-bag meeting today,' someone told me as I went into the first of these *meets*.

I worked towards the middle of a central row and sat next to Trevor Rostrum from Particle Physics, among five hundred rustling academics.

'What the fuck is a brown-bag meeting?'

He stared. 'Where you been?' He looked at my hands. 'Don't tell me you haven't—'

I crouched down: that caught-out schoolboy WTF panic— here it was, yet again.

'*What? Haven't got what?*'

'A bag of *sammies*.' He *hissed* this at me, looking around. 'A brown bag of *sammies*. Don't tell me—'

I looked around, too, I looked down—I didn't even have a bag!

'We're *brown bagging* it,' he whispered.

'Brown bagging *what*?' I kept my voice down, too. Super-Iggo's people were in but the great man wasn't, not yet; they were setting up a large-screen video presentation.

'Issues,' he whispered. 'We come here each Friday and we brown bag the issues.'

Supper-Iggo's face suddenly bloomed on the screen above the lectern. The image pulled back and there he was, all of him, this time in dark charcoal with a pale blue tie.

'Where is he? Super-Iggo?'

'Manila. He's questing a NoSQL database meet in Manila.'

The Super-Iggo on the big screen had just flung his arms wide like a man in a fishing competition. 'Friends, colleagues, scholar-managers!' he cried—out of sync, like Max Headroom.[191] 'Ask me any questions you like!'

'Can he hear us, though?' This was Parsifal Oates, somewhere along to my left. 'I don't think he can hear us, can he?'

We hushed, we listened. The image onscreen began to outline the issues involved in NoSQL databasing—and as soon as it did I began to feel that familiar lift, that belt in the chest as the words hit and took hold of me once again. *Realtime dashboards, downsize assets, holistic concept, key result areas, deck presentation, fungible goals, rich deliverables, windtunnel possibilities.* Soon, a river of words, engulfing us—and there, *there!*—he'd just said it: *a data river—a data lake!* I looked down, I looked around, I fumbled at my flies in the half-dark, I hoped no one could see what was happening—I was starting to *upsize,* for God's sake—

And just then, he crept into the lecture room—Super-Iggo: I'm sure it was him, slipping in through a side entrance down there in the half-dark of the lecture room. I watched him sitting at one end of the front row: for a few minutes, merely a man staring up at the vast image of his speaking self.[192] And a little more time after that to ask myself the obvious question: what was he doing here when he was in Manila? A minute or two more, though, and I stopped thinking about that or anything:

191 Max Headroom was a part-human part-computer-generated video host '[d]irect from a wax and shine at the car-wash around the corner' in a late 1980s UK TV series, whose reliable inanities ('Let's get to the nitty-gritty here and talk about your shoes') now read like propositions from Wittgenstein's *Tractatus.*

192 From *The Wizard of Oz,* of course. But is he even aware of this?

instead, I watched him watching himself, his half-smile and his lips moving in sync with the lips on the screen. *'Leadership,'* the onscreen Super-Iggo was saying. 'When *you* show leadership, *we* have to follow *you!*' And—oh, God—I could have kissed them when he said that, those big rainbow lips on the screen. By now the front of my trousers was *bulging*, simply *bulging—*

That night I found myself making love to Sally in a way I'd never known before. *Fungible goals core competency functioning capabilities best practice buy-in buy-in buy-in drill down drill down drill down leverage-leverage-leverage-leverage—*

DISSEMINATE OUTCOME—

Afterwards, we lay together, both experiencing yield loss. She'd fallen asleep straight away, her body sprawled back, her head to one side, her throat exposed like a victim's, above the tumult of her breasts.[193] I could *just* make out her breathing, but she was somewhere else—we were both somewhere else, but it wasn't the same somewhere else—

And then, from nowhere, '*Háttérkép—*'

I stopped, I froze. Hungarian, I'd just said another word in Hungarian. To Sally. It'd just popped out.

I looked at her furtively—had she picked it? Still she slept, still I couldn't see her face. *Háttérkép, háttérkép*: what did it mean? *Wallpaper.* It came to me from somewhere—nowhere— the way the other words had come. *Háttérkép* meant *wallpaper.*

How did I know that? Why had I said *wallpaper* to my partner whilst in a post-coital embrace? *Background,* it also

193 What's this doing here?—pinched straight from Patrick White's *The Twyborn Affair* (1979): 'He lowered his face into the tumult of her breasts', p.257. Picked up during our man's cursory browsing of the pile in the bookshop foyer, possibly? Maybe he thought we wouldn't notice.

meant *background*. How did I know *that*, why was I suddenly speaking in Hungarian? And would I be able to keep it up long enough to learn the language?

Following Super-Iggo's address from Manila, Houston was the first of us to *show leadership*. *They tried this on in Moscow*, he told us a few nights later: the tiny college in Moscow, Idaho, he claimed as his last employer. *They wanted more ass on seats, wanna know what I did there?* And, lo and behold, what he'd set up there he set up here—a first-year course which drew in the prescribed multiples of *ass*[194] in large numbers just as he'd done (he told us) to save his job *way back stateside*.

A *barbecue* course? I asked him when he first ran it past us. We were in our late poker phase, this time *chez* Dalton Bunn from Plant and Microbial Science, with two or three more of the usual suspects all of whom, of course, were chaps. Maybe it was one of them who asked this—I can't remember, really—but we were all astonished at the thought of what Houston was describing. Dalton wondered aloud what the academic content of a barbecue course was, and Houston guffawed and said *monosodium glutamate*.

The thing is, it worked—if *worked* means—well, getting *ass on seats*. The students queued out to the street to enrol in a course Executive Dean Riordan insisted be called 'American Gustation': part of our Cultural Misunderstanding offerings and specialising, it seemed, in North American eating habits. It began with a barbecue in the quadrangle outside, which filled with perhaps a thousand students once word got out. Later, as the weather cooled and we entered what Houston called *fall*, he

---

194 Multiple of 'buttock'. North American slang. In traditional English, an obtuse member of the horse family, or (figuratively) an obtuse person.

had a hospitality company spit-roast a pig out there and hundreds more scholars arrived to consume it. Word had got back to the main campus out in the north-western suburbs, and we watched the STEM boys turn up and tear the poor animal apart, greasing their mouths with it, smearing their faces, stuffing it down themselves silently, remorselessly, pressing and jostling against one another as we looked down upon them from the English-department windows, reassured of the ongoing relevance of the humanities. And, all the time, Houston's huge cowboy hat, moving through the crowds below us, with Houston beneath it joshing people along, giving his big biting crocodile laugh, nodding and flinging his arms about, wiping his face, telling people he'd shot the pig himself—telling people Super-Iggo had told him to do it, told him to organise the entire carnival.

And there he was, down in the crowd, Super-Iggo himself, in his cream outfit and, yes, a boater, a straw boater![195] Brown-nosers buzzed around him like the flies around the pig. There—*there*: now Houston was talking to him, listening to him, even—now the great man was patting him on the arm! I stared down from my office window like a lover betrayed. Houston was getting *face-time*, Houston of all people, *getting face-time with Super-Iggo.*

Only one thing to do now, I could see that.

>᰾᰾᰾

Back in the shop I tell Bevan about the book exchange at Four Oaks. He looks at me as if I've lost my mind.

195 Straw boating hat with a flat top and horizontal brim, popular in English public schools in the last two centuries and certain colonial institutions because of its lethal potential as a frisbee.

'In a *refrigerator*? They put books in a *refrigerator*?'

'I don't think it's switched on.'

'I've seen them around the place but never a *refrigerator*. Book exchanges. They're a community thing, there's some sort of do-good organisation involved. They've got one near me outside a church.'

In the foyer I stare at the pile of mouldering books. I pick one up: Giorgio Agamben, *Remnants of Auschwitz* (New York: Zone Books 1999). I turn it over. Then I turn it back again.

After work I drive out to Four Oaks. I know the area quite well: genteel, set against the hillside to the south-east. The abandoned bus shelter is a damp, crumbled brick-and-plaster bunker wedged into the hillside with a sad, silent old refrigerator in it. I open it up: books. I open the freezer cabinet: books. The vegetable tray: more books. Tom Clancy, *Clear and Present Danger*. Lian Hearn, *Across the Nightingale Floor*. Celia Rees, *Witch Child and Sorceress*. Forty others. I turn them over one by one.

On top of these, carefully, I place the books I've brought with me. *Remnants of Auschwitz. Humanism in the Renaissance of Islam. The Shock of the New. Anti-Oedipus: Capitalism and Schizophrenia.*

I step back and look around: no one watching. I look at the books, mine on top of the others. I've no idea how they'll go out here in the world, where a brisk wind is coming in off the sea, a touch of diesel in it from the railway.

Chapter 14

Then it's Tim Riordan's turn down the chute. I'm hardly in the Furzes' door, I've barely squeezed the remote at the screen, and here he is, on Sally's *Cut 'em Off!* I haven't seen him since the Dissolution and he looks even more worn than I remember; a despairing, throaty beard doesn't help. I plonk tonight's dinner kit on the kitchen sink bench. The humanities, he's talking about the humanities.

'Example?' Sally, sharply, cutting across him. Sometimes, when I was talking to her, she'd say just that—*Example?*—and I'd know that all, all was lost. Is Tim made of sterner stuff?

'Well,' he says. His voice is thinner now, almost spectral. 'Take for example the IT industry.' He's doing that counting-on-the-fingers stunt where you get marooned on the first finger. 'There's documented evidence that an arts degree increases productivity in the IT industry, especially, but across the board, too—'

'Where? Where's this evidence?'

'Well.' Still that forefinger hooked around the other. 'Obviously, I don't have the details to hand, but—'

'But hasn't your arts degree helped you remember them?' A yelp of laughter from the studio audience. 'Haven't you just said the arts improve the mind?'

A brief burst of machine-gun fire on the audio; TWO crawls across the bottom of the screen—he must have cocked up an answer already. At THREE the seat always starts going back.

She's leaning forward now, she's moving in for the kill, I can tell. 'Here's an alternative argument, professor'—the audience stirs when she says *professor*, they stir and titter—'which goes like this. The arts, what you call the humanities, is where it is because no one reads the stuff, no one practises what it preaches anymore—'

'Well!' he sits up, he disentangles those fingers of his, he sticks one up like a preacher. 'May I just say—'

'—because people like you have failed to communicate it properly—'

'I resent that, I resent that, it's not—'

'—with the result that it's become irrelevant and no one reads it.'

'Some *do*, some *do*, for some people the arts are central to their lives, the arts *explain* their lives, they—'

'Then why would a research library decide to cull over half a million of the books in its humanities holdings?'[196]

'Well, there's all sorts of reasons, some of them might even be *good* reasons, though I can't imagine—'

But Sally isn't interested in this. I can see what she's going to do and that it's going to be ugly.

She's got a list in her lap.

'Essays on Giordano Bruno. Ring a bell?'

'Yes—yes, of course—'

The Making of the English Working Class—?'

'E.P. Thompson? Yes, a crucial text in the social history of Britain—'

'Let's try something a little closer to home.' She flicks a glance down at her notes; she flicks it back up again. 'Here's one that might be easier for you. *Waiariki.*'

196 See David Larsen, 'The National Library cull of 600,000 books could be a disaster for researchers', *The Spinoff*, 20 January 2020.

A pause. Tim stares at her.

'Read it? Just stories, after all?'

'I—'

'I'll take that as a no.' Back to her notes again, and up. *'Death of the Land?'*

Where's she getting this stuff from? She's found everything Tim's never read—she's turning him into me!

He's just staring at her. There's a spatter of applause—they're loving this, her studio audience; there's an edge to things now, there's a nastiness that wasn't in the show before. Tim's starting to panic now, I can see it, there's blood in his face and he's twisting in his seat.

'They're translations—I'm familiar with them, but—from the German, they're—'

'German! *German?*' Now she's spreading her arms, she's opening her palms to the audience. 'Well?—what d'you think?'

YES! YES!—and here's the machine gun on the soundtrack again, *d-d-d-d-d-d-d-d*, and THREE starting to crawl along the bottom of the screen. This is going to be one of those nights, I can sense it, and they're right behind her, the bastards: there's a *thrill* through the audience, a real hum of excitement. Here it is now, the seat jerking back a notch, Tim's feet off the ground, applause and a cheer, a real hoot—

No Ordinary Sun, The Imaginary Lives of James Pōneke, Forbidden Cities, South Pacific Sunrise[197]—one by one the

---

197 The authors of the titles mentioned here to the confusion of both the narrator and Professor Riordan are, in order, Patricia Grace, Rowley Habib / Rore Hapipi, Hone Tuwhare, Tina Makereti, Paula Morris, David Eggleton and J.C. Sturm. However knowingly, this account enlarges a scenario in David Lodge's novel *Changing Places* (1975) in which an ambitious young English academic blurts out a drunken confession that he's never read Shakespeare.

impossible titles chug past, one by one Tim muffs them up to wild shouts and laughter each time, and all through this Sally leads a chant: *Arts improve the mind! Arts improve the mind!*

Now FOUR's crawled past and he's on his back, his head's in the hole the minister of finance went down the last time they executed someone—

'One more chance, Tim!' She's standing now, flushed, excited, she's trying to shush the rhythmic clapping. Slowly it fades and now here's his final chance, his last opportunity to salvage some sort of—

'*The House of the Talking Cat.*'

Silence. Utter silence. Tim's trying to say something but one of the handmaids is taping his mouth. Now—here it is, here it is at last—*d-d-d-d-d-d-d-d*—here's FIVE crawling across the screen, here's his seat going all the way, there are his thin, pathetic ankles, his soles in the air—and he's up-and-over, he's *down the hatch*, the former Executive Dean of Arts is *down the hatch* and gone and Sally's audience is *just going off their heads.* Some of them are up on the stage already—air kisses, *faux* hugs—the rest of them uncontrollable, grabbing one another, kicking their legs around *blood blood blood*—

I squeeze MUTE, one hand still on the meal kit I put on the bench ten minutes ago. I was right, I know that now. It's not him that's just been in the chair. It's me. She's been cross-questioning me.

I turn back to the meal kit. I empty the contents of Packet B onto the contents of Packet A in Blodwyn's Pyrex mixing bowl and pour 300ml of boiling water into one of her measuring jugs. I begin to stir it around, trying not to think, trying not to feel anything. Enchiladas, this is meant to become. Says so on the packet.

Becoming. Rilke. Why am I thinking of Rilke?[198]

>~~~<

I still can't believe what happened after I'd seen Houston cosying up to Super-Iggo at the barbecue. From the start of my career I'd steered clear of committees—students first, after all, and then, of course, one's ongoing commitment to scholarship. But, suddenly, there I was, sitting among strangers in a small mock-neo-Gothic building at a far corner of our quaint College of Arts campus; here I was, looking around a meeting room I'd barely heard of before—at its panelled walls, its north-facing windows with their diamond lead-lights, its long, coffin-shaped mahogany table, its looming portraits of the dead.

I looked up. The vaulted wooden ceiling still invites favourable comment.

Somehow, I'd got myself onto a faculty subcommittee whose purpose was to edit motions signalled to the agenda before each monthly faculty meeting. Or, quite possibly, it received minutes *after* each faculty meeting and edited those instead. At no stage was I ever quite certain which of these was the function of the committee or, indeed, whether its purpose might have been something entirely different again. No matter—I was *showing leadership*, I was following our new vice-chancellor's call to us from Manila or the front row of CG17b, whichever it had been:

198 Because of 'become', presumably, the word he's just said. See Rainer Maria Rilke, *Sonnets to Orpheus* (1923), Part II: 'Want the change. Be inspired by the flame / where everything shines as it disappears' etc. See also the final line of Rilke's earlier sonnet 'Archaic Torso of Apollo' (1908): 'Du mußt dein Leben ändern [You must change your life].' There seems to be some kind of subterranean echo in our narrator's mind here, occasioned by the quick-fix enchiladas.

I'd got myself onto a committee external to the department! It felt like the beginning of a new age. Or, possibly, the end of an era.

It soon became obvious that no one else on this sub-committee was one hundred percent sure, either—about anything, really—and that it would be simply a matter of my bluff-work versus theirs.

I became more confident.

Soon I began to try some of the techniques I'd picked up in English-department meetings over the years. I started to make a point of arriving late—*Sorry, caught up in another meeting*—and always sat directly opposite the *chairperson*. After a minute or two of feigned listening I'd try an ironic smile, then a private shake of the head at whatever was being said by whoever was saying it. Another minute and I'd allow myself a tiny splutter of amusement and (perhaps) a quick, self-important scribble of nothing-much-at-all in the corner of the agenda. *Margarine, fruit, toilet paper, onions . . .*

This performance would rapidly catch the attention of others—even, eventually, that of the chair: *Tom? You've got a comment?* Me: *No! No!*—all innocence, palms up—*I'm not saying anything! But*—and here I'd look around the others as if I knew whereof I spoke—*if we do decide to go down this path*—now I'd pause, and look around the table, knowingly, brow pressed forward, chin tucked in—*then this issue'll come back to us at a future meeting, and—and*—another pause, another meaningful glance around the table—*it'll look exactly the same as it does now!*

A quick double rap of pencil-on-table-top to round things off: *tap-tap!*

See what I mean? A textbook display of simulated competence—completely devoid of content, completely devoid of commitment, a perfect example of the power of *seeming* which I'd back up with further occasional remarks, always taking care *never to initiate anything, always to work off the backs of others*: one of the golden rules of bluff-work. Gone were the days when I'd mix up *Let's park this* and *Let's ballpark this*. Instead: *That's to be seen*, I'd say. *Win some lose some.* Or, *It is what it is. That's certainly a point of view that could be argued.* Or (one of my favourites, completely meaningless but still slightly threatening), *What exactly d'you mean by that?* And, of course, when I could think of nothing better, *Could you just give me the KPIs on that one, thanks*—?

Within a single meeting, I noticed some of my fellow committee members starting to defer to me. Soon, others outside the committee, too—for example, if I was asked to phone a faculty member in a *follow-up* after a *meet*. *I'm ringing on behalf of the faculty subcommittee*—the change of tone at the other end was palpable when I said that—or *the subcommittee feels your submission needs clarification before we action it further.* Soon, I became confident enough to introduce a tiny element of threat: *To tell the truth, we're a little disappointed in the documentation you've provided for your submission.* Or, *We've decided to give you 48 hours to reconsider this.* Saying *we* was always crucial, a hint at the institutional power that had begun to trickle into my veins and, slowly, bring form and style to my essential vacuity.

Then, inevitably, I overplayed my hand. After a couple of months, I felt confident enough to skip a meeting—that sore throat I tend to get, the one I'm never quite sure is actually there. *Apologies, gentlemen, apologies.* (Ladies, too, of course.) Alas—next time I turned up I found I'd been unanimously elected committee chair and appointed associate dean as well! *You mean I'm in charge of the fucking thing*, I demanded of the *now-outgoing* former associate dean, who stood and began to pack his papers the moment I came into the room. *Never turn your back on your friends*, was his silken reply, as he crossed to the door. *Just wait till somebody else skives off for the day and flick the job onto them.* And then this *outgoing* former associate dean—well, *outwent*, slipping through the doorway with relief written all over his departing back, to begin his life again with the help of fresh air, exercise, counselling and a diet of fruit and vegetables.

Dismaying, certainly. I fumbled my way through the first few meetings waiting on-edge for someone to give their apologies. No one did. I was trapped. I fumbled along some more, wild panic surely visible in my eyes from minute to minute. After a few weeks of this, though, something began to change. I had to admit there was a small thrill in this unexpected setback after all, a buzz of excitement mixed into the pit of fear I took with me everywhere I went. What did it *matter* that I had no idea what I was doing? I was an *associate dean* after all, and that had a ring to it, a whiff of power, authority, status: the very things I'd feared and despised throughout my professional career but now, in my own hands and offering some promise of selective head-kicking, a different matter.

Soon, and without my doing anything to make it happen, my new title appeared on my office door—of itself, as if naturally, as if I'd somehow *done the right thing*, as if I'd connected with the larger order of the universe. It felt like a pat on the back from those In The Know—those managerial aliens, perhaps, those Maitlands and Garlands and Gaitskells, those Gaskells and Skellerns and Maskells, always busy, always moving, always muttering into their phones, always open to a hurried nod or a grimace that might just pass for a wink. Or even from Super-Iggo himself, whom I glimpsed one afternoon as I crossed our little campus for one of these new meetings of mine: a distant figure in his latest suit, a light-grey double-breasted this time—more semiotics to be interpreted—and all the time surrounded, of course, by his entourage of brown-nosers, his head down as he nodded *yes-yes-mm-mm-yes*. In my dreams, in my dreams.

In Sally's, too. She was back from Viscera studios—up there three days a week now, on some training course or other. *Welcome to the Dark Side!* she said when I told her my news: she'd *always seen it in me*, it was *great to see me making a commitment*, high time I *stepped away from the lecture room*—I'd heard all this before and tuned most of it out. I'm just an associate dean, I said. Dozens of those around the place. Secretly I was pleased, though—Sally, taking me seriously!

We were on a summer patio at the time, camping in the house of Johannes van der Nacker, a hard-left Marxist on leave from Social and Political Sciences who called everyone *brother* or *comrade* and self-fashioned (I'd just discovered this concept; I saw it everywhere) as Trotsky—the glasses, the goatee and so on. I was working my way through his wine collection, by far the best I've come across (I had a Burgundy Côte de Nuits red in my glass, for God's sake!) and enjoying an unparalleled vista from the much-sought-after hillside suburb of Kashmir.

Self-fashioning. The patio, the lounge, the bookcases full of books I'd never heard of before; the enormous black smart-screen on one wall and the indifferent local art on another; beyond, a tiled, open-plan kitchen with a scullery and cold larder; somewhere else, a spa pool, burbling away. The typical professional's home of a senior academic!—for the first time I felt the pull of it, the sense that it was something that could be *mine*, could be at the other end of the ladder on whose first rung it seemed I'd now set my foot. Is this what Sally meant? The two of us, entertaining in a house like this on a Saturday evening? Entertaining Super-Iggo, perhaps, impressing him— shocking him, even—with my wine cellar? I could almost feel the great man's arm around my shoulder, almost hear his jovial chuckle in my ear: *Tom, we're paying you too much!*

All the time I was working my way through this particular dream, though, here was Sally in front of me on a patio lounger, her phone at her ear as she talked to her new best friend Bonnie. How did Sally fit into my fantasy?—how did Bonnie fit in? I'd never met her but she was something big up at Viscera, apparently, and seemed to ring Sally every evening she wasn't up there; what was this woman doing in our life? Where were we going? I slurped at Nacker's burgundy, aware of a shift in the cargo. Things were threatening to change, we seemed about to take a lurching step forward, Sally and I. Where to, what were we doing?

Or, maybe, we were just riding the tiger: soon—giddily, surprised at myself, shocked at what I was doing—I found myself volunteering for *another gig*, as I heard someone put it, a turn of phrase that made the prospect seem sexier, a bit more *in the moment*, even though I still hadn't any idea what a gig was. This time, I decided, I'd try for something closer to the great man himself—literally; I managed to get myself on to a committee that met high in the Registry building on the main campus out in the 'burbs. The IO committee, everyone called it, but I had no idea what that meant. All I knew was that it met one level below the senior management team and its offices.

I hadn't been out at the main campus for a while. So much going on when I arrived there! I walked past the Norman Iggo water feature with my heart *punching* away in the usual place, diagrammatic fenestration all around me.[199] Ahead, the water-stained brutalist construction that was the Registry building: this monument to the seventies now enclosed by scaffolding and in the process of being heightened from below, the entire structure raised on massive jacks with new floors inserted at ground level week by week.[200] An external elevator took me up five floors to the former Level 1—its resemblance to the Apollo 11 gantry was widely noted. As I rose I gazed down on Super-Iggo's new world, a campus buzzing with unexpected activity and a sense growing all around that *something was about to happen*—something *really* big. We were on our way! Whee!

A challenge, at first, finding the meeting room: then here it was, with a note on the door. *Reserved for IO Committee.* The International Olympics Committee? Nothing about the Olympics in the first few sessions, though; instead, it seemed to be a verb. *IO*, other committee members kept saying, over and over again. *We must IO.* What could that possibly mean?—what did *anything* mean to this strange salad of humanity sitting around what was a much bigger table this time, beneath a far less impressive ceiling but one which held promise, nevertheless, of the great man just above it? Everyone on this committee seemed to *be on task* except me, each of them with a document in front of them the size of a large city phonebook: *Supplement 1a.* For the first time in my life I felt my capacity for

---

199 Where does he get this from? 'Fenestration' is an architectural term for the design and disposition of windows, certainly; but 'diagrammatic fenestration' is a medical term describing a particular kind of surgery. Ambitious bluff-work gone wildly astray, it seems.

200 This process was developed in Germany. See Bumsen P. & Wackelig T., *Hochhausunterleben-Techniken* (Technische Buchhandlung, Berne, 1981). See also https://en.wikipedia.org/wiki/Raising_of_Chicago, about the raising of existing buildings in Chicago after 1858.

bluff-work challenged. Had I got it wrong, was it possible that bullshit really was just an arts thing after all, was there a place where bluff actually stopped and hard reality began, were the STEM people right after all?

Meantime, throughout all this, as we sat in it passing our motions, the Registry building rose centimetre by centimetre. Slowly, a second tower began to rise next to it: U2 to our U1, we were informed. Every few weeks the former paused to let the latter catch up; then, coquettishly, it would start climbing again. Each time we came to our meeting room, the view had improved.

And each week I'd sit there casting furtive looks around the table as the others talked. There were scientists present, and they made me feel uncomfortable. Bryce, the name of the chairperson, Bryce from Engineering, I'd picked that up, and Clyde from Physics, taking the minutes. There was a woman called Muriel, which was quite out of the question, I couldn't help thinking, and a couple of other women whose names passed me by. *Tom is our arts rep*, Bryce told these people at the start of my first meeting, and a couple of the scientists exchanged glances, I'm sure of that. *Tom is from English*, Bryce said—yes, they were definitely smirking at *that*. Pricks. A man called Tyler Waltz who came from Forestry sat staring at me throughout the meeting as if I had a Christmas tree growing out of my head.

For the first few of these IO meetings I crouched there looking down at *Supplement 1a* and riffling through its pages as if I'd read them before. They might as well have been upside down: something about the impact of something on something else. What was it they were all talking about? Slowly, slowly, something began to form itself. *Yes, but what'd be the outcome*, Gus said, a few meetings in, or it might have been Barney or Chester. Then, a few minutes later, someone said it again. *What'd be the outcome if it actually happened,* this man said. *What'd be the impact?*

Impact. Outcome.

IO—Impact the Outcome! But how could it possibly be called the Impact the Outcome Committee?[201] Slowly, over the weeks, I put the rest of the name together: the External/Internal Executive Impact Outcome committee!—in fact, an enabling committee that was setting itself up to *exist*, awaiting its first outcome before it might even Be. *Supplement 1a* was anticipatory; we were working towards a foundational document to which it would eventually be appended. I listened. I became more confident. I was beginning to know where I was. *Undifferentiated relativism—*

I waited for the right moment. Then, here it came, from Muriel, speaking about some proposed cut or other:

'We're not client-facing,' she said. 'Remember that.'

Bingo! It took me by surprise—just like the first time I'd started up in that faculty subcommittee two or three years before. Here I was, sitting up and listening to myself beginning to speak again: where would my voice take me this time? I heard it deepen as the words went on, I felt my back straighten as they came out, I felt the possibility of another temporary self, beginning to assemble itself around me once more.

'I don't agree with that,' this voice said. 'I don't agree with that at all.'

---

201 In fact, IO committees are a known phenomenon; for example, in the formation of the EU, in the early stages of the planning of the Channel Tunnel and at various stages of the Brexit process. EIEIO departments go back to the Kennedy administration in the US, where receptionists were obliged to answer their phones by reciting the acronym many times a day. See Arthur M. Schlesinger Jr, *A Thousand Days* (1965), p.1253.

This Muriel woman had been telling us about some people who'd lost their jobs. *Harden up*, the voice was saying—*my voice, coming out of me.* The others were listening, they were leaning forward and following what my voice was saying, intently, almost as if they were lip-reading me—and, *there*, I made sense, just for a few seconds, I could hear it, I even made sense to myself. *There're hard decisions ahead of all of us*, the voice was saying. *It's tough when individuals we all know are impacted*—but in the end—and here I looked around the table one by one, brow forward, chin tucked in: *In the end, aren't we all client-facing? All the time? All of us?*

Bryce and Tyler nodded side by side and ducked down to scribble something on their copies of *Supplement 1a*. Muriel sat back and cracked her knuckles. Bryce nodded at someone else, Clyde it was, and then began to speak. I didn't really listen but it sounded pretty approving. I waited for him to finish. I leaned forward: *Would you just give me the KPIs on that one, thanks—?* 'Sure,' he said, 'sure.' I leaned back and began to crack my knuckles, too, luxuriously, one by one. *Crack! Crack! Crack! Crack! Crack! Crack!*[202]

And, all the time we sat in our featureless meeting room, there was Super-Iggo, somewhere above our heads, like an idea, like a principle, and the SMT as well, all of them speaking their strange neo-liberal Klingon—and all of us being jacked up, day by day, scores of committees around us steadily rising,

202 Can he possibly know these words are from Laurence Sterne's *The Life and Opinions of Tristram Shandy, Gentleman* (1759): 'Crack, crack—crack, crack—crack, crack—so this is Paris! quoth I'? There seems to be an almost idiot-savant openness at work in the present text already, which brings these naïve echoes from time to time because there is so little to impede them. A negative capability of his own, possibly (see footnotes 188 above and 203 following)?

dozens on each floor, and desks and duplicators and computers and monitors and filing cabinets and one-bar heaters and wall-calendars, pot plants in reception areas, team leaders showing vision and setting goals, personal assistants at their desks writing memos for the team leaders, telling them what to do, people on potties, pants around their ankles: all of us being lifted millimetre by millimetre as the whole building creaked and swayed and, through the window, we watched new vistas come into sight—why, we could see as far as the Beech Forest shopping complex now, and, well beyond it, high-rise buildings and even the spire of Cathedral Mall, just the top of it.

Sally brought me back to earth. Another fine evening, and here we were out on Nacker's patio again, where I was most deedily occupied with his last bottle of Trimbach Alsace Riesling.[203] The sun sagged towards the hills to the west and the light was becoming subtler around his house, imbricated through trees and clouds.[204] Life was looking increasingly positive.

They wanted her to work full-time at Viscera studios. It took me a second or two to catch up, once she'd put her phone down and told me that. *Stay up at Viscera? A thousand kilometres away?*

'You've finished your training, is that—'

I stopped short: her *useless-dumb-fuck* stare coming back at me, hard. Oops.

---

203 The narrator has said earlier that he doesn't 'get' Austen, but here it seems she's got him—this is an unconscious surfacing of a phrase from *Emma* (1815), where Frank Churchill is described as being 'most deedily occupied' in repairing Mrs Bates's spectacles. How the phrase got from Volume II Chapter 10 of the novel past the narrator's short attention span is unknown.
204 'Imbricated'? Does he really mean the clouds are 'layered like tiles'? That's what the word means. Yet again, he gets more than a little out of his depth whenever he tries to impress.

'I finished training *five years* ago, Tom. More, five and a half. Down here. I've been doing general assignment stuff since then, you know that.'

Rilly?

'Sure, sure. Of course. Of course.'

'I can't keep coming and going. I've worked out what I want to do. I don't want to be local the rest of my life, you've seen what they make me do down here—interviewing that guy stuck in a *Portaloo*, for God's sake—'

'Stuck in a *Portaloo*—?'

'Up there I'm working on production, I told you that, and I did that gig on the weather. Anyway, Bonnie says I've—you know, *got* it? She says you either have or you haven't? I've told you all this before.'

Had she? Oops again.

'She wants to give me a shot at anchoring this new show—external work but coming back to a panel thing each night. She watched me do that gig on streetkids—'

'Yeah, yeah.' Working really hard here—when was that?

'—and this is what she came up with.' Sitting back and staring straight at me: Sally, head-on and not to be trifled with: that pale blue gaze. I looked away, I shifted around a bit. I really wanted more about the guy in the Portaloo.

I looked back.

Lára Gifford, at the kitchen window.

Just her face, at the level of the sill—behind Sally, across her shoulder, across the living room and through the dining room, past the dry arrangement and the tapestry hanging above the sofa: there she was, peering in at the kitchen window forty feet away; just a face, there-and-gone but definitely Lára's imp-face, sharp, sallow, a little ravaged. *It can't be, oh God it—*

'Mm,' I said to Sally, a trifle over-brightly. *Oh, please don't turn around—*

'Tom, you're not giving me much help here.'

'Oh, quite!' Lára was back at the kitchen window now, she was holding something close to herself, low down—now she was crouching, she was ducking away again, I couldn't see her—

'I mean, they're hard, commuter relationships are difficult. We're going to have to work on it, same as we've been doing but more.'

'Right.'

'Oh, for *Christ's* sake, Tom, will you fucking *engage* with me, I'm telling you I want to change the way we have our fucking *relationship*, it's like I'm ordering burger-and-chips at McDonald's fucking *drive*-in—'

'I'm—getting my head round it, I—'

Now Lára was back behind her, at the window—something white, struggling in her hands—

'It's sudden,' I was telling Sally. 'I'm a bit—'

'What are you *looking* at—?'—and—*oh, God*—she twisted in her chair, she—

—and Lára bent down again, she was gone, it was like tag-wrestling—

She turned back, Sally, she turned back to me. 'Are you upset, is that what it is—?'

Ah! Of course!

'Yes! Yes!—what d'you *expect?*'

And this moved her, you could tell—she put her head on her shoulder and looked across at me and bit her bottom lip, softly, sort of chewed at it. 'Aw, *Tom*, we can take turns? We can see each other week*ends*—?'

'Great! Great! I want you to succeed!' *That* was it, I was onto something here. I put my arms out to her, trying to remember the routine—no problem, though, here she came, bum-walking along the sofa towards me, full tilt—Sally, snuggling into me with her familiar Sally-smell: Sally in my arms, pleased with me, whispering—

'You're such a *softie.*' She started to do something in my ear with the tip of her nose; now she was biting the lobe, gently, barely a nip. 'A real *meringue.*' Another nip, harder this time. 'No, a *soufflé.*' Then she was fiddling with my flies and out he came, old Woodrow Wilson—oh Lord: the Act of Darkness, here, on the sofa, with the double doors wide open, Old Sol westering in the sky beyond the trees[205] and a mad Hungarian on the loose with a pet clutched to her, a bird or something it seemed to be, a pigeon maybe—*why a fucking pigeon*—

Sally, whispering in my ear now: *Data warehousing solutions. Up-front ETL.* This was our routine now, we were beginning to move together slowly, knowingly. *Nimble data transport path. Agile B2C technologies.* Starting to work, starting to work. *Deploy dot-com paradigms. Global network services. Seamless e-services metrics. Cutting-edge solutions robust outcomes synergistic strategic convergences collaborative platforms collaborative platforms drill down drill down drill down leverage-leverage-leverage-leverage—*
MARKET EXIT—

We lay there, she and I. Evening, the open doors, the spread of the patio, flies in the room: Lára could have been anywhere—I tried to sense her but there was nothing.

'You know I'm writing another book.'

Sally, lying on top of me; she said it just like that, conversationally, close to my ear.

A slight twinge, as before with the other one she wrote, the case study for her degree; another little-boy pang-in-the-chest.

205 Dear oh dear—*Treasury of Verse* stuff.

Couldn't help it. I watched her standing, tidying herself up, making for the doorway.

I pretended to be pleased. 'Another textbook?'

'No, not another textbook.'

'Well, what kind of a book?'

She looked across at me, slyly.

'You'll find out,' she said.

'No, tell me now—'

Again, that sly sweet peek-up-at-me from whatever-she-was-doing, the lips really-and-truly a rosebud. 'You *will* find out, Tom.' She made me an air-kiss, *schmeck-schmeck*, like that. *Mmmwa! Mmmwa!* across the room: *I love you! I love you!* Also: *Piss off and wait. This is private.*

Later, I looked around outside before closing the patio doors and turning off the lights. No sign of Lára; but under the kitchen window there were dabs and smears on the ground, difficult to work out in the fading light but definitely *there*. Green, I could tell they were greenish in colour, and there was an unpleasant smell in the air. Ammonia.

Next day I waited till Gifford passed my office doorway. When I heard his tread up the staircase out in the foyer I shut the door and rang his wife at home.

'Tamás!' when she heard my voice. 'Yes! Me!'

'You mean it's you *now* or it was you *then*—?'

'It's me then—'

'It *was* you then—? Last night? Up at the Nackers' place—'

'No, it was me now. Listening to the trees. They're talking to me.'

A pause.

'Lára, we've got to stop this. We've got to stop seeing each other.'

Silence.

'It's gone too far.'

Nothing.

Another pause.

'What's that noise? In the background?'

'Horthy. Admiral Horthy.[206] *Szarozom a fürdőben.*'

'It sounds like a—'

'*Ő egy kacsa*—'

'Lára, why've you got a—is that what it is?'

'Mm!' Brightly, brightly. 'To look after me!' Always too chirpy these days. Wait—what was this she was telling me?

'Gene is? Where? *Where's* he fucking off to—?'

'Brown rice. Professor Gifford now.'

Brown rice? What in the name of God was she talking about?

The name of Gifford's new employer. He told me the next day while he was clearing his bookcase into boxes. Through the wall in Houston's office something was going on, but it was as if he couldn't hear it.

'Brown–Rice Uni,' he was telling me, in his dry little northern voice. 'West Virginia. In the panhandle. Know it?'

'Yes. No.'

'About eight thousand students. Liberal Arts. A bit more challenging than this.'

Houston, shouting now, bumping against the wall. Was he pissed? *And what was this Gifford had just said to me, suddenly, urgently, leaning across at me—*

206 Admiral Miklós Horthy (1868–1957), Regent of Hungary (1920–1944), whose greatest achievement was to become an admiral in a land-locked country. Hungarian. Ignore.

'Get *out* of here—?' I stared at him. I felt something tighten, deep down inside me. 'Why?—Super-Iggo's got it by the nuts, hasn't he? He seems like a—'

'Tom, the man's about to make massive changes. *Get out while you can*—even school-teaching'd be better—'

School-teaching?—*school-teaching*—?

'Listen, the guy's been hired to *do* things.' *Staring* at me. 'Two colleges are in real trouble and *we're one of them*. We're the worst of the lot. I've seen the spreadsheets.'

'But—'

'He's preparing us, he's softening us up. He can't go on writing off debt month after month. There's rumours he's thinking of closing down units and selling buildings overseas to get some cash.' Those cold fish-eyes of his. 'Such as this college.'

I stared back, shocked, appalled—at him, at his books, at the new photos of cocks on the notice-board behind his head.

'How's Lára?' It surprised me, just coming out of me like that.

'She's fine. Coming with me, of course.'

'Yes. Yes, of course.'

'She'll have to leave Admiral Horthy behind.' A dry, bloodless titter. 'Her emotional support duck.'

'Emotional *support* duck—?'

'Well, she can't expect any from me, can she?' He pointed a finger in the air. '"Remember, the louder he talked of his honour, the faster we counted our spoons."'[207]

'Quite. Quite.'

'This is the vice-chancellor I'm talking about.'

'Oh, quite.'

---

207 Ralph Waldo Emerson, *Conduct of Life: A Philosophical Reading* (1860). Unknown to our hero, no doubt, but plausible in anyone else's mouth.

I looked away. I looked back. Still the gaze.

'You did have halek,' he said, suddenly.

A pause. What was this?

He looked down, he started putting books in the boxes again.

I slipped out. Halek? *Halek?*[208]

Next door, Houston's office door was open. He seemed to have calmed. He had a matchstick in one corner of his mouth.

'Get a load of this,' he told me. Another parcel, this time half opened: he flicked his hand towards it. 'Go on.'

I pulled open the wrapping—coarse brown paper, tissue inside that.

I stared at what I saw.

I took a step back.

I *couldn't believe my eyes*, as they say in books—but it's true, I really couldn't, it was as if a different reality had suddenly entered the room. I couldn't stop seeing it, and I couldn't unsee it once it'd been seen.[209] It couldn't *possibly* be there—

'Shit, Houston, it's a fucking gun,' I hissed at him. 'You've brought a fucking gun to work—'

'It's not a fucken *gun*, man, it's a fucken *handgun*. Get it straight, your *dick* is your *gun*, this is a fucken *handgun*.' He spat a tiny shred. 'Heat,' he said. 'Packin' heat—'

---

208 This is extraordinary. The reference is to Simon Forman (1552–1611), famed astrologer, occultist, herbalist and rumoured Satanic figure in early Renaissance London. He is noted for his diaries, which record his many sexual conquests, marked each time by his unique coinage, 'halek', for 'sexual intercourse' ('Did have halek' was a regular entry). Gifford's use of it here speaks for itself—though not to our man, it seems.

209 Nabokov's *Speak, Memory*: a memoir again (see footnote 124). Now he's repeating his repetitions.

'*Fuck*, Houston—'

In the moment like that, caught off guard, I could do no better. I crept away. *What was happening, what was going to happen?*

These days Sally spent five days a week up north. Five nights a week I was alone. I began to dream of other lovers, vague figures from the past. I dreamed of Houston's gun. *Then I began to dream of Super-Iggo.* I couldn't believe it, but there he was—there we were, the two of us, walking along a beach together, side by side, hand in hand: barefoot, silent, heads down, just the crash of the waves in our ears as we stepped softly through the sand together in wordless communion. Every night this dream, and each night we reached the same point in it, where we stopped in the sand, and turned to each other, and looked each into the other's eyes, and took each other's hands, right in left and left in right, and he started to speak and—

I'd wake up.

What was it—*what was he about to tell me?*

Later that week I go back to the abandoned bus shelter in Four Oaks. It's empty, the fridge is gone—all that's left is a small pile of books on the seat, each one damp out here in the real world and starting to buckle and puff in the usual way of books and water. The one on top is called *Click, Clack, Moo: Cows That Type*. Where the fridge was there's just a drift of crisp blackened leaves. Wind, rustling them a little, off the sea. Nothing much else.

There's a man at the new bus stop across the road. He lifts his hand to me.

'It's been sold,' he calls out. 'The fridge. Some bastard sold it on Trade Me.'

I take *Click, Clack, Moo* back home with me. A kids' book, but it turns out it's quite a good read. These cows find a typewriter, see, and they use it to start asking for things and the farmer gets pissed off, so they withhold their milk? Just crying out for a Marxist interpretation in *Notes and Queries*.

Chapter 15

No one in the shop today, no one at all. Late afternoon: glowering clouds, rain threatening, the foyer dark as the two of us stare down at the book pile. I've brought so many trolley-loads down you'd think it'd be up to the roof, but it's not. The pile's stopped growing, there's only half as many books here— well, two-thirds. They still smell bad, though. I think of the dust mites the specialist told me about, crawling up my nose.

'I've been trying to give books away, but—'

'No, no, that wouldn't account for it. You bring most of those back, anyway.'

There's a bandage on his left wrist. He smells of ointment.

'It must be the tradies. You know, Harrison and—'

'It's a good sign. It means they're reading them.'

'They can't be, not this many. There's something else going on.'

'They ought to return them, of course, once they've read them.'

Over the months he's been sifting through the books as I bring them in and picking out the keepers, as he calls them, and storing them in the office out the back: Trollope, any edition, five different editions of *Vanity Fair*, all of Austen, James, Conrad, Scott, Dickens and so on, in half-leather, quarter-leather, full leather, cloth, dustjackets and bare. Out here in the foyer, though, mostly what he calls the leftovers: I pick some of them up—Saul Bellow, a couple of Elizabeth Bishop collections, Randall Jarrell, Cormac McCarthy, William Trevor. *Orientalism, A Suitable Boy, Shame, The Vendor of Sweets, Midnight's Children.*

We stand there, staring at all this. Then:

'I stayed behind last night. I did a little on the accounts.' He looks around, as if someone's listening. 'I heard voices.'

'*Voices*—?'

'And movements.' Looking around again, crouched over. '*From in the books*—'

He whispers this at me, *hisses* it, and it frightens the life out of me when he does. Splats of rain on the glass, the southerly beginning to bustle against the windows, Bevan's Bookshop empty—

'*Voices* from in the *books*—?'

'The characters. Speaking.'

Ah, God, he's gone at last, he's gone in the head. I should have known. Poor bastard.

I look at my watch: 5:05. We should start shutting up soon. We—

'I'm not making this up.'

Did I ask him that? Outside, on cue, a brief flare of lightning—silly, yes, ridiculous, but on the other hand *you should try it.* I'm standing in front of him, swallowing hard. Static electricity in the air. Then, *boom!*—right above us, there it is, a dramatic, over-the-top roll of thunder. *You should try actually being here.*

'It was like this. Last evening—after you'd gone home, about six, it was dark and stormy—'[210]

---

210 Of course!—'It was a dark and stormy night': the opening sentence of Edward Bulwer-Lytton's novel *Paul Clifford* (1830) and famous in the annals of bad writing. Despite the promise of the first of his two surnames,

'Where were you? Where—'

'In the loo. I'd gone for a leak. Where *you* hang out—where you write that bloody book of yours.'

Help!—how does he know about this book—?

'I looked out into the foyer but there was no one there. It was darker than this, it was after six—and I began to hear them. From in the books. People—speaking to me. Everything back there, it was speaking to me—'

'It must've been people upstairs—'

'No—no, they'd gone out, it was after that, it was dark. There was no one around but the books. I could hear her—'

'Who—?'

'Mrs Proudie. The Bishop's wife. *Barchester Towers*—'

Standing there staring at me pop-eyed, with the rash on his face and his hands. *Here's where reading gets you: forty years of it from when he was a kid, probably.* This is what's going through my mind. *Five decades with your nose in a book and you end up like this, round the bend, covered in spots and broke.*

He's nodding at me: urgent, eager, not a little mad. Another burst of thunder, right above the building.

Next day he rings to tell me he's taking sick leave. Thank God for *that*—but it means I'm alone with the book pile for two whole days. All the time I'm at the counter keeping an eye on the few drifters in the shop, and while I'm moving around the shelves flicking the feather duster, filling in time, I'm thinking of the bloody thing, out there in the foyer. In the afternoon there's a woman who hangs around the cooking-and-recipes

---

the Lord Lytton (1803–73) wrote this straight-faced, though a number of subsequent writers have re-used his words less so. The echo here seems naïve.

shelves and that distracts me for twenty minutes. Then she actually buys a book—early Atwood, *The Edible Woman*—and she tells me there's a talking steak in there![211] I almost laugh in her face when she says that—*another bloody nutter*—but after what Bevan told me about hearing voices it does make me feel a bit odd. And once she's gone, I start thinking of the book pile again, I keep peeking through our double doors to see if it's got smaller or bigger all on its own, and each time I do, it sits there looking back at me like a thing. Nearer closing-time I'm beginning to think these bloody books are starting to drive *me* mad, too.

After five the upstairs tenants start thumping down the stairs to the foyer and out, and then there's the moment when their footsteps and natter have gone and no one's left up there or anywhere, no one at all, there's just me and the books and the last of the light outside. I turn off the bookshop fluorescents, one, two, three, four.

Spooky. Still raining, too.

After twenty minutes the drama starts, almost on cue. A hinge squeaks, a floorboard creaks out there. I stand behind the closed shop doors, listening.

Voices, out in the foyer now. Oh, God, this is silly. I listen, hard up against the bookshop doors. It can't be the books, it just—

There.

Nothing much more than a murmur.

That's a burner—

Who's this—?

---

211 In fact Margaret Atwood's novel *The Edible Woman* (1969) does have a scene in which a steak seems to ask not to be eaten. Our hero, behind the eight ball again (the latter a phrase deriving from the pool table).

There y'go. That'll keep your little buggers warm—
Harrison.

It *is* him, of *course* it's him—
Bastards burn up that quick you need the whole fucken
bookshop every week—
A short sharp laugh, like a dog's bark.
Jason. Of course. Jason. Him, too.
Now they've turned on the foyer light. I watch them through
the slit between the front doors of the shop. They work their way
through the book pile quickly, efficiently, like robbers, grabbing
fistfuls, clutching them, ducking out of the main doors, swearing
whenever they drop one, kicking books along the ground. They
load—who knows? perhaps four or five hundred into their van
out in the quadrangle?—ten minutes of this, no stopping, no
thought, just grabbing armfuls and lugging them out, books
splashing on the floor, books flung into the back of the van and
all the time they're talking, swearing, muttering. By now I'm at
one of the front windows, peeping over the sill, watching them
out in the quadrangle: in and out and calling to each other, in
and out again. The hunger in them, the need.
Then—
We'll drop your half at my place and take the rest out to
Glasnost—
The slam of the van doors, the sound of the engine. They're
off. I watch them from the window as they drive away, slowly,
over the quad's rolling, uneven tar seal, between Old Astronomy
and Old Chemistry and out to the road. Half the books for
Jason's wood burner, half for—Glasnost.
What the hell is Glasnost?
A minute online at Bevan's desk and—there it is, Glasnost!
And I laugh out loud when I see what it is. Of *course*, of *course*.
So bloody obvious! *That's* what they've been doing!

[271]

The second workroom, Tim's room: I work Bevan's key in the lock and here's the stale dark whiff of his Peterson pipe coming out to me. His ashtray on the desk, beside it an old ink bottle, Parker Quink, crusted shut; the *London Review of Books*, piled up with the *Times Literary Supplement*, both of them in piles browning to years back—over there, thirty or forty *John O'London's* extinct on the floor, *PMLA* and *HLME* in a stack. *New Writing*, *The Bookman*, *The Idler*. Dickens, Conrad, Jane Austen; Scott's in there, too, *Redgauntlet* and *Rob Roy* and *Old Mortality*, *The Antiquary*, *The Bride of Lammermoor*. I kick at a pile of them: *Kenilworth*, *The Talisman*, *Maud*, *Pride and Prejudice*, *Youth and Other Stories* and *Sherston's Progress* and *Sword of Honour*.

Ah—this is what I'm after: *The Last Chronicle of Barset*, Bevan's reading place marked with a ginger biscuit. I open the place and there she is, Mrs Proudie, forever clutching her fucking bedpost. I sit on a pile of *Adelphi* magazines, eating the biscuit and reading her for the very last time. My heart rate's up a bit. I know what I'm going to do now, I know what all this is about.

It's dusk when I get to the factory, in an industrial park towards the hills to the south-east of the city. I drive to the side road I've been looking for: anonymous warehouses, a blind end, riverbed shingle, litter caught in wire fencing. There's an office-warehouse complex with a FOR LEASE sign and a loose gravel driveway I jostle the car over, to an opening cut into the tall corrugated metal side of the building. Inside, lights, the thump of machinery, that never-ending factory sound, a couple of men in overalls moving about. Above the door: GLASNOST PULPING. BOUTIQUE PAPER MANUFACTURE. This is where they've been taking our books, the last few months, the ones they don't just burn to heat themselves.

Now here's a man coming out, wiping his hands with a cloth: *What you got?* He calls it out to me and when I tell him it's books and they're in the car he tells me he doesn't pay so much for books. *Warning you*, he yells, and he wipes his hands again. *Telling you that.*

Inside, the light's just dim neon tubes overhead and there's a sweaty-glove smell that gets worse the further we take the books into the factory. Noise, steady, rumbling through the floor, on and on and on, blanking out whatever it is Nikita's trying to tell me behind the racket—that's his name, I picked that up by lip-reading. The racket from the machines: I nod *yes-yes-how-interesting*. This is where it all starts, it seems, the paper comes in here and through to Finishing at the other end and then Dispatch—I pick up bits of this as he shouts through the noise in his Russian English. I keep nodding *yes-yes*, but a lot of it gets lost in the *thump-thump-thump* from the tub that's in front of us. It's the size of a spa pool, perhaps a little bigger, and stiff with a thick pulpy wash covered in bubbles that stretch and pop as it's pushed around in an oval track and through a comb of blades that shred the sludge and send it around and back and shred the sludge again, and then again, and then again. Porridge, think porridge. It never stops, that's one thing I can make out this Nikita's telling me. It keeps on going, day and night. There's another vat working away over by the windows. All the time, that sweaty used-glove smell.

Now he's going to turn on a show, I think. He's picking through a pile of books we've brought in from the car, he's picking one from the top and opening it for me as if he's pulling its legs apart. It's one of the Scotts, it's *The Heart of Midlothian*. He opens it and *look!*—I see him mouthing this at me behind the noise—*look!*—and here he is, turning the black worn covers back on themselves flat together like *stick-your-hands-up*, and then with his other fist he starts *wrenching* at the guts of the book, the pages clutched together and out from the spine, just *wrenching* them, *whoop*, like that, out like the pluck from an animal. Then he starts doing a strong-man-legs-apart-ripping-the-phonebook thing in front of me and slowly, powerfully, starts to push–pull the wodge of tired old pages apart, left and right, pushes and pulls them till the tear gets longer and—*there*, it's done, they're apart and he's really pleased with himself and now he's handing me one of the halves. *Look, look!*—he begins to rip his halved pages into quarters and then into eighths and then into confetti, very quickly, *pick-pick-pick* and the bits flick into the surging wash of the pulp beneath the foam and they're gone.

I go to do the same with my half of the book—but *no no no!*—seems he was just showing off: there's a machine that does this after all! I watch as he rips up the half-book with a plain old-fashioned bandsaw, down and then across and then into smaller and smaller bits with his fingers getting closer to the blade each time he cuts. And the bits into the wash!—all this without ever telling me why he's called Nikita, why he's a Russian, why this place is Glasnost or why he likes destroying books. I stand there in the endless throbbing racket, giving myself over to it, watching him wrench the heart out of *Daniel Deronda* and then *Cranford* and *The Cage at Cranford* and then rip them up with the saw. There they go as the noise becomes a sort of music and what he's doing becomes a sort of dance— *Brideshead Revisited* is getting it now, and then it's *Sleepless Nights* after that, then *Casanova's Chinese Restaurant* and *Books Do Furnish a Room*. He tears the heart out of Anthony Powell and then rips into Iris Murdoch, then two or three of Joseph Conrad, a man I know nothing about, not a thing, and then—

Now he's into Trollope. This is what I came for. I watch as he guts *Doctor Thorne* and one of the other workmen puts him through the saw and into the sludge, then *Phineas Redux*, then *The Warden*, then the rest of them, *The American Senator, He Knew He Was Right, Ralph the Heir*. I'm waiting, waiting—and now here it is, here it is at last, *The Last Chronicle of Barset*. He picks her up, he pulls her open, he begins to tear her body to bits, at last he plucks out her throbbing heart. Mrs Proudie. He's killed her. I hadn't realised I wanted it so much.

I watch him grab others from the pile, *Barchester Towers, The Three Clerks, The Eustace Diamonds*. He opens them up, tears the pluck out of them, saws them into fragments and throws them into the surge and they're gone. The Ocean of Literature. This is where it ends up. I don't know what to think. I pull away—and over there against the bales of paper scrap is the pile of books Harrison and Jason brought in a couple of hours ago. Over the last year I've wiped and dusted thousands of novels and memoirs and histories and plays like these, I've packed and pushed thousands of dictionaries and biographies and autobiographies and manuscripts and music collections and art collections and God knows what else. I haven't read all of a single one of them. Here they are, heaped in a corner with cartons and drums and bales of recycled paper.

I walk over to them as Nikita goes on gutting books behind me, I bend to the titles in the gloom of the neon light. Here they are, here they are, waiting for the end. *Essays on Giordano Bruno. The Colloquies of Erasmus. Inferno. Virgin Soil. Die Juden von Zirndorf. Lord Bacon's Essays. Moby-Dick. Amerika. Song of Solomon. The School for Wives. Adventures of Huckleberry Finn. The Making of the English Working Class. Picasso and Braque: The Cubist Experiment. The Poems of Alfred Lord Tennyson. English Traits. Man's Search for Meaning. Die Blechtrommel. The Fall of Constantinople. Narrative of the Life of Frederick Douglass. The Wretched of the Earth. Nga Tangata Toa. The Story of the Jews. Der Sand aus den Urnen. The Hunger Angel. Tihij Don. The Odyssey. The Age of Empire 1875–1914. Locus Solus. The Double Rainbow. A History of the First World War. Min Kamp. Hyperion. Malaria. De Tweeling. Black Ice Matter. The Guns of August. Mjórtvyje dúshi. Montaigne: Essays. Tangier Buzzless Flies. The Manticore. The Winter's Tale. Anna Karenina. Humanism in the Renaissance of Islam. Te Whiti O Rongomai and the Resistance of Parihaka. Bury My Heart at Wounded Knee. Albertine Disparue. The Federalist Papers. Imperial Leather. Heart of Darkness. Ethan Frome. Aeneid. The Blue Flower. The Republic. I promessi sposi. The Siege of Krishnapur. The Canterbury Tales. The Open Society and Its Enemies. Laocoön. The Downfall of the Liberal Party 1914–1935. Moses Mendelssohn: Sage of Modernity. System of Ethical Life. Le Père Goriot. A Mistake. Enemies of the Enlightenment. Le Grand Meaulnes. Under the Frog. Golden Deeds. Confessioni di Zeno. The Prince. Opus de Antichristo. Sydney Bridge Upside Down. The Long Forgetting. Empire. Fale Aitu. Medea. Religio Medici. Antigone. The Rights of Man. Gravity's Rainbow. One Hundred Years of Solitude. The Arabian Nights. A History of Western Philosophy. The Tragic Comedians. Ocean Roads. The Method Actors. Disraeli: The Novel Politician. King Potatau: An Account of the Life of Potatau Te Wherowhero the First Maori King. Dialogue Concerning Natural Religion. Pensées. Philosophiae Naturalis Principia Mathematica. Les Faux-monnayeurs. Under the Volcano. Leon Trotsky: A Revolutionary's Life. La divina commedia. War Songs. The Adaptable Man. Bulibasha, King of the Gypsies. Geróy náshevo vrémeni. Confessions. Night. Oblomov. La Peste. The Cinnamon Shops and Other Stories. Candide. Die Verwandlung. Natural Light. Human, All Too Human. The Great Gatsby. Alice Munro: Selected Stories. Ritualmord in Ungarn. Du côté de chez Swann. Cultural Amnesia. A History of Aesthetic. Periplus of the Erythraean Sea. The Well Wrought Urn. Satires. Poetics. Crime and Punishment. Dream Fish Floating. Moses: A Human Life. Robinson Crusoe. The Garden Party and Other Stories. Never Enough. In poylishe velder. Piknik na obochine. Lettres Philosophiques. Orientalism. Te Wai Pounamu. Mountolive. Pensées. Bloomsbury South. Cry, the Beloved Country. Riders in the Chariot. Adolphe. Nervous Conditions. Notes Towards the Definition of Culture. Rangatira. Half of a Yellow Sun. The Complete Works of Isaac Babel. Kleiner Mann—was nun? Die Leiden des jungen Werthers. the bone people. Harlequin Rex. The Fatal Shore. A Thousand Days. Cousins. The English Teacher. Voyage au Bout de la Nuit. Eritis Sicut Deus. The Pickwick Papers. Pouliuli. The Diary of a Young Girl. The Carpathians. Il Decamerone. Between Worlds. Kapitanskaya dochka. The Moviegoer. Anatomy of Criticism. Der Eiserne Gustav. Treasure Island. Azazeel. Passagenwerk. Kim. The White Hotel. Der Tod in Venedig. Im Westen Nichts Neues. Monumenti antichi inediti. Orlando furioso. Critique of Pure Reason. A History of the Arab Peoples. The Vendor of Sweets. The Age of Improvement. The Lost Pilot. Atemwende. Le Cid. The Lion and the Honeycomb. Di brider Ashkenazi. Piers Plowman. Literary Character. Se questo è un uomo. Lord of the Flies. The Birth of Tragedy. Juden auf Wanderschaft. Gulliver's Travels. No Fretful Sleeper. The Oxford Movement. Künstlerische Strategien des Fake. Racine. Brave New World. Kisses in the Nederends.*

PART FOUR

The 7 Habits of Highly Effective People

Chapter 16

After two years U1 and U2 achieved full erection, the latter with a helicopter pad beside its penthouse. After three, the University Bookshop nearby had been replaced by a vast shopping precinct featuring exclusive study opportunities. By then the swimming pool near the gymnasium had been rebuilt to face in another direction. The gymnasium was moved further away from it, then, the next year, closer. While this was happening, the Science buildings were replaced by new Science buildings and Engineering buildings by new Engineering buildings, each new building taller, bigger than the one before. Off their windows sunlight dazzled and glittered; window cleaners abseiled up them on ropes, though somebody said it was actually a SWAT team preparing to anticipate an unanticipated crisis. And, every now and then, the *thump-thump-thump* of the vice-chancellor's chopper, going out, coming in, going out again. Our new world, something always happening, something always about to happen, and nobody quite sure what it was going to be. *This was where it was at.*

All through this my IO meetings went on and on, creaking upward each day till Level 5 of U1 had become the seventeenth. Same room, different view; now, instead of seeing across the city we saw—well, U2, right next door, what else. Each time our meeting was done I used to linger at the window and look across at this new tower and the sheer *busyness* of the business inside it, this hive of new management *hard at it* in the first half-dozen floors of what would soon fill to a twenty-layer stack of meaningless activity.

A smart building, this U2, like all the new *builds* around the campus: self-sufficient in energy, air-conditioning, IT and so on, capable of withstanding nuclear attack, natural disaster, more. Houston claimed it even had feelings and was entitled to vote!—and, when challenged, told us a smart building in Philadelphia had recently got loose and attempted to mount the Prudential Life Insurance building nearby. Nonsense, of course—Houston, after all—but it was certainly true (someone slightly more reliable assured me) that the furniture and fittings on the top three floors of U2 were edible in an emergency: any lounge suite in one of the breakout lagoons up there could sustain fifty-to-a-hundred people for a couple of weeks! Well, that was what I was told.

I stood at the window after one of our meetings, watching a bouncy castle being inflated down there, slowly, sluggishly, near the Norman Iggo Water Effect.

'For the Senior Management Team.' Tyler Waltz, standing beside me and stuffing *Supplement 1a* into his briefcase. He pointed across to U2. 'They're moving them up there next. Top three floors.' He looked across and back. He put a finger to his lips. 'Shhh—'

'Shhh?'

'*Verboten.* Secure area.' He nodded to me, an *I'm-sure-you'll-understand* nod.

I nodded back. 'Sure,' I said. 'I understand.'

Verboten. The word made me want to *go* there, into this brand-new second tower, right to the top—made me want to get into those last three floors and have a bloody good poke-round.

What was it up there that could be so important? This gleaming new building—dazzling, refulgent[212]—went on filling with administrators, managers, facilitators, motivators, personal assistants, the personal assistants of personal assistants, IT support staff: all of them rising, floor by floor, while I looked on from U1 after each IO meeting. New hires, most of them, we were told: but who would they administer? Each other, someone suggested. *One* another, somebody else said—as if it mattered anymore.[213]

After a few months, U2 was more than half full and still filling—we could see them in there through the windows, meeting, passing motions, dabbing their mouths with tissues, checking their smartwatches for their next *meet*. Where would all these new salaries come from? I asked Tim Riordan. *We'll just have to sweat our assets a little more*, he replied.[214] I got the sense he was holding something back when he said this.

I watched him chairing meetings, looking weary. He was executive dean now, and in this whirling, seething new world the job was taking it out of him. HR had just asked him if he needed time off—management's most threatening question. *Application of micro-components is progressing*, I heard him say to

212 Really? *Reader's Digest Word Strengthener* territory here: it means 'shining very brightly'. A look-at-me sort of word, though it has to be admitted Richard Ellmann uses it in his final description of Oscar Wilde in his 1988 biography. Our man is trying very, very hard here to be—well, refulgent.

213 For correct use of 'each other' and 'one another', see H.W. Fowler, lexicographer (1858–1933), *The King's English* (Clarendon Press 1906). 'According to Fowler' was a standard usage of his day and his work is still relevant. He is particularly reliable on the use of 'each other' versus 'one another', 'among' versus 'amongst', etc.

214 A surprisingly figurative managerial euphemism for squeezing more from a fixed or reduced FTE base. Related to 'gig' (see footnote 140 above).

a college meeting from outside a door. *We've preferred a targeted operating model, of course, and it seems to be moving the needle.*

Application of micro-components.

Targeted operating model.

Move the needle.

Sweat the assets.

Sweat the assets? This was different, this one, this was beautiful, this was poetry; the first word in it gave life to the last, even gave it meaning—in certain lights, that sense of the ongoing tragedy of existence one finds in Tolstoy, in Dostoevsky, and, of course, in the later novels of Chekhov.[215] Beadsman was right, at its best this new lingo was an art form; like haiku, almost. It was literature, it hung in the mind and followed you around, it had that potential to form one's sensibility, which one always finds in great art. Did they know that, these idiots who spoke it?

Now, back in my office, here was Beadsman again, breezing in with scarcely a knock—'Wakey, wakey!'—and down in one chair before I was half awake in the other. 'The Robert Byng conference!'

I rubbed my eyes, I dragged my feet from the desktop: *CliffsNotes to The Old Man and the Sea* slid to the floor.

Oh, God, he was opening his laptop.

'Last week of September next year—how does that sound?' He rattled at his keyboard. 'I've scheduled the conference to

215 The later novels of Chekhov?—who published one full-length novel, *The Shooting Party* (1884), when he was twenty-four? This aside is hardly worthy of what he calls bluff-work—not necessarily in the claims he makes in it but in the implication that he knows anything at all about the writers he mentions (outside his various readers' guides, that is, on which he seems authoritative).

end on the Saturday so we can have some kind of farewell function that evening.'

Sheduled, not *skeduled*.

'Mm.' Fully half-awake now.

'Tim suggested an evening of bawdy—Wilmot and Etheridge[216] and so on—what d'you think—?' He seemed excited, in the same tittish Oxbridge way of Daresbury, Sophonisba Curry *et al.*[217]

'Mm, mm.'

'I think I've twigged you, by the way—why he's important, I mean. Our Robert. You're right, it's his absence that's the key, isn't it, not his presence? I've been reading Denham again, and Waller—you know, the Fenham group?[218]—and I'm beginning to think you might just be onto something.'

'Quite. Quite.'

'The poems feel *different* when you think of Byng behind them, informing everything. I mean all that *concealment* imagery—Aeneas trying to hide his fleet from Dido—in Denham's passion poem, remember?'

I nodded, dumbly, *yes-yes-mm*. I barely knew what he was

216 'Bawdy' refers to work which is obscene and often sexual in its references. John Wilmot, 2nd Earl of Rochester (1647–80), was a *bon vivant* and author of bawdy verse, as was Sir George Etheridge (1636–92). An evening spent drinking mulled wine and reading verse like this aloud has seemed daring for generations of academics in the humanities, though perhaps less so in recent years. Endless group readings of Milton's *Paradise Lost* have also been reported.

217 Somehow, 'tittish' seems slightly less offensive as used here. *The Collins English Dictionary* (Harper Collins) gives 'testy, irritable' and a Scottish origin, also 'despicable or foolish' in an English context.

218 Denoting an area west of Newcastle-upon-Tyne associated with the mid-seventeenth-century poets mentioned here. Edmund Waller (1606–87) was a minor poet and politician.

talking about. Old Dildo and Anus.

'I mean—that's *Byng* he's hiding, isn't it?—it's an emblem of Byng's influence *on* the text being hidden *in* the text—'

'Oh, quite—'

'—hidden *and* shown—?'

'Quite!'

'Brilliant!' Standing now, closing his laptop. 'Now that's settled I can start advertising the conference—got a title for it, by the way. "An Informing Absence: the Robert Byng phenomenon".'

'Very good. Very good.'

'Old Robert as the ghost in the machine—now, *there's* a title for your keynote address—'

'*My* keynote address?'

'Who else, who else? The dean and I agreed, you're the only one to give it—after all, *you're* the chap who more or less *invented* old Robert, aren't you?'

Old Robert. The bastard had taken possession of Byng; he thought he owned him now—you could see. I watched him leave. It'd begun in bluff, this Byng bullshit, but it was becoming real behind my back. A conference, people turning up—*people* turning up? And what did he mean by *invented* just now? *You're the chap who more or less invented Old Robert, aren't you?*—he looked at me over his shoulder when he said that, looked (I thought) in an insinuating way. Had he? Was he onto me?—yes, *that* was it, he was going to advertise the conference so that *no one would turn up,* and *then*—

I bent to retrieve *CliffsNotes to The Old Man and the Sea*—no, no: it was *Cole's Notes to Derrida.*

Later I was on the Nackers' deck again, listening to Lára's third phone message of the day, that thin needy voice getting more wretched each time. What could she possibly want now? I'd told her I was out of it, she knew I'd had enough. More and more Hungarian in every call, too, and all of it fading away from me, that strange foreign language I once thought I was starting to understand. *Fáj nekem*—she'd just said that and I'd no idea what she meant, that or any of the rest she was rattling in my ear. They were off in a month, the Giffords; he'd declined a farewell ceremony and gift, so he must have meant business. I could feel her falling away from me, Lára, the whole terrifying world she'd threatened me with. The past.

Her voice, still nattering away in my ear.

I looked across at Sally, indoors and on her phone, heard her disagreeing with someone very loudly. 'That's *bullshit*, Tony,' I heard her say. 'No, it *is so*.'

Kérem, segítsen. Lára's voice, tiny and sad. *Fáj a fejemben.*

I turned her off. I deleted her, I deleted all her messages.

A month after that I found a way into U2. The rumours were true, the senior management team was being moved over there, Lyall Boosey told me he'd heard it from someone who'd heard it from somebody else, though that turned out to have been Tyler Waltz, the person who'd told me about it in the first place. No matter: true twice over. They were all going across, those mysterious Maitlands and Gaitskells and Garlands, none of them much more than names to us—people we'd glimpse each day lunching together in *Naseninhalator*, the university restaurant near the boiler-house. We'd peek at them through tinted windows when we walked past, taking in their glitz and hoping (of course) for a glimpse of the great man himself— hardly ever there these days, though, and rumoured to be more and more often overseas. We'd gaze in at these gods as at a new, undiscovered race or intergalactic visitors, while they took no notice of us at all in return. An in-group, feeding off one another, dropping names, checking iPhones and smartwatches, always up for a quick elevator conference[219] or a sausage fest.[220] They fascinated us all the same. Them. Us. We.

High up in U1 our EIEIO committee was getting closer to establishing some of the main principles for writing the enabling document our *Supplement 1a* would eventually be appended to as an *after* to its magisterial *before*. Soon, we would Be. At the end of each meeting, I'd look *down down down* from the window and watch filing cabinets still being rolled from U1 into U2 on hand trolleys, and software and ergonomic office chairs and desks and pot plants and coffee tables and boxes of desktop toys and desk fans and coffee equipment and office photographs. The new order, moving in, tromp, tromp, tromp.

After a few days of this I slid down U1 in a lift and grabbed a pot plant from the foyer on the way out of the building. A manager was pulling a golf cart into U2: I slipstreamed him in and across to one of the elevators, holding the pot to myself, meaningfully, as if I had a purpose in life. *Seventeen*, I told him, and the elevator doors slid shut on us; we were swept up the silver tube. The man's trolley bristled with clubs. I looked around, getting my breath back: brass fittings, steel doors, mirrored walls, that familiar VOC smell everywhere.[221] Whee! All new!

I found myself turning to this manager, I found the words just coming out of me, unexpectedly, like a burp.

219 An exchange succinct enough to be started and finished during a single elevator ride.
220 An all-male management meeting.
221 Inferior bluff-work: '"Volatile Organic Compounds" are organic chemicals that have a high vapour pressure at ordinary room temperature' and can be harmful. I think he's trying to say the new building smells new.

'Questing a NoSQL database meet?'

'A NoSQL database meet?' The man laughed. 'How did you guess?'

'Manila?'

'No, Barry's handling Manila.' The lift slowed, stopped; he stepped out, lugging his clubs. 'Kuala Lumpur, me,' he said, over his shoulder, and was gone.

Up up up some more. I stepped out and looked around. Soft, discreet surfaces, indirect light, that new-car acetone smell again. I touched the walls, bent down and ran my fingertips through the spritzy crackle of the carpeting. All around, that familiar hotel hum. I checked the corridor, left, right. Nothing. I moved left, holding the pot plant in front of me like a passport.

Brand-new meeting rooms, each with a nameplate. Here was one with its door ajar. Nobody about. I pushed in: the lighting sensed me and flickered on to the end of the room. A long, coffin-shaped table; chairs. After a moment of reflection, I put the pot plant on the table, roughly in the centre. I stood back and dusted my hands off. I felt it was the least I could do.

I stepped out and checked the corridor left and right. I stepped back into the room.

The chairs, their backs and the seats of the chairs, the padding there. It couldn't be true, could it? I started to touch them. Surely not—too hard. Another prod. Difficult to tell.

There was only one way to settle this business. I slid down to one knee, I knelt on the floor. The seat smelled of different things—that new-car smell that was all over the place, naturally, but something else far more promising than that. Organic, that was it—was *this* the part you could eat?

I bent forward, as close to the fabric as possible. I sniffed at it, took a nibble, then a bite, sniffed again.

Briskly, busily, headlong, a woman came in the door—

power-dressed; frizz of hair, hint of aftershave. She was holding a clutch of papers. Three steps in she spotted me and stopped short as if she'd walked into a plate glass window.

She stared at me.

I tried to stand up.

There was a tiny bite of the chair-back in my mouth, that was the main problem—not a lot, but it did present difficulties, I could see that. And then, of course, I'd been sniffing the chair seat, something that can easily be misinterpreted.

Just one look back at me—wild, *it-can't-be-happening*—and then—

Behind her in the corridor a man walked past the doorway, right to left, and was gone.

I couldn't believe it. I couldn't believe who I'd just seen. *Really?*

I got to the doorway: nothing, no one. The woman had fled to the right.

To the left, a few doors down, the men's room.

Of course, of course, the men's room—

I stepped in: cubicles empty, no one there.

I sniffed—

Dope, I could smell dope, I could smell dope in the air.

Dope, in my life again—?

By now we were the Department of Text Management,[222] but my office was the same sad, featureless room it'd been for years now, and still right next to you-know-where. I paused to listen

---

222 With acknowledgements to Emeritus Professor R.D. Robinson, Victoria University of Wellington, originator of this concept of safeguarding arts departments from managerial interference. See also the Author's Note at the end of this main text.

through the wall: surely this was Dylan Edgie (*Joseph Conrad the Gay Clown*, Simon & Schuster 1989)? We hired him only last year and I was still learning the subtleties of his performance.

Three phone messages: Biddle, trying to organise yet another resistance meeting, Lára yet again, and—well, it took me twenty seconds to understand the third.

I listened to the voice. A cough, with a slight hoick in it . . .

I stared at the boiler-house wall, still there, ten feet beyond my window.

It was true. He was back.

There was a number at the end of it all: I pushed it into my phone. A pause, a clatter—then—yes, that voice. *That voice.*[223] After how long?

Was it?

'You! I can't believe it!'

'Yeah, yeah—'

'You were into bullfighting, I heard that, you were in Tbilisi, directing—'

'Yeah, Shakespeare and shit, yeah.'

'And the Olympics in the Maldives, you were—'

'Naah, Caymans, shame about that—wouldn't—y'know— *gel*? No vision, that's the pricker, some people got no vision?'

'Then what? After that?'

I listened as he told me about it—his American years, the doctorate from the Institute of Health & Strength; teaching at a tiny college in Wisconsin; women problems; escape to a university above the Arctic Circle where everyone went around with a rifle; a relationship with a bear—Houston, he was beginning to sound

223 From Conrad, *Heart of Darkness* (1899)—describing the voice of the megalomaniac Kurtz; used naively here, naturally, any appropriateness accidental. Overheard and half-remembered, presumably.

more and more like Houston; but no, he said, no, he didn't know any prick called Houston, and no, it wasn't in the States anyway, this last college, the nearest town was called Pessary.[224]

All through this I couldn't believe it was him. That voice, in my ear again. It couldn't be true.

'So—what are you doing now?'

'Change management consultant.'

'The *dark* side? *You?*'

'Yeah—used to be a stoner but I've matured, now I'm a pothead.'

'Right.'

'Or the other way around.' I heard him fumbling with the phone. 'Listen, what's the first thing you remember about the sixties, the seventies?'

I didn't even have to think, of course. 'Dope. Smoking dope—'

'Right. Smoking dope. What's the first thing you think about when you think about smoking dope?'

'You *know* what I—'

'Yeah, yeah, but *tell* me—'

'Good times. Feeling good. Happiness.'

'And how's this new guy of yours make you feel?'

'The new vice-chancellor? When he's talking? Well—he makes me feel—happy, he makes us all—'

'He makes you *feel* good, he gives you a good *time*, he makes you *happy*. Euphoria, you told me that, you said you got high listening to him.'

Did I? When? It was true, though, that's what always happened—what was this he was asking me now, though?

224 Mis-hearing of Peschany, possibly, a town south of Murmansk and certainly within the Arctic Circle; but a university college there? Unlikely.

'Add up? How do you mean? Does he—'

'Make sense? The boss? When he's talking? Giving a speech?'

'I don't know. I don't know.' I thought about it. 'I can't always remember where he's started from—'

Down the line, a light, confirming cough. 'He talks like a *stoner*—can't you *see* that? Remember trying to remember things when we got stoned? All those times we'd jump track?'

'When we were talking? Of course, I—'

'Start a sentence, halfway through you can't even remember where it began, what the fuck you been *talkin'* about—?'

'Yeah!'

'Spend a whole fucken evening, end up neither of us'd know what in God's name we'd been—'

'Yeah! Yeah!'

'But we were *happy*, and that's how *he* talks to *you*. He makes us feel the way *we* used to feel, we never gave a fuck what we'd forgotten, we were just *happy*, the same way *he* makes you *feel*—'

He was saying *fuck* more often now—I could hear him feeling his way back into my memory of him. I still couldn't believe it, though. How could it be Manatine, after all these years?

'Listen. The whole of managerialism—the whole fucken neo-liberal thing—comes out of smoking dope. Just think about it: it really went big in the sixties, seventies, right? And when did managerialism—y'know, the neoliberal thing—when did that start to—'

'Yeah, yeah, yeah—' I was starting to get it. 'Same time, it started at the same time, you're right. But it comes out of the Harvard Business School—'[225]

225 'The Harvard Business School is the graduate business school of the Harvard University in Boston, Massachusetts,' was established in 1908 'by the humanities faculty', and has been helping people all over the world ever

'Biggest pack of stoners on the planet. Listen—it's *in* the words—*marijuana*—*managerial*—can you hear it? If you say it fast—?'

Marijuana. Managerial.

Manatine—

Of course—*of course*! Why hadn't I thought of this before? As soon as he said it I realised it was what I'd have thought if I had. The discontinuity that had taken over as soon as the new vice-chancellor arrived—the way we'd woken up and found we'd turned from a faculty into a college overnight, the way that old wooden lecture room had become a row of offices over the summer break: *that's* what he meant. The new people in the new offices, as if they'd been there as long as the tiny histories they put on their walls—instant tradition, like the brown-bag meetings, or the fireworks displays in the southern quadrangle whenever an essay was handed in on time. Whee!—so *obvious*, so incredibly *obvious*.

But what was this he was saying now? Oh, it was all tumbling out again, the full tirade, the full vista—of *course* he'd ended up in management, Manatine, of *course* he'd become a manager. *What else could he be?* God, I'd missed him, I'd missed that sense that he could explain everything, anything, show how it all added up. I drank him in, after all these years.

Afterwards I sat there with the receiver in my hand. It hadn't happened, had it? I'd woken from one of my office naps, that was it. It'd *sounded* like him, though, that was the thing about it—he'd sounded more and more like himself the more he went on. It was just like *being* with him, the discontinuity, the wild

since. The claims being made here are ridiculous—this is a stoner fantasy, typically compelling on the face of it but not standing up to the slightest inspection.

swoops of thought, the chaos that always began to form itself when he was on a roll—I mean, a relationship with a *bear*—?

Now, a tap at the door: Clodagh Bacon (*Jane Austen, Quilt-Maker*, Hamburg: Quilt-Veröffentlichung 2005), one of my many younger colleagues—a plump, tense young woman who was next door these days, in Alun Pismire's former office. She stood there, sniffing.

'Are you smoking something naughty in here, Tom?'

I stood, and sniffed the air.

Dope. Pot. Grass. Mary Jane . . .

In *here*—?

She looked at me, reproachfully. 'You can smell it next door in my room,' she said. 'It's out here in the corridor.'

A day or two later, *hors de bleu*, a plastic swipe card arrived in the internal mail. I remembered the way *Associate Dean* had appeared on my office door years back like a magical thumbs-up from the System. Acceptance again: *yes*, I really was *part of something*. Except in this case the man in the photo wasn't quite me. I kept taking the card out and looking at him during the day. He was like someone I knew. My Platonic self? My electronic being? Or Manatine, was it Manatine? Was it his card? Whoever it was, it was obviously something to do with him. Things always started to happen when he was around.

I lay there in my weeknight bed, letting all this assemble itself for me. He'd gone from my life, all those years ago, and Sally had come into it. Now, Sally was away in another city most of the week—and here was Manatine, back in my life again. Apparently. Is that how it worked?

I let my new card take me back into U2, and up the tower to the nineteenth floor. I stepped out: a reception area—breakout lagoon, long executive front desk, ergonomically appropriate chairs, receptionists, pot plants, meaningless modern sculpture in wood.

The receptionist on the right looked up. 'Professor!' She smiled at me. 'You're early for your appointment!'

Professor? 'I—'

'Tom!'

I turned. Behind me, Maisie Jago, from the Senior Management Team—in charge of parallel parking. She smelled of influence, reeked of it, that distinctive whiff of burnt chlorine I'd begun to notice around managers now—sharp, electric, differentiating. *Someone from Senior Management was talking to me!* But how did she know my name? Smiling at me now, too, as she came up, smiling and—

'We were just talking about you!'

Now, from behind me, a hand on my shoulder. 'I'd be very careful, Maisie, talking to this chap.' The hand came around, an arm settled about me, tightened, ended up patting against my chest. 'He's far too clever for his own good.' A squeeze, the hand against my heart, a light, firm press-and-hold. It stayed there. The *strength*, the *warmth*. 'This boy.'

Oh, God, the power of it. You've no idea, you've no idea. All the life went out of my legs. Acceptance after all these years. Part of the team, after all these years.

Super-Iggo's penthouse—that's what was on top of U2, on the twentieth floor, that's where he lived, with his mysterious wife. Maisie Jago's PA's PA took us there early on a Friday evening, shot us up in a private elevator and led us across a padded foyer into the great man's card-entry Xanadu. One look inside and Johannes van der Nacker's Kashmir Hill paradise turned to dust behind us. *This was it: we'd made it.* We were going to spend the next six weeks of our lives *at the top*. I stood at the rack of north-facing floor-to-ceiling windows and squinted into a blowtorch of sunlight captured, mellowed—given meaning, even—by tinted glass.

I was here at last. I'd arrived.

Behind me, Jacinda, Maisie's personal assistant's personal assistant, checking us out. 'No, no pets,' I heard Sally tell her. 'No, we don't smoke, either of us.' And then: 'Ushak? Really? Genuine Turkish? How much is that worth? Insured for *how* much?—did you hear that, Tom?' But I was too busy trying to be Super-Iggo, trying to get into his mind, just for a moment, trying to get into the feel of being *him*. I looked around: a wine cellar?

We moved in the next day, Sally's home gym coming up the lift-shaft with us along with the ironing board and the collapsible sofa and all the rest of our junk—so shabby amidst the glory of the vice-chancellor's world! We stuffed it into the great man's study and closed the door.

That first night we sat with a simple chablis from the wine cellar in the pantry and watched the sun go down behind the mountain range. For dinner we ate parts of a pair of 1940s Louis XV–style fauteuils,[226] which had a hint of salmon with roasted grapes and thyme. Outside, the city started lighting up for us and we could see the fluoro sign on Cathedral Mall: *For God's Sake, Shop Here!* I thought of Super-Iggo on the other side of the world, negotiating with the mighty, and then I thought of him sitting right where we were, sipping wine and watching the coy flutter of the city lights. *Here we were, here we were—*

---

226 French, alas. What armchairs become when sold in fashionable boutiques, along with Sheraton refrigerators. 'We buy junk and sell antiques.'

That night we lay together on the vice-chancellor's super-king-sized waterbed, in the unfamiliar darkness. Sally was so far from me I wasn't even sure she was still in the room.

Her voice, out of the darkness and the hum of the building. 'We're babysitting the *building*?'

'Apparently.'

'Are you levelling with me?'

I'd noticed she'd started using phrases like this. Viscera, that must have been Viscera talk. I tried to explain what had happened but without mentioning that Manatine was back in my life: about Maisie Jago, how I'd thought I was about to meet Super-Iggo but I'd turned and it was a man who looked like him, a lot like him but who was his—

'Bovril Anderson? *Bovril*? Is that a nickname or something?'

'I don't know. He's the boss's stand-in or stunt-double or something. I'm not quite sure how it—'

'No one's called *Bovril*, Tom. And what's a vice-chancellor need a *stunt*-double for, for God's sake?'

Good point. Good point.

I tried to tell her the rest—about smart buildings, how they were so attuned to humans they were virtually organic themselves, how they needed a constant human presence in order to be: everything Maisie Jago had told me.

'*Lonely*? Smart buildings get *lonely*?'

'Well—that's what Maisie said.'

I told Sally nothing about Manatine, though, nothing about that sense of being drawn into his world again. Nothing about that.

After a few minutes I heard her breathing settle, her familiar slow drift into sleep, the tiny cat-sounds she used to make during each night. In the background, the familiar low hotel-hum of the air conditioning, the sound of distant functionaries so far away as not to be there at all—that big-building here-and-not-here hum. Instead, something else taking over, another sound, something that was quite new—

A voice. Surely it was, surely that's what it was—? I sat up in the dark, half-sat-up, my weight on my elbows. Somebody was saying something, weren't they, someone was saying something to me? No, not quite *saying*—communicating, that was it. Like a tune, like music: sadness, melancholy, loss. Who was this— what was this?

Chapter 17

Early evening and I'm pushing my way into Cathedral Mall, down the side of a stopped tram and past shoppers and through their babble and smell and the Sound of Muzak. There it is, ahead of me, down near the chancel: the lights, the natter of the diners, that familiar yum cha scent as I close in on it—

I come up to the windows. And here she is, Sally, back in town at last, at a table across from the bullied diners and surrounded by her coterie, left and right. I half-recognise one or two of them, onscreen faces looking less than their images, and a large woman who must be Bonnie, dabbing chopsticks at her plate. Beside her, Sally, oblique to the windows and nodding *mm-mm* just as she did when I was watching her last night on her show, and the night before that and the night before that: listening to the man across the table from her. I move along the window: still Sally, as she leans towards this man, still the woman I've been telling you about but Sally in her prime now, Sally where she was always destined to end up, all the time I had my arms around her and whimpered silly rot in her ear, begged her forgiveness for this cockup and that. The man who's talking to her is Yousef, the Palestinian, looking like the rest of her brave new world.[227]

---

227 The title of Aldous Huxley's novel *Brave New World* (1932) is the more likely source for this smuggled quotation than Shakespeare's play *The Tempest*, where it appears in Act V—far too late for our man.

My hand slides into my pocket. There it is, I can feel the weight of it.

Now she's standing, Sally, and here's her little child; Yousef takes this little olive from her strawberry-blond mum. I watch him put his arms around her, hold her tight to himself as he sits down, I can see the look on Sally's face—

Now—

I rap at the restaurant windows so she'll see it's me doing what I've come here to do. She looks straight at me—she looks right through me. *I've changed that much?* I'm pulling the damn thing out of my pocket. Here we go. Here we go—

>~~~~<

By the end of the year U1 and U2 had filled up with new managers. What next? Slowly, bit by bit, one tower began to manage the other, the former the latter or possibly the other way around. After a few months they began to take turns, dominating and submitting like lovers. Soon, wholesale de-layering began in one tower as mass re-layering[228] began in the other. Rumour, all this, just rumour; so much gossip going around these days. Lots more managers about the main campus now, no doubt about that, and back in our little college in town, too—snooping around, measuring up, taking pix. Eyeing us as we went past.

228 'De-layering' is the process by which a 'vertical' or hierarchical organisation is made into a flat structure through redundancies; 're-layering' is the reverse, brought about, inevitably, by a prior de-layering, itself brought about by prior re-layerings. Not to be confused with 're-basing', the process by which high-salaried staff are dismissed and replaced by smaller numbers of younger staff, often temporary and always lower-paid, the latter being the point of re-basing.

Sometimes when I passed U1 and U2 I saw figures emerging at ground level that were almost familiar to me but not quite, like former schoolmates half-recognised in adult bodies. Maitland was one of them, I'm sure it was Maitland—except when he got closer it was not quite him after all but perhaps another person who'd gone through the same structural processes and become as he was, dark-suited with a tie in a single colour— teal, puce, whatever—and with tanned skin bonded teeth designer spectacles sculpted hair; or perhaps no hair at all, just the bared skull, shaven to the wood. Whoever it was swept past me, talking urgently into his hand or his wrist or his lapel, networking with the world, the cosmos. Gaitskell, that was his name—no—no. It wasn't Gaitskell. It wasn't Maitland, either.[229]

I was still babysitting the vice-chancellor's penthouse, still hearing in the depth of each weeknight a deep unhappiness in the workings of the building, an *mmmm* in the air conditioning that made me think of Lára Gifford, gone to the States with her husband. But, then, each Friday evening: Sally, back for the weekend!—I'd clutch at her like a kid each time she reappeared, cleave intensely to her.[230] She completed the scenario that

229 There we are again—he can't possibly have read Lacan on the masked ball; besides, Lacan was French and hence incomprehensible. Nevertheless, there's a clear echo of him here: overheard in the common room again, or a more complex influencing from that 'ocean of literature' around us?

230 Straight from D.H. Lawrence's *Women in Love*, where Gudrun is highly contemptuous of Gerald's dependency on her. 'Like a child at the breast, he cleaved intensely to her, and she could not put him away' (p.345). On holiday in Austria, she tells him bluntly that on that night 'I had to take pity on you. But it was never love' (p.442). Penguin edition used here. The late page number for this passage suggests, however, that it's almost certain our man would never have got that far.

seemed to be forming now we'd got—well, to the top: the two of us, twenty storeys up, a pair of high achievers reflected in the mirrors that began to surround us each Saturday and Sunday evening as light faded beyond the tinted double-glazing. In the glass we could see ourselves as others might have seen us: movers and shakers in a young executive's penthouse, acting ourselves out against the glimmer of a night-time city—quaffing the vice-chancellor's wine, peeking out at our reflections as we shared silences both lambent and profound; and every night nibbling at his furniture. *Made it.*

Here's me, suddenly, inspired one of these evenings by what I could see of myself out there, a huge imago hovering over the city, reflected back with a wineglass in its hand:

'More changes.' Words, just words, just what drifted into my mind, anything that sounded right, sounded big. 'New managerial appointments.'

'Changes?' Sally was sitting on a sofa upholstered in the distressed skin of the unborn elk. She looked across and away, over the city, playing her part. 'About time.'

I straightened my shoulders and took a sip—a Domaine wine, very expensive.[231] 'Of course, they'll pay for themselves. By the end of the Quinquennium. The changes.'

'Through retrieved academic salaries? Yes—but of course, one can't just *throw* people out of their *jobs*—'

'Oh—of *course* not! Of *course* not!'

'I mean, these are people who've spent their—'

'I know! I know! Their *entire life*—'

'Right! *Almost* their *entire life*! People like Back Passage—'

---

231 Very expensive indeed, but this is genuine bullshit—the kind of wine he's claiming here is probably beyond even the average university executive's range, starting at around $4,000 a bottle.

'Or Maxine Tapwater. Maxine's been here forever.'

'Right. Maxine Tapwater. I mean, what would they *do*, what would they *live* on—? If they got the boot—?'

'As if they don't matter anymore, as if they're just—' A well-managed pause. I looked out again: there I was, still reflected—huge, magnificent, executive, hovering over the twinkling city. 'She's been here forty years. Maxine. At the uni.'

'*Forty*? *Has* she? *God*, that's a long time. I had no idea.'

'I mean, someone like that could—'

'Yeah, yeah.'

'Well, y'know—'

'Yeah.'

'I mean, she must have something put away—'

'Back Passage, too. They must have a bit stashed away, people like that—don't you think?'

'They could probably *buy* you and me!'

'Yeah! But you have to think of, you know, how they'd feel after—'

'Yeah. Yeah.' A pause. 'Beadsman. He's a shit.'

'But he's *young*, Tom, he's just starting his career—'

'Yeah, but he's a shit. We could do without him.'

'Tom, you're getting so *hard*—'

It surprised me when she said that, it even shocked me a little. Had I *really* become hard? But then, after a moment, I found I liked the feel of it. Hard! Me! I squared up and straightened, and the hovering imago that stared back at me from above the city squared up and straightened, too. He turned and looked at the woman beside him, who reached up as he bent down to her; he placed his wine glass on a carved Chinese rosewood side table, he took her in his arms—

She whispered up at him. It began again:

Application of micro-components. Targeted operating model.

Move the needle. Sweat the assets sweat the assets robust outcomes robust outcomes drill down drill down drill down drill down leverage-leverage-leverage-leverage-leverage—

Afterwards, we faded away, motion passed *nem con.* We lay together, limbs entwined on the skin of the unborn elk.

Far too early in the morning a drone appeared outside the window and hovered there for twenty minutes—backed off a little, returned, backed off again and returned again.

Sally was in the shower and I called her but she didn't come out till the thing had gone—suddenly, there-and-not-there, *boom!* like that.

'There was a drone here looking in,' I told her.

'What?' A dressing gown, and her hair clamped wet in a towel. 'Nonsense, there can't've been.'

Or a UFO, I didn't want to say a UFO.

The next time he rang I could smell it straight away, as if it was coming at me through the phone. An illusion, of course—as *he* was: no more than a voice in my ear, an occasional *erm-erm* in the throat. Wasn't he? Just like the good old days, though, as I sat listening to him rattling on about the meetings he'd just been in, how the one the night before had gone *on* and *on*— they'd been trapped two days and two nights trying to make it finish but it just *wouldn't* till in the end they'd got a hostage negotiator in.

I listened to all this until—

'Refluxicorp?'

'Yeah! This international outfit I work for now! Change management solutions. Listen. *Refluxicorp is dedicated to leveraging existent potentials in leading-edge communities via disintermediated and frictionless e-tail supply chains—*'

'What's this?'

'Start of the presentation I made at the meeting last night. That's when they got the hostage negotiator.'

'Re*flux*icorp?'

'Think gastric bands. That's what we do. Find fat, strangle fat. Tie it off. Shrink the institution. We strangle jobs, we strangle careers. We get down to essentials. Like, take attachments for example—'

'Attachments?'

'Yeah. Not necessarily part of our vision going forward, man.'

Attachments? It takes me a moment. He means—

'Students? They'll work from home—?'

'Right!—attachments are optional! Gotta remember, we're shifting paradigms here, we're rationalising the student option entirely.' That cough again, *hoick-hoick*. 'Students. Out of the schema.'

Another moment to catch up. 'No students at *all*, then?'

'Yeah, no attachments. We've ballparked this, we've run the numbers on a negative paradigm and the gains in efficiency you *wouldn't believe*—they're through the roof, through the fucken ceiling LED fittings.'

'Staff? What about—?'

'They're attachments too. Got no students, what you need staff for?'

'No *staff*?—you mean they're closing the place down?'

'No no—place stays open.'

'What's left, then? No staff? No students?'

'Well, work it out for yourself—'

A pause.

'*Management*? Just *management*? What are you *on*?'

'Listen, I'm *in* management now, man, I *am* management,

I'm fucken *mari-ju-ana*. I'm giving you our vision here—pure management, nothing else, it's the logical outcome of everything, the last forty years, fifty, that's what we're driving at in Refluxicorp—a world where everyone manages everyone else, there's nothing else but management—it's Hegel, it's the end of history—*he* smoked the blaze, man, you should read his *System*—'[232]

So—this was where he was heading, all those years ago. He made sense, as long as he was speaking. When he stopped, he made no sense at all. Classic Manatine.

Hold on, what was this he was telling me now—

'What d'you mean, I'm toast?'

'If your man buys what we're offering in Refluxicorp. That's why I'm here. That's what we do, we help failing institutions market-exit to a business sublime.'

'By cutting out fat?'

'If he buys into our programme, you'll lose your job.'

Here it was at last. I sat there, swallowing and swallowing.

'It was never going to be about syllabus. It was never going to be about how you taught. It was always going to be about this. Money. Once you monetise a place like this people like you are fucked. If *anyone* can do what you do, *no one* can do it even better.'

So simple. The death sentence, after all these years. Gifford had been right. All that was left was the sound of Beadsman, on the other side of my office wall now, with his tinkling, maidenly performance.

232 Here he might be referring to something in the area of system level interconnect prediction. IT. Ignore. Alternatively, he might be referring to Hegel's *System of Ethical Life and First Philosophy of Spirit* (1802). Georg Wilhelm Friedrich Hegel (1770–1831), influential idealist philosopher. German. Also ignore.

I tried to focus on Manatine's voice again. What was this?

'Me?'

'You snow them? The students? When you were teaching?'

'Well, I suppose I—'

'Bullshit 'em? Make out you knew things they didn't know?'

'Of *course*. All the time. We both did, you—'

'Research?'

'Complete and utter bullshit. What there was of it. *You* remember.'

I told him a little about Robert Byng—I could hear him laughing back at me down the line, that old-times laugh of his. Yes, definitely Manatine, I was sure of it now.

'I'm sick of it.' It took me by surprise when I said it, but it was true.

'Me, too, man. That's why I got out. Couldn't stand the students, couldn't stand the lecture room, couldn't get published—then I realised there was only one place left to go. Management. And I've never looked back.'

'*Management?*'

'We're all failed academics, man—well, not all of us, some of us've failed at other things, business, law, television. Sport, even.' More coughing. 'You should try it.'

'Management—? But I don't have any vision—'

'See yourself in a top job? Huge salary? Expense account? Company credit card? Isn't that what vision means?'

I stared out of the window.

'Listen. I'll try you out some more. What's the key to a visionary project—any visionary project?'

I thought for a second. 'Underfunding. You underfund the project.' The words just seemed to come to me.

'Right! And then—'

'You find a scapegoat—'

'Yeah, yeah—'

'—and then when you've fired him you—sweat the assets to make up the deficit—?'

'Right! Brilliant! Listen—you're *made* for it, you're a natural. Come our way, man. It's eternal life—'

Out there, the blank heave of the boiler-house wall. *Management—*

Later, as if she'd been listening from her office next door, here was Clodagh Bacon again. This time she came in and shut the door behind her. A nervous titter. She sniffed the air.

Then, suddenly: 'Could you get me some?'

'Some—?'

'Stinkweed!'

'*Stinkweed?*'

Standing there in front of me, tittering, blushing, tittering some more, blushing some more. *Stinkweed?*

Outside again I walked through the cloisters and into the northern quadrangle—and here was a black silhouette, only just painted on a wall of the humanities library: a man, a little more than life-sized, sitting in a pensive pose with suggestions of an academic gown and a squared mortarboard on his head—*à la* Rodin's *Thinker,* someone suggested. Further into the quadrangle and here was another of these painted black silhouettes, another man in academic regalia but this time with a finger up to emphasise an imaginary point to an invisible class. More of these images were planned (someone told me who'd been told by someone else) to represent the daily work of a university life.[233] Then, soon, a further rumour, more

233 Silly as this may sound on a university or college campus, it has been the practice in certain smaller colleges in the US to paint on the external

sinister this time: *there was more behind these silhouettes than mere imagery.* But what, what?—always rumours these days, nothing direct, no one seemed to know what was really going on anymore. Unease, settling around us; worried scholars, scurrying about, attending to their CVs, talking to their fund managers.

The hyperreal, Beadsman said, he who was really beginning to irritate me with his Oxbridge ways. The black silhouettes, he meant.

I was so buffled[234] by this I quite forgot to say *quite.* He explained the hyperreal to me, languidly, condescendingly, knowingly, all the time under the soulless tearoom gazes of Borin and Gotch: in the usual way of these things I took in but a *soupçon* of what I was being told, just enough to get it creatively wrong at some later date. *Content hollowed out and replaced by form,* that's the only part of it I remembered: the inside-becoming-the-outside. Oh, *quite,* I said as I tried to keep up with him; *quite*—but I think he'd rumbled me by now and he spelled it out as if to a moron. *The more they cut back funding, the less we can teach,* he said. *Right? Quite so, quite so,* I replied.

He was doomed, too, of course, but he didn't know that yet.

The less we can teach, he said, patiently, irritatingly, *the more we get images of us teaching painted on the walls as a compensation. Right?*[235]

---

walls of certain buildings larger-than-life images of academics reading, teaching and reflecting.

234 A neologism, presumably, possibly even a nonce word particular to our man or one he's heard and thinks is genuine currency. A fusion, made however wittingly, among some or all of 'baffled', 'rattled', 'battered' and 'ruffled'?

235 See footnote 7 above. He seems to have forgotten this earlier mention of the hyperreal.

Oh, quite, quite, I said.

But did I *really* think that? I'd stand in front of these glistening black shapes in the quadrangle and sometimes I'd think he was right, and then at other times I'd think he was just being silly. Why were they there if he was wrong, though, what *were* they for? Things were becoming so difficult to pin down, that was the problem. Not hard to understand the logical end-point of all this, though, if he was right. No-staff-and-no-students, Manatine had said, and he'd given one of those laughs that isn't a laugh at all. Just administrators. Just management. And of course I thought of what Beadsman had just told me when he said that. These mad ideas were getting into the tapwater, they were getting real.

Then, days later, a counter-counter-rumour—wild, terrifying, raging from mouth to ear to mouth again like mad cow disease. Our buildings were going to be sold all right, *but not rented back for teaching after all*—teaching was to be *franchised out, franchised overseas* and *taught to our students online.* Dickens would come to our students via Zhengzhou, *The Rape of the Lock* from Belgrade, *Lady Windermere's Fan* from Dar es Salaam. *Could that be?* Oh yes, Reg Pye assured us, worldly-wise as ever: yes, yes, in point of fact it had been happening overseas for some time already. But what about the classroom, then, what about that intimate connection that builds over a period of years between pedagogue and pupil, and which forms the basis of a genuine, ongoing life-learning?

I don't know what you see in me.

After that, words began circulating in a different direction: Super-Iggo was back in town, something big had happened, some kind of breakthrough had occurred overseas, in the Northern Hemisphere, possibly—even somewhere beyond the solar system! The planets, it seemed, had aligned at last—how, though, why? You could *feel* the excitement as we crackled our way into CG17b for our Friday *brown bag*. I was an old hand at this by now, and, for its positive connotations, had chosen a service-station hot dog over egg and mayonnaise. It poked out of my brown bag, hopefully, as I went in.

You could feel the excitement as the great man entered, behind the Senior Management Team and his advisers, people I was beginning to know by sight and more. They lined up behind him like an identification parade.

We settled in. He was back! He had good news for us! He—
Something else happened instead. *He said the word at last.*

He began as he always began, by talking about great things, about the places he still wanted to take us, all of us, destinations which when he described them made me think again of that comet with the spacecraft behind it—of our own spacecraft, too, the UFO Houston and I had seen or thought we'd seen some time ago now; of U1 and U2, our own rockets, pointing to the skies, side by side, ready for lift-off.

Friends, colleagues, scholar-managers! he cried, and as soon as he said those words again I felt myself begin to rise once more, just a little, felt that first dizzy whiff that always came when he began to talk. Here they were, here they came, all those wonderful words again: *unpack, unpick, interface, synergy, ideate, incentivise, client-facing*—more, more—I could feel my heart beginning to thrill—

But, then, a pause.

This had never happened before.

Around me, five hundred scholar-managers began to look up from their brown bags, caught mid-munch. I stopped halfway along my service-station hot dog: it jutted amorously from my mouth. What was this?

He was standing behind the lectern, head down, just standing there.

We waited.

Waited.

Silence.

Then he began to speak, softly, gently, in a voice full of regret.

First, he said, *we're going to have to make some changes . . .*

There it was at last, the word which I realised as soon as I heard it had been hiding behind everything he'd said from the day he arrived. Here was the spacecraft behind the comet, come to take us away. I could feel my heart give a big double bump; around me, the crowd in the Great Hall went silent—*completely* silent, as if no one was there at all, as if the room was empty, as if we'd already taken the phenobarbital. Then, from across the room, I heard the tiny, meaningless *bzzzt, bzzzt, bzzzt* of Back Passage's pacemaker, swathed deep inside the wax of his body fat. Every breath in the room, held. Almost: *Prinny has let loose his belly,* someone whispered nearby, which made no sense to me at all.[236]

Changes. As he said the word Super-Iggo bit his lip and dropped his head, just a little, and half-turned from the lectern, and let his arms down slowly, slowly, till they hung beside him as if he'd given up on them or they on him. *Despair*—I felt its wet, detumescent droop upon me, upon us all. *Changes,* he said again, and looked up, looked sad, looked rueful; and,

236 Rather a good, though somewhat recondite, witticism here. 'Prinny has let loose his belly, which now reaches to his knees,' a courtier's comment on the decision of the then Prince of Wales (later George IV) to discontinue further use of a corset in his middle years; see Thomas Creevey, *The Creevey Papers* (London: 1904, Vol.1, p.279), and Lytton Strachey, *Queen Victoria: A Life* (p.12).

yes, I felt sad and rueful, too. I turned and peered around the rows of staff stacked behind me: all of them looking back at Super-Iggo, each man, each woman caught up in him, hanging on every word just as I was, and each face like mine, like his, rueful and sad. *All* of us were *sad*—everything was, even the half-bitten sandwiches held motionless across the room seemed drooped and forlorn. He'd brought us all together, he'd united us at last.

We watched him look down again, look up again, gather himself and meet our gaze, and hold it as we held his.

He was *right*, that was the important thing—*right*, we knew that as he spoke and that *that* was what mattered. Changes *were* jolly well needed, of *course* they were. He'd just said that, *jolly well needed*, and it made me feel—made us all feel—*close* to him, *part* of him, part of a *team*. Now, though, here was a joke, perfectly pitched—and suddenly the hall was rocking with laughter; there were tears on five hundred faces; mine, too, mine most of all. *But what was it he'd just said?*—gone in a nanosecond, but, oh, *God*, it'd made me feel so *happy* when he said it. We were a *team*, for God's sake, we were all *on the same page* (he'd just said that, too, *on the same page*). He'd turned back to us when he told the joke, and when he said we were *all on the same page* he lifted his arms a little so his hands looked now as if they were giving us something—happiness? Reassurance? Love, even, even love its very self? Now his arms were coming down again, with the hands opened, pink clean palms showing, spatulate fingers spread: he had *nothing more to share with us*, we could see that, we could see he was *played out* with honesty; this was a man with *nothing to hide*, a man we could *trust*. We could see it in the way he stood, the way he looked, the very *being* of the man. God, I loved him. At that point I loved him as I'd never loved anyone before.

[314]

He had come amongst us. Was it wrong to think that?[237]

A silence, a moment of silence.

And now I began to stand, I was standing up—I'd stood, my body had stood itself up on its own! Here I was—the most amazing moment of my life, this—well, of my life till that moment, surely. Super-Iggo's words had simply lifted me— mere *Mr* Flannery, middle-rank nonentity, bluffed-through senior lecturer trapped halfway through the flatulent peristalsis of the promotion system—here was I, up and exposed and naked to everyone but most of all to *myself*, with every eye upon me and no idea what I'd say. Yet here they were all the same, words, bubbling up from somewhere in me: here were my hands, placing themselves confidently palm-to-palm in front of me as if frozen mid-clap, and, now, here was my voice, thanking the vice-chancellor for his visionary address, reassuring him that we all understood what he was saying but knew, *knew* he was right, simply *right*. Time to grasp the nettle! To seize the moment! *There's a war on!*—I even said that, to a nervous sputter of laughter, though where it came from I know not. Smiles on some faces, I could see that, not many but on some; other faces I had to admit were looking quite pissed off, and that puzzled me, that took me aback a little.

Here I was all the same, though, carried along, turning to my colleagues as I spoke. I was starting to know something of what all this was about, I was becoming confident, I could feel myself being picked up and swung along by the moment, by the language, simply by my own words. 'And *now*,' I said—found I was saying—'*now*, a special thankyou to the older staff with us today. I guess we all know'—turning to look around the mass of faces, from right to left—'how these things go at times like

237 Yes. Without a doubt.

[315]

this!' A rueful smile—Super-Iggo's rueful smile, I could feel it, transmigrated now and attached, somehow and momentarily, to my face. My hands parted and, slowly, met again in a moist clap. They held there, fingertip to fingertip. I listened to myself thanking the senior staff for their long, selfless contributions, the professors and the associate professors—everyone ranked above me—and wishing them a long and fruitful early retirement for their research. We all knew of the need for renewal, knew that change was a process which consisted, in turn, of individual changes in life, and that for newer growth to have a chance, some of the older growth had to be—well, slashed away. I think I might even have said something about winning some and losing some. *To everything,* I reminded them, *there is a season—*

Where was all this crap coming from?[238]—I'd no idea, but it seemed to be going down well enough all the same: there were the SMT members, like an identity parade against the whiteboard below us at the front of the room and most of them smiling, nodding—were they? Yes, *there* was Maisie Jago, looking straight at me and nodding her head *yes-yes!* There was Eric Camp next to her, whispering something that made her smile and whisper something back—now they both laughed, little approving splutters. *There* was the great man himself, smiling up at me, nodding as I spoke—and all through this, my voice coming out of my head like somebody else's, talking about unity, and sacrifice, and our gratitude to all those academics above us, an older generation in fact, who were, I knew (and I knew they wouldn't mind my saying this on their behalf!), only too willing to lay themselves down for the younger generation below them, to take the hit and *resign—*

238 From King Solomon, actually (Ecclesiastes 3: 1–8), but more likely to have reached our man via Pete Seeger and the Byrds.

I stopped. It seemed I'd come to the end of things. The whole show stopped, people were standing even before I'd finished, pulling on their coats, murmuring together against the rumble of seats snapping back as the room began to empty. Not quite the finish to things I'd expected—no applause, no nods of approval, no pats on the back. I looked down to the SMT but they were standing, talking to one another, many of them heading off through the side doors already, phones-out and gone. I threw a yearning look at the vice-chancellor's departing back, but—

Here was Henry Bumb, though, clumping towards me down the aisle—Henry, an Aspro[239] from American Text Management—here he was, lunging his head at me:

'You *fuckin' asshole*,' he hissed.

I couldn't believe it. 'What—'

'You *fucken two*-faced *ass*hole.' He grabbed me by the shoulder and shook it so hard my jacket came half off.

Jennings, now, going past as I scrambled my coat back on—he too lunged at me: 'Thanks a *million*.' He looked back at me once he was past. 'You arse-licking bloody quisling.'[240]

I had no idea what he meant, but oh, the *look* on his *face*. *What was happening?* Irina Oates next, silently, sarcastically pretending to clap her hands at me as she went past—someone else, doing the same, behind her—more, there were half a dozen of them pretending to applaud, women, disdainful, bitter, contemptuous. Why, why?—I hadn't had a relationship with any of them, had I—?

'Know where *you're* headed,' one of them called out. And: 'Congratulations!'—this from someone else, anyone—who

239 Associate Professor. Informal.
240 Vidkun Quisling (1887–1945), leader of pro-Nazi puppet government in Norway 1942–45, whose name has become synonymous with betrayal.

cares; I had to be out of there. 'Hope you know what you've done,' someone murmured as he smeared his way past me: Beadsman, it was Beadsman looking back as he adjusted his collar and went off through the door with Amanda Cupmark; they were both shaking their heads, both of them talking— about me, obviously talking about me.

Hope you know what you've done?—what *had* I done?

I was a pariah from that moment. Colleagues avoided me, people stood up and left the tearoom when I came into it, someone let the air out of my bike tyres—it was like being back at Anthrax High. When I told Sally she couldn't believe it:

'You said *that*? Those actual words? What d'you expect? Whose side are you on?'

I've often thought of that episode in CG17b. Yes, a trifle impulsive, a little badly judged, perhaps; perhaps the timing *was* poor. But did they *really* have to start calling me *Tom Flattery* behind my back, which was something (after all) that did tend to stick? I began to spend more and more time at the main campus, in one or other of the Registry towers, hoping to run into one of the suits, hungering for them when I saw them go past, my tongue out like a dog's. Sometimes a nod, rarely more.

Not a friend in the world.

Super-Iggo, meanwhile, was off overseas again, people said. One last attempt; though for what, no one seemed to have the slightest idea.

Chapter 18

And after all my hand comes out of my pocket empty, as if it's a sensible hand that belongs to someone else. Some part of me I don't know makes me turn away from the restaurant window. *Why, why, what does it want?* Whatever it is, I let it take me off and away. *That was my big moment, and that's all there is to it?* I'm walking back through the nave now and through the babble of the muzak and the racket of the shoppers and the tourists. I let that push me along the side of another tram that's creeping in, this one full of schoolkids with their party-party-party racket just above my head. I look up for a moment—and there're the Riordans, high in the mezzanine above me, Tim and Yvette, both of them looking shabby and older but holding hands, walking past the tiny boutiques up there and holding hands. *Why didn't I knock on the window?*

Out in the cathedral porch an amateur choir is preparing to humiliate shoppers. Here's David Peach!—looking older, in walkshorts and with socks to his knees. He starts telling me about his new, school-teacher life: best thing that ever happened to him! 'Really?' I say, '*That's* good news,' and 'Fine! Fine!' when he asks how I'm doing. 'Yes, with Bevan Panter! Old Bevan!' We laugh knowingly together, almost in barbershop harmony. Back in the real word he's losing that American accent.

Suddenly, furtively, I'm looking around and blurting it out at him and he's screwing his eyes up at me, I can see he's thinking *what's this guy on?* Then I show him the gun. I pull it out of my pocket—and seeing it there just takes him to another universe, you can tell, it takes him somewhere he's never been before in his *life*. I show it on my palm, just a second or two, then I slip it back in my pocket. Hard, cold; the bulk of it, the fear.

'For God's sake, man, what're you *thinking*?' He's looking around; he's hunching forward to keep his head near mine; here we are, hissing at each other amidst the push-and-pull of the shoppers. He stares at me, point blank: 'You remember Houston?'

'This is Houston's gun.'

'This is Houston's *gun*?—how'd you get hold of Houston's *gun*—?'

'I took it out of his drawer. So he wouldn't use it.'

He stares at me.

'I just want to get away from *books*.'

He's still staring. '*White Noise*,' he says. 'There's a gun in there.'

Really? 'Oh, yes, yes, quite. So there is.'

'*Lolita*. *Lolita*, too.'

He stops, he half-points at me and then pulls out of it.

'You went there with a gun to shoot your ex, and you changed your mind when you saw her in there with her partner and her kid—?'

I shrug at him. In fact, I've no idea what I just did. Yes, okay, I do know, it was that.

'*Herzog*.'

'*Herzog*—?'

'Bellow. Saul Bellow. You're acting out *Herzog* by Saul Bellow.[241] You know—he has a scene just like that? Second half of the novel—?'

---

241 Don DeLillo, *White Noise* (1985); Vladimir Nabokov, *Lolita* (1955); Saul Bellow, *Herzog* (1964).

'Second? Not a chance—'

'He's looking through a window with a gun, a pistol. Moses Herzog. He looks in but he decides not to shoot because it's all so, you know—mom-and-apple-pie?' Staring across at me, as if he's waiting. 'You *must*'ve read it—otherwise you wouldn't have done what you've just done—'

So, this Herzog character looks in the window and sees this guy who's married to his ex, bathing his little daughter, and he decides not to shoot him? I know, I know, it's not *exactly* the same. But so close, unnervingly close. If it's true. I've never read the book, of course, but—

'It's not loaded. I don't know how to load it.'

'Not *loaded*—?'

'He didn't have any ammo, I couldn't find any ammo in his room—'

I pull away. I have to sort this stuff out. It's sinking in, though, it's beginning to sink in. They're all around us, they're in everything, they're everywhere. Books. You can't get away from the fucking things.

He raises a hand to me, half-mast, and watches me back off. The choir starts singing an Xtra Penis number, 'Too Tall to Kiss'. I'm out of the Cathedral now, can't get away fast enough, I'm out and into the Square—where, wildly, passionately, a lone madman on a box is addressing almost nobody at all. One or two people scurry past him, embarrassed, looking down, looking away, as he bawls out the words he always bawls when he stands here each day on his wooden box with the label that says PEACHES. I recognise the voice, the face, the magnificent, ruined head, I recognise the whole performance from long-gone faculty meetings: Parsifal Oates, ex–Art History, whose house I baby-sat with Sally all those years ago. Now his foghorn carries across to me in the wind—hoarse, empty, completely without hope. *Fourteen hundred years of institutional knowledge,* he's telling all the world and no one. *That's what the bastards've wiped their arses on—*

⤛⤜

Suddenly, an all-staff email: *Urgent Meeting CG17B 2:00pm*: no time for brown bag or hot dog, hardly time even to shuttle out to the main campus and find a place in the expectant hubbub of scientists and engineers and teachers of business and the law and of something called education as well. We waited, we waited, till the lights went down almost to darkness and the murmuring fell away. Then—boom!—*there* he was, our man: a crackle of static and he was before us, lit, glittering, made up of colours, coming and going till he settled down and became the man we thought we knew. And in his creamy-white outfit, for God's sake!—though minus boater and cane: what were the semiotics of *that*?

He started to speak and for two seconds it was as if he was chewing air, there was nothing—then, the voice, *his* voice, but out of sync and with a message-from-Mars quality to it, there-and-not-there until the lips began to fit the words: *Friends, colleagues, scholar-managers—*

Someone behind us started whispering: the woman next to me turned back and hissed *no, it isn't.* What was this? *It is,* the bloke whispered back down at her, and the bloke next to him muttered the same thing, *you can see it is, it's obvious.* The woman said *nonsense* and turned back; *shhh!* from somebody nearby.

I stared down at the great man in his nimbus of light, as he *pulled* his arms to his chest, *clenched* his fists, *flung* his arms back out at us again, imploring, yearning, all the time talking, talking, his mouth chewing at words, biting them—a *hologram*? Is that what they'd just said, the two behind? And if it was, what was it here to tell us? No changes? The mouth, still chewing words a little out of sync, yes, but otherwise it was hard to tell—no, it *wasn't* a hologram, it was *him*, it was the man himself, wasn't it? It was—

No changes—is that what he'd just told us? All around me, people stirring, waking to him, looking around, murmuring, starting to take in what it was he'd just said. *We were free*—suddenly, out of the blue, we were back in the black! I can't remember exactly what he told us, but I can still remember the huge, collective gulp of euphoria when we realised what he was saying: we were *free*—yes, it was *true*, it was *true*—*ding dong the witch is dead!* When he was done we tumbled out of the lecture hall, sleepers awake,[242] babbling, laughing—kissing, even, I saw two women from Film Studies kissing as we crowded into the foyer and then across to the sculptured oasis outside—kissing and hugging and crying as if they were in some foreign movie; off to one side somebody sobbing into a hankie. French, or Italian, surely; definitely Modern Languages Text Management people.

And all the time all of us laughing, gabbling, trying to get it straight even as we left the campus: *what had we actually been told*? No one had heard quite the same thing, it seemed; we were still putting it together among ourselves as we walked—dear God, someone even lighting up a cigarette over there!—ran, babbled, even *gambolled* our way through the sensitively sculpted environment. We agreed, all of us as we waited for the shuttle back to town, that, yes, there were to be *no changes after*

242 Bach? What's he doing in here? Is there an Ocean of Music as well as an Ocean of Literature?

[323]

all (he'd definitely said that), but that didn't mean *No Change* (he'd said that too). *Change* was fine with us, though, once *changes* was gone—we were scrambling aboard the shuttle now, ready to go back to our lives as we'd always known them, and when some prick said after a few minutes it was all bullshit, what we'd just been told, Super-Iggo was playing games, just toying with us—he was shouted down. He kept on bawling at us: it was a funding problem, that was what was at the bottom of it, it was anti-arts, anti-humanities. 'Trust the boss!' someone called out, and that's how we felt. We wanted to believe in Super-Iggo, in the promise of him—*I* did, I trusted him I *trusted* him—

On the shuttle we argued whether the great man had been a hologram or not. Some who'd been in the front rows said they'd smelled ozone, a burnt ozone smell, and soon after we got back to the College of Arts a rumour went around that he'd been killed, Super-Iggo, I mean, killed or held captive in a cave somewhere with Elvis and JFK, hence the fake. No one believed that, of course—well, not all of us did—but it seemed we were back in the world of rumour again, where we'd all been living for some time. In a way, it was a relief not to know, to feel happy, to feel safe like that—to hear that wash of laughter around the place, for example, when we turned up the following day and found that someone had painted an unauthorised extra black silhouette on a wall in the cloisters, showing an academic engaged in core business with a female student. Completely inappropriate, of course, completely inappropriate. I'd found I was becoming increasingly sensitised to the question of how men treat women on campus. I came back to the new silhouette several times each day to check out the exploitation.

A few days later Oscar Sceese threw a party to celebrate—Oscar from Experiencing Animals, on his lifestyle block on Dairy

Road. Sally was still up at Viscera Enterprises and I went alone: a long country drive, cows on one side and sheep on the other, then Oscar's lifestyle block and his little renovated farmhouse and, closer, The Sound of Muzak again—Pet Shop Boys singing 'Being Boring' and, by the time I'd got to the brick patio out the back where the barbecue the people and the booze were, the Pointer Sisters starting up with 'I'm So Excited'. Here was Oscar, a little drunk already and trying to dance: Great fancy dress! I told him as he twisted and turned in front of me—I meant the flared trousers and the jerkin top. He paused and said *It's a disco party, for Christ's sake* and then *the punch is over there*, and danced off as if he'd been wedgied. Who else could I offend? Earth, Wind & Fire next, 'Let's Groove', and here was the woman I'd sat next to in the CG17b meeting, Monica somebody. *It's just a reprieve*, she called out as I tried to brush past, and *don't get your hopes up* as I succeeded. I put my bottle of Cold Duck on the drinks table and had two or three shots of someone else's scotch. I needed to get this end-of-the-world stuff out of my mind. We were free!

Amanda Cupmark, alone by the windows. She was pissed, painfully, tragically pissed, something I'd never seen before— she was in a far worse state than I was. I must have spotted an opportunity; something like that. No idea how we ended up in Oscar's shower cabinet together later in the evening but we did, behind the curtain, with the party raging two rooms away: Dire Straits now. She kissed like a first-timer but seemed to get the idea quickly, pushing her face against me and then her lean body. *People always took her for granted, she was always on the edge of things, she always felt underappreciated*—the gist of what she was whispering in my ear in the middle of the wet work, that and *thankyou, thankyou* when she wasn't pushing her pointy little tongue against mine.

After a few minutes of this I began to wonder about the possibility of more. There was something I was beginning to find attractive in her neediness, her loneliness, the sexiness of her despair.

I popped the question. There had to be an unoccupied bed somewhere—*quid non?*[243]

She stopped and pulled back. Whitney Houston playing now, 'I Will Always Love You'.

'I'm sorry,' she said. 'I'm having my visitor.'

I couldn't believe it! I told her that. 'I can't fucking *believe* it!' I started to laugh.

And that's what seemed to tip her over the edge. 'It's not a joke,' she said. 'It's not funny.' She was pushing at the shower curtains. 'You should try it sometime.' Out there, the party, the music, the babble of revelling middle-aged academics at least a decade and a half out of date.

She was halfway out of the shower cabinet now. She turned back at me.

'There's a reason they call it the curse. A week out of every fucking month and I get torn apart every fucking time.'

Was she was trying to tell me something? I suppose some people are just born unhappy. I followed her out between wet curtains.

Lára Gifford, right in front of me, as if Amanda had turned into her. *What in the name of God was she doing here?—hadn't she gone to the States with her husband?*

She turned and went off, just like that; I followed her out

---

243 'Why not?' Dropping in Latin phrases like this as if he's familiar with the language is typical of the academic pseud. He's actually admitted before that he's never learned the language. Bullshit, naturally, but certainly not particular to him as an academic.

to the barbecue, where the flames were dying the death. She'd been listening to us outside the curtain.

I stopped when she turned to me:

You think with your sétapálca, she said.

And was gone—into the shambles of jigging, groping, middle-aged academic bodies flirting with obesity. Mike Mareen singing 'Don't Talk to the Snake', as if Lára herself had requested it. *Sétapálca* means *walking stick*, you see; somehow, I knew that, somehow it was still there, that piece of her that I'd picked up. It was to be the very last of those strange Hungarian words that had taken me over while I was with her. I looked for her on the edge of the Sceeses' patio as the revels wound down: more familiar green-brown smears on the brickwork.

At the end of the week I ran into Monica again, the woman from CG17b who'd been at Oscar's party: I was caught, outside English Text Management, beneath the gingko tree and the late summer stink of its rotting berries.

'Still a believer?' she asked as I attempted to walk past her. 'We're being *targeted*,' she said. 'We're a threat because the humanities critiques ideologies, so it's the only means of showing managerialism up as just another ideology.'

'*Mm, mm.*' I looked around—God, the stench of the berries.

'*That's* why they want to close us down.'

'But they told us, the arts are the beating heart of the university.'

'That means we're dead. Don't trust the bastards, they're slippery, they'll jump ship. Then it'll be good-cop-bad-cop. They're softening us up, that's why we don't know anything, there's no background to it, we're always catching up, it's deliberate, they're wrongfooting us—why this sudden change? What's behind it? Mm?'

[327]

She stared up at me and I had no idea, I just wanted to get away from this terrible, doom-laden woman, away from having to *think* about everything.

'It's deliberate,' she said. 'This is when they strike.'

Who? I wanted to know. Who's this *they* that people kept talking about?

I broke away from her. I could see Marketing and Outreach on the far side of the quadrangle, two dozen of them now, jogging across the quad in a black-uniformed phalanx. They hadn't been here on the arts campus before. They looked threatening, they looked impressive. I stood and watched them drilling for a minute or two. I felt drawn to them, more than I expected, more than I wanted.

A few days after this I took the shuttle back to the main campus and walked home to U2 in the cabernet sauvignon light of a late afternoon.[244] As I reached the forecourt, here was Sally, walking out of the building with suitcases pulling her arms down and a rolled travelling rug over one shoulder. She walked right past me as if I wasn't there, to a car that was parked in the vice-chancellor's parking space. She dumped the suitcases and lifted the boot open: I could see that orange bag of hers in there and a couple of paintings. There was her ironing board, squeezed in at the back.

I knew in a second what was happening. *At last—why'd it taken her so long?*

Another woman now, coming out of Super-Iggo's tower and

244 Oh, for goodness' sake—does he mean the skies are dark red? He knows no more about wines than he knows about anything else! Sauvignon blanc, maybe, or Chardonnay, perhaps, if he's trying to evoke an early evening light, or maybe a Reisling. So much for his expert musings about Nacker's wine cellar earlier on.

past me, loaded up. I could see Sally's vegetable blitzer clutched against her with the boxing gloves and the Bullworker, across one shoulder Sally's home gymnasium packed up on itself. That large, strong body—Bonnie. At the car she stopped and looked back at me across her shoulder, lingeringly, with real loathing. She slid the home gymnasium through a car back-window like a stiff corpse and made for the driver's side.[245]

Now here was Sally, coming back to me from the car. She was terribly upset, I could see that; her eyes were sucked-in, red, wrecked, wet. Behind her the car's windscreen wipers started and stopped, just once.

She stood there, in front of me.

'Fuck *you*, Tom,' she said.

Not the way you're thinking, not FUCK YOU or even just offhand *fuckya*, but quietly, as a statement, a piece of information. I was surprised at the poignancy of it, I was surprised how well I understood. That I'd stuffed up, I mean, stuffed up a good thing she'd *really* wanted, however unfathomable that fact had always been for me: stuffed up something that, somehow, had *really* mattered to her.

Fuck *you*, Tom. Like that. Fuck *you*.

Me. No one else.

And she walked off and stepped into the car. The sound of the door chuffing shut, the sound of the chassis creaking, and the car eased off. Bonnie, her big, hulking bruiser's shape against the wheel;[246] beside her Sally, the back of her head. Just like that, the last how-many-years of my life: going: going: gone.

---

245 So much fear of women in a description like this—as elsewhere in this book, of course.

246 And again. What is it that he's afraid of? We learn nothing of that.

Inside U2 the dazzling silent elevator slid me up the lift-shaft to the penthouse. At the top its doors murmured open; I was across the foyer with my card against the entry pad. Another murmur and I was stepping into the blowtorch dazzle of Super-Iggo's penthouse. Immediately, a smell that was all wrong, and, two steps in, my feet going from under me—a slip not a skid, but enough to make me start back up again carefully, on tiptoe. *What the hell was this?* Another step, another slip—pale green slime, sticky on the floor tiles, soapy, horrifying dark lumps in it, and all the time that stench—ammonia, of course it was ammonia. Oh, God. I peered down, tiptoed forward another step, two. It was taking me seconds to catch up with all this, but then: of *course*, of *course*—

Admiral Horthy.

Lára Gifford's emotional support duck—loose in Super-Iggo's penthouse. I could hear her now, *quack-quack*, beyond the sun-splashed second sofa, over by the windows with their unparalleled vista of the cityscape and the faraway range of the Snow Kings. *Quack-quack*—there it was: she shat as I watched, a splat on the tiling, a contemptuous waggle of her tail and then a couple of steps more—

Quack-quack—

She was heading for the Ushak rug.

I flung myself past the nearer of the two upholstered fauteuils, slipping on duckshit as I went. The Admiral was leaving a trail of it now, crapping with every stupid, waddling, lumbering step, a widening trail of sticky white–green splats with those brown smears at their centres, like nouvelle cuisine. I lunged, and the bloody thing leapt and squawked and fluttered, and shat again—

Quack-quack—

She'd been here, Lára, she'd turned up with this fucking thing, she'd left it here for me to deal with, together with whatever else she'd brought along with it. *Quack-quack.* She must have spilled the beans, even without knowing it she was sure to have let something slip—but she didn't have to, Sally was smart enough to work it all out, wasn't she? *Quack-quack.* She'd probably known anyway, some of it, guessed it. *Quack-quack.* All this going through my mind as I stumbled and squished around the sun-drenched penthouse living area, trying to shepherd the wretched, meaningless animal away from Super-Iggo's priceless rug. *Quack-quack.* I got between the two, I backed the thing up against the windows again, I saw a note on the stone-topped coffee table, I picked it up: *A friend of yours dropped by and left this specially for you. I've fed it up with lettuce and pond-water. It'll probably stop shitting sometime tomorrow night.*

I turned back: Admiral Horthy, on the precious carpet at last.

Quack-quack—

I stood there and watched pale green slime sinking into the luminous, silken Anatolian wool. My past, catching up with me, my life, going by my eyes.

Quack-quack—quack-quack—

I began to live at the Giffords' house. I used the key Lára had given me at one stage back then and waited for her inside. The little phonebox hallway, the grandfather clock, those flat square Hungarian pillows again, the brightly patterned bedding, the vivid curtains, the exhausted dining suite from that mad dinner party—family photos, left on the wall, old soot-and-silver shots of her grandparents, her godawful children in colour, herself with Gifford. Her scent, too, that I'd never tasted anywhere else and was everywhere, in everything. I lay on her bed and remembered the feel of her, and those strange Hungarian words that had started to pop out of me, all that nightmare jousting with trains. *Are you my Jewish boy?*

And Sally. Each evening I watched her show on the Giffords' telly, waiting, madly, for some kind of reference to me; each morning I checked for her email. From Lára, too—I was waiting for both women, aware that in some strange way I didn't understand their stories ran together. Would the air hostess turn up to make an end-times trifecta?

Instead, a bright yellow FOR SALE sign appeared in the Giffords' lawn: MAUREEN B. PARSONS REALTY above a face with the happy-despairing gun-at-your-throat smile of a real estate agent.

I pulled their sign out of the grass and threw it in the gutter. Inside, I sat spooning cold creamed corn from the tin and watched Sally, this time in a doco. Her career had taken yet another leap: here she was with a young Palestinian who worked for GLAAS, a United Nations outfit handling sanitation and drinking-water supplies. He was telling her this in excellent English: *mm, mm,* she nodded, taking care to keep her head covered against the eastern Mediterranean sun wind and more. He looked young, this earnest, globalised, twenty-first-century man, busy doing good in the world, giving us all hope. *Naturally we cannot take a step back in an environment like this,* he told her. *Mm, mm,* she said, and nodded up to him as if she hoped for the world.

Next day the Parsons Realty sign reappeared in the Giffords' lawn. I pulled it out again and threw it in the gutter. Inside, an abruptly handwritten note on the ruin of my breakfast: *Please ring this number.*

Instead, I watched Sally—*being* interviewed this time, in one of the big US network studios and live, talking about a new book. *Just coming out,* the interviewer was telling us: he looked knowingly at the camera. It was on his lap: he flipped it over and began to read from the back cover. *Remorseless, dispassionate, the unforgiving anatomy of a doomed relationship—like a detective slowly unpicking a crime*—he stopped reading and looked up for a second, knowingly, and down again—*a certain kind of male, pinned forever to the page*—

The hair on the nape of my neck began to prickle.

He sat back and looked across at Sally. *There really is a kind of love at work here*—? He slapped the book with the back of his knuckles, as if he'd read it. *The love of the title*—?

Oh, sure, sure—Sally now—*don't get me wrong, Bob, it's like the title says, written out of real love*—

A squinty, knowing smile. *Right throughout?* Head cocked to one side. *There's some fairly intimate passages here, Sally—somebody's surely squirming*—

Laughter—knowing, shared laughter, audience laughter, too.

Oh, God, oh, God. There was more, there was more. Sally the social scientist, the dispassionate observer, writing down only what she'd witnessed over the years, like a lab report?—adding nothing, taking nothing away? I could see it as if I was reading the damn thing, I could hear the rhythm of it, watch the details expanding. Anyone would be drawn in, taken over: a man, under a microscope that showed *everything*—the skidmarks, the circumcision marks, the appendectomy scar, the tiny birthmark that showed him heir to the Austro-Hungarian throne, the interim pimple you-guess-where, the Tiger Balm afterwards—the spinach on the tooth, the strange noises he made working the toothbrush, his democratic approach to flatulence, even the tiny *erm erm erm* in his throat whenever he shook out pepper and salt, the way he ducked his head into his neck like a scheming turtle when caught lying—

I stood up, sweating like Farkap.[247] I turned off the sound—I didn't have to listen to this shit, I could hear it all in my head. The smell of other women on him, the comical, furtive fear in his eyes when he came back from each tryst sodden in aftershave. Even the racket he made when he was spilling the beans—she'd written about that, surely she'd written about that. *She waits, she waits—and here it is again, the little shudder-and-flap of his feet, like a little kid swimming, the—*

Back on the screen Bob was holding the book up to the camera. On the back cover, a photo of Sally looking Plathishly up and to her left. On the front, an image of a dead man seen from straight above, spread out naked on a slab, with the resting bitchface of the dead. Lower, covering his Woodrow Wilson, the book's title: *A Higher Kind of Love.*

My title. I could kill her.[248]

Nine in the morning and already the smell came up to me as I walked into the quadrangle: they were roasting another pig. I checked it out and turned away. Over there, a training group in a row with a management instructor, practising simulated spontaneity outdoors—*raise-your-arm-two-three-say-hi!-two-three-lower-your-arm-two-three-pretend-to-smile-two-three—*

I took a step back towards the pyre. I bent into the sizzle-and-fumes of the roasting, and screwed up my eyes, and looked into the heat.

247. I think he might mean Phar Lap (1926–32), a champion thoroughbred New Zealand racehorse which occasionally ran in Australia and the United States.

248 Ah! Makes (sort-of) sense of his mad present-tense visit to the restaurant with a gun in his pocket at the end of Chapter 17 and the start of this chapter: he gets the idea here. Cf Anton Chekhov (famously): 'If you have a gun in Act 1 . . .' Mae West also comes to mind, of course.

Surely not—*surely not*. I turned away again.

A few steps off, and I stopped and turned back. It *couldn't* be, could it?

Up came Crispin Deadmarsh from Journalism Text Management. I pointed at the animal as he went past. 'What?' He stopped. 'So, they're roasting another pig, so what?'

'Yes, but look closer.'

He looked. He shrugged.

'No, closer—'

'I *have*.' Turning away. 'So what?'

'Look at the face.'

'It hasn't got a face, it's a pig.'

'It's not a pig.' So *mad*, but said aloud now, escaped from the growing jungle in my head, and into the world.

He'd stopped, twenty steps away, and turned back. 'So, what is it? If it isn't a pig?'

Behind him the Science and Engineering boys were starting to turn up for the barbecue: their lunchboxes, their walkshorts, their Roman sandals, a couple of them kicking a hacky-sack around.[249]

I shrugged, I turned away. 'Doesn't matter.'

But it did. It was *Back Passage*, for God's sake—wasn't it? *Surely* it was—*surely* that was what they were roasting, not a pig, surely it was Professor Becker-Paysage on the spit, Leon Becker-Paysage, L-ès-l, University of Paris, M-ès-l, Université Louis-Ferdinand Céline—?

---

249 A stuffed mini-football kicked about in mid-air among players, with the point of keeping it off the ground. Popular among STEM students, less so amongst the arts and humanities students, where the concern tends to be over what the hacky-sack is made of.

Several times during the afternoon I came back as the crowd thickened and the animal started to be pulled apart and eaten. The first time I wasn't so sure, but later, looking down from my office window, I was. *Back Passage.* I watched them as they stood about, the STEM boys—after a while some of their lecturers, too—exchanging jokes, laughing, wiping grease from their faces, and munching their way through the last of the Professor of French.

Back in my office, an email just in from Perry in Ontario: *Tight, or Chosen?* So Sally's book was there, too. Then another, from Gifford in the States:

Tom—
Lára killed herself last night. Sleeping pills etc. I can't decide which of us is more to blame, you or me.
Kind regards.
Gene.

Chapter 19

And then Super-Iggo was gone!—one minute, here and moving amongst us, talking to us, urging us on, pointing to the skies—the next, vanished, gone before we knew he was going. His work here was done, we were told it was said he had said; he'd taken us to the heights and shown us the stars and now he had other, even higher challenges to meet. The United Nations, some said, though others said the European Union or maybe NATO or the World Bank.

No one knew. Words had become strange things during his time with us, more and more unstuck from what they'd once been stuck to, and the reality they came from had come unstuck as well. Who knew now what they really meant, these words, who knew the meaning of the unstuck world caught up in them, that series of mysterious shapes as it seemed now to be? Rumours, of course—he'd been booted out, he'd agreed to sell some of the university buildings to the local iwi and rent them back, he'd tried to do the same with all of Engineering—wild stories like this which nobody could believe except in those times when they woke, suddenly, in the middle of the night, smelling the stench of the void.

Then, after several months and at last, something to grasp hold of: there he was, coming in on overseas news feeds, a *would-you-believe-it* novelty item following the weather-forecast, a last glimpse of the stars: Super-Iggo, weightless, slowly rotating in midair, thumbs up as he rolled onto his back, coming over again now in slow motion, smiling that everlasting front-grille smile, his knees tucked under his chin as he mugged for the camera—Super-Iggo, part of the SpaceX programme, training to blast off for Mars on the BFR rocket and soon (the voice-over assured us) to set up a university there—the first extra-terrestrial tertiary institution, the University of Olympus Mons! Tumbling, turning and smiling, always smiling as he tumbled and turned, thumbs forever up even when the rest of him was down: constantly turning, slowly, in middle air,[250] forever smiling to us his very special smile.

Another conclave, a thousand rumours, weeks of a confidential process in first-class convention centres around the city: a puff of white smoke. Or, alternatively, an enormous UFO seen in the middle of the night by Houston, who insisted he'd watched it land outside the city and let a ladder down.

Either way: welcome to our new vice-chancellor, Professor Dod.

From Bidness, he told us at his official welcome. At first, given his furtive, side-of-the-mouth delivery, we thought he'd said *bigness*, but his people assured us he'd been the CEO of a gigantic aluminium smelter somewhere, before that the boss of an energy conglomerate somewhere else. *Business*, then—and he really did mean business: we soon found *that* out, quite contrary to our initial perception of him as yet another easy-beat, yet more mist to our grill.

At first, we were completely taken in by his dazed, accidental quality, by the sense that he'd just been defrosted or rehydrated

250 Sounds like a loose memory of Yeats's poem 'Those Images' ('Find in middle air / An eagle on the wing'); to what purpose cited here, who knows? Yet again, his Ocean of Literature at work.

or woken from a long coma and was improvising as he went along, until he'd worked out which century it was, which country he'd arrived at, which institution he'd ended up in this time. Immediately after the usual introductory speeches at the usual introductory buffet luncheon, he was engulfed by Super-Iggo's former brown-nosers, who swirled around him, talking, swilling, nibbling, pretending to listen, feigning amusement, seeking his touch. Maitland was with him—I saw him looking across at me at one point, really hard. There were others I knew, throwing their heads back and pretending to laugh at whatever was said, nodding *yes-yes* to this, the latest place of power.[251]

Even as the great man said absolutely nothing at all. Experienced point blank, he responded to conversation sparingly but did nothing to initiate it; at times he seemed puzzled by what was said back. He kept checking his watch, like a fat kid at a school formal. Soon, he drifted away from the official party and hung about alone against the walls, touching them with his knuckles from time to time, uneasily, as if to confirm that—yes, yes, they really were there, and he really was out in the world again, in the twenty-first century now and having to deal with people. One by one they, too, began to drift away, discouraged by his long silences—baffled, confused, without a home.

I remember the first of the handful of arid exchanges he was to have with us before he melted our jobs away and our lives, then flew back to Proxima Centauri: '*Speckso*,' he said, in his

251 An echo of 'place of power'—Dr Johnson, describing obeisance to what the monarch represents, not his person. Another overheard common room fragment, surfacing in the Ocean of Literature?—it can't possibly be anything else. Samuel Johnson (1709–84), poet, lexicographer, author of *A Dictionary of the English Language* (1755) and *Rasselas, Prince of Abissinia* [sic] (1759).

dry, rustling voice, to any observation that was made: 'I expect
so'—the sound of a rodent escaping a feared human presence,
and very nearly the sound of nothing at all. He had the look
and feel of an impostor—the former commandant of a death
camp on the run, perhaps, fearing exposure at every minute,
or a person who'd committed some terrible private crime for
which he'd been forgiven but which had nonetheless robbed
him of his sense of himself, condemning him to spend the rest
of his life just getting by, living day to day and always on the
surface of things, in some sort of spiritual motel.[252]

All this we discussed afterwards at one or another of the
bars and bistros across the willow-trailed river nearby: the
parking-meter quality of his personality, his KGB clothing,[253]
his strange, shaven head, shaped (as Colin Moist from
Mathematics assured us) rather like the frustum of a road-
cone.[254] We talked about the curious sense he gave of becoming
a little taller the further he moved away, in a sort of personal
Chinese inverse perspective. 'How long do you think this one'll
last?' somebody called out, to a general heave of laughter amid
the rattle of glasses and the muzak, all this so nostalgic to think
of now—Rod Stewart and Dire Straits and something else after
that, new stuff I couldn't recognise. 'How long till he gives up?'

252 Feel an improvement in the quality of thought and expression here?
That's because he's based it on part of Alice Munro's story 'Tricks', from
Runaway (2004). This man is shameless.
253 KGB—the Westernised initials of the terrifying Soviet Committee
for State Security 1954–91, after which the KGB was split into two other
committees. The reference here is to the utilitarian tailoring of Soviet
clothing, said to feature jackets with more buttons than buttonholes,
sleeves of differing lengths, trousers with enormous turnups, etc.
254 Odd to see a recondite word like this in such a text. He means that the
new vice-chancellor's head was shaped much like a road cone but one from
which the upper part has been removed by a horizontal slice.

someone else wanted to know. More drunken laughter—beer spilling, a glass rolling on the floor.

Pye it was who spoke those words, Reg Pye from Theatre Studies Management, that in-the-know insider I mentioned in Chapter 12 above: he whom I was to glimpse barely six months later, bouncing along aboard one of the city council's mechanical mowers in the Botanical Gardens, his hands slack on the tiller, his overalls loose on his frame, his eyes flickering at me for a second and away with the unrecognising recognition that was to become the mark of so many meetings between the members of the newly dispossessed, the diaspora of the humanities Professor Dod was to fling across the city and the land, into streets and malls and supermarkets, onto park benches for long, solitary afternoons spent alone, blinking into sunlight.

Little had we known what he meant, any of us, little had we understood the strange power of his emptiness, the implacability of his lack of charisma, the sheer strength of his nonentity. For this was not just Professor Dod, our new vice-chancellor. This was *Hamish* Dod—Little Hamish, developmental steps completed, here to bring me to justice. Here he was, my fate, arrived after all these years, in barely human form—

And he did for us all with his plan of attack.[255]

To some degree, I feel responsible for this. These days I shuttled from our little college to the main campus every day, for committee work but also because I felt increasingly at home over there. I'd hang around the new breakout lagoon on

255 Another theft—borrowing, I suppose he'd say, of course, or another of his wretched acts of so-called hommage. We all know where this quote comes from—Siegfried Sassoon. Again, something overheard in the common room.

Level 15 of U2 and use the direct-vent water-heater to make coffee. Sometimes I'd find myself showing a newcomer how to use the thing, where to go in the building, and began to feel I was starting to belong there.[256] *Down to Level 13 and turn left out of the elevator*, I'd say, or, *Ask Maggie at Level 3 reception*. And there was the simple business of walking along the corridors—no reason to be there, just *doing* it, head down, behind a couple of managers, past people arranging a meeting, then pulling aside as if I really was about something, stepping into an elevator and going up two, three floors and stepping out again to try a different corridor. After a while I began to realise that *they* were what really mattered in this new world: it was the corridors that were important, not the rooms they connected. Movement, quick exchanges, words called out in passing, promises made, nothing happening, everything deferred, just *movement*, movement without end. *This was where it was at.*[257]

It was there that I got *my first nod from a member of the Senior Management Team!*—Maisie Jago, it was, who *actually remembered my name* as she went past. *Tom*, she said. My voice cracked as I replied. *Maisie*, I said back, with a nod, of course; just *Maisie*. Joe Cool on the outside, of course, but, *God*, my heart was *bumping*, I can tell you. Later I saw Bovril Anderson going into the men's room at the far end of the same corridor, and hurried down and creaked the door open and listened, awe-struck, to the familiar sounds—the seat coming down, the

256 Hmmm . . . seems he might have read the first few pages of *The Great Gatsby* at some stage.

257 In fact, Roger Luckhurst's *Corridors: Passages of Modernity* (London: Reaktion Books 2019) is probably where it's at. Overheard being discussed in the common room? Or (less likely, given the greater-than-a-page word-length involved) from a review he's read in the *London Review of Books*? (Vol.41, No.24, 19 December 2019, pp.11–12).

belt unbuckling, worse. Obviously, he'd agreed a contract with his bowel to remove waste from his body.

There was still that buzz out here, even after Super-Iggo had gone—still that sense of *going somewhere fast* and *who knows where* and *the devil take the hindmost*.[258] I'd stand before the topless towers of U1 and U2[259] and remember those moments when, not often, I used to spot the great man himself coming out of one or the other of them like a Renaissance pope surrounded by his cardinals, and watch him proceeding across the vast launch-site of the courtyard in front of them to inspect everything a man might see. Pointing upward, he always seemed to be pointing upward as he went, showing his entourage this site of excellence and that—then across to other *builds*, at that stage not yet *buildings* since tradies still clung to their sides. Always, each time I hung about for him, I used to yearn for that initial rock-star moment when he appeared; always, each time, I used to follow him wherever he went. *What would happen, what would happen?*

Now, as I stood there one afternoon remembering all this, out came his successor instead. He seemed buffled, Dod, almost as if he'd escaped from something; he looked around, left, right, up, down; sunlight glinted on his lenses. Then he spotted me. Oh, God—here he came, here he—

That strange, whispering rattle, that voice that wasn't a voice at all. I leaned closer. It seemed he wanted to know where something was. There was a food stain ironed into his tie.

258 Proverbial, so he can be forgiven for using it here. First written in Beaumont and Fletcher, *Philaster, or Love Lies a-Bleeding* (1611) (phrases. org.uk).
259 What's this, though—'the topless towers of Ilium'? I can see his ongoing interest in toplessness, certainly, but the rest of it is from Christopher Marlowe's *Doctor Faustus* (1592). What's it doing here?

Now here was Maitland, out of the U2 exit and running towards us like a zoo-keeper. No, no—as he got closer he turned into one of the others, Garland, maybe, or Gaitskell. So hard to tell.

He bent to Dod's *bzzzt-bzzzt-bzzzt*—

'The College of Arts?' Garland, to me. 'He doesn't know where the College of Arts is.'

'It's in town.' I spoke loudly, carefully: 'It's a separate campus. It's five miles away.'

Bzzzt-bzzzt-bzzzt. Those tin-foil specs, staring up at me.

'We'll have to drive there,' Garland was telling him.

I couldn't get back to our safe, smug little campus fast enough. 'He doesn't even know how to find us!' I told them as I tumbled into the common room. 'Dod! He didn't even know there's two campuses!'

They laughed, of course, laughed so much I told it all again to regain a little favour, and to newcomers as they came in, too, and the newcomers told it to others. The story got around; someone told it back to me that evening at the bar of the faculty club. I laughed—everybody laughed. What next, what next? What an idiot!

It wasn't till later that the thought occurred to me. I sat up in bed in the middle of the night. *Why had I told Dod how to find us?*

He turned up at the College of Arts, with his full entourage—suddenly, there they were, in the southern quadrangle, under the gingko tree in front of our English Text Management building. Eight or ten of them, less than Super-Iggo's entourage but disconcerting all the same in their dark suits, and ties the wind whipped across their shoulders. I watched them strolling around with a plan held amongst their various hands, and pointing at things and then back at the square of paper, which flapped and fluttered in their grip. *There*—jabbing at it as they struggled against the wind—*there, there.* What were they pointing at, *why were they here? Changes*, their movements reeked of *changes*; you couldn't fool us now, not after our recent experience. Those sweeping gestures as they looked up at us, pointing, those mouths working inaudibly in the breeze, those nodding heads around Dod's bald, obscene, pink-frustum-cone-of-authority: changes. A couple of Super-Iggo's Marketing and Outreach chaps as well, standing around in their black uniforms and looking almost like bodyguards now; staunch, their eyes narrowed, iPhones in their holsters like pistols.

After ten minutes I slipped down the staircase and past them. Hard to make out anything in the wind, but I did hear one of them say, 'No idea this place was even here!' 'Same!'—this was one of the others—and 'Me neither!' from somebody else. Another voice: 'What do they actually *do* here?' Maitland, I could see Maitland at Dod's shoulder, and Dod giving me a vacant look from somewhere behind those spectacles as I passed. Again, Maitland, looking at me, looking at me *hard.*

Not long after this, we got our first hint of what was coming.

'For A read B,' Tim Riordan told me in the Level 2 corridor of English Text Management, in the sardonic manner he'd seemed to be cultivating to cope with the slow bleeding-away of what power he'd once had. He showed me his phone.

An all-staff email: OPERATION CONTRACT in the title-bar, the rest misspellings, sentence fragments, no capitals. Dod—the written version of his *bzzzt-bzzzt-bzzzt* death-rattle, but signed by someone else.

'Can he really be called Bovril Anderson? This flunky who's signed it?'

'I think Dod's dreamed him up.'

'What happened to Operation Expand?'

'It's being contracted.'

Both of us, staring down at his phone. Simple enough, really: Operation Expand had made things bigger. Operation Contract would make them smaller again! There might be some in-flight turbulence along the way, which we should ignore. Enjoy your flight!

Operation Expand.

Operation Contract.

Rolling five-year horizon.

Days later, Johannes van der Nacker came into my office, white-faced: he thrust his phone at me. 'Read this.'

Another all-staff communication. Restructuring. Rationalisation. Changes—*changes*—

'He says it's not us. Look.' I pointed at the tiny display. '*No changes to academic staffing levels are envisaged in this process.*'

'God, man, can't you see what that *means?*' Beads of sweat along his hairline. 'It means they're targeting *us*—'

'But it says here that they're not—'

'Don't you know how these things *work*—? It's obvious, they're lining up the academic staff—if they *weren't* they'd be telling us they *were*—'

Tim called a college meeting, to dispel fears, he said, to reassure us, particularly about a nasty rumour that had started to go around to the effect that *we* were the target—arts, the College of Arts! He looked haggard as he spoke.

'I'm confident the VC values the arts. The humanities.' His voice trailed off, then firmed up a little. 'Remember, the humanities exist to prevent normal people from turning into managers.'

Nods of agreement, a splatter of applause.

'We've all got to face this head-on. Show them we mean business.'

'Quite. Quite.'

'United. Pin them to the wall.'

'Yes! Yes!'

A pause.

'Any ideas?' Looking around the room.

'We could march somewhere.'

'Fine Arts and Music did that last week. They marched into town.'

'And—?'

'Well, they haven't come back. No one knows where they are.'

Silence.

'A petition?'

'Done that.'

'A press statement, then?'

This attracted attention; people twisted around to see who'd said it. A little man in porthole glasses.

Someone called out, 'Stand up when you address the meeting.'

'I *am* standing up.'

A shout of cruel, baying laughter—that pure, academic belch of Shady Joy[260] when a man is down and wounded and the hounds are in full cry. Ah, the humanities, the humanities.

Tim tapped the rostrum with his folded spectacles. 'What would we say in a press statement?'

'Humanities. We're speaking for the humanities. That's the point.'

'Right. Right.' A ripple of applause.

---

260 'Schadenfreude' means something more like 'danger-joy' or 'harm-joy', delight in seeing others in some sort of trouble. *Priceless, simply priceless.*

'There've been other periods of humanism in history. We need to say we're pissed off in a Western humanities way—'

'—concerned, we're concerned—we could say "we've been observing developments lately, and as humanists"—'

'Good, good, nice touch—'

'—"we're very concerned".'

Another pause. Tim was writing this down. He looked up.

'Are we happy with that? With—'

'—"concerned"? It's a bit—'

'Strident? D'you think it's a bit—you know, OTT?'

'*Very concerned* is definitely strident—perhaps it should just be, you know, "We are concerned"—something like that—'

Tim put his glasses on again and wrote it down. He began to read it back. '"Tertiary academics in the humanities met today to discuss proposed changes to their institutions"—'

'Good, good, nice touch—'

'"And wish to state their concern at proposed changes to academic staffing levels"—'

'"With particular reference to"—'

'—"and wish to state their concern with particular reference to—'

'No—no—"and wish to state that they are *not unconcerned* at"—'

'Ah! Perfect! "*Not unconcerned*"!'

General agreement around the meeting—not a little enthusiasm, it was not untrue to say.

Tertiary academics in the humanities met today to discuss proposed changes with reference to their institutions and wish to state that, with reference to plans for academic staffing levels, they are not unconcerned.

This appeared in online news aggregators that night, next to an advertisement for a bicycle.

In U2 the elevator doors opened: I hurried in, the doors closed, I felt my weight begin to melt, I turned and—*Dod, Dod in the elevator with me, just standing there next to me oh say it isn't so—*

We slid down together. He stared up at me and didn't speak; I looked away. I looked back. He looked away. We slid down together. He looked at me again. I looked away.

Thirteen, twelve, eleven—

He turned to me, abruptly. His mouth opened a little: teeth in there.

'Optimum growth potentials.'

—ten, nine, eight—

I waited, I stared at the display, the numbers flickering by.

—seven, six—

'Integrate deliverables.'

—four, three—

The sensation of weight returning, the pause, the doors opening. He stepped out. He stopped. He turned back to me.

'World-class granular portals.'

I watched him move off. Overalls: somehow, he was wearing overalls. The years melted away—Gotch's rubber waders, I remembered Gotch's rubber chest-waders. No one knew why he wore those, either. You can't get away from these bastards, you can't escape them.

And it was true, it was true after all, it was going to be us and no one else, everyone else was to be left alone but the College of Arts. I couldn't believe it, but at the same time I'd known it all along. *Significantly enhanced*, the entire college was to be significantly enhanced, that was what we were told. *Enhanced!*—it could mean only one thing. *We were finished—*

Deadlines were announced. A final legal challenge from

our union, another from the students; more letters to the paper. A silent vigil in the centre of town one Friday night, almost universally ignored by the populace; much fine oratory, many statements of principle. A speech in the University Senate that had everyone *cheering to the rafters*, as they say: something about laying down your life when the bulldozers came. Trouble was, no bulldozers. Nothing much happened at all. Books went first, because books took up more space than warranted by their face value: books, and then, naturally, librarians; after that the common rooms and their tea ladies, then the gardeners and the parking men and the security staff. Arts academics came in one morning and found their desks and computers being taken out, then the shelves and filing cabinets. At the end of it all, our pay stopped. Reapply for your position? What position?

That was the point, that was how they did it, that was how Dod got the business done. All of us became redundant; arts simply stopped being. It was towards the end of the summer vacation; there were hardly any students left and none of the staff; the emptiness was almost indistinguishable from six months before. Someone organised a rally of sorts in one of the quadrangles with several quite witty banners, but none of the local television stations sent news teams or cameras. We were yesterday's news. The legal challenges went on— they're still going on now, a year later—and there were one or two individual acts of protest: by a political scientist who simply went on lecturing at the usual times, to lecture halls only marginally emptier than they'd been during term-time; by Parsifal Oates, who stood on a box haranguing the public outside Cathedral Mall every day; by Justin Beadsman, who mounted a stepladder nearby one Friday night, and started his standard lecture on Coleridge, 'Fancy and the Imagination', to jeers and threats from skinheads.

In the real world beyond our diminutive mock-Gothic buildings, the great unwashed simply went their doggy way. When we marched a few quavering blocks into the centre of town one last time, the public still seemed not to give a stuff, and, after speeches infused with pathos and a banner-jiggling chant or two, we turned back in a gaggle, dazed and confused. There was simply nothing to be done. The land filled, as in Elton's great description of the Dissolution of the Monasteries, with wandering, bewildered monks and friars living off the countryside, carrying their votaries[261] and their bags of relics as they went, threatened by the populace and without a safe house willing to take them in.[262] Leaving behind this, the former campus, and its constellation of crumbling, locked-up buildings being made over into something else, something unimaginable, with workmen wet-sawing sandstone and sandblasting gargoyles in the parts of the former campus that were to be kept, it was said, as replicas of themselves.[263]

The final act. Houston, suddenly, in the doorway of my room: that gunslinger's stance, those long, long legs of his, the thrust-forward pelvis, his Redneck Rivieras spread wide on the floor and his Stetson on the back of his head. At last it was happening—he'd got the *handgun*, for God's sake, he was twirling it backwards-a-couple-of-times then forwards-a-

---

261 This is sheer nonsense—a votary is a follower; a monk or a nun, perhaps.

262 This is bullshit plain and simple. Nowhere does Elton describe the Dissolution like this; in fact, he hardly deals with it in any part of his *oeuvre*.

263 A whiff here of Max Beerbohm's parody of Joseph Conrad, in *A Christmas Garland* (1912): '... the stars, which are but reflections of themselves ...'

couple-of-times and into-the-holster like Alan Ladd after he shot Jack Palance in *Shane*; it flew off and clattered to the floor. He picked it up. He'd *located* some *ammo*, he told me.

He stood there. 'This fucker is loaded.'

'*Fuck*, Houston?'—one of those whiny Vienna Boys' Choir squeaks only Sally had ever got out of me. He gave the gun another twirl and my innards went with it; I cringed away from him, I couldn't stop myself. *Cole's Notes to Wuthering Heights* slid to the floor.

Now he had it pointed at the window. He closed his right hand around the grip and his left over his right and sighted along it like a US marshal. The venetian blinds clattered with each move he made.

One final protest, he told me, on the main campus. That afternoon. They were going to break into U2 and find Dod.

Even a couple of hundred yards from the Registry towers I could hear them: *Not Just Artholes! Not Just Artholes!*—and then a huge cheer and a spout of water starting up—the Iggo Memorial Water Effect, they must have torn it out of the ground—up and up and up, water in the air and down over everything, water everywhere, I was soaked in seconds. Oh, yes, they really meant it this time, I could see *that* as soon as I got there, they were fighting already—skinheads sodden among the banners, pushing, wrenching bodies, water, water all over us. Near me someone was going down amongst the shoving and the kicking, a club bounced on his head till he was on his knees—no, not skinheads, this was Marketing and Outreach, working in a phalanx, NUMBER ONE VARSITY EXPERIENCE on their T-shirts, blood smeared into the white-on-black. Digby Hose it was, the man down, from Digital Humanities Management, with the same club still working on him—now, bodies collapsing and he was gone, just his feet showing, one shoe lost. A female voice, yelling *you fucking shits, you fucking shits*—

I stopped short of this. They were bringing a woman out with blood trickling from under her cycle helmet, another being carried like a baby. *Get me out of here*—but I was caught up in it anyway, I was being forced backwards into—the bouncy castle, I was being shoved against the bouncy castle. Air was coming out, the whole thing was slackening enough for me to scramble up the side. Beadsman, I could hear Beadsman somewhere above me—there he was, up in the rubber barbican and yelling in that posh fucking Oxbridge voice of his *Don't Let the Orts Die! Don't Let the Orts Die!* I worked my way closer to him, clutched at the rubber, worked myself around behind him while he tried to fight off a man wrenching at his sign, twisting the pole—*I say! I say!*—half gone now but he held on to the last of it: *I say! I say!* And I got to the little prick, got to him while bodies fought down there and the man pulled, I got behind him just as the banner came out of his hands, got him by the collar from behind, Beadsman, I mean; I pulled him back and began to punch him *hard* in the back of his neck *thump, thump, thump*, I *thumped* him and *thumped* him with my pointy little fist, worked at it till my knuckles bled. And all the time he was squealing *I say, I say* and *crying*, the poor little prick had started *crying*—I kept my spare fist in his collar to stop him from seeing me but he twisted around so I punched him some more. Then someone came between us and I lost him—Maxwell from Design Management, dragged down by someone else so I got him, too, in the head, twice, and behind the ear, and it felt so *good* I kicked him again, in the eye this time, and I pulled away and slid down the side of the castle—

Over to the left, Marketing and Outreach were hard at it, clubs *digging* and *digging* into academic bodyfat with the boys from Works and Services hard in behind them. I watched a couple of academics take it on the head and go down, Guyon Puce from Philosophy Text Management and someone from History Text Management—bleeding from the head, whimpering and whining in the middle of the noise. I got another guy in the balls, hard, don't know who but he looked like a prick, got him *hard* in the knackers. And then—*there was Henry Bumb*—the prick who called me an asshole!—there he was, caught by Marketing and Outreach, someone's arm round his throat, his head going back, nothing he could do. He pushed his hand at me when I got there, into my face, and I bit it hard like a sandwich, edge-on, and when he squealed and pulled it away I bit him in the back like a dog, near the neck, I didn't care anymore. *This is what it's all about, this is what they want*—going through my mind, suddenly, I knew it at last in the middle of all this rage and chaos; Dod, I meant, Dod and everything he stood for. He was *right*, that was the thing, I knew that now, he was *right* and it made you *feel so fucking free*—

Exactly then, a shot went off. Squeals. Another. *Another*—shouting, people scattering, the courtyard beginning to clear. *Houston was here.* I looked around the mass of heaving, shouting, kicking academic bodies—there, there he was, crouched behind the remains of the fountain and firing into the air. I could hear his voice, that unlocatable North American bellow: 'Creative Writin' over here!'—waving his pistol—'Creative fucken Writin' over here!'[264] I watched Amanda Cupmark scurrying across to him, a hand to her head, blood in her fingers. Someone began shooting back. That's the last I saw of Houston—of any

264 This sequence is familiar but I can't place it—I'm sure this is another unacknowledged theft.

of them. One of the Marketing guys grabbed me and pulled me out—I was one of *them* now, I could feel it—pulled me onto the steps of U2. I saw the doors opening in front of me.

In the foyer inside, here was a frightened little man in an overcoat and a trilby hat and with a trolley case stooped from his hand. There was a tiny fleck of blood fresh on his cheek. What was he asking me? I leaned over and tried to hear—what, what was this he was saying? *I have just arrived from the University of Essen.* I leaned forward. *I wish to know*—looking around, shocked, terrified, completely out of his depth. Now something went *hard* into the glass behind me and he staggered back and dropped the handle of his trolley case. He bent to pick it up, he straightened. He was shouting above the racket now—I could hear him better, here it was:

I wish to know please, is this the Robert Byng conference?

Further down the corridor I found the downstairs men's room—but here was a plumber in one of the cubicles, crouched over the cistern with his back to me. When he heard me come in, he straightened and looked over his shoulder. Humming to himself, I could hear him humming to himself, *mm-mm-mmmm.*

That nude, frustum-shaped skull—

Dod, Professor Dod, in overalls and holding a spanner. The vice-chancellor, working on a lavatory cistern—

Outside, the riot, getting louder after the shooting: babble, screams, shouting. A voice on a bullhorn, a siren starting up. I could hear the threat in it. Tear-gas, for God's sake—

Dod turned back to me. I stared at him, I watched his face widen slightly again. On anyone else it would have been a smile. Now he was pointing the spanner at the cistern. I couldn't hear what he was saying. Well, I could, but—

Someone broke this. Now it's fixed. I think that's what it was. He waved me closer, pointed into the cistern. *Y'turn off the supply tap, y'flush the cistern*—I was starting to make some of this out. *Y'unscrew this, see, and y'take this bit off*—he was pointing into the abyss—*then y'replace this valve here*—tapping with the spanner.

You wouldn't believe it, the fill valve needed fixing but then it turned out the flush valve was shot, too! New unit, under three years old!

Happy, he was happy, he was chuckling, almost. What was this he was saying now? I bent closer.

Best day I had in years—

That was what he was telling me. He was down low, twisting the supply tap: pipes, starting up in the walls, the cistern beginning to fill again. He straightened. He turned to me. His face seemed rich, full of blood.

'Gotta break things. Break things, you get opportunities, right?'

Staring at me.

'Chaos. Find it or make it.'

Staring at me, staring at me.

'What's *your* name, anyway?' Sudden, abrupt, terrifying. 'How long you been teaching here?'

Outside, the sound of glass shattering.

He stared up at me, point-blank—soulless, vicious, unforgiving, unconflicted: man, after the humanities.

I am become death, destroyer of worlds.[265]

---

265 From the *Bhagavad Gita* and famously claimed by J. Robert Oppenheimer, 'father of the atomic bomb', to have been his response to witnessing the first nuclear explosion, in July 1945. His physicist brother Frank later claimed that Oppenheimer actually said, 'Well, that seems to work.'

Chapter 20

So there you are, folks, that's what happened!—now you know how I came to be sitting here in a cubicle each day with a laptop on my knees and power-drills and wet saws whining in the distance, tradies calling out to one another, hammering so high above me it echoes.

By now they've completed the upgrade here in the men's room. No flies anymore: instead, the entire ceiling flickers on when I come in the door. Light ripples across the room and bounces back from the new lino, which is colourless but with a colour all the same if you look for it hard enough. There's a quiet hum in the air, too, which goes away if you try to listen to it, and the tiniest *mm-mm* when the door shuts, as if it's thanking you. There's a Dyson Airblade, too, and noise-activated toilet roll dispensers in the cubicles.

Boldest move of all, though, the metal urinal has been hauled away at last and replaced by two dainty plastic bowls— white, like shells, and obviously obliging close attention from the user. We aim to please.

The rest of the old English-department building around and above is being made into *an executive precinct*. The upstairs rooms have been emptied out—the Canadian potter's gone, the transactional analyst and the others who were up there as well, the wymmin if they ever existed—even a masseuse I didn't know was there in the first place! The lawyer and her PA have exited, too—*Satisfied now?* she hissed at me as she stalked through the foyer and out of the building for the last time, her arms stacked with ring-binders. Did she think all this was my idea? Ma'am, this is *history*—

Meantime, the humanities library is cleared out, the last of the books gone to the people at Glasnost thanks to Harrison and the others. We've been given a week to clear the handful left in the shop and get them across to Bevan's country estate, there, presumably, to complete their decay. He's been talking a big game about starting again, pooling capital and getting new premises and so on, the usual stuff, but when I told him I've *got* no capital, nothing to show for all these years, I think he started to go off the idea. Something about a mobile rare-used-books shop, that's his latest crackpot idea, I believe. He's baffled about the Barchester sequence, still looking for it and the other Trollopes—I think he suspects me and that's another reason he doesn't mention me anymore when he talks about his plans. His rash is clearing up, by the way.

All this time I've been warming a pie in the Dyson Airblade. It's almost too hot to hold when I take it out. I munch it down quickly, disgustingly, watching myself in the new mirror that takes up nearly all the freshly tiled wall above the sinks. Ah, those slumped shoulders, the shabby jacket, the tragic, balding dome with its trailing strands, that abandoned single tuft at the widow's peak. What will Manatine make of me?

Back in the cubicle, I close the door and wait with my laptop. Today's meeting is scheduled for the Old Registry building at the corner of this campus-that-was—in that room with the remarkable carved ceiling, do you remember it? Full circle! In other ways, too: he'll be here in a minute. 'Time to meet up!' he said in our last call. 'Gotta make sure you look right for the big meet.' My first management meeting. Twenty minutes.

And now, here he is, here he is—the sound of the pneumatic

arm on the door and I'm up and peeping over the top of the cubicle wall. *Is it him, what's he look like now, has he changed?*

Maitland. Down there it's Maitland, unzipping at one of the paired white china troughs: I might have guessed he'd be back. I wait. Now he's turning to the trio of sinks beneath the mirror—there, he pumps gel onto his pink executive palms and begins to work them together.

He spots me reflected behind him, peering down. He nods into the mirror.

I nod back. 'Maitland?'

'In Manila.' Working up a froth in the sink now, cuffs rolled back, hands awash. 'He's questing a NoSQL database meet.'

Then who *is* this? I look closer. A man exactly Maitland's height and build and wearing Maitland's brand, it seems—the same *faux* handmade brogues, dark formal trousers in blue worsted plus a white shirt with a sharp collar opened at the neck. No jacket this time and with shirt cuffs rolled back, nicely calibrated to bare the wrists enough to represent *busyness*, the state of being forever caught between important assignments, never in the moment of actually performing them—definitely a manager, an executive *moving forward*, a man *thinking outside the box*. Maitland, yes, but the face in the mirror's different, just a little, and his hair, too, shaven high at the side and the top combed over at the front and forward, a bit fashy. But for that, he could be Maitland. But he isn't, not quite.

I look at him again, the face in the mirror. Hold on, hold on—

I watch him, bent forward, rinsing his hands, his wrists, under the tap.

He butts the tap off with an elbow, like a surgeon, and turns to the airblade with his wet hands out in front of him as if he's just found them somewhere. The blade starts up.

I keep looking at him. I step down and open the cubicle door.

'You're Maitland,' I tell him: it just pops out.

His hands, blowing in the airblade. 'Does it matter?' Still looking in the mirror. 'We all use product.' There, he's found my reflection, he's looking at me. 'Is that you?—Christ, you look fucken terrible.'

Manatine, now he's beginning to sound like Manatine— and *there*, just for a second, a tiny whiff of something, behind the gel on his hands. Was it? No, I was imagining it, I—

'Watch this.'

He begins to massage his face with his fingertips, under the eyes, around the mouth, along the lips, gently, painstakingly, as if he's pressing dough. Then, something extraordinary begins to happen—he starts to adjust his entire face in the same way, he starts pressing his fingertips against the sides of his forehead, pushing it into shape, pushing further down to compact his underjaw; after that a tweak to the ears to press them closer to the skull: and, finally, a rough upward finger-and-thumb twist to the nose, that leaves it more nearly like—

He steps away from the mirror, he turns to me.

'You!'

'Me!'

Is it? I'm still not sure about this. Who *is* this man? Do I believe everything that's happening in front of me? I want so much for it to be *him*, I want us to hug, I want to hear that laugh of his, I want so much for the old days to be back—

What's he doing now, though—hands in his pockets, fumbling something out, head crouched forward, looking back at the door for a moment—licking at paper, furtive, quick, lick-lick and now here's the stuff, he's—

This is him, this is where it happens, this is where—

The match flares, his head goes back: *Manatine, he's Manatine at last.* I'm starting to make him out through the wisps of smoke, starting to see the man he used to be—nearly, almost. Here's his arm, coming at me, here's my hand, taking the joint from him, here I am, drawing it in again—

It doesn't last long, sixty seconds, less, but it's enough for me. He's already over the toilet, flushing the joint, now he's back at the mirror, crouched forward, pushing and pulling at himself, quickly, urgently. I watch Maitland come back bit by bit as he pulls at his ears, pushes his cheeks, I watch the single downward movement that straightens out his nose.

'Remember, we're organics, we're made of the soft stuff.' He steps back and he's Maitland again, present, managerial, brushing himself off. This has all come with the dope, it's not been—

He's bending down to a bag on the floor, a plastic bag: he pulls something out.

'We need to get you ready for this gig. You still look terrible.'

And then—you won't believe this—he reaches out and moves my nose, adjusts it—what Sally tried to do, remember? I hardly feel a thing. I've been distracted for a few minutes now by the possibility that I'm not being reflected in the mirror—or that I *am*, but only barely so at best: off-centre, a shadow to one side, something that moves away from me when I try to pin it down. Merely a player.[266] There—there I am, looking a tiny bit different, a tiny bit better. A tiny bit like Maitland, to tell the truth. In the mirror I stare at him, I stare at myself staring at him. Which side am I on?

He turns back. 'Slip into this before the big meet.' He's

266 Ah, yes—not quite a theft, really, since it's commonly used. Do you think he knows where it comes from?

holding a laden clothes-hanger out to me. 'One of my suits. You can have it till you get your own. And the rest of it, the shirt and the tie.'

'Right, right—'

'Oh, yes.' He leans towards me: 'Be sure you shave your wrists.'

I stare at him.

'*Shave my wrists*—?'

'Before you start. It's important. Just a hint.' He's looking me up, down. 'There's other work-ons but you could start there.'

'Oh. Right. I—'

'And always use a proper foam when you shave.' He points at the canister he's left in front of me. 'Keep away from gel.' He nods at me, once, and there's almost a wink in it. He's half out the door. 'Back in a minute—'

'Right,' I tell him. 'Right.'

He's gone. The pneumatic muscle on the door, the sound of its slow electronic submission. All this feels as if an offer has been made, as if some sort of transaction has taken place.

I'm standing here, pushing at my jaw, aware of the bristles, the looseness of its flesh. Trying to push back at its *organicity*, its fallen state.

Slowly, I begin to shave my wrists, using the foam and not a gel. The right wrist is harder than the left, but the job gets done in the end.

I'm about to empty the sink and try some wax when I catch myself in the mirror. Still that used, anybody face, above it those sad, purposeless wisps, the widening patches front and back where there's no longer very much of anything left on the skull. That lone, silly tuft, the last of my widow's peak—my final, tentative semicolon.

Something's beginning to come together for me.

I pick up the canister of shaving foam again. Shake well, it says in the instructions on the side.

I shake well.

It takes a minute to massage the foam into what's left at the back. I begin to shave by feel, scraping and rinsing. The hair comes off in clogged clumps; every few minutes I scrape these together and flush them down the loo. Fifteen minutes at least, scraping, wiping, feeling. At the end of it there's almost nothing up there, just the nude feel of the skin and the bone.

That lonely forelock. It's all that's left now. Above it, the bared skull looms, awaiting completion. I begin to work the foam into the tuft and then the razor through the mess—two or three strokes, that's all, and it's a last soapy blob in the sink.

I stare at myself, at me. Left-handed. I'm left-handed in the mirror. It's my left hand that's got the razor in it. Lára, I think of Lára for a moment, left-handed Lára Gifford. But am I on the other side, am I in the mirror anymore? I can't quite tell, I'm not quite sure.

I look down. The razor's definitely in my left hand now.

Looking up at myself again. My head looks like a balloon with my face on it.

I turn and peek into the mirror over my shoulder.

Closer, I look closer.

Dod. His strange, cone-shaped head.

I look like Dod. I'm turning myself into Dod.

Of course I am. Of course I am.

Cautiously, a little frightened, I begin to squeeze at the sides of my face, at my cheeks.

Nearly there.

He's back soon after: he leans in the door.

'Maskell?'

I shake my head. 'Maslin.'

'Where's Maskell?'

'With Gaskell and Maitland.' The words come easily, inevitably, without thought. 'They're questing a NoSQL database meet in Manila.'

He smiles at me in the mirror. 'New hair stylist?' He seems to approve, he seems pleased—I feel a thrill, a buzz in the middle of my chest.

'Five minutes.' He slips out, he's heading off for our *big meet*.

Time for a last, quick, nervous bio-break. I bustle into my cubicle: I'm a man of affairs. Got a contract—got a gig—back in the swim lane!

There are outcomes to be leveraged.

I unbuckle and settle myself onto the familiar plastic oval. In front of me, a fresh spreadsheet waits to be scrolled down on my laptop: I can scent its immanence coming up to me already. I want to give this meeting 110%, but I'm not even sure yet of the KPIs. Marketing has overspent its budget, I think that might be the issue. Or, on the other hand, the problem might be that it *hasn't* overspent its budget and the close of the fiscal year is impacting. All notional money, of course, written off if overspent. But no one wants unspent non-official notional moneys to accumulate, naturally, since unspent accumulation always has implications going forward. Everything has implications going forward. Everything is going forward.

Such are my learnings now I'm part of a Tiger Team. I couldn't believe it when Maitland blue-skied me. Part of a Tiger Team, he said, tasked with drilling down to a point where—who knows—if we manage to leverage the learnings we've made so far, we might transition to a SWAT team and *open the kimono at last!*

Moving parts, moving parts.

Best practice! Punch a puppy!

Boil the sea—

I've started. Paper offers itself from the cubicle wall. I crumple it in my fingertips. I wipe robustly, with vision, moving forward, and let the sullied wodge of paper drop into the pan beneath my research outlet.[267]

I reach out to the paper dispenser once more—

And then, out of nothing, as if the thought's come with the paper, I stop. I stare down at the unsullied strip between finger and thumb. Is it?—could it be? I bring it up to my eyes. Surely not? I squint at it from arm's length. Yes. Yes. A brand-name, stamped into each square of paper. It's there. It's definitely there.

I bring the tissue close again:

Glasnost Boutique Toilet Paper.

Nikita—his little factory, that pool of pages slowly turning into sludge in his pulping pool, the Western humanities' answer to the data lake.

Then who is it I've just Made Contact with? Poe, surely, of all writers it must be Edgar Allan Poe? Or is it Dickens? Herrick? Southey? Thackeray? One of the Brontës, maybe— *all* of them, all three sisters and their pisshead brother as well, mixed together in the paper? And if so, which of them have I just become closer to, which of their imaginings has just given me pause for thought? Heathcliff? Mr Rochester? The Heathcliff–Rochester clone someone told me was in the

---

267 This sequence is revolting, and inappropriate to Art. *But is it?*—here is the great James Joyce in *Ulysses*: 'Quietly he read, restraining himself, the first column and, yielding but resisting, began the second. Midway, his last resistance yielding, he allowed his bowels to ease themselves quietly as he read, reading still patiently, that slight constipation of yesterday quite gone.' *Ulysses* was selected by 'a panel of scholars' as the greatest novel of the twentieth century. See https://www.chicagotribune.com/news/ct-xpm-1998–07–21–9807210312–story.html

other sister's novel—what was it called?—haven't read *that*, either—*but have I just met him at last all the same*? Or Roderick Random, is it Roderick Random, a name that comes belching out of my unconscious mind from nowhere? Or one of Bevan's minnows instead, caught in the toilet paper?—Sturge Moore or Mary Alcock perhaps, or Charles Reade, author of the imperishable *Peg Woffington* (1853)? Susan Edmonstone Ferrier? Lyly, Horton, Watts-Dunton, Ralph Roister Doister—*who the hell is Ralph Roister Doister, where is all this stuff coming from?* Oliver Goldsmith, is he in there? Henry Handel Richardson? Miles Franklin—who? Emily Dickinson, wound around upon herself in perpetual night? Edith Wharton, dreaming among the fibres?

I tear off another section and bunch it between finger and thumb. I ready myself again. Wordsworth this time, perhaps?— the *Lyrical Ballads*? *'Tis eight o'clock, a clear March night, / The moon is up, the sky is blue—*

And thus I proceed, caught in what I know will be the larger meaning of my life: Benjaminian, almost, despite the fact that, of course, I haven't really read any of him, either. Though in that, perhaps, I am most like his Angel: I remember overhearing part of an absolutely *sublime* conversation about this last detail in the common room—Gifford, surely, surely Gifford was involved in it—about the way Benjamin's Angel of History works only if you see it as having no consciousness, like history itself. Or was that Rilke's Angel they were talking about? Yes, I think it might have been—Rilke had angels, didn't he? And Milton, Milton definitely did, I remember someone telling me so. *Me miserable*. See—I do know something, after all! Complete and utter bullshit, of course, wherever it comes from, whoever was saying it, whatever they might have meant as they did. But brilliant nonetheless, dazzling, stunning: the very peak of the dreaming towers, the core of the world itself. Seeming. Seeming. *Seeming to be.*

Thinking these thoughts, absorbed in my work, my sense of purpose reborn, I accept more paper from the dispenser, and crumple it, and set it about its final task.

I am an agent of History at last. *I am become*[268] *a child of the age.*[269]

268 A final unwitting echo, perhaps from Tennyson's 'Ulysses' ('I am become a name, for always roaming with a hungry heart'). Maybe Gotch's lectures were not in vain, after all.

269 And, thus, we reach the conclusion of this rather uneven text. I'm afraid that, all things considered, it can't be recommend for publication. There's just too much in it that's unreliable, too many claims that are just plain wrong. I've made my comments along the way, but I must record here my final disappointment, in the poor treatment of the Brontë sisters in particular. Charlotte Brontë's *Jane Eyre* is one of the great works of English literature (though I must say I've never understood why she took so long to write *Wide Sargasso Sea*).

AUTHOR'S NOTE

Many readers will see that this novel is full of bits and pieces—sometimes more—pinched from other people's work, and that to some extent it is about that process as a part of the business of writing and of everyday life. Some of these thefts are acknowledged in or below the text as they appear, others are more generally acknowledged here as existing unowned. As Cosmo Manatine might have said, these are acts of *hommage*, to be detected, rather than acts of plagiarism, to be concealed. How much in *Bluffworld* did you fish out of the great Ocean of Literature? How many details come from the world of popular culture? How many of your own lines did you spot unacknowledged?

The same principle of acknowledged unacknowledgement applies to my use of other people's one-liners: when these are unidentified as to source, it is because I am genuinely unsure whether they are yours, mine, or belong to the ages. For a fuller account of my theory of the role of plagiarism/*hommage* in the creative act—which, naturally, is not original to me—see my novel *The Back of His Head* (VUP 2015). Not all of that novel was original to me, either, and parts of it and of *Salt Picnic* (VUP 2018) and *Bluffworld* are believed to have been written by John Fletcher, Francis Beaumont, Thomas Middleton and other hands.

In honour of the larger themes of this book, no background research has been undertaken during its writing that might involve the use of a library, the reading of real-world books, consultation with living people for factual information, or any online text lacking sexual images. Unless otherwise indicated, any footnote that seems to show informed knowledge may safely be assumed to be sourced in

Wikipedia. Knowledge that seems less reliable is likely to have been rummaged up elsewhere on the internet, itself well-known as an enormous treasure chest for the *Bullshit-Künstler*. No native speakers of the Hungarian language have been consulted in the writing of this text: the few Hungarian words and phrases that occur in it came via https://www.bing.com/translator, an invaluable tool which enables the barely monolingual to fake knowledge of a large range of foreign languages, including English. Elsewhere, when it has not been possible to verify details of certain sources, for example page numbers and publishing details, they have been made up. Much of *Bluffworld* is unreliable, including this sentence.

Three texts in particular have helped form my mind and create the *textuell imaginär* of *Bluffworld*. Martin Seymour-Smith's imperishable *The Bluffer's Guide to Literature* (Mass Market Paperback 1971), which I first read as a student, showed me how to write and speak with confidence about books I haven't read and things I know nothing about; its influence is everywhere in this novel as in my life. Emeritus Professor K.K. Ruthven's remarkable *Faking Literature* (Cambridge University Press 2001) remorselessly revealed to me the inherently factitious nature of the entire literary project—the fact that, consciously or not, texts replicate other texts, meaning that bluff and bullshit are irretrievably at the heart of Western humanism's great literary project. Professor Harry Frankfurt's study *On Bullshit* (Princeton University Press 2005) is a philosophic enquiry into the status of bullshit as opposed to other forms of dissimulation and a book I believe may be seen as giving the *Bullshit-Künstler* a long-deserved formal status in the world of scholarship.

Further to footnote 222 above, where I acknowledge his ownership of the phrase 'Department of Text Management', I thank Emeritus Professor Roger Robinson of Victoria University of Wellington for allowing me use of his dying-to-save-expense joke near the end of Chapter 6. He has also graciously allowed me to place my protagonist in a version of the office in which he began his academic life, and to mention the sound effects he regularly reported from this room during his tenure. More generally, he has encouraged me over the years to see that campus life is best enjoyed as a comedy, and that its greatest comedians are those who take themselves most seriously.

In writing this novel, as with *Gifted, The Back of His Head, Salt Picnic* and many other things, I have been sustained throughout, as ever, by my son Nathan Evans. I pay particular tribute to Paul Millar, John Newton and James Acheson, who read early drafts and unfailingly kept me going. I have also been sustained by the encouragement and advice of Simon Garrett, Cynthia Brophy, Nicholas Wright, Reg Berry, Robyn Toomath, Andrew Dean, Bruce Harding, Gail Tatham, Quentin Wilson and Mandala White. I am very grateful for their ongoing interest in my work, their expertise, their advice on my drafts, their editorial work—frequently substantial—and especially for their kindness. For *Faecem in Caenum Mutare* I thank Enrica Sciarrino, for the *Spinoff* reference below I thank Catherine Chidgey, for the final footnote I thank Richard Scragg. I thank Fergus Barrowman once again for his constant encouragement and for further evidence of his ability to get books out of writers, and the team at Victoria University Press for their help in bringing this book to the public. Special thanks to Jasmine Sargent for her searching and sympathetic editing work. As ever, the processes of publication have been rapid and pleasant for me.

The most common question I've been asked while writing this book is 'Am I in it?' The correct answer is, 'No. You live in the material world, caught up in history. How interesting do you think you are?' No character in *Bluffworld* is intended to represent any person living, dead, or just resting.

OBITUARY

for the book you are working on right now

Born

[I]n good London bookstores a new novel has nineteen days to live. If after nineteen days there hasn't been any press, media attention, news that it's becoming a best-seller, the book-sellers announce, 'Sorry, we don't have room for it,' and it's either returned to the publisher, sold to remainder houses who sell it for a third of the price, pulped, or tossed into the garbage.

(George Steiner with Laure Adler, *The Long Saturday: Conversations*, University of Chicago Press 2017, p.71)

Died

Internal Affairs briefing, Hon Tracey Martin, Minister of Internal Affairs
Title: Management of the National Library's Overseas Published Collections
Date: 11 December 2018
Action sought: Approve the removal of all overseas publications from the Overseas Published Collections, excluding those in subject areas identified as collecting priorities in the Overseas Collecting Plan, and in alignment with the 2015 National Library Collections Policy.
Note that due to evidence of low demand and the age of the material, secure destruction of removed items is the most likely outcome.

(Quoted in David Larsen, 'The National Library cull of 600,000 books could be a disaster for researchers', *The Spinoff*, 20 January 2020.)